CITY OF DREAMS

Don Winslow is the author of twenty-three acclaimed, award-winning international bestsellers, including six *New York Times* bestsellers (*Savages*, *The Kings of Cool*, *The Cartel*, *The Force*, *The Border* and *City on Fire*). *Savages* was made into a feature film by three-time Oscar-winning writer-director Oliver Stone and a screenplay by Shane Salerno, Winslow and Stone. Winslow's epic Cartel trilogy has been adapted for TV and will appear as a weekly series on FX in 2023. *The Force* is soon to be a major motion picture from 20th Century Studios starring Matt Damon with James Mangold directing from a Scott Frank screenplay. Additional Winslow books are currently in development at Netflix, Warner Brothers, Sony and Working Title and he has recently written a series of acclaimed short stories for Audible, narrated by four-time Oscar nominee Ed Harris.

don-winslow.com

/DonWinslowAuthor

@donwinslow

ALSO BY DON WINSLOW

CITY
OF
DREAMS

A Novel

Don Winslow

HarperCollins*Publishers*

HarperCollins*Publishers*
1 London Bridge Street,
London SE1 9GF

www.harpercollins.co.uk

HarperCollins*Publishers*
Macken House, 39/40 Mayor Street Upper,
Dublin 1, D01 C9W8, Ireland

First published in Great Britain by HarperCollins*Publishers* Ltd 2023
1

First published in the United States by William Morrow,
an imprint of HarperCollins*Publishers* 2023

A catalogue copy of this book is available from the British Library.

ISBN: 9780008507824 (HB)
ISBN: 9780008507831 (TPB)

This novel is entirely a work of fiction. The names, characters and incidents
portrayed in it are the work of the author's imagination. Any resemblance
to actual persons, living or dead, events or localities is entirely coincidental.

Typeset in Ehrhardt MT Std

Printed and bound in the UK using 100% renewable electricity
at CPI Group (UK) Ltd

To teachers
Without you, these books would never be written.
Or read

Of wars and a man I sing,
An exile, driven on by fate . . .

Virgil
The Aeneid
Book I

CITY OF DREAMS

DAYBREAK

Anza-Borrego Desert, California
April 1991

At last the day was breaking, the
morning star on the rise . . .

Virgil

The Aeneid

Book II

DANNY SHOULD HAVE KILLED THEM all.

He knows that now.

Should have known it then—you rip forty million in cash from people in an armed robbery, you shouldn't leave them alive to come after you.

You should take their money *and* their lives.

But that ain't Danny Ryan.

It's always been his problem—he still believes in God. Heaven and hell and all that happy crap. He's pushed the button on a few guys, but it was always a him-or-them situation.

The robbery wasn't. Danny had them all zip-tied, flat on the floor or the ground, helpless, and his guys wanted to put bullets in the backs of their heads.

Execution style, like they say.

"They'd do it to us," Kevin Coombs said to him.

Yeah, they would, Danny thought.

Popeye Abbarca was notorious for killing not only the people who ripped him off but their entire families, too. Popeye's head guy had even told Danny that. Looked up from the floor, smiled, and said, "You and all your families. *Muerte*. And not fast, either."

We came for the money, not a massacre, Danny thought. Tens of millions of dollars in cash to start new lives, not keep reliving the old ones.

The killing had to stop.

So he took their money and left them their lives.

Now he knows it was a mistake.

He's on his knees with a gun to his head. The others are tied, bound wrist and ankle, stretched on poles, looking down at him with pleading, terrified eyes.

The desert air is cold at dawn and Danny shivers as he kneels in the sand with the sun coming up and the moon a fading memory. A dream. Maybe that's all life is, Danny thinks, a dream.

Or a nightmare.

Because even in dreams, Danny thinks, you pay for your sins.

An acrid smell pierces the crisp, fresh air.

Gasoline.

Then Danny hears, "You watch while we burn them alive. Then you."

So this is how I die, he thinks.

The dream fades.

The long night is over.

The day is breaking.

PART ONE

In Some Neglected Land

Rhode Island
December 1988

. . . exiles now, searching earth for a
home in some neglected land . . .

Virgil
The Aeneid
Book III

ONE

THEY LEAVE A LITTLE AFTER dawn.

A cold northeast wind—is there any other kind? Danny thinks—blows off the ocean like it's giving them the bum's rush. He and his family—or what's left of it—with his crew in cars behind him, spread out so they don't look like the refugee convoy they are.

Danny's old man, Marty, is singing—

Farewell to Prince's landing stage,
River Mersey fare thee well
I'm bound for California . . .

Danny Ryan's not sure where they're going, just that they have to get the hell out of Rhode Island.

It's not the leaving of Liverpool that grieves me . . .

It's not Liverpool they're leaving, it's freakin' Providence. They have to put a lot of miles between them and the Moretti crime family, the city cops, the state troopers, the feds . . . just about everybody.

What happens when you lose a war.

Danny's not grieving, either.

Even though his wife, Terri, died just hours ago now—the cancer took her like a slow-moving but relentless storm—Danny doesn't have the time for heartbreak, not with an eighteen-month-old child asleep in the back seat.

But my darlin', when I think of thee . . .

There'll be a mass, Danny thinks, there'll be a funeral and a wake, but I won't be there for any of it. If the cops or the feds didn't get me, the Morettis would, and then Ian would be an orphan.

The boy sleeps through his grandfather's caterwauling. I dunno, Danny thinks, maybe the old Irish song is a lullaby.

Danny's in no hurry for him to wake up.

How am I going to tell him that he isn't going to see his mommy anymore, that "she's with God"?

If you believe that stuff.

Danny's not sure he does anymore.

If there is a God, he thinks, he's a cruel, vengeful prick who made my wife and my little boy pay for the things I did. I thought Jesus died for my sins, that's what the nuns said anyway.

Maybe my sins just maxed out Christ's credit card.

You've robbed, Danny thinks, you've beaten people. You've killed three men. Left the last one dead on a frozen beach just an hour or so ago. He tried to kill you first, though.

Yeah, tell yourself that. The guy is still dead. You still killed him. You have a lot to answer for.

You're a drug dealer; you were going to put ten kilos of heroin out on the street.

Danny wishes he'd never touched the shit.

You knew better, he thinks now as he drives. You can make all the excuses you want for yourself—you were doing it to survive, for your kid, for a better life, you'd make up for it somehow down the road—but the truth is that you still did it.

Danny knew it was freakin' wrong, that he would be putting evil and suffering out into a world that already had too much of both. Was doing it even as he was watching his wife die of cancer with a tube of the same shit running into her arm.

The money he would have made was blood money.

So minutes before he killed the dirty cop, Danny Ryan threw two million dollars' worth of heroin into the ocean.

THE WAR HAD started over a woman.

At least that's how most people tell it: they blame Pam.

Danny was there that day when she walked out of the water onto the beach like a goddess. No one knew this WASP ice maiden was Paulie Moretti's girlfriend; no one knew he really loved her.

If Liam Murphy knew, he didn't care.

Then again, Liam never cared about anything but himself. What he thought was that she was a beautiful woman and he was a beautiful man and so they belonged together. He took her like a trophy he'd won just for being him.

And Pam?

Danny never understood what she saw in Liam, or why she stayed with him as long as she did. He'd always liked Pam; she was smart, she was funny, she seemed to care about other people.

Paulie couldn't get past it—losing Pam, getting cuckolded by some Irish charmer.

Thing of it was, the Irish and Italians had been friends before that. Allies for generations. Danny's own father, Marty—who's now thankfully dozed off, snoring instead of singing—was one of the men who made that happen. The Irish had the docks, the Italians had the gambling, and they shared the unions. They ran New England together. They were all at the same beach party when Liam made his move on Pam.

Forty years of friendship came apart in one night.

The Italians beat Liam half to death.

Pam came to the hospital and left with Liam.

The war was on.

Sure, most people lay it on Pam, Danny thinks, but Peter Moretti had been wanting to make a move on the docks for years, and he used his brother's embarrassment as an excuse.

Doesn't matter now, Danny thinks.

Whatever started the war, it's over.

We lost.

The losses were more than the docks, the unions.

They were personal, too.

Danny wasn't a Murphy; he'd married into the family that ruled the Irish mob. Even then he was pretty much just a soldier. John Murphy and his two sons, Pat and Liam, ran things.

But now John's in a federal lockup awaiting heroin charges that will put him away for life.

Liam is dead, shot by the same cop that Danny killed.

And Pat, Danny's best friend—his brother-in-law but more like his brother—was killed. Run over by a car, his body dragged through the streets, flayed almost beyond recognition.

It broke Danny's heart.

And Terri . . .

She wasn't killed in the war, Danny thinks. Not directly, anyway, but the cancer started after Pat, her beloved brother, was killed, and sometimes Danny wonders if that was where it began. Like the grief grew from her heart and spread through her chest.

God, Danny loved her.

In a world where most of the guys fucked around, had mistresses or *gumars*, Danny never cheated. He was as faithful as a golden retriever, and Terri even teased him about it, although she expected nothing less.

She and Danny were there that day Pam showed up; they were lying on the beach together when Pam came out of the water, her skin glistening from sunshine and salt. Terri saw him looking, gave him a sharp elbow, then they went back to their cottage and made frantic love.

The sex between them—delayed so long because they were Irish Catholics and she was Pat's sister—was always good. Danny never needed to look outside the marriage, not even when Terri was sick.

Especially not when she was sick.

Her last words to him, before she slipped into the morphine-induced terminal coma—

"Take care of our son."

"I will."

"Promise."

"I promise," he said. "I swear."

DRIVING THROUGH NEW Haven on Route 95, Danny notices that buildings are decorated with giant wreaths. The lights in the windows are red and green. A giant Christmas tree pokes up from an office plaza.

Christmas, Danny thinks.

Merry freakin' Christmas.

He'd forgotten all about it, forgotten Liam's sick stupid heroin joke about dreaming of a white Christmas. It's in a week or so, right? Danny thinks. The hell difference does it make? Ian's too young to know or care. Maybe next year . . . if there is a next year.

So do it now, he thinks.

No point in putting it off, it's not going to get any better with time.

He gets off the highway at Bridgeport, follows a street east until it takes him to the ocean. Or Long Island Sound, anyway. He pulls into a dirt parking lot by a little beach.

Within a few minutes, the others pull in behind him.

Danny gets out of the car. He pulls the collar of his peacoat up around his neck, but the sharp winter air feels good.

Jimmy Mac rolls down his window. His friend since they were in freakin' kindergarten, Jimmy gets a little chubbier with every year, has a body like a laundry bag, but he's the best wheelman in the business. He asks, "What's up? Why did you pull off?"

Get it over with, Danny thinks. Just say it, short and sharp. "I dumped the heroin, Jimmy."

Jimmy's shock is plain on his bland, friendly face. "The *hell*, Danny? That was our shot! We risked our lives for that dope!"

And we shouldn't have, Danny thinks.

Because it was a setup.

From the get-go.

A Moretti captain named Frankie Vecchio had come to them with the proverbial offer you can't refuse. He was in charge of a forty-kilo shipment of heroin that Peter Moretti bought from the Mexicans on the come. Frankie thought the Morettis were going to have him whacked, so he came to ask Danny to hijack the shipment.

Danny saw it as a chance to cripple the Morettis and end the war.

So I went for it, Danny thinks now.

They jacked the forty keys, it was easy.

Too freakin' easy, that was the problem.

A fed named Phillip Jardine was in bed with the Italians. The whole plan was to have the Murphys hijack the shipment, then bust them. Most of the heroin would find its way back to the Morettis.

It was all a trap to finish off the Irish.

And it worked.

We fell for it, Danny thinks, hook, line, and sinker.

The Murphys got busted and the Morettis got the dope.

Except for the ten kilos that Danny had stashed away.

It was their safety net, the getaway money, the funds that would let them go off the radar until things cooled down.

Except now Danny has given it to the ocean, to the sea god.

Jimmy is just staring at him.

Ned Egan walks up. Marty's longtime bodyguard, he's in his forties now. Built like a fire hydrant but a hell of a lot tougher. You don't fuck with Ned Egan, you don't even joke about fucking with him, because Ned Egan has killed more guys than cholesterol.

Marty stays in the car because he isn't going to get out in the cold. Back in the day, you said the name Marty Ryan, grown men would piss their pants, but that was a lot of days ago. Now he's an old man, more often drunk than not, half-blind with cataracts.

Two other guys come over.

Sean South couldn't look more Irish if you stuck a pipe in his mouth and shoved him into a green leprechaun suit. With his bright red hair, freckles, and clean-cut appearance, Sean looks about as dangerous as a day-old kitten, but give him a reason and he'll shoot you in the face and then go out for a burger and a beer.

Kevin Coombs has his hands jammed into the black leather jacket he's worn since Danny first met him. Unkempt brown hair down to his shoulders, three days' growth of beard, Kevin looks like the stereotypical East Coast punk. Add his boozing to that and you have the whole Irish Catholic–alcoholic combo plate. But if you need some serious work done, Kevin is your man.

Collectively, Sean and Kevin are known as the Altar Boys. They like to go around saying that they serve "Last Communion."

"What are we doing, boss?" Sean asks.

"I dumped the heroin," Danny says.

Kevin blinks. He can't believe it. Then his face twists into an angry snarl. "Are you fucking kidding me?"

"Watch your mouth," Ned says. "You're talking to the boss."

"That was millions of dollars there," Kevin says.

Danny can smell the booze on his breath.

"If we could lay it off," Danny says. "I didn't even know who to approach."

"Liam did," Kevin says.

"Liam's dead," Danny says. "That shit brought us nothing but bad. We probably have indictments chasing us, never mind the Morettis."

"That's why we needed the money, Danny," Sean says.

Jimmy says, "They'll all be coming after us. The Italians, the feds . . ."

"I know," Danny says. But not Jardine, he thinks. Maybe other feds, but not that one. He doesn't tell the others this—no point in giving them guilty knowledge, for both their protection and his. "But the heroin was evidence. I got rid of it."

"I can't believe you did us like that," Kevin says.

Danny sees Kevin's wrist move a little above his jacket pocket and knows the gun is in his hand.

If Kevin thinks he can do it, he will.

Sean too.

They're a pair, the Altar Boys.

But Danny doesn't go for his own gun. He doesn't need to. Ned Egan already has his out.

Pointed at Kevin's head.

"Kevin," Danny says, "don't make me drop you in the ocean with the dope. Because I will."

It's right on the edge.

It can go either way.

Then Kevin laughs. Throws his head up and howls. "Throwing two mil in the water?! The feds after us?! The Italians?! The whole freakin' world?! That's wicked pisser! I *love* it! I'm with you, man! I'm with the Danny Ryan crew! Cradle to the freakin' grave!"

Ned lowers his gun.

A little.

Danny relaxes. A little. The good thing about the Altar Boys is that they're crazy. The bad thing about the Altar Boys is that they're crazy.

"Okay, we don't need a parade here," Danny says. "Spread out. We'll stay in touch through Bernie."

Bernie Hughes, the organization's old accountant, is holed up in New Hampshire, safe—for the time being, anyway—from the feds and the Morettis.

"You got it, boss," Sean says.

Kevin nods.

They all get back in their cars and head out.

We're refugees, Danny thinks as he drives.

Freakin' refugees.

Fugitives.

Exiles.

TWO

PETER MORETTI IS FREAKING THE fuck out.

Waiting for Chris Palumbo.

Sitting in the office of American Vending Machine on Atwells Avenue in Providence, Peter's tapping his right foot like a rabbit on speed. The office is decorated like a mother, because his brother Paulie goes nuts at the holidays and because this was supposed to have been a very good Christmas, what with the heroin money coming in and the Irish going out. Wreaths and shit festoon the walls and a big artificial silver tree stands in the corner with wrapped presents underneath, ready for the annual party.

Maybe I should take some of the presents back, Peter thinks, because if Palumbo doesn't show up, we're all going to be broke. Last thing he heard from his consigliere, Chris, he was headed down to the shore to get the ten kilos of horse Danny Ryan had tucked away in a stash house. That was three hours ago and there isn't anywhere in Rhode Island it takes three hours to get to and get back.

But Chris *hasn't* come back, hasn't called.

So ten keys of horse is in the wind with him.

After you step on it like Godzilla on Bambi, ten kilos of heroin has a street value of over two million dollars.

Peter needs that money.

Because he owes that money.

Sort of.

Peter had bought forty kilos of smack from the Mexicans at a hundred thousand a key because he was desperate to get into the drug business. Guys like Gotti in New York were making money hand over clenched fist with dope, and Peter wanted in on the windfall.

But no way did Peter have four million in cash, so he and his brother went out to half the wiseguys in New England, generously letting them in on the investment opportunity. Some guys bought into it because they liked the potential, others because they were afraid to say no to the boss, but for whatever reason a lot of people had a piece of the shipment.

It would have been fine, but then Peter let Chris Palumbo talk him into doing a very risky thing.

"We send Frankie V to the Irish," Chris said, "and let him pretend that he's flipping on us. He tips them off to the heroin shipment and gets Danny Ryan to boost it."

"The fuck, Chris?" Peter asked, because what the fuck kind of idea was it to get your own dope boosted, especially by a gang you've been at war with? Christ, was Chris high himself?

Chris explained that he had a fed, Phillip Jardine, on the arm. The Irish take the heroin and Jardine busts them, effectively ending the long war between the Moretti family and the Irish.

"Four mil is too high a price tag," Peter said.

"That's the beauty part," Chris said.

He explained that Jardine would keep some of the heroin to make it look legit, but the bulk of it would come straight back to them. They'd have to give Jardine a big cut, but by the time they cut up the drugs, there'd be more than enough in street value to make up for the loss.

"Win-win," Chris said.

Peter went for it.

Yeah, and it all went according to plan.

Officially, Jardine seized twelve kilos from the Irish in a highly pub-
licized raid. John Murphy, the Irish boss, got popped on thirty-to-life
federal charges.

Good.

His son Liam got dead.

Even better.

Okay, twenty-eight keys is a fucking fortune and everybody gets paid.

Except—

Chris Palumbo and Jardine were supposed to go bust Danny and take
his ten kilos.

Fine.

But—

No one's heard from either of them since. And Jardine supposedly has
the other eighteen keys.

Peter does more math.

There were forty kilos of dope.

Jardine officially busted twelve.

Liam had three keys on him when Jardine caught him.

Danny Ryan had another ten.

Frankie Vecchio took five.

That leaves ten kilos.

Peter ain't too worried about that. Jardine claimed twelve to satisfy
the government and didn't report the other ten. Probably gave a few of the
cops on the raid a taste and will show up with the rest.

If he fucking shows up.

Ryan's gone, too. Left the hospital where his wife was dying, somehow
got around Peter's guys, and no one's seen him since, either.

Billy Battaglia comes through the door.

He looks shaken.

"What?" Peter asks.

"Me and some other guys went with Chris to get that dope from Ryan," Billy says. "Chris goes in, comes out ten minutes later—without the dope—tells us to go home."

"What the fuck?" Peter's heart feels like it's going to jump out of his chest.

"Ryan had shooters outside Chris's house," Billy says. "Said he'd have them kill Chris's whole family if he didn't back off."

"Why isn't Chris here telling me that?"

"Chris hasn't come?"

"You think you needed to tell me this if Chris already came?" Peter asks. "Where is he now?"

"I dunno. He just drove away."

The phone rings and Peter jumps.

It's Paulie. "I just got a call from a Gilead cop. They found a body on the beach."

Peter feels like he could throw up. Is it Ryan? Chris?

"It's Jardine," Paulie says. "One in the chest. Had his gun in his hand."

"What about Chris?"

"Nothin'."

Peter hangs up.

The news about Jardine is devastating. The fed was supposed to deliver the rest of the heroin to them. And why did Chris take off? Shit, could he and Ryan have cooked up some deal? That redheaded guinea Chris triple-crossed everyone? It would be just like him.

Merry fuckin' Christmas, Peter thinks.

We won the war but lost our money.

All of it—the years of fighting, the killings, the funerals—all for what?
Nothing.

Unless we find Danny Ryan.

DANNY AIN'T FIGURING on being found.

He drives at night, all night. Pulls into a motel in the morning and sleeps most of the day, or as much as Ian will let him. Every day or so, he and Jimmy boost a couple cars and plates, switch them around, smear mud on the plates. Drive them for a few hundred miles and then dump them.

Rinse and repeat.

It's stressful as hell, always checking the rearview mirror, holding his breath every time he passes a cop car on the highway, praying he doesn't spot the cruiser pull out and come after him. Tense, too, at gas stations—does he see something in the clerk's eyes, a small extra glance, a flick of fear?

He chooses motels on the outskirts of town, those places where people don't ask a lot of questions, where they see nothing and remember less.

Funny thing of it is, this is a trip Danny's always wanted to make. Never having been out of New England, he's dreamed about driving cross-country with Terri and Ian, seeing new stuff, experiencing new things.

But in the daytime, like a real person.

Not running at night, like an animal.

Yet the romance of the road is there.

Danny gets this thrill seeing the highway exit signs with the new names—Baltimore, Washington, DC, Lynchburg, Bristol—as the road rolls under his tires, the radio stations change, the distance stacks up.

It's the freakin' American dream, Danny thinks as he drives. The road trip, the migration west. This wagon train of theirs, spread out over miles, stopping at phone booths to check in with Bernie to coordinate.

Meeting every couple of days in some cheap motel, safety in numbers in case the Italian Apaches show up.

Not easy, what with a baby's needs and an old man's bladder. Too many stops, every one a risk. Sometimes Marty rides with Jimmy Mac, but most of the time he's with Danny, sipping on a bottle, singing or just yapping, telling Danny old war stories about his times on liberty in San Diego—"Dago," as he calls it—the bars, the women, the brawls.

Danny left Rhode Island so fast he didn't really think about where he was going, but now that he's on the road, he has empty hours to consider it. He's always wanted to see California, used to talk to Terri about moving there, but she always dismissed it as a pipe dream.

Now it seems like a good idea. It would be hard to put much more distance between himself and Rhode Island than San Diego, and it would make Marty happier than a pig in shit, so why not?

But first I have to get there, Danny thinks.

Long road.

DANNY FINDS A motel out by the highway and gets on the horn.

Before the war with the Morettis, Danny's relationship with Pasco Ferri had always been pretty good. He and the old New England boss used to go crabbing together; Danny and Terri used to lie out on the beach in front of Pasco's house in the summer.

And Pasco and Marty go *way* back.

"Pasco, it's Danny Ryan."

"I heard about Terri," Pasco says. "I'm sorry for your loss."

"Thank you."

Long silence, then, "What can I do for you, Danny?"

Danny notices that Pasco doesn't ask where he is. "I need to know if you have a problem with me, Pasco."

"Peter Moretti thinks I should."

Danny feels like he can't freakin' breathe. "And?"

"I'm not happy with Peter," Pasco says. "He's got himself involved with drugs—which I always told him not to—and now he's in trouble. He lost a lot of people a lot of money, and there's nothing I can say to them."

Meaning, Danny thinks, that Peter is under a ton of pressure, there's nothing Pasco can do to take the weight off, and he doesn't particularly want to.

"So I'm good with you?" Danny asks. "Because I want you to know, I'm out of this thing. I just want to find a place to set my feet."

"You're out of this thing?" Pasco asks. "How can you be 'out of this thing' with ten keys of *banania* in the trunk of your car? It's a sin, an *infamnia*."

"I don't have the dope."

"Don't insult me."

"It's the truth, Pasco," Danny says.

Silence.

"The Morettis won the war," Danny says. "I get that, I accept it, I just need to find a way to live. But if you're after me, Pasco, I know I'm a dead man."

"Stop whining," Pasco says. "It's unmanly. Your problems with Peter are your problems with Peter. As far as I'm concerned, Chris Palumbo has that H."

"Thank you, Pasco."

"It's for your father's sake," Pasco says. "Not for you."

"I understand."

"You have your life," Pasco says. "You can start over. Build something for your son. That's what a man does."

He hangs up.

Danny sums up the conversation to Marty.

"That's good," Marty says. "If we don't got to worry about Pasco, we'll be okay."

Yeah, maybe, Danny thinks.

But Peter Moretti won't let up, he'll try to track us down, and we don't know about indictments yet.

Danny lets Ian watch a half hour of television before getting him into bed and reading him a story, something about a farmer that Danny could basically recite from memory, he's read it so many times.

Tonight Ian goes down quickly.

THREE

A GRAINY IMAGE OF RYAN POPS up on a screen in a meeting room of the FBI office in Boston.

Brent Harris isn't happy about being at this meeting, having had to take a red-eye to freezing New England from sunny San Diego. He's not even FBI, he's DEA, an agent with the Southwest High Intensity Drug Trafficking Area Task Force. But his bosses told him to play nice with the Bureau, so Harris is playing nice.

He looks at the surveillance photo of Danny Ryan, the ostensible purpose of this interagency clusterfuck. Ryan is a solid six feet with the shoulders you'd expect from a former dockworker, unkempt brown hair, deep brown eyes that look like they've seen a few things they wish they hadn't. The photo was taken in winter—Ryan wears an old navy peacoat with the collar turned up.

A little white electronic arrow nestles under Ryan's chin as Reggie Moneta, recently promoted to the FBI's national subdirector for organized crime, says, "I want Ryan *found*. I want him found and I want him brought in."

Moneta is one of those intense little Sicilian types, Harris thinks. Maybe five-five, short black hair with just a trace of silver woven in, dark brown eyes, with a well-earned reputation for being a ball-buster. She worked out of Boston until recently, so she has a personal investment in this shit.

Bill Callahan, the New England special agent in charge, is classic Boston Irish—pasty face, red hair fading to rust, broken veins in his nose, big and beefy with the face of man who never met a scotch or a steak he couldn't love. "Danny Ryan? He was a donkey, a beast of burden. Why are we talking about him?"

Moneta says, "I like him for Phil Jardine's murder."

Callahan says, "We have nothing connecting Ryan to Agent Jardine's murder."

Moneta turns to Harris. "Brent?"

Harris hides his annoyance at having flown all night (in economy, at that) to give a briefing about what they already know. "The Abbarca organization, operating out of Tijuana, sent a large shipment of heroin to Peter Moretti in Providence. Domingo Abbarca—aka 'Popeye' because he lost an eye in a gunfight with a rival narco—is a bad piece of business, a sadistic psychopath who ships tons of grass, coke, and heroin into the U.S.

"Agent Jardine had a CI named Francis Vecchio, who alerted Jardine about the shipment. It appears, however, that Vecchio was engaged in a conspiracy with Danny Ryan and Liam Murphy to hijack that shipment.

"As you know, twelve kilos of heroin were seized in a raid Jardine conducted at the Murphy-owned Glocca Morra bar. It's rumored that Ryan had ten keys in his possession when he fled. Agent Jardine's body was found on a beach near Ryan's father's house and in a location that Ryan was known to frequent."

Moneta says, "We can postulate that Jardine went there to arrest Ryan and was killed in the process."

"That's a big leap, Reggie," Callahan says.

"It's enough to bring Ryan in for questioning," Moneta says.

"Even if we can find him, are we sure we want to?" Callahan asks. He leans forward. "Let's say what no one has been saying: Jardine was dirty."

"We don't know that," Moneta says.

"Don't we?" Callahan asks. "Three kilos of that heroin were found in the trunk of his car."

Moneta says, "He might have been on his way to log them in when he got information about Ryan's whereabouts."

"And he went alone?" Callahan asks. "Come on. Harris, how many kilos did Abbarca sell to the Morettis?"

"Our sources say forty."

"Forty," Callahan says. "Minus the twelve Jardine booked equals twenty-eight. Minus the three found in Jardine's trunk equals twenty-five. Vecchio turned his five in when he entered the program. Let's say Ryan did take ten. Where are the other ten?"

"You're alleging that Jardine took them?" Moneta asks. "He went into Murphy's club with a task force—FBI, DEA, state and local police. There were witnesses everywhere."

"And it would be the first time in history," Callahan says, "that a group of cops siphoned off some dope before it got to the evidence locker. I'm just asking, do we really want to dig all this up for public consumption? If this dog is willing to lie down, I say we let it sleep."

"An FBI agent has been murdered," Moneta says. "We do not *let that sleep*. Ryan's wife's funeral is tomorrow. I want it covered."

"You think Ryan is going to show up?" Callahan asks.

"No," Moneta says, "but if he does we're going to be there. And I want the family interviewed as to his whereabouts."

"You're asking us to harass these people," Callahan says, "as they're burying their daughter."

"I'm telling you to do your job," Moneta says.

She's out of the door maybe five seconds when Callahan pisses on it. "I don't know about you, but my office has too much shit on its plate already to stop everything and look for some washed-up mick. I'll make a show, go through the motions. But I'm not busting my budget or putting anything else on the back burner in order to chase Reggie Moneta's wet dreams."

Harris asks, "Why does Moneta have such a hard-on for Ryan?"

"She was sleeping with Phil Jardine."

"No shit," Harris says.

"One of those Route Ninety-Five affairs," Callahan says. "She was in Boston, he was in Providence. When she got the bump to Washington, they'd hop on Amtrak and meet in Wilmington."

"Wilmington?"

"Love is a powerful thing."

"Do you think Ryan did Jardine?" Harris asks.

"Who cares?" Callahan says. "A dirty agent? He had it coming."

"It begs the question, though . . ."

"Whether Moneta was in on the drug boost with her lover?" Callahan says. "I don't think so, because if she were, she wouldn't be chasing Ryan. I practically gave her a gilded invitation to let him skate. I've known Reggie Moneta since she was a road guard. She's ambitious, but she's straight."

Harris leaves the meeting with one mission in mind.

Find Danny Ryan before Reggie Moneta does.

A MOTEL OUTSIDE Little Rock.

Kevin and Sean picked up some women. Or the women picked them up, whatever. The Altar Boys had logged a couple of hours of sleep, then went across the highway to a bar to search out beer and some pussy and found both.

Linda, Kelli, and Jo Anne were regulars at the bar, the boys could tell that right away, and could also tell they were pleased to see some new guys instead of the "local jerks and truck jockeys" they were used to. Wasn't fifty-eight seconds before they joined the boys to play a little pool, and then in a booth for some shooters, and it was Linda who brought up the idea of a "party."

"You got a room at the motel?" she asked. Maybe midthirties, dark red hair, nice tits under a purple silk blouse.

"We each have a room," Kevin answered.

"Let's have a party," Linda said.

"We have a little numbers problem, don't we?" Sean asked. "Three of you, two of us."

Linda shook her head. "Kelli and me are a team."

Kelli was a tight little blonde, looked maybe in her twenties.

Sean blushed. "I'm just a simple Irish Catholic boy . . ."

Linda turned to Kevin. Ran her hand up his thigh and squeezed his cock. "*You* aren't a little Irish Catholic boy, are you? You like the idea, I can tell."

Yeah, turns out Kevin did.

He left with the two teammates and Sean took Jo Anne to his room. She was short and black-haired and a little plump, but Sean liked her big boobs and full lips and the little beaten-puppy expression she carried around, so he was happy.

Kevin, he had a party.

Which ended abruptly when he reached into Linda's pants and felt a dick. "What the fuck?!"

"What's the matter?" Linda asked.

"*You're* the fuckin' matter," Kevin said. "You're a fuckin' *guy*!"

"Only in my body," Linda said. "Not in my heart."

"Yeah, well, it's your body I'm concerned with," Kevin said. "Get the fuck outta here."

"Not before you pay us."

"Who said anything about paying you?"

"Did you think it was for free?" Linda asked.

"We didn't even do nothin'!"

"Our time is worth something."

"Get the fuck out before I beat the shit out of both of you," Kevin said.

"Give me my money, asshole!"

Now Sean came out of the adjoining room, having made a similar discovery. "Kev, they're dudes!"

"No fucking shit!"

"I want my money!"

Inside his room, Danny hears the yelling. Last freakin' thing they need—noise. Stepping out on the landing, he sees Kevin in the doorway of his room, bare-chested, his jeans open around his waist, a woman by the wrist. She's shrieking at him and clawing at his face with her nails while a shorter blond girl kicks at Kevin's shins.

Danny runs down his set of concrete stairs, across the courtyard, and up the stairs to Kevin's door.

"What's going on?" Danny asks.

"This son of a bitch doesn't want to pay me," Linda says.

"She's a he," Kevin says.

"Pay the woman," Danny says to Kevin.

Something in Danny's eyes, in his tone, tells Kevin to do what he's told without an argument. He pulls some bills out of his wallet and tosses them at Linda.

"Just take the money and go," Danny says to her.

Linda picks up the money.

Kevin can't let it go. "Freak."

The knife comes out of her purse. She jabs it at Kevin's throat. He weaves and adds, "He-she. Faggot."

"Shut up," Danny snaps.

Linda starts shrieking and Kelli chimes in.

Jimmy looks up from the courtyard.

"Get my old man and Ian and head out," Danny orders. "I'll be along with these clowns."

"Yeah, get the fuck out of here," Linda hisses. "And take your dirty-mouthed boy here with you. The cheap prick. He'll eat with plastic forks from paper plates his whole life, the loser."

Danny holds his hands up. "We're leaving. Why don't you go, too, before the cops get here?"

Linda takes Kelli by the hand and leads her down the stairs. Jo Anne kisses Sean on the cheek and follows them. Kevin goes back into his room.

Danny and Sean go in after him.

"Jesus Christ," Kevin says, "that freak makes my blood run cold."

Danny grabs him by the shoulders and rams him into the wall. "I already have one child to take care of, I don't need another. You could have brought the cops down on us."

"I'm sorry, Danny."

"I'm trying to take care of my family," Danny says, "and with that, you don't fuck around. I love you, Kevin, but you put my family in jeopardy again, I'll pop two in the back of your head. You got it?"

"Yeah, Danny."

Danny lets him go and looks at both the Altar Boys. "You have to use your brains. Stay out of situations."

"We will," Sean says. "I'll make sure."

"Get your stuff together."

Danny goes to the motel office. The night clerk stares at him, pissed off. Danny takes a hundred out of his pocket—a hundred he *needs*, God damn it—and slides it across the counter. "I'm sorry for the trouble. Are we good?"

The clerk takes the bill. "We're good."

"I have to know the truth, friend. Did you call the cops?"

"No."

"Have a good one."

Ten minutes later, like so many before him, Danny gathers what's left of his family and heads west.

Oklahoma City, Amarillo, Tucumcari . . .

Albuquerque, Grants, Gallup . . .

Winslow, Flagstaff, Phoenix . . .

The American road.

FOUR

STANDING AT HER SISTER'S GRAVESIDE, Cassandra Murphy shivers under her coat. Snowflakes fall and then melt on the amber hair that flows over the upturned collar.

Two funerals in two days, she thinks. Exceptional even for the Murphy family.

Yesterday they put her brother Liam in the ground. Beautiful, flawed, selfish Liam, the cause of all the trouble. The police said it was suicide, a bullet to the head, but Cassie doesn't believe it—Liam was far too in love with himself to do his favorite person any harm.

The suicide determination had been a problem, though, because the fucking church didn't want to bury Liam in hallowed ground. Cassie had to go to the priest, explain to him how much money the Murphy family puts into the parish and how much money they wouldn't be putting in if Liam weren't laid to rest with the priest mumbling the sacred words and flicking holy water around.

Cassie was, of course, raised a Catholic, but she checked out of that motel. Now she calls herself a Baddhist—a bad Buddhist—part of her search for some higher power now that she's going back into the program.

She's shooting smack again.

Had been off the shit for coming on three years, but then, within hours, her father was carted off to prison, her sister died, and her brother Liam was killed in an other-assisted suicide.

Cassie went back to the needle.

She got high this morning, just to get through Terri's funeral, and she'll probably pop a little this afternoon, but after that she's planning on quitting. Not going back to rehab—she's done with that—but going back to the meetings, anyway, because it's going to kill her and her parents can't take another loss.

Cassie is their one surviving child.

Patrick—her beloved Pat, her older brother, protector, and confidant—went first. He was the best of them—brave, honest, devout, loyal—and none of that saved him from being killed. She managed to stay clean after he died, mostly to honor him.

Cassie glances over at his widow, Sheila, standing there with her hands on her little boy's shoulders, her thick hair as black as her coat. Sheila was always the solid one, the practical one, the leader of the women in this close-knit tribe. Now she's a solitary figure. Cassie has tried to get her to start dating, but Sheila won't even consider it. It's like she has her dead husband on a pedestal—the house is practically a shrine to him—and she wears her loneliness like a dutiful cloak of honor.

Liam's funeral was a nightmare.

Her mother, Catherine, shrieked like a banshee, inconsolable. Liam had always been her favorite, her baby boy, and they had to drag her off his coffin before they lowered it into the ground.

Her father had just stood there, his coat discreetly draped over his cuffed hands. A judge—fortunately a local guy, Irish—had issued compassionate bail for John, allowing him several hours out to attend his son's and daughter's funerals. Two federal marshals flanked him at all times.

Cassie looks over at him now.

Same old Dad, she thinks—stoic, too proud to show emotion. But he looks old, fragile, a broken man. His business destroyed, three of his four children dead, and Cassie can't help but wonder which hurts him more.

And poor Terri, she thinks.

All she ever wanted was a home and a family. She got both. But for such a short time. She married sweet, loyal Danny, had a darling little boy, and just months later she was diagnosed.

So let this priest drone on about a loving god.

It's bullshit.

The funeral is well attended, like Liam's.

All the Irish are there. Back in the day, the Italians would have been there, too, but that seems like another lifetime. Terri had been friends with all of them, with the Moretti brothers, Chris Palumbo—*all* of them.

They're not at the funeral and they're right not to come.

It would be offensive.

Instead, Cassie sees a couple of cars patrolling the avenue along the cemetery, and knows they're Peter Moretti's people, looking for Danny.

The cops came, too.

Providence police, plainclothes state troopers, and feds stand at the edge of the cemetery like jackals, waiting for Danny to show up, she thinks.

She hopes he doesn't. If Danny got away, she hopes he stays away, that he and Ian are long gone and never come back to this cursed place or this cursed family.

His mother is here, paying her respects to her daughter-in-law.

Madeleine the sex goddess, Cassie thinks as she looks at Danny's mother standing like a statue. The former showgirl had used her beauty to become rich and powerful and has flown in from her Las Vegas mansion.

Even as a child Cassie knew how Danny's mother had abandoned him when he was a baby, given him up to his drunken old man and disappeared. Danny had practically been raised in the Murphy household, was basically a brother to Pat.

Madeleine had only reappeared a couple of years ago, swooped in like a mother bird when Danny got shot, saw that he had the best medical care, that his bills got paid. Her son resented her for it, but Terri grew to like her mother-in-law, was always pressing Danny to reconcile with her.

Now she has to be worried sick about her missing son and grandson.

Cassie feels another shiver.

Her shoulders quiver and she's not sure if it's the cold or if she's jonesing.

THE SERVICE FINALLY ends.

MADELEINE MCKAY WALKS back toward the waiting limousine. She's tall, regal, her head held high, her startling red hair tied back severely, her makeup perfect, subtle.

The funeral was so terribly sad, she thinks. Terri had been a good wife to her son and a good mother to her grandson.

She hasn't heard from Danny since she called him at the hospital a few hours before Terri passed, urging him to get away from the potential indictments and the murderous Italian mob. Apparently he did, taking his son and his father with him, because none of them has been seen since.

And, thank God, no body has been found.

Except Jardine's.

Madeleine hopes Danny does get in touch with her, if only to let her know that he and Ian are all right.

But she doubts he will.

My son, she thinks, is still angry at me.

She's halfway to the car when a man in an overcoat and suit walks up beside her. "Ms. McKay?"

"Yes?"

"Agent Monroe, FBI."

"I have nothing to say to you."

Looking around, she sees that the feds are swarming around the Murphy family and their friends, like seagulls diving on a garbage dump.

"Do you know where Danny is?" Monroe asks. "Has he called you?"

"If you have questions," Madeleine says, continuing to walk, "call my attorneys. If you ask me anything else, *they'll* be calling *you*."

"Do you know—"

"Or perhaps I should call your director personally," Madeleine says. "I have his private number in my book."

That stops it.

Monroe backs off.

The chauffeur opens the door. He's left the engine running so the car is nice and warm. Then a burst of cold as the other door opens and Bill Callahan slides in.

He rubs his gloved hands together. "Madeleine, this wasn't my idea."

"I hope not," Madeleine says, "because it's extremely distasteful. Whose idea was it?"

Callahan tells her about Reggie Moneta's obsession with Danny.

"I don't need this," Callahan says. "I'm pulling the pin soon, have a nice corporate job lined up."

Madeleine says, "If my son is harmed in any way, I will destroy everyone involved. Including you, Bill."

"We're old friends, Madeleine."

"I hope we remain so," she says.

Callahan knows a dismissal when he hears one and gets out.

"Airport," Madeleine says.

She has no reason to linger in Providence.

There's no one here that she wants to see.

DANNY LIFTS IAN onto the little plastic slide and then lets go, but keeps his hands near as the boy rides down laughing.

The small playground is by the beach and Danny looks out at the blue water. He's always liked the ocean. In another existence—in his twenties—he worked the fishing boats out of Gilead back in Rhode Island and it was, in many ways, the best time of his life.

Ian points to the top of the slide—he wants to go again.

Danny lifts him back up on the slide for the umpteenth time, hoping to wear the kid out so he'll take a nap. He's just now fed him lunch, a peanut-butter-and-jelly sandwich, grapes, and apple slices, so with the food, fresh air, and exercise, he should go right out for an hour or so.

No more than that, though, because Danny doesn't want him awake too late with the sitter at night. But the boy needs the nap and so does Danny, who works nights and then is up early with Ian, so he catches sleep when he can.

Ian points again.

"Last one," Danny says.

Ian slides down, laughing.

Danny picks him up at the bottom of the slide and hoists him on his shoulders because it's time to catch the bus. He has the bus schedule down pat because this is their routine. The bus picks them up across the street from the park and drops them a block away from the little apartment in a nondescript neighborhood in downtown San Diego.

When they first got to California, Danny took whatever low-level, off-the-radar jobs he could find. Night clerk at a motel in exchange for a room, custodian at a trailer park in lieu of rent, fry cook at a diner, driving a gypsy cab.

But after three months of that he decided that he had to stop moving Ian all over the place, so he found an off-the-books job tending bar at an Irish pub in the Gaslamp, serving old Harps who'd retired to sunny California but still wanted a feel of their northeast alcoholic lives.

At first the number of retired cops who come into the place scared the bejesus out of Danny, but he soon learned they were a lot more interested in their beers and chasers than they were in him.

Calling himself John Doyle, he cut his hair and grew a cheesy mustache, and no one cares as long as he doesn't water the drinks and he tosses in a freebie now and then to the steady customers, even though none of them seem to be able to dig a tip out of their pockets.

Danny minds his own business, pours the booze, lugs the kegs and the ice, mops the floor, cleans the bathrooms, goes home and pays the sitter.

Short nights and then up early with Ian. Making his breakfast, letting him watch a few cartoons, then off to the beach or the park to find other kids and let him play. Couple of opportunities in the park with some of the divorced mommies who throw hints that they wouldn't mind, but Danny doesn't catch them.

Something Marty taught him—when you're on the run, you leave the skirts alone. You don't believe him, ask Dillinger, ask any of them. Danny believes him, but also he isn't close to being over Terri and it seems wrong to hop into bed with another woman, even for a meaningless roll.

Anyway, Danny's too busy doing the daddy thing.

Jesus, who knew?

How much work a toddler could be.

How constant it is.

Between making meals, cajoling Ian into eating, then keeping him busy and occupied, playing with him, giving him baths . . . then there's the diapers, and Danny is glad that Ian is in the potty-training phase now, into Huggies and "big-boy pants." Danny had no freakin' clue how to go about this, so he walked down to the library one day and looked up books on the subject.

Which about drove him nuts, because they all offered contradictory advice. Do this or you'll fuck your kid up forever. No, do the opposite or you'll fuck your kid up forever.

Marty was no help because, for one thing, he was a lousy father, and for the other thing, he can barely remember last week, never mind thirty years ago.

Thank God for the women at the playground, who took pity on a single father and told him what to do.

They also told him to relax.

"Of course you'll fuck your kid up," one said. "Didn't your parents fuck you up?"

Oh hell yes, Danny thought.

"Kids are hard to break," the woman said. "Just love him, that's all."

Danny hopes that's enough.

Hopes he gets the chance.

There's still the possibility of federal drug indictments—God only knows what grand juries are out there. Then there are potential Rhode Island charges for robbery, weapons, homicide, a grab bag of counts that could put him away for longer than life.

This morning he called his lawyer, Dennehy, back in Providence.

"No news is good news," Dennehy said. "No indictment on the drug charges."

"What about that other thing?"

Jardine.

"Did you ever have any dealings with a fed named Regina Moneta?" Dennehy asked. "Was out of Boston in your day, now she's in Washington?"

"No. Why?"

"Apparently she's been pushing you for the Jardine homicide," Dennehy said. "The Rhode Island AG's office pushed back, said they have nothing linking you. But she's trying to lay a U.S. Eighteen on you."

"What's that?"

"U.S. Code Title Eighteen, Section One Fourteen," Dennehy said. "Murder of a federal law enforcement officer. Carries the death penalty."

"I'm so glad I called."

"She's got nothing. Can't get the federal prosecutors interested."

"What's her beef with me?" Danny asked.

"Word is she was banging Jardine," Dennehy said. "Anyway, better you still keep your head down for a while."

Danny hung up, not feeling much better about things.

Now he goes and catches the bus with Ian, whose eyes are already getting heavy. Danny hopes the boy goes down for a nap, because his naps are Danny's naps, and his chance to grab a shower.

Ian's asleep before the bus stops, and Danny picks him up, carries him into the apartment and lays him on the bed. Danny sleeps for fifteen minutes himself, takes a shower, then shoves dirty laundry into a pillowcase.

He has the sitter coming over early so he can go to the laundromat, because they're about out of clean clothes.

"There's mac and cheese in the fridge," he tells Chauncey when she gets there. She's a neighbor girl who goes to community college, and Ian likes her.

"Cool."

"Let him watch some cartoons and the VHS of that farmer thing he likes," Danny says.

"Got it."

"I'll come back with the laundry and give him a kiss before I go to work."

Danny walks down to the laundromat and sticks dollar bills into the change machine to get quarters. He separates the darks from the whites—again, thank God for the women in the park—and finds two available machines.

Jimmy Mac comes in a half hour later and sits down next to him.

Jimmy lives in an apartment over some old lady's garage. She's grateful for the rent in cash and doesn't ask questions, and he got himself an off-the-books job in an auto body shop.

He and Danny get together, but not too often, and never at each other's homes.

Jimmy gets right to it. "I'm thinking of bringing Angie and the kids out."

"It's too soon."

"I gotta do something," Jimmy says. "Angie's bagging groceries at Almacs, for Chrissakes. I dunno, maybe I should go back."

"You can't do that, either."

"There's no indictments on me."

"Tell that to Peter Moretti," Danny says. "I'm sure he'll give you a pass."

"I'm not leaving my family forever, Danny."

Danny hears the unspoken rebuke. You have your kid with you. And this is your responsibility—you dumped the drugs that would have given us a different life.

The washers stop. Danny gets up and loads the clothing into the dryers.

Jimmy comes and helps him. "I need to earn. Real money."

"I know."

"So?"

"So a little while longer, Jimmy."

Danny closes the dryer door.

"Until when?" Jimmy asks. "What happens that changes things?"

Danny doesn't know.

This Moneta woman gives it up?

Peter dies?

Neither of those things is likely to happen.

"What are you thinking about?" Danny asks.

Jimmy lowers his voice. "Cars. You can boost cars here, drive them over to Mexico and get better than book price."

"And if you got busted?"

"I'd never give you up, Danny."

"I know that," Danny says. "But the feds, the Morettis . . . just give it a little more time, Jimmy."

Danny isn't going to do any work and he isn't going to let Jimmy do any, either. All they need, one of them gets popped and they're on some extradition van back to RI. And what is Ian gonna do, with his mom dead and his dad in the joint? And even if they pull something off and don't get caught, word gets around.

To the worst places.

It's like a law.

But Jimmy will do what he asks, because Jimmy always does.

He's loyal.

Danny worries more about the Altar Boys.

He doesn't hear much from South and Coombs, but they check in. Every couple of weeks they call Bernie Hughes, let him know where they are—up in the Bay Area for a while, then down in Anaheim going to Disneyland every day.

Bernie is still holed up in New Hampshire, a little too close to Providence for Danny's liking, but not in any real danger because he's never done any wet work.

Jimmy's right, though, he thinks. When I left Providence I just left. I had no real plan and I still don't. And things can't go on like this much longer.

When Danny brings the laundry home, Ian is up and playing with some big Legos on the floor with Chauncey.

"Daddy!"

Danny lifts him up and kisses him on the cheek. "Love you."

"Love *you*."

He sets him down. "I'll be home when you wake up."

"Okay." Ian's eager to get back to playing.

Danny walks down to the bar.

It's a hard time.

Mourning Terri, taking care of Ian, dealing with the old man, making shit money, worrying about indictments, worrying about getting recognized, worrying about what the hell he's going to do with his life, how he's going to provide for Ian as he gets older, sweating how he's going to provide for Ian *now*, what with his small take-home barely able to cover rent, milk, cereal . . .

And then he always has his head on a swivel, is always paranoid. Was that guy who looked at him for an extra second one of Moretti's scouts? Was the new guy who came into the bar a fed?

It wears Danny down.

Danny doesn't love his life, but it's life and who said you were ever going to like it anyway? He isn't in a cell or a grave, he isn't killing anybody or getting killed, and maybe that's all you can ask for in this world.

You get that, maybe you keep your head down and your mouth shut, show a little gratitude, a little humility.

He's raising his kid, what he's doing.

Being a father.

FIVE

A LOT OF PEOPLE ARE UNHAPPY with Peter Moretti.

No one got paid, the investors lost their investments.

He tries to tough it out. *Hey, you knew it was a risk. It got boosted, what can I tell you?* Yeah, and Peter's the boss, so no one is going to hold him accountable, but Peter is smart enough to know this truth: A boss stays a boss as long as he's making other people money. When he starts *costing* people money, they start looking around for a new boss.

Peter's heard the drumbeats. They're muffled, but they're out there. Now he sits in the office with his new consigliere, Vinnie Calfo. "Any pings on Ryan?"

"The cocksucker is off the radar," Vinnie says.

Vinnie is just out from a three-year bit pumping iron at the ACI. He likes to wear tight-fitting T-shirts to show off the guns and the triceps, and he is one good-looking guinea. But Vinnie is no dumb stooge, a smart fucking guy with a string of his own strip clubs, car washes, and an asphalt business. Peter doesn't like Vinnie all that much, but there weren't a lot of choices.

Sal Antonucci dead.

Tony Romano dead.

Chris in the wind.

And his brother, Paulie, he's no help. He just took his *buciac* of a wife, Pam, and moved down to Florida. Doesn't want to know from any of this shit, doesn't lend a finger, never mind a hand.

The Morettis won the war but it left them depleted, and Peter tasked Vinnie with getting some new guys on the books. Whatever else you might want to say about him, Vinnie is an earner, which Peter desperately needs now that he's lost his drug investment. Without enough people on the streets, there isn't a lot of money coming in.

So Peter's working like a motherfucker, pulling scams he wouldn't have touched a year ago. Bullshit like stealing city-owned asphalt and selling it to contractors, swapping out parts at car repair joints for cheaper merchandise and selling the real stuff to dealers, that kind of nickel-and-dime shit.

Except it's not enough nickels and dimes.

"It could have been Chris *and* Ryan," Vinnie says. "They could have been in what-do-you-call-it—cahoots."

Peter stares at him. "'Cahoots'?"

Vinnie shrugs.

"What about Jimmy MacNeese?" Peter asks. "He still has family here, right?"

"Yeah . . ."

"So go talk to the wife," Peter says. "I'll bet she knows where her husband is."

Vinnie looks sketchy.

"What?" Peter asks.

"We don't do that kind of thing, do we?" Vinnie asks. "I mean, we got rules. Families are off-limits."

"You're saying you won't do it?"

"I'm saying it's a bad idea," Vinnie says. "The guys won't like it."

"Then let 'the guys' come up with the money," Peter says, realizing as he says it that it's a bad thing to say. The guys, including Vinnie here, already came up with the money.

"What about Chris's wife?" Vinnie asks, as long as they're talking wives here.

"Cathy? What about her?"

"Maybe she knows where *her* husband is," Vinnie says.

"I'll talk to her."

But Peter doesn't really think Chris has the dope.

It's Danny fucking Ryan. If that Irish prick is somewhere playing Jimmy Buffett on my money, Peter thinks, I'm going to make him hurt before I kill him.

VINNIE RINGS MACNEESE'S doorbell.

Angie MacNeese comes to the door. She looks like hammered shit, face pale, eyes swollen like she's been crying. "Yes?"

"Sorry to bother you," Vinnie says. "I'm an old friend of Jimmy's."

"No, you're not," Angie says. "I know all of Jimmy's old friends. Are you a cop or did Peter send you, or both?"

"I'm not a cop," Vinnie says. "Can I come in?"

"No."

Vinnie smiles. "You're going to leave me standing out here in the cold?"

"What do you want?"

"Where's Jimmy?"

"I don't know," Angie says. "And if I did, I wouldn't tell you."

"He hasn't called you or anything?" Vinnie asks.

Angie doesn't answer. She tries to shut the door but Vinnie sticks his foot in it. "Angie . . . it's Angie, right? It would be a lot better for you . . . and your kids . . . if you told me where Jimmy is."

He feels like shit saying this. It isn't right, and like he told Peter, the guys aren't going to like it because they'll think if Peter would come down on MacNeese's family, he'd do it to theirs.

Angie's eyes fill with tears. "I don't know where my husband is."

Vinnie moves his foot.

Angie closes the door.

PETER SITS IN Chris Palumbo's kitchen.

He's been there a thousand times, but always with Chris, never just sitting there at the kitchen breakfast bar with the guy's wife. Peter's known Cathy Palumbo forever, since high school; he was Chris's best man at the wedding.

"You want to know where Chris is," Cathy says, getting right to it.

She's a looker, Cathy Palumbo, Peter thinks. Always has been—long blond hair, blue eyes. No tits to speak of, but you can't have everything. Chris used to joke, "If I want to look at tits, I own a strip club."

Peter says, "This isn't like him, just taking off. I'm worried about him."

Cathy smiles. "You're worried about *you*, Peter."

"That too."

"I don't know where Chris is," Cathy says. "Maybe with his *gumar*."

"I didn't know he had a *gumar*," Peter says.

"Bullshit."

"Okay, bullshit," Peter says. He's already talked to Chris's mistress, who didn't know where Chris was. "I really need to find him, Cath."

"You think I'm going to help you kill my husband?"

"I just want to talk with him."

"Fuck you, Peter."

"It would be better for you—"

"You threatening me?" Cathy asks. "What is *that*? I mean, there used to be rules to this thing. I accepted them. My husband has *gumars* . . . okay, he has *gumars*. I accepted that. He don't talk about his business, okay, he don't talk about his business, I accepted that. He might not come home some night. I accepted that. But now you come into my house and threaten me? That, I do not accept."

"Tell me where he is and—"

"Get out of my house, Peter."

He gets up and leaves.

PETER HAD TWO fucking drinks before leaving the city—two fucking vodkas . . . okay, three—and now he sits in his car pulled over on Route 4 and waits for the state trooper to walk up.

When he does, Peter rolls down the window.

"License and registration."

Peter hands him both and knows that will do it. Once a cop sees his name, it's *Sorry, Mr. Moretti. But hey, be a little more careful the next time.* So he's surprised when the trooper says, "Get out of the car, please."

"What?"

"Get out of the car, please."

"Why?"

"Because I asked you to."

Peter looks at the trooper's nameplate—O'Leary.

Figures.

"Do you know who I am?" Peter asks.

"Please get out of the car," O'Leary says. "I'm not going to ask again."

Peter gets out.

Traffic streams past them. It's humiliating.

"Do you know why I stopped you?"

"I was speeding," Peter says.

"Have you been drinking today, sir?" O'Leary asks.

"No."

"Your breath smells like alcohol."

"Mouthwash," Peter says.

"I don't think so."

"I may have had a drink."

"*A* drink?"

Peter doesn't answer. Fuck this shit. You'd have a drink or two yourself, you mutt, if you were down millions, your own guys are looking at you funny, and you're headed home to a wife who's only going to present you with more headaches.

O'Leary administers a Breathalyzer test.

Peter blows a 1.1.

"The legal limit in Rhode Island is zero point eight, sir," O'Leary says. "I'm going to place you under arrest for driving under the influence. Turn around and put your hands behind your back, please."

"You been on the job long?" Peter asks. "Because you're not going to be on it much longer after I call your boss."

"Turn around, please."

O'Leary does cut him a break, though, and doesn't have the car towed. Lets Paulie come pick it up.

Peter's out on bail in an hour.

Vinnie picks him up and drives him down to the big house along the Narragansett shore, the "Italian Riviera," that his wife insisted they needed. Pulls under the stone arch onto the driveway.

A fucking mansion is what it is, Peter thinks as he gets out of the car, but Celia had to have it.

"You're the boss of New England now," she said. "You can't live like some old *paisan*, it doesn't look good."

They had a perfectly nice house in Cranston—modern, four bedrooms, two and a half baths—but that wasn't good enough for Celia.

No, she had to have the place overlooking the ocean, a stone archway over the driveway, five bedrooms, three bathrooms, a guesthouse, a tennis court, and a swimming pool. A swimming pool, right next to the fucking Atlantic, you'd think that would be enough water for her, and neither of them plays tennis, although Celia has started taking lessons.

The money the place cost, never mind the upkeep, he's millions in the hole and Celia's throwing parties in there that are like that movie, what was it, with Robert Redford and somebody.

Peter takes a deep breath before going in, because he knows the second he walks through the door, Celia is going to hit him up with a problem.

It could be the water heater isn't heating water fast enough, or the decorator doesn't understand her "vision," or the cheap vodka he got won't suit the guests she's invited, but these days the problem is usually Gina.

The Morettis have three kids—a son and two daughters.

Peter wanted more, but Celia, she didn't want to be like one of them old-style Italian mothers, cranking out bambinos. She wanted Peter to get a vasectomy, which he resolutely refused to do.

"You get cut or I'll cut you off," Celia told him.

"Go on the pill."

"It has side effects."

"Cutting on my balls don't?"

"What do you care, anyway?" Celia asked. "You can always fuck your *gumar.*"

This was true, Peter thinks. Still and all, a man has a right to have sex with his wife, especially one that costs as much as Celia, with her parties and her make-overs, and her closets full of clothes.

She did go on the pill, but they only screw occasionally, mostly when she's had a few at one of the parties and is feeling good after the guests have left. When Celia wants it, she really wants it and she's a tigress in bed. And beautiful, no one can take that away from her. As much as she spends keeping herself up, it's worth it.

Anyway, they had Heather, then Peter Jr., then Gina, and stopped at that.

Heather is twenty, Peter is eighteen, Gina sixteen, perfectly spaced at the ideal two years apart.

Heather's away at college down at URI, a smart kid studying business. She and Peter are close, tight, and he misses her because she don't come home on weekends a lot, likes to party, but what the hell, that's what college kids do, right?

Peter Jr. is everything a father could want. Handsome, athletic—a star at baseball and basketball—respectful, good with the girls, a leader among the boys. Peter adores him.

And they've already had "the talk."

Not the sex talk, the Mafia father talk.

Peter Jr. knows what his father does to put bread on the table—he isn't an idiot—and when he was sixteen, Peter sat him down and said, "That's me, that's not you. You can do better—a doctor, a lawyer . . ."

Except Peter Jr. didn't want that, either.

Not yet.

First, he wanted to go into the military.

The marines.

"Why?" Peter asked his son. "Why not college?"

"It's my duty," Peter Jr. said. "First the military, then I'll go to college. Besides, that way, they'll pay for it."

"Money isn't your problem in life," Peter said.

Which was true.

Then.

Peter questioned his son's decision about this, and Celia was dead set against it, like most mothers would be, but secretly he was proud of the boy. So Peter Jr. enlisted in the Corps.

He's not the problem.

The problem is Gina.

Peter could never understand it.

The girl is as beautiful as her mother, maybe more so, but she can never seem to be happy.

Gina is depressed.

Gina was anorexic, then Gina was bulimic. Gina cries all the time, all the time she isn't throwing temper tantrums, screaming at Celia or Peter, or just lying on her bed staring at the ceiling.

She's a "gifted" student who couldn't pull good grades, a cheerleader who quit the squad, a gymnast who gave up on that, too. Over Peter's objections, Celia took the girl to a shrink, then another when that didn't work, then another, who prescribed a cocktail of medications that only seemed to make things worse.

Now, as Peter walks through the door, Celia is waiting, martini in hand, not for him, for herself.

What she has for him is more agita.

"She's in her room," Celia says.

"Of course she is."

"She's been cutting herself."

"The fuck you mean?"

"Cutting herself," Celia says. "She takes a little knife and slices her legs. Not deep, but enough to bleed. I guess it's a thing."

"A 'thing'?"

"Rosa saw the blood when she was changing the sheets," Celia says. "It was embarrassing. I confronted Gina about it."

"And?"

"And she admitted it."

"Did she say why?" Peter asks.

"She said it makes her know she's alive."

"Cutting herself does," Peter says.

"That's what she said."

Peter walks over to the bar and pours himself a vodka. Jesus Christ, his daughter taking a knife to herself.

"I called Dr. Schneider," Celia says.

"And that quack said what?"

"There's a place," Celia says. "In Vermont."

"A 'place.'"

"For girls like Gina."

"The fuck does that mean," Peter says, starting to get angry, "'girls like Gina'?"

"Girls that cut themselves."

"I'm not sending my daughter to some nut house."

"It's not a nut house," Celia says. "It's more like a boarding school, or a resort, but with doctors."

"*I'd* like to go to a resort," Peter says. "Can I?"

"Dr. Schneider says she needs inpatient treatment."

"What do you want to bet he has a piece of this joint? Do you know how much these places cost?" Probably not, Peter thinks, because Celia isn't one to look at price tags. "Or how long she'd be there?"

"They won't know," Celia says, "until they see how the treatment is going."

"No, of course not," Peter says. "I'll tell you how long—for as long as we keep paying the bill. The second we don't, she's cured. 'It's a miracle.'"

"We're talking about our daughter here," Celia says. "It costs what it costs."

"We don't have the money."

"What do you mean?"

"What do I mean?" Peter asks. He knocks back a swallow of the vodka. "What about what I said was unclear? We . . . don't . . . have . . . the . . . money. *No abbiamo la escarole. Capisce?*"

He rubs his thumb and forefinger together.

"Since when?" Celia asks.

"Business is bad right now."

She stares him down. Classic Celia, in her gold silk blouse unbuttoned enough to show a little cleavage and the tight pants to show off the ass he paid for in the gym membership and the personal trainer, she arches her trimmed eyebrow at him and stares him down. "But you have enough money to put diamonds on your *gumar*'s neck, I'll bet."

He slams the glass down on the bar. "You want to send her to this school, mental hospital, spa, whatever the fuck, let's sell this house and we'll have the money. Sell that rock on your finger, we'll have the money. Go upstairs, empty out your shoe closet, for fuck's sake, we'll probably have the money right there."

"Peter, we're going to do this."

"No, Celia, we're not," Peter says. "She just wants attention."

"Because you never give her any," Celia says. "You're always too busy working."

Yeah, I'm busy putting clothes on her back, a roof over her head, food in her mouth, which she pukes up anyway, Peter thinks. "The kid needs to toughen up. She scratches herself and you want to reward her by sending her on a vacation. *Basta*. Enough."

Celia glares at him. The full *malocchio*. "I hate you."

"Get in line."

Peter finishes his drink and walks upstairs to the bedroom suite with its sweeping view of the ocean. Strips, gets into the shower and stands under the spray. Gets out, puts on a robe and calls his lawyer about the DUI.

"The best I can do for you," the lawyer says, "is a thousand-dollar fine. No jail time, though."

"The fuck is happening to this state?" Peter asks.

"And you have to go to meetings."

"You mean that twelve-step shit?" Peter says. "Forget it. I'm not some alcoholic."

"You want to keep your license, Peter?" the lawyer asks. "What's the big deal, you sit through a few sob stories, they sign your paperwork, you're done."

Peter hangs up.

I have to go to fucking meetings, he thinks.

My daughter is a wack job.

My wife hates me.

I'm going fucking broke.

My guys are about to mutiny.

If this is winning a war, I'd hate to see what losing looks like.

I have to find Danny Ryan.

SIX

ONE OF THE RISKIER THINGS Danny does is to go check on his old man. Marty and Ned are holed up in an SRO hotel in the seedy Gaslamp District under fake names, but everybody who's looking for Danny knows he left with his kid and his father, so the visits are potential exposure.

At least Marty fits in at the Golden Lion, which is full of old alcoholics on their way out.

Danny brings the usual groceries, but this time the guy at the front desk stops him. "Need a word with you."

"What's up?"

"It's your uncle," the guy says. "He can't stay here no more."

"Why not?"

"He can't take care of himself," the guy says. "He don't know where he is half the time."

Danny looks around the lobby, where a half dozen old men sit staring into God knows where and a couple of others stagger around having conversations with ghosts. "And these other guys are what, Magellan?"

"He shits his bed," the guy says. "We get complaints. The smell."

Danny knew Marty was getting worse, but he didn't know it was that bad. And Ned would never rat Marty out about something like this. Danny has seen Marty's lapses in memory, his legs getting shakier and shakier, a couple of times he's asked how Terri is, but shitting the bed?

"The owner says he's gotta leave. I can give you a week."

"Okay. Thanks."

Now what? Danny thinks.

He browbeats Marty into going to a clinic with him, gets him checked out. Marty calls him every name in the book but goes.

The doctor comes out of the exam room to talk with Danny. He's young but pragmatic. "Look, I could run a battery of tests, but it's readily apparent that your uncle has dementia, exacerbated by late-stage, chronic alcoholism. His liver is shot, he's losing control of his bodily functions, his mental acuity is fading fast. He'll show flashes of his old self, but he's going to need full-time residential care."

Danny thought his old man would put up more of a fight about going into a home, but he doesn't.

"I get my own room?" Marty asks.

"You get your own room."

"And the nurses will give me hand jobs?"

"That you have to negotiate for yourself," Danny says.

"See if I don't."

Money is another issue. Danny doesn't see how he's going to pay for it, but Marty says, "I got insurance. 'Long-term care.'"

"You do?"

"Your wife made me take it out," Marty says.

Which makes sense, Danny thinks. Terri was always the cautious one, the one who thought ahead.

It's risky, though, because Marty will have to use his own name to access the policy. There are no charges or indictments against him, but it's still a connection to Danny.

I have to take the risk, though, Danny thinks.

I don't have a choice.

He finds a place in North Park that has a vacancy.

Marty gets a little misty-eyed when it's time to say goodbye, maybe the first time Danny has seen him show any actual human feeling.

Ned is stoic, like usual, but Danny can see it's hard on him. He tells him he can get a bus and visit every day if he wants.

"And I'll come over a couple of times a week," Danny says.

"Okay, John," Marty says to Danny.

"Dad, it's Danny."

"I'm fucking with you, dipstick," Marty says. "Be careful, huh? I don't want anything to happen to you. Who'd bring me my Hormels?"

THAT NIGHT DANNY has a dream.

Wicked weird dream.

He's in a cemetery, Swan Point, walking, looking for Terri's grave but he can't find it. Then he sees Sheila Murphy standing at Pat's headstone. She has a bottle of Narragansett in her hand, and she's pouring the beer on his grave.

She sees him.

"Danny?" she asks. "Is that you?"

"Sheila? What the—"

"I come here every day," she says. She stares at him, like she can't believe he's real. "I thought you were dead."

"No."

"Ian? Is he alive?"

"Yeah. he's fine."

"But Terri isn't," Sheila says. "She's here with Patrick."

"I can't find her," Danny says.

Sheila says, "I got married again."

"You did?" Danny asks.

"To Patrick's brother."

"Liam?" Danny's shocked.

"No," she says. "Liam's dead. He's here. To Patrick's other brother, Tommy."

Danny's confused. There were only two Murphy brothers, Patrick and Liam. But then a man walks up, he looks a lot like Patrick, only older and heavier, settled and content.

"Nice to see you, Danny," Tommy says. "But you don't belong here. I mean, you think this is the place for you, but it isn't."

"Where is, then?"

"I dunno," Tommy says. He wraps his arm around Sheila's shoulder. His hands are big. "But Pasco told me."

"When did you see Pasco?"

"I see him all the time."

Sheila is knitting. She hands Danny a green sweater. "For Ian. So he'll remember where he came from."

Then Danny wakes up. It takes him a minute to remember where he is and even then he feels a little shook. Danny's not a big believer in dreams, that they mean anything, but that was fucked up. Pat never had another brother; Sheila would never remarry.

And what did he mean, this place isn't for me? And what does Pasco have to do with it?

And why couldn't I find Terri's grave?

Maybe because you know you'll never be able to go there, visit her.

He hears Ian babbling, and goes in to get him and make his breakfast.

Oatmeal, maybe, or a scrambled egg if he can get him to eat it.

SEVEN

CHRIS PALUMBO HAD A SERIOUS problem.

He brokered a deal with the Abbarca people for forty keys of H, got Peter Moretti and half the wiseguys in New England to put their money in, and then got Danny Ryan and his Irish crew to jack it.

It was classic Chris Palumbo: find a way to fuck everybody.

He was going to fuck Ryan by getting all the Irish busted with the dope. Then he and the fed Jardine were going to fuck Peter by making off with the drugs themselves, and letting Peter take the blame for losing everyone's money.

Chris's way of pushing Peter off the throne and taking it himself.

Because Chris was sick of having to fix all of Peter's mistakes, sick of kicking up to the guy, sick of cleaning up after his idiot brother, Paulie.

But it all got fucked up.

Chris was supposed to take the ten kilos that Danny Ryan had stashed away. But Danny somehow grew a pair of balls and faced Chris down, threatening to kill his whole family. Okay, they could have lost the ten keys—not great but not fatal—but then Jardine got himself killed.

Inconsiderate prick.

So none of the heroin that was supposed to come to Chris got there. His deal for immunity for his past indiscretions was as dead as Jardine. And Peter Moretti doubtless suspected him of ripping off the heroin and was just as doubtless looking for his head.

So Chris Palumbo, who loved complicated machinations, took the simplest solution.

He ran.

Just because Peter has issued a death sentence, Chris thought, doesn't mean I have to show up for the execution.

They can hold it without me.

Chris blew his chance to take the corner office, but the truth is that he wasn't all that unhappy to leave. He was tired of the goombah wiseguy thing, tired of the inbred, suffocating, everyone-living-up-everyone-else's-ass Rhode Island scene. The Sunday family dinners, the weddings, the christenings, all the mandatory events that started to bore him breath-less.

Sure, he had a family, but the kids were pretty much grown up now and his wife, well, Cathy was always pretty able to take care of herself.

He'd send her some cash when he had it to send.

And he fully intended to come back, he really did, as soon as things cooled off. Maybe when people finally got tired of Peter's bullshit and decided to do something about it.

In the meantime, he was sure that his family would rather have a missing husband and father than a dead one. So Chris took the hundred K in mad money he had stored in his *gumar*'s crawl space, gave her a peck on the cheek and took off.

Thought about Florida but then thought better of it. Every wiseguy in the northeast goes down to Miami or Boca for weekends or vacations. His next choice would have been Vegas, but same thing.

He wanted someplace warm, though, someplace with some fucking sun.

So now he sits in Scottsdale, Arizona, sipping on a beer and looking across the table at Frankie Vecchio.

Frankie fucking V, he of the big ears and the bigger mouth. Hears everything, tells everything he hears and then some.

It was Frankie that Chris manipulated into gulling Ryan and the Irish into the heroin boost, Frankie who promised to testify against them in exchange for immunity and a new life in the Witness Protection Program.

Frankie is so fucking dumb that he turned his whole five keys of heroin over to the government when he went into protection, leaving himself broke, and then so fucking dumber that he got bored selling aluminum siding or what-the-fuck-ever and left the program.

So Frankie's in the wind, too.

What Frankie's mostly useful for is being used, Chris thinks.

At this he never fails.

Frankie hates Arizona, at least that's what he tells Chris. "*Marone*, the heat. I feel like my head is going to explode."

Chris doesn't feel that way. One thing that has surprised him is how much he likes the desert. The sun, the heat, how you never have to think about getting into a coat, boots, gloves. He wears shorts and a polo shirt most of the time. Sandals. You don't like the heat, you got air-conditioning. You go out, play a round early in the morning, maybe again around sunset.

He wishes he'd come to Scottsdale years ago.

Maybe Cathy would like it here, if she could stand being away from her sisters, fighting with them all the time.

Frankie's also concerned about the ethnic composition. "A lot of Mexicans here. You notice that?"

"It used to be Mexico."

"Still is, far as I can tell."

This does not bother Chris in the least. He's developed a taste for Mexican food, although he could do without the mariachi bands.

No, he likes Arizona.

He found himself a woman, the real estate manager who hooked him up with his nice one-bedroom condo, didn't ask a lot of inconvenient questions on the application form, and then helped him test out the bed.

Chris has actually tried to feel homesick, mostly out of guilt, tried to miss Cathy and the kids, but the fact is he just doesn't. Not yet, at least. This is a good life, the sweet life, and he's happy here.

The one problem is money.

It's leaking out his ass.

A hundred K sounds like a lot of money, and he's fine for now, but it isn't going to last forever. He's going to need money. What he'd really like is to open a car dealership, but he can't do anything legit or out in the open. That's the thing about this life of ours, Chris thinks, you cross a certain bridge, you can't ever come back to the other side.

"So what do you want to do?" Frankie asks. Because he's never had an original idea in his life.

"I'm thinking of getting back in touch with the Abbarca people," Chris says.

"Because it worked out so well last time?"

"Hey, the Mexicans got their money," Chris says. "They have no beef with us. But I'm thinking coke instead of horse. Better class of customer."

"What? Crack whores?"

"No, rich white guys," Chris says. "Doctors, lawyers, Indian chiefs. Those motherfuckers on the golf course, they're always looking for blow."

"You got the money for it?"

"I've got credit."

"You think so?"

Yeah, I do, Chris thinks. That's why I said it.

Next day, him and Frankie get in Chris's Caddy and drive to Ruidoso, New Mexico, where one of Popeye Abbarca's top guys has a horse ranch.

VINNIE CAN FUCK.

The man is tireless.

Celia gets out of bed and starts to dress. She debated with herself whether to shower at the motel or wait until she got home, but decided on the latter because Peter won't be home anyway, and the less time her car sits outside the Holiday Inn the better, even though she parks it out back.

Vinnie lies on the bed with that smug look on his face.

Yeah, I know, Celia thinks—you got me off. But I got you off, too. Christ, it was like a busted hydrant shooting into me.

"So, Wednesday?" Vinnie asks.

"Here?"

"We should mix it up," he says.

Fucking the boss's wife, you can't be too careful.

PETER GOES TO the meetings. They're boring as shit, but the stories these drunks tell can be kind of funny and they have coffee and cookies. After a few meetings, he gets to almost liking them. There's something about the quiet, the peacefulness, the soulfulness of it.

His sixth one, he sees a young woman with long red hair and a sad expression.

He hasn't seen her in years.

Cassie Murphy.

SHE RECOGNIZES HIM.

In another lifetime they were even sort of friends, used to hang out on the beach, go to Pasco Ferri's clambakes together. That was back when she was clean and sober, doing pretty well, off the booze, off the smack.

Before all the shit happened and the Murphys and Morettis went to war against each other. Back before her brothers were killed and her father went to prison and she started shooting up again. Now she's trying to get clean, she's back in the church basements, but it isn't going so well.

They come face-to-face on the steps outside the church.

"Cassie."

"Peter."

They don't know what to say. What is there to say? He destroyed her family, ruined her life.

No, that's not exactly true, Cassie thinks. Everything we did, we did to ourselves. She had begged Danny Ryan, her good friend, not to do the heroin boost with Liam, but he did it anyway.

Peter Moretti didn't make them do that.

She says, "This is one of the last places I'd expect to see you."

"DUI," Peter says. "You?"

"You know, it's an old story with me."

"Yeah, I kind of remember."

A long silence but neither of them walks away. They're the only ones on the steps now; everyone else has gone.

Peter says, "I know this is weird, but you want to get coffee or something?"

It is weird, Cassie thinks. Very weird. But she's still a little high from her last fix, and she knows that unless she does something different she's going to go out and fix again, so she says yes.

They have coffee, that's all.

Talk about the program.

Peter finds himself talking about Gina.

How he tries to pay more attention to her because he sure as shit isn't going to ship her off to some five-star booby hatch in Vermont.

But paying attention to Gina isn't easy because she spends most of her time in her room with the door locked. And he isn't home a lot, because he's out scuffling money.

Cassie, she sits and listens. Surprised that Peter Moretti, a stone goombah, is opening up like this.

"You should share in the meeting," Cassie says.

"Fuck that," Peter says.

CHRIS ACTUALLY HAS to explain to Frankie V that "quarter horse" doesn't mean one-fourth of a horse.

"It's a *breed* of horse," Chris says in the car as they're going up the road to Neto Valdez's ranch. "They use them for herding cattle."

"Then why do they call them quarter horses?" Frankie asks.

"The fuck do I know?" Chris says.

The fuck do I *care*?

There must be a lot of money in horses, though, because the fucking ranch is beautiful. Chris is impressed as he drives beside long white fences that border beautiful green pastures.

Irrigation sprinklers hiss rhythmically.

Neto meets them outside the house.

White cowboy hat, denim shirt with mother-of-pearl snaps, brown Lucchese boots.

Neto is one handsome motherfucker.

He greets Chris warmly. "Chris, it's been too long."

Yeah, they ain't seen each other since Chris arranged for the heroin shipment.

"Neto," Chris says, "this is a friend of ours, Frankie."

"*Bienvenido*," Neto says.

He shows them around the stables. Turns out his quarter horses go for about $150K or more. "The real money, though, is in stud fees."

He explains how they freeze the semen and ship it to buyers.

"You mean there's money in horse come?" Frankie whispers to Chris.

"I guess so."

"Who knew?" Frankie asks.

And Chris knows that no racetrack in America is ever going to be safe again because even now Frankie is figuring out how he can go around jacking off the horses.

After the tour, Neto leads them to a patio for lunch. Beautiful lunch, beautiful food—carne asada, shrimp, fresh fruit, ice-cold beers.

They get down to business. Chris says he wants to buy some coke.

"How much do you want?" Neto asks.

"I'm thinking ten kilos," Chris says.

"I can give you that," Neto says, "for seventeen K a kilo."

"That's the gringo price," Chris says. "What's the price to a Mexican?"

"You're not a Mexican," Neto says, but he's smiling.

"But I think of you as a brother," Chris says.

"I like you, Chris," Neto says. "You up your order a little bit, I could go down to fifteen."

"Fifteen at fifteen?" Chris asks.

"Done," Neto says.

"I have fifty of it in cash," Chris says. "I'll put that down, pay you the rest when I lay it off."

"Oh, Chris."

"Come on," Chris says, "you know I can get double the money in Minneapolis, Omaha, any of those Midwest towns. In a heartbeat."

"I can't forward you one-seventy-five," Neto says. "I like you, Chris, I don't want to see you get in over your head. Tell you what, I'll sell you five at that price, carry you for the rest. You sell it, you come back and pay it off, we do it again."

"Deal," Chris says.

"But I'll need collateral," Neto says.

"I'm a little short on that," Chris says.

"You're on the run," Neto says. "I heard all about it. But you have to leave me with some security, Chris."

Chris does.

He leaves him with Frankie V.

It's like a pawn shop.

If Chris comes back with the money, he redeems Frankie.

If he doesn't . . .

Frankie's seriously fucked.

PETER GETS HOME and walks through the door just in time to hear the screams. They're Celia's and they're coming from upstairs. He takes the stairs three at a time and sees that Gina's door is open.

Celia is standing there.

Her screams are shrieks, the worst thing he's ever heard.

Peter shoves her aside and sees Gina on her bed.

The covers are red, Gina's head is thrown back across the edge of the mattress. Her eyes are open, staring at the ceiling, her mouth agape, her tongue lolling to one side of her mouth.

A knife lies on the floor by her left hand.

Peter grabs her and pulls her up. Her body is limp. He sees the long, deep gashes down her wrists.

Peter slaps her face. "Gina! Gina! Wake up!"

She doesn't answer.

Peter turns to Celia. "Go call 911!"

Celia stands there and keeps shrieking.

"Go fucking call 911!"

She looks down at him.

"It's too late," Celia says. "She's dead."

"No, no, no . . ."

Celia says, "She's dead and you killed her."

GINA MORETTI'S FUNERAL is pathetic.

Well attended, for sure. Every made guy, connected guy, most politicians, more than a few cops, all the friends and neighbors and all their wives are there, at both the church and the cemetery.

Peter Jr. came home on compassionate leave to bury his sister.

It's so sad.

The bereaved parents stand together but don't talk to each other. Celia is tragically beautiful in her black dress, but even under the veil you can see she's tranquilized with pills and probably booze.

Peter is silent as stone.

The whispers, the questions . . . *How could a girl so pretty . . . a girl who had everything . . . What was going on in that house . . . You never know what happens behind closed doors . . .*

Peter is a pallbearer, carrying his child to a hole in the ground. Peter Jr. is another, with Paulie, Vinnie, and two of their crew.

Celia loses it at the graveside. She tosses a handful of dirt onto Gina's coffin and then her knees buckle. Peter tries to hold her up but she shrugs him off. Paulie and Pam grab her before she falls and hold her up as they walk her back to the limousine.

Peter can hear her sobs and howls from the graveside.

PAULIE MORETTI LOOKS through the open bathroom door of the motel room and watches his wife get out of the shower and wrap herself in a big white towel.

Which she could have bought at fucking REI, he thinks, because Pam has put on a few pounds, more than a fucking few. He liked her better when she was doing coke and skinny; now any white powder under her nose probably comes from a doughnut.

It wasn't always like this. It wasn't all that long ago—a handful of years—when Pam was the most beautiful woman he'd ever seen, hell, the most beautiful woman *anyone* had ever seen.

Which was what started the whole fucking thing in the first place— Liam Murphy jealous that Paulie had a woman like that, getting drunk and assaulting her after a beach party, Paulie and Peter and Sal, God rest, beating the shit of Liam. Then Pam had gone to see the Irish fuck at the hospital and ended up leaving with him.

It started there and didn't stop.

How many bodies? How many funerals?

And then Chris came with this fucking genius idea to set the Irish up with this drug boost and here we are. The Irish are finished, we got New England, and I got Pam back, but was it worth it?

Pam is starting to look like the "Before" picture in a Weight Watchers ad.

"That was so sad," Pam says, coming into the bedroom.

"Gina? Yeah." The kid was always a fucking fruitcake, Paulie thinks.

Pam unwraps the towel, lets it drop on the floor and gets into bed. Great, Paulie thinks—a damp towel on the rug.

Fucking slob.

"You want sex?" Pam asks.

"Not really."

She rolls over with her back to him.

Paulie turns up the volume on *Letterman*.

PAM'S RELIEVED THAT Paulie doesn't want sex. When she first went back to him, it was all he wanted, and it was always the same thing—*Am I better than Liam? Did he do this to you, did he do that to you? Did he make you come? Did he make you come like I do?*

She knew the right answers—*You're the best. Liam never did this, never did that. I never came with him. You're the only one who can make me come.*

Getting off the coke hadn't been that hard—she'd mostly done it to keep up with Liam anyway, and because they were so miserable together— but she knows she's replaced the blow with food, just like she knows on some level that she wants to get fat so maybe Paulie will leave her.

She's afraid to leave him.

Afraid, with good reason, that he'll track her down and kill her. He did it before, almost, except she seduced him into fucking her instead. It still comes up on the increasingly rare occasions when he wants sex. The gun comes out and it's *Suck on this first, bitch. What if I just pull the trigger, huh?* Sometimes he keeps the gun barrel in her mouth while he fucks her, thinks she gets off on it too, like she pretends to, because what else is she going to do?

Pam knows now what she *shouldn't* have done.

She shouldn't have given Paulie the dope.

The ten keys of heroin that Liam—beautiful, too-clever-for-his-own-good, arrogant Liam—had left in his coke-fueled rush to get out of the safe house. He had shoved three bricks into a suitcase and the other ten under the bed and left them there.

They ran and kept running until she flipped on him.

The fed Jardine came and busted him and she never saw him again. What she did see was Paulie come into her motel room. Pointed the gun in her face and said, "Hello, bitch."

She thought he was going to shoot her and she begged, "Please. No. I'll fuck you, I'll blow you."

"You think I want Liam Murphy's leftovers?" He pulled the hammer back.

"I'll let you have my ass."

"Murphy didn't have that, too?"

"Please," she cried.

"You got nothing I want."

But it turned out she did. She knew where ten keys of heroin was, if Jardine didn't get to it first. "Let me live, I'll take you there," she said. "We can get out, go somewhere together, have a life.

"I love you," she said. "I've always loved you. Let me prove it."

She took him to the safe house, and thank God, the heroin was still there. Paulie stashed it and a few weeks later headed down to Florida, where they stayed until they came back for poor Gina's funeral.

The money from the dope bought them a decent house in Fort Lauderdale and enough cash to live on and do, well . . . nothing. Paulie never thought about helping Peter out of his financial jam by giving him some of the heroin money.

"Fuck him," was what Paulie said.

Now he falls asleep.

She quietly takes the remote and turns the TV off.

FINALLY. *FINALLY.* THE mourners and the relatives and the morbidly curious leave the house and Peter Jr. and Heather are alone in the living room.

Celia is upstairs in the master bedroom, tranquilized, out cold; Peter is outside on the grounds smoking a cigar.

Peter Jr. says, "I thought they'd never leave."

"They all love this shit," Heather says. "Drama, tragedy."

"It is tragic."

"Strictly speaking, it isn't," Heather says. "It's just sad."

"Is Mom going to be all right?"

"Has she *ever* been all right?" Heather asks. "It's Dad I'm worried about. He holds things in. And it builds. It eats at him."

They sit quietly for a while, then Peter Jr. says, "Poor Gina. I feel like, I don't know, we could have done more or something."

"Don't do that."

"What?"

"Get all guilty," Heather says. "Gina was always selfish and this was just her last, most selfish thing."

"That's harsh."

Heather loves her brother but he's so naive. Of course he is—he's the only son in an Italian family, the Chosen One. Dad made every one of Peter's games, every one of them. Gina, her events were an afterthought and Dad made more apologies than appearances. But he was busier when Gina was growing up, and Heather knows why.

She reads the newspapers.

In fairness to Dad, Gina stopped going to her events, too.

"She blames him, you know," Heather says.

"Who blames who for what?"

Heather rolls her eyes. "Mom blames Dad for Gina killing herself."

"Because he didn't send her to that place in New Hampshire?"

"Vermont," Heather says. "But yeah."

"Maybe it would have helped."

"I doubt it."

"Don't do what you're thinking about doing," Peter Jr. says.

Heather smiles. "What am I thinking about doing?"

"Dropping out of college to move back here and take care of Dad," Peter Jr. says. "He'll be okay."

"Says the kid who ran away to the marines," Heather says. "Don't you do it, either."

"Yeah, I don't think the Marine Corps will let me."

"You know what I mean."

He knows what she means—come back from the Corps and join the family business, become the heir apparent and take over from Dad someday. It's the last thing Peter Jr. wants—hell, it's the last thing Dad wants. "Don't worry, I won't."

Heather says, "I mean, this shit has to end."

Sometime.

EIGHT

REGGIE MONETA PUTS A CASSETTE player on Brent Harris's desk. "We have intelligence that Mr. Ryan might be here in San Diego. One of my brilliant subordinates finally noticed this on the old audio surveillance of the Murphys."

She pushes play and Harris hears, *"So what if the Morettis connect us to the hijacking? What are they going to do? Kill us? They're trying to do that already."*

"That was Liam Murphy," Moneta says. "This is Ryan—"

"They'll try to get their dope back."

"Which is why we should move it now. Don't you want to get to California?"

"What's this?"

"That was John Murphy," Moneta says. "Now listen to what Ryan has to say."

"I've been meaning to tell you, the right moment never came up, but yeah, I'm going to use this money to move out to the West Coast. I'm thinking maybe San Diego."

She shuts off the tape.

That's the intelligence? Harris thinks. *"I'm thinking maybe San Diego"*? Moneta is grasping at any straw. He doesn't need this. He has his hands full already with drug violence seeping across from Tijuana as the Abbarca organization tries to take control of the San Diego gangs. He has exactly zero interest in Moneta's hard-on for Danny Ryan.

He also knows that Moneta's own people feel the same way. No one in the Bureau wants Ryan testifying about Phil Jardine. Which is why Moneta is talking to me, Harris thinks.

Great.

"We know Ryan has connections with the Abbarca organization," Moneta says. "I'm hoping maybe some of your sources might give us something on Ryan."

"Actually, we don't know that," Harris says. "We know that *Chris Palumbo* was hooked up with Abbarca. I'm more interested in finding him."

Moneta says, "Take a walk with me."

"Sure," Harris says. He can't say no, offend the woman, and besides, he's interested in what the head of OC has on her mind that she doesn't want to discuss in the office. So he takes the short walk with her down Broadway to the harbor. They walk north and look out at the small pleasure boats bobbing on the incoming tide.

"I'm guessing you've heard the rumors about Phil Jardine and me," Moneta says.

Embarrassed, Harris shrugs. This day is only getting worse.

"They're true," Moneta says.

"Okay." I don't care, he thinks. I just don't care. Please stop.

Moneta says, "You've doubtless speculated that if Phil was dirty, so was I."

"I haven't speculated at all."

"Phil wasn't a perfect person," Moneta says. "He had his demons. Was he corrupt? Honestly, I don't know. But I'm not."

"You don't have to—"

"I just want to make sure there are no misunderstandings," Moneta says.

There aren't, Harris thinks. He understands her perfectly. And even though she isn't his boss, she wields some power in DC. All she has to do is complain that she's not getting cooperation from a task force colleague and it would fuck his career.

So he'll go through the motions, shake the tree a little and see if Ryan falls out.

Then Moneta says something that makes Harris understand why they're out taking a walk in the cold and damp, instead of sitting in the office or bellied up to the bar in a warm hotel, why she flew all the way out here to have this talk in person.

"DANNY RYAN IS a very dangerous man," Moneta says. "If he puts up any resistance at all, well, the safety of you and your personnel comes first. Do we share an understanding here?"

Harris shares the understanding.

Moneta wants Ryan delivered like KFC.

In a bag or a box.

Well, Harris thinks, that would solve the problem of his testimony.

A HUNTED ANIMAL develops a sense.

Of when something is not quite right.

Maybe a sound, or the absence of one; maybe something from the corner of the eye that hasn't been there before; maybe it's a facial expression, a glance, a word, a question.

Danny has a sense when the guy walks into the bar.

He isn't a regular, not one of the sad veterans of a losing army. His clothes are off by just that much—the floral-print shirt looks a little too new, his loafers have shine on them. His skin is pale but sunburned, like he just got to California.

And his eyes widen, just a touch, when he sees Danny behind the bar.

Danny whispers to the other bartender, Carl, that he's taking his break and goes down the stairs into the storeroom and then out the delivery door into the alley.

"YOU SAW DANNY Ryan," Vinnie says.

He looks at the degenerate gambler sitting across from him and Peter in the American Vending office.

"I think I did," Benjy Grosso says. "I'm pretty sure it was him."

"What were you doing in San Diego?" Peter asks.

"Vacation."

"Vacation?" Vinnie asks. "You don't have the money to pay us, but you have the money to go on vacation?"

Benjy looks abashed.

"And you go into some Irish bar?" Vinnie asks. "How come?"

"To get a drink."

"If you're lying to us, Benjy," Peter says. "If you're making up a story . . ."

Benjy holds his hand up like he's in court. "I'm not."

"You knew Ryan back in the day?" Vinnie asks.

"Enough."

"You were what, friends?"

"No," Benjy says. "Of course not. I'd see him around, you know."

"Okay, you can go," Vinnie says. "We'll be in touch."

Benjy stands up. "If it's him, will that do me some good? On my debt?"

"If it's him," Vinny says, "your debt's wiped out. Now get outta here, let the men talk."

When Benjy goes out the door, Peter asks, "What do you think?"

I think I'm fucking your wife upside down, inside out, and sideways, Vinnie thinks. "I don't know. The guy owes money, he's desperate, he comes to us with a story."

"But if the story is true," Peter says, "we can lay hands on Danny."

"What's Pasco going to say?"

"He's retired," Peter says, "and, anyway, what he don't know . . ."

"You don't think we should check it out with him first?" Vinnie asks.

No, Peter doesn't. If he checks it out with Pasco, the old man will say no, and then Peter is fucked. If he obeys Pasco and doesn't go after Ryan, he loses his chance to get his money back; if he does, then he disobeys Pasco and gets himself clipped.

Which is pretty much what Vinnie is counting on.

IAN IS CONTENT playing with his truck in the sand.

Sitting at a picnic bench in the park, Danny watches him while he talks with Jimmy Mac.

"You're sure this guy made you?" Jimmy asks.

"No," Danny says. "I just had this feeling."

"The guy never came back in?"

"No."

"So there you go," Jimmy says. "Probably nothing."

"I dunno."

They sit and watch Ian play. Then Danny says, "You miss your boys."

"Sure," Jimmy says.

"I was going to tell you, bring your family out here," Danny says. "But now . . ."

"I know."

"Let's see what happens."

Just to be on the safe side.

Like there is such a thing, Danny thinks.

He's seen the inside and the outside, the upside and the downside, but he's never seen the safe side.

Danny can't keep his kid close to this kind of danger, and besides, the boy has no kind of life. He needs a stable home, which Danny can't give him.

He does what he never dreamed he'd ever do.

So now the abandoned son takes his child to the abandoning mother, which Danny figures is the irony the nuns tried to teach him about in high school English class.

I get it now, Danny thinks.

LAS VEGAS IS a hallucination.

Nothing is real, not the pyramids, the palaces, the pirate ships. Then you have Circus Circus—like one of them wasn't enough, Danny thinks; hell, the whole place is a circus.

He drives through the Strip and out to Madeleine's place. "Place"? Danny thinks as he pulls up. This is a *palace*.

And Madeleine is all too real, standing in front of the big door in a flowing white dress like the goddess she thinks she is. Red hair shining, tan glowing, perfect white teeth as she smiles.

She walks to the car, opens the passenger door and sweeps Ian into her arms. "My baby, my precious grandson."

Ian is scared freakin' shitless and starts to cry.

"No, baby, it's Grandma," Madeleine said. "Grandma loves you."

Danny got out. "I'll take him."

Madeleine sets Ian down and Danny holds his hand. "This is your grandmother. Why don't you say hello?"

"Hello." Ian stops crying.

"Hello, darling."

Her eyes are all moist and Danny wonders when it was his parents got so soft. It's a fairly recent development, anyway.

The words taste like dirt in his mouth. "I need your help."

NO ONE REALLY knows why damaged people find each other.

But they do.

There's an attraction of pain to pain, a magnetism of hurt, a mutual recognition that creates a haven of understanding. With that person, you don't have to explain why you're down, you don't have to hear "suck it up," you don't have to pretend to be happy.

The other damaged being just understands.

Cassandra Murphy is sufficiently self-aware to acknowledge some of that, but she'd be hard-pressed to explain why she went with Peter Moretti, why she keeps going back.

He was her family's worst enemy, the man who practically destroyed them, a man she should hate.

Maybe that's the attraction, she thinks as she walks to the little apartment that Peter rented for their assignations. Maybe doing something so wrong, such a betrayal of my family, confirms my worst opinion of myself, and that's what I really want.

An excuse to get high.

Stay high.

Because if I think I'm a worthless piece of shit, I can treat myself like a worthless piece of shit.

But it's more than that.

There's something about Peter that's soft, soulful, something that's come to him recently, as a result of his daughter's suicide. Cassie understands grief—she's lost two brothers and a sister. But to lose a child? A daughter who kills herself?

The pain is unimaginable.

She can feel it in his body as they hold each other after they've had sex. It sings through his skin like a dirge, and she holds him tighter. His back stiffens like a taut wire and then slackens.

They do have sex—Cassie wouldn't call it "making love"—but it isn't the focal point of their relationship. Mostly they talk, over cups of instant coffee or small meals that come from cans or boxes. They discuss what was said at the meetings—by other people; neither of them ever speaks—what it means, if they can apply it to their lives or not; they talk about the steps, how much they like the meetings, how much they hate them.

Sometimes Cassie shows up straight, other times she comes in high and he doesn't berate or criticize or shame her. The wounded, they understand failing, they understand losing. And if she needs money to go out and score, he gives it to her.

Cassie isn't high tonight.

She's hurting, she's jonesing, she's fighting it hard.

Peter's sport jacket is draped over the back of the kitchen chair. He's in shirtsleeves standing by the stove, heating up some fettucine alfredo mix that comes from a box.

"How's it going?" he asks.

"It's going," she says. "I hit the seven o'clock at St. Paul's."

"Was it any good?"

"I'm clean," she says, sitting down at the table. "Three days now."

"That's great."

She shrugs. We'll see if it lasts.

They eat and then sit around talking over coffee and then go into the bedroom. Cassie always turns the light out, she's shy about undressing because she's junkie skinny and has track marks on her arms. She never orgasms—that's a casualty of the dope, because nothing can match that first blast from the needle—but it feels good to be held, feels good to have him inside her because it lets her know that she's alive, it's contact with the world outside her addiction, outside her aching self and her need.

Sometimes after sex, while Peter sleeps, she's awash in memories, pulled by an undertow into the deep-water current of the past, swept out to sea. Fourteen years old when Pasco Ferri snuck into her bedroom and told her don't tell anyone, they won't believe you, and she didn't, though she swore to never let another man inside her and she didn't, even though they all thought she was a whore, she didn't let a man touch her and no one did until the night after years of staying clean she went back to the needle and lying dull and high on a dirty mattress in a shooting gallery a man held her down and raped her, she so high she didn't know if it was a nightmare or real, so Peter was her third man, but the only one she chose, because the wounded find the wounded, washed up on the same sad shore.

NINE

A FLAT TIRE FUCKS CHRIS.

Good as his word, Chris had no problem doubling his money selling coke in the Twin Cities and then in Omaha. As he predicted, it was a relatively untapped market, and no one ever said that Chris Palumbo wasn't a good businessman.

So he's driving back to Ruidoso on a two-lane blacktop because he read *Blue Highways* and was inspired to see the real America, which gets too real on Highway 34 east of Malcolm, Nebraska, and sticks a ten-penny nail into his right rear tire.

He's on the side of the road looking for the spare when a bright yellow VW bug pulls over and a woman gets out.

Tall, zaftig, fortyish, with wild blond hair exploding from under a cowboy hat with a hawk feather stuck in the band, she's otherwise dressed entirely in denim—denim jacket, denim shirt, denim jeans—and cowboy boots. "Can I help you?"

Looks like it, Chris thinks, because he finds that he doesn't have a spare tire. "I dunno. You have a 205/7OR15 on you?"

She laughs. "I know where you can get one. Come on, I'll give you a lift into town."

Chris gets into the bug with her. "I'm Joe."

"Laura. What brings you here?"

"Looking for America," Chris says.

"Let me know if you find it."

She takes him to the only repair shop in Malcolm, which, as far as Chris can see, is a couple of streets, a diner, and a water tower. The repair shop guy says he doesn't have the right tire in stock and it will take a day or so to get one from Lincoln. In the meantime, though, he'll tow Chris's car and store it.

"I guess I'll get a motel room," Chris says.

Laura laughs again. "Not in Malcolm."

"Could you give me a ride to Lincoln?" Chris asks. "I'll pay."

"I'd rather give you a ride to my house," Laura says.

"What, you have a bed-and-breakfast or something?"

"Well, I have a bed," Laura says, "and I guess I could make you breakfast."

They drive back out to his car, Chris picks up his bags—including a gym bag stuffed with cash—and then they go way the hell out into the country (like there's anything else, Chris thinks), into some low hills and then down into a narrow little valley to her farmhouse.

White, two-story, with a steeply pitched roof and broad front porch.

A barn is off to the side and a line of trees sits between the yard and a field of crops that Chris doesn't recognize.

"Eighty acres," Laura said. "I inherited from my aunt."

"You're a farmer?"

"I rent out the acreage to my neighbor Dicky, he plants milo," Laura says. "I'm a yoga instructor. And a healer."

Chris doesn't see any neighbors. "Is there a lot of call for yoga out here?"

"Not a lot."

"How about healing?"

"Everyone needs healing, Joe."

She proves it to him. Takes him upstairs to her bedroom, into her soft bed, and heals him. What Laura doesn't know about sex hasn't been invented yet, Chris learns. He doesn't know if he's found America, but she sure as shit takes him on a tour of the world.

And cooks him breakfast.

Bacon and eggs, although she has yogurt and fruit, because of course she's a vegetarian.

He doesn't ask why she has the bacon.

His tire arrives that afternoon.

Laura takes him to pick up his car and then he doesn't get back on the highway to New Mexico, he follows her right back to her white farmhouse and her big bed.

And stays.

That night, she tells him that she's a Wiccan.

"What's that?" Chris asks.

A witch, she tells him.

HARRIS CATCHES A break.

An illegal Guatemalan staring down the barrel of a federal coke rap is lucky enough to have a sister-in-law who empties bedpans at a local old-age home. Turns out some of the shit comes out of a dying old man named Martin Ryan. She liked the old guy and told her husband about him. Her husband told his brother. The brother had heard the name Ryan in connection with some of Harris's inquiries and starts hopping up and down in his cell, squeaking "I know something you don't know" to his public defender until the lawyer gets tired enough of it to bust a phone call.

Harris pulls a file photo and shows it to the sister-in-law. Martin is a lot older now and very sick, but she confirms it's the same man.

Sister-in-law gets a different job, her husband's brother gets a Santa Claus plea bargain, and Brent Harris pays an old man a visit.

"HE'S GONE," BENETTO, the guy from San Diego, says.

Peter had reached out to the family there to ask for someone to hunt down Danny Ryan, and they gave him Benetto. Supposed to be a good worker who knows how to take care of this kind of thing.

"What do you mean, 'gone'?" Peter asks. Puts Benetto on speaker so Vinnie and Paulie can hear.

"What do you mean, what do I mean?" Benetto asks. "We went to the bar where he works, he didn't show up for his shift, hasn't shown up for weeks. He's gone. Your bird flew the coop."

"Shit," Peter says. He hangs up, looks at Vinnie. "Someone tipped Ryan off."

"The fuck you looking at *me* for?" Vinnie asks.

"I'm not looking at you," Peter says.

"Yeah, you are," Vinnie says. "You're looking right at me right now."

"Because I'm talking to you," Peter says. "Jesus."

The guy is getting stranger and stranger since his daughter died. He's losing it, Vinnie thinks. The boss is walking toward the edge of the cliff and it will only take a little shove to push him over.

A lot of people aren't happy with him.

First there's the money they lost.

Then there's Peter going to these AA meetings, which is a place where people spill their guts. Sure, it's court-ordered, but it isn't a good look, a boss sitting in a basement with a lot of losers, nibbling on cookies.

Then there's the other thing, which is simply unacceptable.

Peter being seen with Cassandra Murphy.

Old Man Murphy's daughter.

The sister of the guy who blew Tony Romano to bits, the sister to another guy who killed Sal Antonucci.

A buddy of Danny Ryan's.

Talk about a bad look.

What the fuck is Peter thinking?

And now any chance of getting some of their money back just flew away with Danny Ryan.

HARRIS WALKS INTO Martin Ryan's room and closes the door behind him.

The old man says, "Danny?"

Harris peers into Marty Ryan's face and realizes that his eyes are blanks. They see nothing. Marty Ryan is withered and shrunken. Needles stick out of him, tubes run to bags hanging on stainless steel racks. One of those bags must be full of dope, because Ryan looks out of it. His breath comes in jagged rasps.

Old men smell bad, Harris thinks. Dying old men smell *horrible*.

"Is that you, Danny?" Marty asks again. He lifts his head off the pillow. It seems to take a lot of effort.

"Danny sent me, Mr. Ryan."

"Is he coming?" Ryan asks.

"Did he call you, Mr. Ryan? Say he was coming?"

"I don't remember," Marty says.

"I'm supposed to meet him," Harris says. "Pick him up, bring him here. But I don't know where he is."

"I'm tired."

"If I just knew—"

The old man lays his head back on the pillow, as if the effort of keeping it up has exhausted him. Soon his eyes close.

Harris goes down to the front desk and asks the nurse, "Does Mr. Ryan get any other visitors?"

"There's a man who usually comes every day, but he hasn't been here for a couple of weeks."

Harris shows her a photo of Danny. "Is this him?"

"No," she says. "This man is much older."

As she describes him, Harris realizes it's Ned Egan.

"The man in the picture usually comes on Thursdays," the nurse says. "But he didn't come this week or last week."

Shit, Harris thinks. Did Ryan and his crew get hinky and fly? Abandon his old man here and take off?

"Do you have an emergency contact number regarding Mr. Ryan?"

"That's confidential."

Harris shows her his badge.

She comes up with a phone number for a David Dennehy.

A Rhode Island number.

Harris leaves his card. "If any visitors show up, please call me right away."

Turns out Dennehy is a criminal defense lawyer. Harris thinks about calling him, advising him to turn over his client, but then thinks better of it. Dennehy will probably just warn Ryan that the feds are close to him and Ryan will take off.

So Harris puts the home under surveillance, lets Reggie Moneta know that he has a lead, and waits for Danny boy to show up.

Then he gets a call from Washington.

THE NURSE DOES what Mr. Ryan's son gave her five hundred dollars in cash to do.

She calls the emergency number.

•   •   •

DANNY GETS THE call in Las Vegas.

Dennehy says, "The feds found Marty."

"Did they bother him?"

"Danny, you can't go see him."

"It's my father, Dave."

"You have to stay away from him," Dennehy says. "Stay in Vegas for a while. Go see the tigers or something."

HARRIS PULLS HIS car onto the Key Bridge.

It's jammed, like it always is, so he has time to enjoy the view of the Potomac, to the extent that he's enjoying anything right now what with the Danny Ryan thing about to bust open.

He drives across the bridge into Georgetown, then up the steep hill to its eponymous university. It's good to be back among the old stone buildings and quads, just turning green in the late spring. He misses university life. Harris did his doctorate here, under the same professor he's about to visit, back in an endowed chair after his stint with the agency.

It takes Harris a good fifteen minutes to find a space in the visitors' parking section, then he walks back up the hill to the classroom building across from the main quad, a walk he can never take without hearing the tubular bells from the soundtrack of *The Exorcist*, which was shot here.

He walks into his old classroom building, stands in the back of the crowded lecture hall and watches Penner do his star turn. The place is packed with undergraduates who won places in the class through a lottery—it's not every day nor every semester that you have the chance to study international relations under a former director of the CIA, one whose term was brief but eventful.

And Penner is a star, Harris thinks with admiration, watching his old prof speak sans notes for twenty minutes without as much as a stumble or a missed beat. The man is brilliant, his resignation a loss to the nation if a gain to Georgetown, and Harris is caught between his loyalty to his beloved country and his equally beloved alma mater.

Penner notices him standing in the back of the hall and gives him an almost imperceptible nod. Harris smiles back. It was Penner who persuaded him to go with DEA, Penner who talked him into being an unofficial liaison to the Company. "Do you want to stand on the sidelines," the professor had asked him, "or get in the game? Be a Monday morning quarterback or take your place on the field?"

Harris had taken the field. He's still in the game.

After the lecture is over and the swarm of admiring undergraduates dissipates from around him, Penner makes his way to the back of the hall and shakes Harris's hand.

"It's good to see you," Penner says.

He looks remarkably youthful. Well, Harris thinks as they walk out of the building onto the quadrangle, he *is* young, was in fact the youngest director in the agency's history. Penner was to have been the new wind that blew the cobwebs and dust out of the old agency. And, to a great degree, he did it. It was a shame and a tragedy that his reforms came just a little too late.

They go back to Penner's office, where he changes into a sweatsuit and tennis shoes, then walk down the hill to the track and start to jog. Penner does six miles a day; Harris tries to run daily, but his frenetic schedule usually gets in the way. Now he struggles to keep up, and then feels Penner slow his pace to make it easier.

Penner stops at Key Bridge and puts a foot on the rail to retie his shoe. "I understand that you're close to locating one Danny Ryan."

"Reggie Moneta at the Bureau's been pushing me on it," Harris says. "I gather it's something of a vendetta."

"And you've kept her informed of the latest developments," Penner says.

"I have."

"Ryan's not in San Diego," Penner says. "He's at his mother's house in Las Vegas."

"How do you know this, sir?"

Penner doesn't answer and Harris feels stupid for asking.

Then Penner says, "Moneta has doubtless intimated to you that she desires Ryan to be killed in the process of arrest."

"Not in so many words."

"We have better uses for Mr. Ryan," Penner says. Looking down toward the Washington Monument, he sighs and says, "The American public wants it all—energy, security, and lawfulness. It wants to be warm in the winter, safe from terrorist attacks, and it wants all of this while maintaining its self-image as the pristine city on the hill. The American people want the entire omelet but don't want to know about the breaking of eggs."

He takes his shoe from the railing, bends over to stretch a bit, and then says, "But eggs have to be broken."

Penner starts running again.

Harris falls into step.

HEATHER MORETTI RUNS out of quarters.

She's in her dorm about to do her laundry and realizes she doesn't have enough of the right change to wash *and* dry and then thinks, Fuck it. Her parents' house is just a fifteen-minute drive away, she could save a little money and get some cred for making a home visit. Maybe raid the fridge while she's at it.

So Heather drives home and sees the car in the driveway.

Vinnie Calfo's Lincoln.

Nothing unusual there, except her dad's car is gone and Vinnie always comes to talk with her dad.

Heather grabs the laundry bag out of her little Toyota, walks into the house and hears the sounds.

Unmistakable sounds if you live in a dorm.

She walks right out again.

Her mother is fucking Vinnie Calfo.

"I HATE HIM," Celia says.

Vinnie just listens.

"He could have saved Gina but he didn't," she says.

Vinnie gets up and grabs his briefs from the floor. He's getting a little tired of this record, Celia's Greatest Hit. It's annoying, but he's crazy about her and the kick of fucking her in Peter's bed is too good to pass up.

He picks up his shirt and puts it on.

She switches it up. "And he's fucking Cassie Murphy? Some Irish junkie whore? She's not even pretty, she dresses like a pig—"

"Celia. Time out."

"What?"

Vinnie pulls his slacks on. "I gotta talk to you about something."

She sits up in bed. "What is it?"

"A lot of people are unhappy with Peter," Vinnie says. "They want a change."

"So?"

"They want me to take the chair."

"So?"

"So we don't exactly vote, you know what I mean?" Vinnie says. "It's not like he takes a cardboard box and cleans out his desk. Like he gets a gold watch and a party."

Celia doesn't say anything.

Vinnie sits down in a chair and puts on his shoes. He looks across the room at Celia and says, "If you don't want me to do this, I won't. I mean, he's your husband, he's the father of your children. If you say the word, I won't do it. I'll find a way to quash this."

Celia says nothing.

HARRIS ROLLS UP to Madeleine McKay's house outside Las Vegas and stops in the circular crushed-gravel driveway.

By a freaking fountain with some Greek goddess standing in the center.

The tall shrubbery is manicured; behind that he sees the tennis court, what looks to be a putting green, and farther away, a white-fenced pasture with several horses.

He gets out of the car, walks up to the door and rings the bell.

A minute later a butler opens the door.

"Brent Harris."

"Ms. McKay is expecting you," the butler says, and shows him in. "She'll be down momentarily."

Madeleine has done okay for herself, Harris thinks.

He knows her story from her file. She started life as trailer park trash from Barstow, took her long legs down the 15 to become a Vegas showgirl, married and divorced manufacturer Manny Maniscalco, had a kid out of wedlock and gave him up, then started a highly successful career as a courtesan, sleeping her way from Hollywood actors to Washington politicians to New York financiers, acquiring money and influence all along the way.

Her former lovers are bank presidents, heads of brokerage houses, cabinet secretaries. Most of them remain friends and business partners. Madeleine has videos of federal judges sucking cocks, prosecutors taking it up the ass, DOJ officials going down on underage girls, proof of cabinet secretaries engaging in insider trading.

She's powerful.

When Manny died he left her this mansion and the ranch with the acreage because he never stopped loving her and they never stopped being friends.

Now she comes into the room and gives him a dazzling smile. She still has that Vegas showgirl statuesque look as she leads him into the living room and beckons him to sit down on a sofa that is probably worth more than half his annual salary.

A maid brings in a pitcher of iced tea and glasses, but Madeleine asks, "Or would you like something stronger?"

"This is fine, thanks," Harris says. "Evan Penner asked me to pass on his regards."

"That's kind of him," Madeleine says. "But I hope you've come with something more substantive from Evan than a polite greeting."

"I should take that up with your son," Harris says.

"Danny and I have a difficult relationship," she says. "You don't care about our Oedipal drama, but the point is that Danny almost reflexively resists my efforts to help him. So it's preferable that you downplay my role in this."

"We tracked him down because we always check on family," Harris says. "But Evan wanted to make sure that you do understand there are risks involved."

"I understand," Madeleine says, "that the FBI is looking to judicially murder my son and that the Mafia is tracking him down with the same intent. I believe you are the only harbor, perfectly safe or no, into which Danny can sail."

Harris spots something under her chair. A child's toy—a little locomotive—Thomas the Tank Engine or something. "May I see him, then?"

She gets up.

•   •   •

DANNY SITS ON the white wrought-iron chair under an umbrella and looks across the table at Agent Brent Harris.

It's hot out.

The pool behind Harris looks inviting.

"You're on the Endangered Species List," Harris says. "The Moretti family wants you dead, and powerful factions in the FBI want to stick a needle in your arm for the murder of Agent Jardine. We know Jardine was in bed with the Morettis; we don't know if Moneta was in bed with Jardine in any more than the literal sense."

"What about you?" Danny asks.

"I don't care about Phil Jardine," Harris says. "I care even less about the Moretti brothers. I can't help you with the mob, that's your problem. I can help you with the FBI."

"How?" Danny asks.

Harris lays it out.

The heroin Danny hijacked came from the Baja Cartel, run by one Domingo Abbarca, aka Popeye. Popeye's guys in the States collect money and stash it in remote houses way out in the desert east of San Diego. Then, periodically, they load it into trucks and drive it across the border into Mexico.

"They have so much cash," Harris says, "they can't even count it. They weigh it."

"What's this have to do with me?" Danny asks.

"We've located one of the stash houses."

"So hit it."

"It's more complicated than that," Harris says.

"Life is complicated," Danny answered. "Try me, see if I can hang in with you."

"Even if we can get a warrant," Harris says, "which isn't a slam dunk, we can't connect the stash house to Abbarca. He sits over the border, safe and protected by his government."

"But you'd hurt him taking the money."

"Maybe the money would be better used elsewhere," Harris says.

And there it is, Danny thinks. Another dirty fed. "Like in your retirement account."

"I'm not Phil Jardine," Harris says. "Certain agencies in the government have run overseas operations against terrorists who are backed by drug traffickers like Abbarca. Congress has defunded those operations. We need money to continue those ops and not leave our allies in the lurch. You don't need to know anything beyond that."

Then Harris starts talking about a "symbiotic relationship." Ivy League for "one hand washes the other." You do a little something for us, we do a little something for you.

"You hit that house, keep half of what you get," Harris says. "We protect you against any federal charges. You walk away clean and rich. We're talking tens of millions of dollars. Makes your Providence score look like small potatoes."

"I don't want anything more to do with dope," Danny says.

"That's the beauty of it," Harris says. "There's no dope. Just money. And you'd be hurting a heroin slinger. You'd be doing a service to your country."

Danny says, "I'm trying to go straight."

"One last score will set you up for life."

"You know who the last person was who said that to me?" Danny asks. "Liam Murphy. No, count me out."

"It won't be just you," Harris says. "Moneta will put your pal Jimmy away, Sean South, Kevin Coombs, Bernie Hughes, Ned Egan, all of them. She'll even make sure your old man dies in the joint. A federal lockup, a supermax, Pelican Bay, the worst she can find."

"And if I say no to this," Danny says, "you'll help her do it."

"In a word, yes."

Danny thinks for a second, and then says, "I'll take my chances."

"No, you won't," Harris says. "I've studied up on you. You like playing Jesus Christ, 'nail me up,' all that, but you won't see your friends and your family crucified with you."

He's right, Danny thinks.

"If I do this," Danny says, "I want protection for myself, my crew, and my family."

"You have my word."

"Is your word any good?" Danny asks. "Does this 'certain agency' have the swag to go up against the Bureau?"

"These people are higher up the ladder," Harris says. "Top rungs. Danny, you don't have a lot of choice here. You know your current situation is unsustainable. Your string is played out. If *I* could find you . . ."

He doesn't need to finish.

Danny knows it's true. He can't hold the crew together much longer. They'll go out and do their own things, and the results could be catastrophic for everyone.

And personally he's tempted.

The thought of handing something substantial over to Ian . . . generational wealth . . .

And then there's the simple fact of not wanting to go spend the rest of his life in prison. Keeping everyone else out as well.

Harris is offering salvation.

This might be your last chance.

And face it—you do this "poor Danny Ryan," innocent-victim shit. "Anything bad I've done it's because someone else made me do it." Grow up. You're a leg-breaker, a stickup man and a killer.

You've made your choices.

Now make this one.

TEN

DANNY FIGURES NEVADA'S NEVER GOING to run out of desert.

There's ample empty spaces to train for the hit on Abbarca's stash house.

So now they're out in a canyon not far from Vegas where Harris built a mock-up of the Abbarca stash house. They've pored over maps, diagrams, and aerial surveillance photos. The compound is a series of low, one-story stuccos with corrugated iron roofs behind fences topped with strands of coiled barbed wire screened by tall casuarina hedges.

A dirt road runs eighteen miles south from the two-lane blacktop that traverses the desert from east to west. It's the only route in or out of the compound.

Not good, Danny thinks.

He likes to have options.

Danny's done a lot of truck hijackings—often with the cooperation of the driver, who got a cut—some warehouses, a few small stash houses around Providence, a few card game boosts, but never anything like this.

This is almost a military operation.

The stakes are far higher—millions instead of a few thousand dollars. And the victims sure as shit aren't in on it. For that kind of money, they aren't going to give up, they're going to fight.

Surprise is essential, Danny thinks, which makes the single road entrance more of a problem.

Harris disagrees. "They won't have guards out on the road. Their security is to be inconspicuous, not to call attention to themselves. That's why the casuarina hedges."

Another thing, Harris tells him, maybe more of a concern—the Abbarca organization's chief method of self-protection is sheer terror. Nobody in the drug business would dare to stage a *tombe*, a robbery, because they have relatives in Mexico and the retaliation would be brutal.

"Abbarca would kill the whole family," Harris says.

Great, Danny thinks. That's very comforting. He turns to Jimmy. "What do you think?"

"Four-wheel-drive vehicles," Jimmy says. "Headlights off. We can get close."

But we can't get *in*, Danny thinks. There's a gate and it does have a guard—we'd have to shoot our way into the compound.

It's sixty yards from the gate to the house where the cash is stored, Danny thinks. Sixty yards of flat, open desert with no cover. Even at night, we'd get mown down from inside the house. And that's even if we can get through the gate.

No, we're not going to do that.

We're going to have them open the gate for us.

BRINGING THE ALTAR Boys to Las Vegas is like dropping a ten-year-old off at Disneyland with a platinum card.

Danny stores them at a motel on the outskirts of town and gives them strict orders to stay off the Strip, because you can't swing a dead cat in any of the major casinos without hitting a fed, a cop, or a wiseguy. But that doesn't stop Kevin and Sean, because if you can't find a game or a hooker in Vegas, your seeing-eye dog probably can.

He lets it play out, lets them get it out of their system, knows it won't last long.

Three days later, they come to him, strung out, fucked out, and broke.

"The party's over," Danny says. "You show up for work drunk, high, or hungover, you're done. You're here to work."

He works them hard.

First in the cool dawn out at the mock-up, then he switches to nights, when the actual job will take place. Danny's plan requires precise timing, each man knowing and performing his assignment, or they'll all get killed. To their credit the Altar Boys take the sessions seriously. They know it's the score of a lifetime; they also know they won't get that lifetime if they fuck it up.

Jimmy Mac is professional as usual, all business. Danny's decided not to bring Ned—he needs someone to look after Marty. Besides, this job requires speed, and Ned is getting a little long in the tooth; new weaponry, and Ned is fixed on his old .38.

The weapons that Harris supplies are a big part of the training. The fed produced AR-15s, a MAC-10 machine gun, and a freakin' M203 grenade launcher—all seized from narcos. Danny's carried a MAC-10 on jobs before but never had to fire one, but neither he nor any of his crew have ever used a freakin' grenade launcher.

Same with the flash-bang grenades.

Harris instructs them.

Which makes Danny wonder who this guy really is, what his background was. He presses Harris on it.

"You sure you're DEA?" Danny asks one night as he watches the Altar Boys work with the M203.

"Pretty sure," Harris says.

"Because I was thinking maybe other letters," Danny says.

"The federal alphabet soup can get stirred up sometimes," Harris says. Then he walks away to supervise the Altar Boys.

They train for two weeks, every night, all night, until the sun comes up. Then they go back to their rooms and sleep a good part of the day.

DANNY, HE GOES to his mother's house to get some rest and spend time with Ian.

The boy loves it there.

Why not? Danny thinks. His grandmother pulls him around the swimming pool, puts him on the back of a pony, makes him nice meals, gives him ice cream and cookies. She reads to him, watches videos with him, they go for walks, hand in hand.

Danny joins them for a lot of this.

His reconciliation with his mother isn't dramatic.

There's no emotional moment, no mutual declaration of forgiveness and mutual love, no tight embrace.

That isn't Danny, that isn't her.

It comes gradually, recognized but unacknowledged, just an accepted matter. He's grateful that she's taking good care of Ian; she's thankful that he's letting her. With that as a given, they exchange polite small talk that evolves into conversation, then the small jokes shared by people inhabiting the same space.

Madeleine is too smart to push it, to force some dramatic moment. She sees Danny's slow softening, and it's enough for her. It's heaven, actually, having her son and her grandson with her, and she doesn't want it to end.

One day, sitting out by the pool, Ian down for his nap, Danny says, "You set this up, didn't you?"

"What do you mean?"

"You reached out to old friends in Washington."

"Does it bother you?"

"It should," Danny says. "It used to. Now? For some reason it doesn't."

"I'm glad," she says. "I'm worried, too. Are you sure you want to do . . . whatever it is you're doing for them?"

"It's not just for me," Danny says. " It's other people, too. I have to do this."

"Is there anything I can do," Madeleine asks, "to help?"

"You're doing it," Danny says. "Taking care of Ian. Look, I'm pretty sure it won't be necessary, but if anything happens to me, will you keep taking care of him?"

"Of course," she says. "I'm leaving you everything, if that's useful for you to know."

"You don't have to do that."

"I know." Madeleine knows that her son is proud, doesn't want to live off her wealth, is already sensitive about accepting her hospitality, so she lets it go.

That's their reconciliation, that's it.

It's enough.

REGGIE MONETA'S NOT happy.

Shit flows downstream. From, apparently, Pennsylvania Avenue to the director and then to her. And this particular floating turd stinks to high heaven with its "Lay off Ryan" message.

Touches off one of those Law Enforcement v. Intelligence border skirmishes, this time with the knives out. She doesn't dial down the rhetoric, either; it's all "Fuck Harris, fuck Penner, fuck POTUS for that matter, if that's what it comes to."

The director looks at her like she's stone-cold crazy. "I got a personal call. He brought a very clear and succinct message which I am going to repeat to you for the last—italics the *last*—time: Ryan is a no-fly zone. You don't enter it. If you have any assets in this particular Area Fifty-One, you pull them out the day before yesterday. Do we understand each other?"

Yeah, Moneta understands. Her problem isn't comprehension, it's acceptance that Danny Ryan has managed to cloak himself in an officially sponsored mantle of invisibility.

Probably his cunt of a mother.

But if her own government won't do anything about Ryan, she knows people who will.

PETER'S ABOUT TO leave the office when the phone rings. "Yeah?"

It's a woman's voice. "The person you're looking for will be going to . . ."

She gives him the address of some old-age home and hangs up.

Peter calls that guy Benetto in San Diego. "I want him bagged, not killed. He has to tell us where the dope is, or where he has the money."

Make him tell you, but make him hurt first.

Before you kill him.

DANNY RYAN LOOKS up at the night sky.

Lying in a ditch beside the dirt road waiting for the cash car, Danny feels he can almost reach up and touch the stars.

The desert night is soft, the air still, the silence overwhelming.

But now he hears an engine.

It's not as close as it seems because sound travels far in the desert.

Then Danny sees headlights come down the road.

Tires crunch on rock and gravel.

Danny thinks his crew is ready.

They've practiced a hundred times, but you never know what's going to happen.

Anything can.

He's warned the Altar Boys. "Killing is the last option, not the first."

"Got it, boss."

He hopes so. If this goes right, there's no reason for anyone to lose his life. There's been too much of that already.

He sees the cash car.

Like Harris said, an old VW Westfalia van like so many use to go camping in the desert. A rack on top holds folded-up tents, sleeping bags, and jerry cans of water.

It rumbles past Danny.

He pulls the black ski mask down over his face. The whole crew has them.

Then the van hits the spike strip and rolls past it for a second until the front left tire blows.

The driver opens the door and looks down at the tire.

Then he gets out.

Kevin is out of the ditch and on him. Gun to the side of his head. Sean is as fast with the passenger side, the AR-15 at his shoulder and ready to blast.

The MAC-10 stuck out in front of him, Danny walks toward the back of the van, eases to the side and slides the door open.

If it's going to go off, it's going to go off now.

But the man sitting in the back already has his hands up. Danny gestures with the MAC-10—"Out."

The man gets out, kneels on the ground, his hands still up.

The crew moves efficiently. In a few minutes, the passenger and the man in the back are tied up, gagged and dragged to the side of the road.

Jimmy drives up in another old VW van, geared out to look like the Westfalia. He and Sean get in the back as Kevin puts the driver behind the wheel. Danny crouches behind him, shoves the gun barrel into the back of the seat. "One wrong word, I blow your spine away."

"Okay."

Sean collects the bags of cash from the Westfalia and climbs in the back of the new van with Kevin.

Danny says, "Go."

They drive the half mile to the compound.

Kevin, in the passenger seat, says, "We're coming up on the gate."

"You got kids?" Danny asks the driver.

"Daughters. Two and four."

"Don't leave them without a father," Danny says. "Be smart, you live through this."

Kevin pulls the hood of his sweatshirt over his head as they pull up to the gate.

A guard walks up.

The driver rolls down the window.

Danny shoves the gun barrel harder into the seat as he listens to the guard and the driver speak in Spanish. He doesn't know what they're saying; the driver could be playing along or he could be warning the guard.

If the latter, we're dead.

Then he hears the gate swing open and feels the van move forward.

"Smart," Kevin says.

The gate closes behind them.

"Now," Danny says.

Kevin rolls down the window, rests the grenade launcher on the sill, and aims it at the garage.

Pulls the trigger.

The explosion is loud, a red ball of flame goes up, and then more explosions as the fire hits gas tanks.

Danny sticks his head up and sees three men run out of the house toward the garage.

"Go!" he yells.

He opens the door and gets out, his crew right behind him.

The driver jumps out and runs.

Spotlights come on, flooding the ground with light.

Danny fires a burst in the air and yells, "Get down! Get the fuck down and spread your arms out!"

Two of the guys do it.

A third goes for his gun.

Sean cuts him down.

Shit, Danny thinks. He didn't want that. He didn't want anyone killed on this job.

Kevin turns the grenade launcher to the house and aims for the front door.

It hits and the door falls open.

He reloads and fires a flash-bang grenade inside.

Danny is the first through.

A stunned man, clearly concussed, sits on the floor with a Glock on his lap. Danny kicks the gun away from him.

Jimmy's right behind him, throws the guy to the floor and zip-ties his hands behind his back.

Sean's out in the yard doing the same to the other two.

A man comes out of the bathroom.

Looks at Danny's MAC pointed at his face, holds his hands above his head and smiles. "You're making a big mistake, friend. Do you know who we're with? Domingo Abbarca. Popeye. You'll never live to enjoy this money."

"Lie down."

The man lies face-first on the floor. As Jimmy zip-ties him, he says, "You and all your families. *Muerte*. And not fast, either."

"Shut up."

Danny hears shooting from outside.

Has to be Sean and the gate guard.

"Not good," the man says. "Not good at all."

"Let's go," Danny says.

They move through the house. It's freakin' ridiculous—there's cash everywhere, in neat, plastic-wrapped stacks. Just sitting on the floor, or behind cheap fake-wood siding, above ceiling panels. They scoop it up into plastic bags and keep moving.

The shooting outside stops.

Danny hears Sean yell, "Clear!"

Kevin goes into one of the bedrooms and then Danny hears him yell, "Jesus Christ! Boss! Get in here!"

Stepping into the room, Danny sees a guy sitting on the bed.

Danny blinks.

He can't believe what his eyes are telling him.

That it's Frankie Vecchio.

THE BATH HAS become a ritual.

The hot water soothes Peter's sore back and Cassie sits behind him and lays a steaming washcloth on his neck. Relaxed, he talks about them leaving together, going off where no one knows them.

He's going to get his money back.

It will fund their new lives.

He's just waiting for the phone call from San Diego saying that it's done.

Cassie listens but knows it's a fantasy. Peter will never leave Rhode Island, never leave his kids. She doubts he's even capable of leaving Celia, as much as he bad-mouths her, says how unhappy she makes him.

A realist, Cassie knows they're never getting out of here alive—neither of them will escape their mutual addictions. But she doesn't say this to him; he wouldn't believe her anyway and it would be cruel to take his dreams away from him.

So she keeps quiet, listens, and rubs his neck.

The bathroom door opens.

The light comes on.

Cassie sees the man standing in the doorway.

Peter looks at the man and says, "Vinnie, what the fuck, you're supposed to be in Flor—"

The gun comes up so quickly.

Muffled shots, two of them.

Into Peter's forehead.

Cassie screams inside herself but no sound comes out and she feels like she's choking, knows that she's going to die.

Her last, weird thought is *Great, just when I got clean.*

Vinnie says, "Sorry."

Then shoots twice more.

"DANNY, THANK GOD it's you," Frankie says.

"The hell are you doing here?"

Frankie starts crying, almost blubbering how him and Chris made a coke deal with the Mexicans, with Abbarca, how Chris left Vecchio here as a hostage. "Jesus Christ, Danny, you wouldn't believe the shit that goes down here. These people are fucking animals. The shit I've seen. They boil people, they put them in vats and melt them, and they laugh. Keep telling me I'm next if Chris don't come back. He just left me, Danny. The son of a bitch just left me."

Kevin turns to Danny. "You want me to do him?"

Danny should kill them all.

The Mexicans and the Italian, too.

But that ain't Danny.

It's always been his problem—he's soft-hearted and believes in God. Heaven and hell and all that happy crap. He's hit the button on a few guys, but it was always him or them, not like this. Not when he has them all zip-tied, flat on the floor or the ground, and his guys want to put bullets in the backs of their heads.

Execution style, like they say.

So he hesitates. "They'd do it to us," Kevin says.

"No, Danny, please," Vecchio says. "Take me with you. I'm begging you. They'll think I was in on this. You don't know what they'll do to me."

"Fuck him," Kevin says.

Jimmy walks up, pulls Danny away by the elbow. "You gotta do him, Danny. He can ID us."

"Not if we take him with us."

"Are you kidding me?" Jimmy asks. "This is the guy who set us up!"

"Chris set us up," Danny says. "Frankie was just the tool."

"So what?" Jimmy asks. "Kill the motherfucker. You don't have the heart, I'll do it."

"Put him in the van," Danny says.

"He'd kill you in a heartbeat," Jimmy says, "the roles were reversed."

"I'm not him."

"Danny—"

"Did you hear me?"

Jimmy glares at him. "Yeah, I heard you."

Shaking his head, Kevin hauls Vecchio up, walks him out.

"We got all the money?" Danny asks.

"I think so," Jimmy says.

No time to count it now, but Danny thinks it's twenty, thirty, maybe even forty.

Million.

Untraceable, and no one is going to go to the cops.

The score of a lifetime.

Literally, because this is his last job.

"Then let's go," Danny says.

As they walk through the living room, the guy on the floor says, "He'll make you beg to die. He'll make you watch your children scream."

Danny doesn't answer him.

They walk out into the yard, load the cash into the van, and they take off into the soft desert night.

Jimmy drives the van like he stole it.

Which he did.

Back up the long dirt road, past the original van, past the guys they left tied up out there. A two-lane blacktop, then up and out of the desert into some low mountains, then down a twisty road onto the flats toward San Diego.

On the edge of town, Danny tells Jimmy to pull over, and when he does, orders Frankie Vecchio to get out.

"Where am I supposed to go?" Vecchio asks.

"Not my problem," Danny says.

"He'll go running to Abbarca's people about us," Kevin says.

"He's too scared of them," Danny says.

"Thank you, Danny," Vecchio says. "I swear, I'll never forget this."

"No, forget this," Danny says.

Vecchio walks away.

"It's a mistake," Jimmy says as he drives into the city proper. "We should have killed him."

Danny counts out twenty grand for each of the Altar Boys.

"When we get into San Diego, split up, find places to hang. Spread out and lay low. Stay under the radar."

By which he means no cowboy crap. No partying, no fights, no throwing money around, above all, no jobs.

Kevin shakes his head like *This is a mistake, too.*

"You got a problem?" Danny asks.

"I got no problems," Kevin answers, pocketing the money.

"A few months," Danny says, "four or five, six *tops*, the money comes back clean, we share out. Then we get on with our lives. The past is dead and buried."

"What do you mean, Danny?" Sean asks.

"I have assurances," Danny says, "that cases back east go into the deep freeze and stay there."

"You made a deal?" Kevin asks. "Shit, Danny, what did you give them?"

"Nothing," Danny answers, starting to get pissed. "We did a job for them, that was part of the deal. You don't have to thank me or anything, Kev, for getting you immunity. But you're a citizen from now on. You take your share, buy a bar, a club, a car wash—I don't care, but you keep your nose clean. You don't track any of your dirt into my house. *Capisce?*"

"Yeah, I got it."

Yeah, he gets it but does he *get* it? Danny wonders. Does he get how rare the chance for a new life is?

But you don't really get a new life, Danny thinks. You might get a fresh start, a second chance, but your old life stays with you. The killings, the deaths, the losses, the guilt, the loves, the memories—good and bad—all come along.

Danny had fought a long, losing war and then fled, but took the survivors with him. A widower with a toddler son, he's also a son with an aging father and he has both of them to take care of.

But with this money, he can do it legit.

Same with his crew.

They can take their cuts and set themselves up with something good. Danny owes it to them—he threw their last stake away.

TWO PROVIDENCE HOMICIDE detectives, O'Neill and Viola, responding to an anonymous tip, go to the apartment.

"Jesus Christ," Viola says. "It's Peter."

"Who's the woman?"

O'Neill takes a closer look at Cassandra's corpse. "You know who this is? John Murphy's daughter."

Viola shakes his head. "I didn't believe it. I mean, I heard things, but . . . You know what we have to do."

O'Neill knows.

Peter Moretti has been good for a monthly envelope and a fatter one at Christmas for a number of years. They owe it to him and his widow to do the right thing here. So they wrap Cassie's body in a blanket and lug it down to their car, then dump it near a shooting gallery in South Providence.

Then they call in the murder of Peter Moretti.

BENETTO WAITS IN a car outside the old-age home.

The Providence guy, Moretti, told him that Ryan would be showing up here sooner or later, and Benetto wishes it was sooner because he and two other guys have been taking shifts for days now and it's getting boring.

Moretti is paying good money, Benetto thinks, but shit, if I wanted to do stakeouts I'd have become a cop.

"What are you laughing at?" one of his guys asks.

"Just a funny thought," Benetto says.

"This donkey ever going to show?"

Benetto shrugs.

He thinks Ryan's going to show. His old man is in there, and what kind of a son doesn't come see his father?

CELIA ANSWERS THE early-morning doorbell.

Two Providence cops—O'Neill and Viola, she knows them from a few Christmas parties—stand at the door.

Viola says, "Mrs. Moretti, we regret to inform you that your husband, Peter, is dead. He's been murdered."

They will later note that she took the news stoically.

In fact, she smiled.

HEATHER MORETTI DROPS the phone in her dorm room and screams and screams and screams.

THEY MEET HARRIS at a beach parking lot north of Camp Pendleton. It's empty at 3 A.M.

The DEA agent is waiting in his car when Danny and Jimmy roll up.

"How did it go?" he asks.

"We're here," Danny says.

Harris gets in the van and counts out the money.

Forty-three million dollars in cash.

"More than I thought," Harris says.

"You remember our deal," Danny says. "I have Abbarca to worry about, I don't want to have to worry about the feds, too."

"You have my word," Harris says. "Just keep your head down."

"Don't worry."

They split up the money and then Harris takes off.

"Can we trust him?" Jimmy asks.

"Can we trust anybody?"

They drive back down toward San Diego, to a suburb called Rancho Bernardo, where Bernie is staying at a Residence Inn. When they get to his room, the old man is sipping on a cup of tea. "I've been worried about you."

"Everyone's okay," Danny says. "Twenty-one million, five hundred thousand."

Bernie gives a soft whistle. "It's going to take some time to launder all this. I'll have to go to a lot of banks, make a number of small investments, casino visits . . ."

"You do your thing," Danny says. "Ned will come up, get a room here, guard the cash, keep you safe."

Danny takes fifty thousand for himself and gives Jimmy the same. "Don't bring the family out for a while. It's okay to send them money, but . . ."

"I heard what the guy said."

Bernie's phone rings. He answers it and hands it to Danny.

"Thank God I found you," Dennehy says. "I don't know how to tell you this. The home called. Your father is dying. They say it's a matter of hours."

Danny doesn't really know how to feel as he drives down to San Diego in a Camry that Jimmy had boosted.

Marty was never much of a father.

A neglectful, abusive drunk.

And his quality of life had become about zero, so this is probably a mercy.

Still . . .

He was your dad.

Danny drives to the home.

•　　•　　•

BENETTO IS DOZING off when he hears—

"Hey. Someone's coming."

Benetto sees a Camry pull over and park along the curb.

"Is that our guy?"

"That's him."

About time, Benetto thinks.

DANNY SEES THE car coming down the street toward him, an SUV driving just a little too slow, and he knows what's going to happen. A guy will jump out, jam a gun into his back and then push him into the car.

And that will be that, because once they have you in the car they have you. First thing you learn in this kind of life: Never get in the car. Make your stand in the street, die in the parking lot, but never get in the car.

I have two things going for me, Danny thinks as he keeps walking, forcing himself not to hurry, to keep the same pace. One, they can't just shoot me, they have to take me alive. Two, they don't know yet that I've made them.

It ain't much, Danny thinks, but it's what I got.

Early in the morning, the streets are quiet, and it's what these guys are counting on. Get me in the car and drive off before anyone sees. Then it's a basement or a warehouse, the blowtorch and the meat hook or both.

Danny pulls the Glock out from under his shirt and keeps walking toward the car. Aims to the right between the headlights and fires two shots. Give the motherfucker something to think about other than his job.

A guy jumps out the passenger door.

Hesitates for just that fraction of a second, thinking about his orders to take Danny alive.

He who hesitates is fucked.

Danny steps toward him and shoots him twice in the face.

The guy's gun clatters on the sidewalk.

The SUV drifts into a light pole. The driver is slumped over the wheel, but another shooter gets out. He lays a Glock on the open car window and aims at Danny but his forehead blows open in a spray of blood.

Ned Egan walks up to the SUV, throws open the back door and aims his .38 inside.

Danny sees the flashes.

He runs back to his car and takes off.

PART TWO

Lifeless Pictures

California
November 1989

"Trust me, this fame of ours will offer some haven."

So Aeneas says, feeding his spirit on empty, lifeless pictures.

Virgil
The Aeneid
Book II

ELEVEN

THE PACIFIC IS A SUNSET coast.

The sun doesn't rise over this ocean, but Danny Ryan gets up at dawn anyway to watch the sky and the water change as clouds take shape, the sea becomes visible, and a horizon appears.

It's his favorite part of the day.

Danny's early mornings are almost ritualistic. He gets out of bed, flips on the electric kettle, and brushes his teeth while the water heats up. Then he goes back into the little kitchen, makes a cup of instant coffee and sips at it as he pulls on jeans and a hooded sweatshirt. He shoves a gun into the sweatshirt's pouch, then walks out of the mobile home and across the Pacific Coast Highway to Capistrano Beach, where he stands and watches the dawn.

The winter morning is chilly but Danny still wears sandals, not willing to make too many concessions to the season. He's a summer man and always has been, loves the sun and the warmth, and even now, transplanted to California from cold New England, he can't get over the dread of snow and biting winds.

This has been his dream, this warm and sunset coast, where even the dawns are soft in pastels of pink and rose, and he stands on the deserted beach until the sky turns that sharp California winter blue, the horizon like a line drawn across a sheet of paper.

The gun in his left hand is cold. Danny doesn't like the feel of it, doesn't like carrying it at all, and wishes he didn't have to. But there are still people out there who can't forget, people who would like to see Danny Ryan dead.

Danny walks back to the trailer, the "mobile home."

There's a concept, he thinks.

Mobile home.

This life in the wind has to end.

It's no life at all.

But that's been reality since he left Rhode Island. On the road, under the radar, out of reach. He's been in this "home" for months now, which has been somewhat stable, has allowed him to establish the routine that has become ritual.

He puts two slices of bacon into the little cast-iron pan and turns the burner on underneath. As the bacon cooks, he lays a sheet of paper towel on a plate and gets a fork and spatula out of the dish rack. When the bacon is done, crispy, he sets the strips on the paper towel and cracks two eggs into the pan.

Danny likes them over hard, can't stand runny yolks. Terri knew this and always cooked them "like rubber," she said, with the edges brown. While the eggs fry, he pops two slices of white bread into the toaster and then watches them. Unlike his eggs and bacon, his toast he likes light.

Terri used to call him a pain in the ass about it.

I suppose that's true, Danny thinks. I suppose I am.

She's still a hole in his heart.

He pops the toast up before it gets too brown, flips the eggs and breaks the yolks with the spatula. Then he lays his gun on the table and pulls off his sweatshirt as the sunshine coming through the windows warms the "kitchen area."

Looking out the window, he sees Mrs. Mossbach out walking her Yorkie and he waves. She's out there every morning, the leash in one hand and a plastic bag to pick up the poop in the other.

She waves back.

Danny's learned it's good to be friendly but not intimate with his neighbors. Too friendly, they know too much about you, but if you're too standoffish you become that weird guy, that mystery man in the mobile home park, and you don't want to be that, either.

You don't want people thinking that you have something to hide.

Danny takes the paper towel out from under the bacon and drops it in the garbage under the sink, then slides the eggs out of the pan onto his plate and sits down. He eats quickly—too quickly, Terri always said—then gets up and washes the dishes right away. It's become a discipline in small spaces, to keep everything clean and neat as he goes. He waits for the pan to cool a little, then swipes a wet cloth around it and puts it back on the burner. He pours a little oil into it and heats it on low, something Mrs. Mossbach taught him about caring for cast iron.

The mobile home came fully furnished and equipped—turnkey—and he wants to give it back in the same condition when he leaves.

Which is hopefully soon.

Missing Ian like crazy, Danny wants to go back to Las Vegas, to reunite with his son and pick up a life together.

But Popeye Abbarca is looking for the people who stole his money, his enforcers are ripping through the San Diego–Tijuana area, leaving bodies stacked up. So even though they don't know of Danny Ryan's existence and have no way of tracing him, Danny isn't going anywhere near his family until things cool off.

It wasn't Abbarca but Peter Moretti who tried to hit him outside the old-age home, and even though Peter is dead, some of the Providence people might still be gunning for Danny Ryan.

So he found the trailer park and dug in.

Danny wanted to at least make a trip to Vegas to see Ian, but Harris nixed it. Same with phone calls—Danny had to keep them "short and sweet" and make them from phone booths away from the trailer park.

It was heartbreaking, hearing his kid's voice, "Daddy?"

As time went by, Danny could tell Ian was less and less interested in talking with him. Little kids have short memories; Danny knew his son's was dimming, that "Gramma" was increasingly the boy's world.

Danny didn't blame him.

He knew the feeling of being abandoned from his own childhood; he was only grateful that the boy had Madeleine—the irony of which wasn't lost on him.

Harris wouldn't let Danny be a father. He also prevented him from being a son.

"I can't even bury my father?" Danny asked.

"It was taken care off," Harris said. "He was a veteran, right? We buried him at Rosecrans. It's nice."

"I want to go to the grave," Danny said. I dunno, lay flowers or something. Pour some whiskey on the headstone.

"People might be watching it," Harris said.

"What people?"

"Your old Italian friends?" Harris asked.

"Peter Moretti's dead."

"Vinnie Calfo isn't," Harris said.

The new boss, Danny thought. You'd have expected the corner office to have gone to Paulie, but Peter died in such big stink that it covered his brother. And after all, it was Vinnie who did the job on Peter, so he got the crown.

Danny had confirmed this when he made a risky but necessary call to Pasco Ferri, the old boss of New England.

"Well, we don't have to worry about Peter Moretti anymore, do we?" Pasco said.

"I had nothing to do with that."

"No kidding."

So there it is, Danny thought. Pasco gave the green light on Peter, if he didn't outright order it. It's good news. "Who's going to take over there?"

"It's none of my concern anymore," Pasco said. "But if I was a betting man, I'd put my money on Vinnie Calfo. Do you remember him?"

Sort of, Danny thought. Years ago, before he went to the joint, Calfo had run a small crew out of East Providence and Fall River.

"He was Peter's consigliere after Chris," Pasco said. "He was also sleeping with his wife."

Pasco, Danny thought. Always such an old lady, can't resist a piece of gossip. "Did Calfo kill him?"

"I don't know who killed him," Pasco said. "How would I?"

Meaning, Danny thought, you absolutely know that Calfo killed him.

"Where are you now?" Pasco asked.

Danny didn't answer.

"I'm hurt you don't trust me," Pasco said. "So why call me? Why are we talking?"

"I just want to make sure we're still good."

"As far as I'm concerned we are."

"How about as far as Calfo is concerned?" Danny asked.

Long silence, Pasco thinking, then, "If Vinnie got the money back he lost, I'm sure he'd be willing to let sleeping dogs lie. Is that a possibility, Danny?"

"How much are we talking?"

"Maybe two hundred."

It's beautiful, Danny thinks. Always the same old hustle. If I kick

Vinnie two hundred thousand dollars, he fucks the other Providence guys and makes peace with me. And Pasco will take a taste as a finder's fee. "I'd need a couple of months."

"I think that's doable."

"I want a clean slate, though," Danny said. "I don't want Paulie or any of the others coming after me."

"I think Paulie's gotten the message," Pasco says. "I'm sure everyone understands."

Understands, Danny thinks, that everyone signed off on Peter's killing—Pasco, a majority of the New England mob, certainly Boston and probably New York as well. Killing a boss requires a lot of initials.

"And it covers my guys," Danny said.

"Everyone wants this put to bed," Pasco said. "It's bad for business."

"Okay."

"It's a shame about that girl Cassie," Pasco says. "She was such a sad creature. She always had problems with the alcohol and the drugs. I've always said, the drugs are the devil."

"I'll be in touch," Danny said.

Two hundred K was a cheap price to pay for peace.

He settled into his routine and waited.

Waited for Bernie to launder the money, waited for Harris to give him the all clear.

He walked the beach, drove up the coast, strolled along Dana Point Harbor looking at the boats, wandered Encinitas, Laguna Beach, and Corona Del Mar. He took naps, watched TV, went to the grocery store, cooked meals, all the mundane stuff that goes with normal life. Sometimes he went out, had lunch somewhere, went to a movie.

Danny thought a lot—about what comes, what he's going to do, where he's going to live, how he can build a life for Ian.

He knew he wanted to be here in California; beyond that, he didn't have any real answers.

Now he sits and eats his eggs, like every other morning.

Like every other freakin' morning.

Then the phone rings.

HE MEETS HARRIS in the parking lot outside a supermarket in Laguna Beach.

The agent's black Mercedes is already there when Danny pulls in, driver's window to driver's window.

Harris is smiling.

"What?" Danny asks.

"Today is a very good day," Harris says. "God is in his heaven and all is right with the world."

"What are you talking about?"

"The world is a better place today," Harris says, "without Popeye Abbarca in it."

The *federales* ambushed Popeye in Rosarito, Harris tells him. Killed five of his *sicarios* and riddled him with bullets. The story goes that one of those bullets took out Abbarca's remaining eye.

Champagne corks are hitting the ceilings in DEA offices all over the country.

"You want to hear the weird part?" Harris asks. "Popeye's guys busted into the morgue and took his body. Hauled it into the hills for some kind of Santa Muerte religious shit. Anyway, Danny Ryan, you are a free man. Live your life."

Live my life, Danny thinks.

Okay.

DANNY MEETS JIMMY at a taco stand on San Clemente State Beach near the train station.

It's a beautiful California day—blue sky, blue ocean.

They sit outside.

Jimmy reads the menu board and says he wants a cheeseburger.

"It's a Mexican place," Danny says. "The burgers are probably awful."

"Yeah, but I want a burger," Jimmy says. "I'd give my left nut for a couple of White Castles and a Del's."

Del's Lemonade, Danny thinks, the slushy, icy drink sold out of trucks back in Rhode Island. He knows that Jimmy misses home, that he'd go back to RI in a heartbeat if he could.

Danny orders two fish tacos. Jimmy gets the burger and fries. When they come, he asks for vinegar. The guy behind the counter looks at him blankly and Jimmy gives up after a couple more tries and settles for two plastic packets of ketchup.

"Fries without vinegar," he says as he sits across from Danny at the picnic table outside. "Barbaric."

They're the only customers there. Jimmy says, "So?"

"So it's over," Danny says. He tells him about Popeye's demise and the proposed peace deal with Calfo. "We'll have Bernie send him the two hundred and we're done."

Because the money has finally been laundered and Bernie has pronounced it "clean as a whistle."

"Thank God." Jimmy bites into his burger, then says, "Bernie is still cooling his heels at Residence Inn. He likes the free breakfasts."

"Cheap old bastard."

"What you want in an accountant."

"Sure." Danny takes a bite of his taco, and then pours more salsa on it. "Put out the radar bings. Bring the guys in so I can pay them out."

He's worried. He hasn't heard from Ned, Sean, or Kevin. Ned Egan is one thing—they could lock him down in hard solitary in the max wing and Ned would whistle through it. Sean? Solid, but you never know. Kevin is tough as nails, but his drinking problem makes him a loose cannon.

"You're right," Jimmy says. "This burger is horrible."

"You really gotta go with the local food."

"Fish doesn't belong in a taco," Jimmy says. "Fish was meant to be deep fried in batter, set beside chips with vinegar."

"Dave's Dock," Danny says.

Jimmy smiles. "Now you're talkin'."

"Good days," Danny says.

"Pisser."

"But they're over," Danny says. "We can't get them back."

Then he's sorry he said it, because Jimmy almost looks like he's going to cry, like he's going to break down right there.

So Danny says, "Look, you're a freakin' millionaire, there's no warrants on you, no indictments. You bring the family out, you get a place, they'll love it here. The beaches, Disneyland . . . We did it, Jimmy. We got out of Dogtown. We have a new life here."

Danny goes back to the trailer and packs.

Looks out the window and waves at Mrs. Mossbach.

She waves back.

This life in the wind is over.

TWELVE

B ERNIE HUGHES KNEELS AND LIGHTS a candle.

They're comforting, these old rituals, he thinks as he prays for the soul of his late wife. Gone seventeen years now, and there's not a day he doesn't miss her. Bernie was headed toward priesthood with the Franciscans when he saw Bridget Donnelly walking on Weybosset Street and that was it for the holy orders. He courted her, wedded her, and took her to Block Island for their honeymoon. He'd never forget the sweetness of that first night together, the sweetness of all their nights and days together. When Bridget came to him in tears and sobbed that the doctor said she could never have children, he held her in his arms and whispered, "It's all right. You're all I want, all I need."

True, and also, truth be known, he hated the damn rubbers anyway. Of course, the priest told him that now he and Bridget should live as brother and sister, but what did the priest know about loving a woman? About the look in Bridget's eyes and the feel of her skin, the joy of her in his arms?

Every other month since she died, he went to a whore and did his business. Then he made confession, said his prayers of penance, and lit a candle and asked for Bridget's forgiveness. A man has needs and flesh is weak. It meant nothing.

And I'm an old man, Bernie thought. How much longer can lust survive in this shell? A flickering flame, surely.

Now he prays for the soul of Martin Ryan.

Two souls on the one candle, but Bernie was always thrifty. Knows where every penny comes from and where it's going. Mind the pennies and the dollars take care of themselves.

Unlike Martin.

You were always too easy with the money, Martin, he thinks. It was part of your charm, but you were left with nothing, my old pal. Nothing for the rainy day, except that old broken-down house and just enough dosh to keep you in the booze that killed you. My poor old friend.

It was that woman that did you in.

The oldest story in the world, Eve coming straight from a natter with the devil himself, bearing the apple, offering the irresistible taste.

Christ, but the tits on her, and those legs . . .

Shame on you, Bernard Hughes, he tells himself. In *church*, and at the altar.

Shame.

He goes back to praying for Martin's departed soul, asking the Lord to accept him into heaven. Which might be overshooting, Bernie thinks. Purgatory is the more realistic goal, hell a sad but distinct possibility. Maybe Martin did receive the last rites, so perhaps he's skated through. Take him, Lord, he did what he had to do to live in the world that You created. No offense to Yourself, understand.

Bernie gets up from his knees. They creak and pop, one reason that Bernie goes to church every day but never goes to mass, with all its sitting and kneeling and standing. One thing the Proddies have on us, he thinks, their church services don't resemble gymnastics classes. The first—and one of the last—fights Bernie ever had was when a thick Prod bastard from Eddy Street called him a "kneeler" and Bernie answered, "Let me show you where your *sister* kneels." A fat lip and blackened eye later, Bernie decided that his future lay more with his mathematical than his fistic abilities.

Mathematics, Bernie thinks as he makes his way up the aisle to the back of the church. The only tongue that never lies. Numbers are what they are, nothing more, nothing less. A lovely precision. Balance and beauty in an otherwise chaotic and ugly world.

He walks out of the church and blinks at the bright sunshine. The sun feels good, though, on old bones, and Bernie can see why this town started as a retirement community, and why so many elderly live here. It's lovely and peaceful—flower gardens flank the sidewalks. Big, clean supermarkets within walking distance. Restaurants, movie theaters, bookstores . . . he hasn't found a whorehouse yet, but there must be one in downtown San Diego, just a twenty-minute bus ride away.

Now he looks for a place to have lunch. He had the free breakfast at Residence Inn before walking to the church—pancakes, scrambled eggs, sausage, and tea that he enjoyed in the dining room while watching the news on the big-screen television set.

Four nights a week, he can also get supper at the motel; the complimentary happy hour "snacks" they serve—tuna casserole, little hot dogs, small bowls of beef stew—are sufficient for an old man's appetite. And every Wednesday is Cookout Night, when the staff grills burgers and hot dogs out by the pool.

But he has to provide for lunch himself. Now he has to decide from among TGI Friday's, Applebee's, California Pizza Kitchen, New York Bagel, and China Fun. Bernie hasn't really enjoyed Chinese since Wong's closed back in Dogtown. It had been a Friday night ritual for him and Bridget, going to Wong's for chop suey. They would sit in that hot little place and listen to Wong and his wife scream at each other in the kitchen.

Wong always gave him the family price because the Murphys protected them against the local punks who would otherwise pick on the "chinks."

Today he decides on Applebee's because they have a $5.95 lunch special going. Tomato soup and half a sandwich, choice of roast beef, chicken, turkey, or tuna salad. He decides on the chicken salad and to drink, something called an Arnold Palmer, which he's never heard of before—half iced tea, half lemonade.

This will be a nice place to retire, Bernie thinks. He finishes his lunch and goes back to his room to take a nap. The maid is still there, finishing up the kitchen.

She has nice legs.

NED EGAN MOVED up to Los Angeles.

He wanted to be in a freakin' city.

He found one of the dwindling number of SRO hotels among the burgeoning condo redevelopments down on the Nickel. His room is small as a cell, the way he likes it. Having spent eight years in the Adult Correctional Institute in Cranston, Rhode Island, Ned feels more comfortable in small spaces with low ceilings. And he likes downtowns; you can get to places without a car. There's a little joint a half block from the hotel that still serves real breakfasts—fried eggs, bacon, potatoes, toast, and coffee with free refills. Not a bad place for lunch, either—you can get soup and a sandwich.

Ned went out and bought an electric hot plate that he smuggled into the room against the rules. So nights he listens to the radio even though he can't get the Sox, and heats canned beef stew or Campbell's chicken noodle soup on the hot plate, eats out of the can. That and a piece of bread make a pretty good supper. Before he gets into the sack he slides the hot plate under the bed, because he knows they don't clean under there. His neighbor down the hall smelled the stew one night, knocked on the door, and threatened to tell the manager unless Ned shared the stew with him.

"The manager comes up about the hot plate," Ned said, "I'll beat you to death."

The neighbor believed him, which was smart, because Ned wasn't kidding. Maybe the neighbor took a look at Ned's Popeye forearms, flat broken knuckles, or his barrel chest. Ned has beaten a man to death, but his ACI stint was for *attempted* murder, when some joker in a pub slid his hand up the waitress's dress and didn't want to apologize. Ned beat him until the bones in his own hands broke and then beat him some more, even while Danny and a half dozen others tried to pry him off. Blew his chance at parole after four years when he told the board that he'd do it again if the situation arose. Ned didn't want parole anyway. "When I get out," he said, "I intend to consort with known felons and nobody's going to tell me I can't."

Ned Egan gets the newspaper every morning and reads it over breakfast.

Like most guys who've spent a lot of time in prison, routine rules his life. So before he leaves his room, he makes sure he has two quarters in his left pocket so he can get a paper from the machine on the sidewalk. This morning he sits down to eat, checks the sports pages, skips all the shit about the Dodgers and reads about the Sox.

Then he checks the classifieds, running one thick finger down the columns. Every other morning for the past few weeks, his search has come up empty, but today he spots what he's been looking for: an ad for a bright yellow 1989 Trans Am.

Jimmy sending the signal.

He finishes his breakfast and goes to make a phone call.

THIRTEEN

MADELEINE PICKED SOMEONE LIKE HERSELF.

Well, not *exactly* like her, Danny thinks as he watches the young woman swing the shotgun up and gracefully arc it at the disk flying through the air, but the same statuesque body, long legs, and red hair.

Much younger, of course, maybe in her late twenties, but otherwise a virtual copy of Madeleine.

With the same icy competence—the woman (Danny thinks her name is Sharon) squeezes the trigger and the disk shatters into satisfying fragments. She lowers the gun, turns and smiles at Danny.

"Are you sure you don't want to try?" she asks.

"I'm sure."

"You don't like guns?"

"They make me nervous."

Her smiles intensifies. "Really? You don't look like the nervous type to me."

Danny knows this is the cue for him to ask, "What type do I look like?" but for some reason he doesn't want to play the game. Maybe because Madeleine made up the rules. So he says, "I like watching you."

That seems to satisfy her. Sharon turns back, yells, "Pull!" and blasts another defenseless clay pigeon out of the sky.

Leave it to Madeleine, Danny thinks, to have her own shooting range. And a stable, horses, a pool, a screening room, a gym . . .

Las Vegas, Danny thinks, makes Los Angeles look Amish.

He's been here for a month, about twenty-nine days longer than he'd intended, but inertia has set in and besides, it's been harder to tear Ian from his grandmother than he thought it would be.

For both of them.

Ian's become very attached, and Madeleine . . .

Well, it's her grandson.

So Danny has lingered at her estate just outside of downtown, yielding to the lethargy of heat and luxury, the truth being that he doesn't know what he's going to do next. He knows he wants to go back to California, but exactly where and to do what he has no clue.

He doesn't need to work, he has millions now and his millions have been wisely invested, so his money is working for him. But Danny can't quite fathom a life without some kind of labor, so he has to figure out something to do.

Danny just doesn't know what it is, so he's gradually drifted onto the chaise lounge by the pool with an icy cold beer at his hand, or into the screening room watching cartoons with Ian, even taking walks with his mother in the early morning's relative cool.

It's on these walks that Madeleine started in on the subject of women.

That is, his need for one.

And Ian's.

"Ian needs a mother," Madeleine said.

"He has you."

"And I love it," she said. "But I'm a grandmother, and there's a difference. Besides, don't you have . . . *needs*?"

"If you think I'm discussing this with you—"

"Have you been with anyone since Terri?"

"Jesus Christ."

"Oh my God, it's only natural," Madeleine said.

She started bringing young women by under the guise of visiting her, but Madeleine always found an excuse to get away and leave them with Danny, which was painfully obvious to both him and the lady in question.

They were all pretty, all smart, all funny, and all apparently available, but Danny just couldn't bring himself to pull the trigger, as it were.

Not that he doesn't have . . . *needs* . . . it's more that he can't bring himself to give in to his mother's attempts to run his life. He knows that it stems from resentment—if you didn't want to mother me then, don't start now.

And it feels creepy, like incest.

"You're aware," he said to her on one of their walks, "that these women you're pushing at me are all younger versions of yourself."

"What are you talking about?"

"Oh, come on," Danny said. "They all look like you."

"You could do worse," she said.

"You think a lot of yourself, Madeleine."

Danny can't bring himself to call her Mom or Mother, only Madeleine.

Madeleine accepts it, grateful that he calls her anything at all. It wasn't that long ago that he wouldn't even speak to her.

Their relationship has always been difficult, conflicted, laden with past baggage and future uncertainties, but it is a relationship. They bond, of course, over their love for Ian, but it's gone beyond that now and Danny has to admit to himself that she's smart and funny, warm and even caring, and that they share an outlook on life that's pragmatic and wry.

But God, Danny thinks as he watches Sharon crack open the shotgun and then sit down across from him, will she please stop running these women at me?

Sharon takes a bottle of cold beer from the cooler, lifts it to him in a toast, and says, "So I guess this is Madeleine's version of setting us up on a blind date?"

"She's as subtle as a sledgehammer."

"I don't mind. Do you?"

"No," Danny says. "It's just that I'm not looking for a relationship right now, Sharon."

"Neither am I," she says. "I was just hoping to get laid."

Oh, Danny thinks.

KEVIN COOMBS IS fucked up.

He pours a hit of JD into his breakfast beer and momentarily ponders his fucked-up-ed-ness before he tosses it back.

It feels good going down—the burn spreads through his stomach and across his chest—but not good enough, not as good as it should, so he pours more whiskey into the opening of the can, spilling a little around the edge because his hand is trembling.

The next pop takes care of the shakes so he can enjoy the rest of his beer. A few minutes later he rummages in the kitchen for something to eat and comes up with a chocolate-covered doughnut left in a cardboard container. Thank God for Entenmann's, he thinks as he holds the dough-nut in his teeth and walks back across the apartment, opens a curtain and blinks at the bright white sunshine.

He goes out through the glass slider and sits down on the white plastic-lathed chair on the little balcony that overlooks the apartment complex courtyard with its swimming pool, outdoor tables, and "sports court."

One of those extended-stay hotels in the Valley, just off the 101 on the edge of Burbank, it caters to businessmen on long trips, families who are relocating and looking for a house or waiting for escrow to close, and recently divorced women with their kids.

Kevin finds the place sad as sin on the weekends, when the divorced dads come from out of town for their mandated visits and make sad stabs at normal home life with their children. The kids are usually in the pool all day because Dad doesn't know what the fuck else to do with them and they'd rather be home with their friends anyway. Or he hauls them up the road to Universal Studios, but how many times can you do that? So most of the time the divorced dads end up sitting poolside with the divorced moms and get into desperate new relationships that will lead to another "blended family," another divorce, and more business for the long-stay hotel.

Another class of people—really strange—inhabits the place.

Kids—with their mothers—looking to break into show business.

Weird, hyperactive, attention-deficit miniature drama queens running around the hallways singing Broadway show tunes, getting dolled up like molestation victims to meet with their pimp/agent at the picnic tables out by the pool. The agents—who charge the parents up front for "representation and development"—book the families into this complex because it's near the studios and so they only have to go to one place to rip off their clients. One-stop unarmed robbery is what Kevin calls it, and what the fuck, he wonders, am I doing in honest crime?

Poor fucking little bastards, Kevin thinks, believing they're going to be stars, flashing their fake, forced smiles at anyone who'll even pretend to care, being dragged off to endless open casting calls or acting classes taught by out-of-work adult actors sticking their snouts into the kiddie trough.

Used to be pipe dreams were at least free. Now they cost: agents' fees, photographers' bills, acting classes, dance lessons—and who the fuck dances in the movies anymore, by the way—speech therapists, voice coaches, makeup and hair consultants . . . Kevin hears the conversations among the mothers as they sit around the pool during the rare times—usually at night—when the kids are allowed to be kids and just mess around in the water playing Marco Polo and shit. The moms tell each other about all the money they're spending on what, and then the mother who wasn't forking out for the new flavor of the month runs back to her room and jacks the Mastercard limit up to pay for a "life coach" or a "smile expert," any stupid fucking thing that might give her kid the edge, might get her a commercial or a one-liner on a cable sitcom that would pay for one more month of chasing the dream. "Investments in the future" is what they call it when they phone the husband, who's back home busting his ass to pay for all this crap.

Yeah, investment in future psychiatric bills, Kevin thinks. He's surprised that the shrinks aren't just lined up in the lobby, taking a number to cash in on the bonanza of neurotics in the making. He's grateful that he had a relatively normal Irish Catholic alcoholic childhood with the Saturday night domestic disturbance followed by Sunday postchurch pot roast, served with carrots, onions, potato, remorse, regret, and shame.

Anyway, what with the displaced families, visitation fathers, stage mothers, and their freakish offspring, the complex is one of the most depressing places on the face of the earth. A refugee camp with air-conditioning, swimming pool, a petri dish hot tub, and complimentary continental breakfast—stale muffins, fake orange juice, weak coffee and artificial frozen "waffles" you heat up in the toaster and try to smother with plastic packets of "syrup food"—served in the hospitality suite.

The fact that the place doesn't host more suicides than the Golden Gate Bridge is a testament to something, Kevin thinks, but he's not quite sure just what. Maybe to a dogged determination to survive, or maybe to a lack of hope that there's anything else out there anyway, that you can expect anything better than a fake home, faux food, feigned love or false hope.

And then there's me, he thinks.

Speaking of refugees.

Just another lost pup from Dogtown.

Well, a pup with three million bucks.

That Danny Ryan won't let me spend.

Not much of it, anyway.

They finally got their money from the Abbarca job—"Popeye's spinach," Kevin calls it—and Danny told them to keep most of it in their pockets; in fact, to keep most of it in the accounts that old Harp set up.

"You're out there buying sports cars and coke," Danny said, "it's conspicuous. We don't want to be conspicuous. So cool it for a while."

"For how long?" Kevin asked.

"Until I tell you otherwise," Danny said.

So far, he hasn't told them.

The beer can is empty.

Kevin gets up to go back into the kitchen for a fresh one and walks smack into the glass slider. The pain makes him dizzy, rocks his knees, and for a second he thinks he's going to faint. He touches his forehead and it feels wet. Looks at his hand and it's bloody. He sees the smear of blood on the slider.

That'll freak the maids out, he thinks.

He opens the slider—Sure, *now*, he thinks—and goes into the bathroom to check the damage in the mirror. He really hopes he won't need stitches because going to the E-room is a drag. But the cut doesn't look too bad, although there's going to be a nice bump, and the pain is starting to subside. What he mostly feels is stupid—unwitting kamikaze missions are something that birds do, and even most of them can usually tell the difference between empty air and solid glass. Yeah, he thinks, but most birds aren't as drunk as you are, so they have an unfair advantage. He yanks some toilet paper off the roll, wads it into a ball, and presses it against the cut, then walks back to the kitchen for another beer.

The phone rings.

There are only two possibilities—the front desk asking him how long he intends to keep the apartment, or Sean.

It's Sean, the only other person who knows where Kevin is.

"You up?" Sean asks.

Which is like a stupid-ass question, Kevin thinks, because obviously I'm up, I answered the fucking phone.

"Yeah."

"You sound fucked up. Are you fucked up?"

Mother Sean, nagging him about his drinking. If I wanted to catch shit about my drinking, Kevin thinks, I'd find a woman to do it, because at least there might be intermittent sexual side benefits. Actually, he has his eye on one of the better-looking stage moms, who seems so stressed out she might throw him a mercy fuck just for a diversion.

"I hit my head," Kevin says.

"On what?"

"A door," Kevin says.

"A door," Sean asks. "How do you hit your head on a door?"

"I dunno. I did, all right?" Kevin says. Sean sounds way too cheerful, truly amused, like he's heard some great joke he can't keep to himself.

"Dude," Sean says.

Dude? Kevin thinks. This redheaded mick is doing "Dude"?

"Dude," Sean repeats, "you're not going to believe *this* shit."

I'm in L.A., Kevin thinks.

I'll believe *any* shit.

A MOVIE.

They're doing a fucking movie.

Kevin sits across from Sean in a booth at Denny's, within walking distance from the hotel because Kevin's not dumb enough to drive anywhere and risk a DUI. Now Sean is sitting there, grinning so hard Kevin thinks the freckles might pop off his face.

"Seriously?" Kevin says.

"Seriously."

"A movie."

"A movie," Sean repeats.

"The fuck," Kevin says.

"Truly, huh?"

"How weird is that?"

"Wicked weird," Sean says.

Kevin looks at the menu, which has glossy photos of the items. Last thing Kevin wants to do is look at pictures of food, so he sets it down.

"You should eat," Sean says.

"Yeah? Why is that?"

"You have to eat. A person has to eat."

"What's the movie called?" Kevin asks.

"*Providence.*"

"Well, I guess that says it."

"I guess."

Kevin looks over Sean's shoulder. One of the stage mommies he aspires to bang is sitting in a booth with her neurotic daughter. There's the Hollywood dream, Kevin thinks. You come out here for little Ashley whatever-the-fuck to be a star, you end up getting lunch at Denny's. He smiles at her. She looks at him but doesn't smile back, or at least the smile is noncommittal. Can't blame her, Kevin thinks, I must look like hammered shit. Maybe I can manage a shave later without actually slicing my throat and bleeding out.

He asks, "Who's playing me?"

"I don't think anybody," Sean says. "I gather it's mostly about the older guys. You know, Pat Murphy and them."

"Okay, who's playing Pat?"

"Sam Wakefield."

"Big star."

"Pisser."

The woman's peeking over her menu at Kevin. Hell, he thinks, they're making a movie about people I know, and she can sniff out the faint scent of opportunity from over there. Yeah, like movie producers "do lunch" at Denny's. Amazing, a truly amazing place they got here. He tries another smile, turns back to Sean and asks, "Isn't he Australian or something like that?"

"He's taking dialect lessons," Sean says.

"How'd you find out about this?" Kevin asks.

Through his new girlfriend, Ana, Sean says. One of those things—he was on the train heading up to L.A., and it was pretty crowded, so this Latina chick took the seat next to him.

Black hair, honey skin, full lips . . .

"Blow job lips," Kevin said when Sean described her to him.

"Yeah, if you want to go there," Sean said.

"Who doesn't want to go there?" Kevin asked.

Ana's petite, but with a nice rack and these killer dark eyes, and she and Sean started to talk on the train ride. About whales. Sean couldn't figure out anything else to say, so he broke the ice by saying that he'd heard you could sometimes see whales from the train.

"If it's the right time of year," Ana said.

"Is this the right time of year?" Sean asked.

"Not quite," she said. Usually it's more like April when the whales start their northward migration back up from Baja.

"Have you ever seen whales from the train?" Sean asked.

"Yes. Yes, I have."

Sean got up to go to the club car and asked if he could get her anything. She declined at first.

"Nothing?" Sean asked. "You don't want a glass of wine or a beer or a soda or something?"

"Maybe a Coke?"

"How about a sandwich?" Sean asked. "Long ride."

"I guess maybe a sandwich would be nice."

He came back with a Coke, a turkey sandwich. Bag of chips and a big cookie.

"I'll get fat," she said.

"I can't see you getting fat."

They talked all the way up to L.A. Turned out Ana was a hairstylist who worked for the movies.

"That's got to be pretty interesting," Sean said.

"It is," Ana said. "It beats working in a salon, and it's good money."

"Do you, like, do any famous person's hair?" Sean asked. "Like a movie star, something like that?"

"Well, I do a lot of work with Diane Carson."

"No shit?!" Sean was impressed. Diane Carson was like the biggest star there was. Blond, big rack, long legs, blue eyes, a modern-day Marilyn Monroe. "What's she like, can you say?"

"She's nice."

"Yeah?"

"Yeah, very polite, down-to-earth."

"Diane Carson," Sean said. "Wow."

"I know," Ana said. "Guys get all crazy. Like, Diane walks into the room and all the rest of us become invisible all of a sudden."

"Not you," Sean said.

Sean's no idiot. He knew there was no way outside his fantasies that he was ever going to do Diane Carson, but he might have an outside shot with Ana.

"You're sweet," she said.

"You don't know the half."

She gave him her phone number as they were getting off the train. He got himself settled in a little motel in Culver City, waited a day or two so as not to look too eager, and then called her. They've been seeing each other for two months now, although they were five dates in before she'd let him get anywhere near the main prize.

"Good Catholic girl," she explained during one heated session as she pushed his hand away from her panties.

"I know Catholic girls," Sean said. You can't get them started, but once you do, you can't get them stopped. Three dates later, when she gave it up, she gave it *all* up.

Then, just last night, she told him that she was really excited because she just "got" a new film, a feature, with Diane.

"Cool," Sean said. "What is it?"

It was called *Providence*, and it was about gangsters from Providence, Rhode Island. About how the Irish and Italians fought each other for control of New England. Like, apparently they'd been friends before, but they had a falling-out and started killing each other.

"And," Ana continued, "it's based on things that really happened."

"No shit?" Sean said.

Now Kevin looks across the table at Sean and says, "We should do something about this."

"What do you mean?"

"I mean we should get in on this," Kevin says. "It's our fucking lives they're turning into a movie. Don't they, like, owe us something?"

"I dunno, I guess."

"You *guess*?"

They drop it when the waitress comes over. Sean orders a club sandwich and an iced tea. Kevin gets a couple of scrambled eggs and a coffee with cream and extra sugar. He looks over at Stage Mom eating her chef's salad and decides from the way she chews her food that she'd be good in bed. He likes her hands, long fingers on her fork, and thinks he'd like them wrapped around his dick.

"So where did they get all this shit, anyway?" he asks.

"What shit?"

"The shit about us," Kevin says. "All this cool shit that really happened."

Sean grins again. "You remember Bobby Bangs?"

"Bobby . . ."

"Bangs," Sean says. "Bangs like a girl? We thought he was a queer but he wasn't?"

"Oh, yeah, that guy," Kevin says. "What about him?"

"He wrote a film treatment."

"He did?" Kevin says. Bobby "Bangs" Moran was a joke, a bartender at the Glocca Morra barely tolerated at the tables of men who did the heavy lifting. Now he's going around making it out like he had some weight? "Bobby didn't do shit in the wars. I mean, he was around the edges . . ."

"Yeah, well, I guess you read his treatment, you'd think he was in the middle of it."

"That mook," Kevin says. If Bobby got anywhere near a gun going off, he'd shit his pants.

"Can't fault a guy for making a buck."

Can't fault him, no, Kevin thinks. But he owes us, doesn't he? A piece, a slice, a lick of the ice cream cone. I mean, the guy did precisely jack shit back then except hang around the bar listening to other guys' stories, and he turns that into a payday, gets to see movie stars and fuck actresses and shit like that? While I'm walking into glass doors, trying to get by, only hoping to hit some yummy mummy if she can dump her ugly kid long enough at tap class?

Speaking of which, the woman wanders over, her check in her hand, the chunky little wannabe Ashley skulking behind her. "I'm sorry," she says, "I don't mean to interrupt, but I couldn't help overhearing you talk about a movie?"

"Yeah," Kevin says.

She has shoulder-length frosted brown hair, trim body, a nice face, and tired brown eyes. "Are you producers?"

"Consultants," Kevin says. "More like consultants."

"On a Sam Wakefield movie, that's something," she says. She holds out her hand for him to shake. "I'm Kim Canigliaro. This is my daughter, Amber."

It comes out of her mouth "Ambuh." Jersey or Long Island, Kevin can't make out which. And her makeup is definitely East Coast, a little heavier with the mascara than the California women do.

"Hi."

"Haven't I seen you around Oakwood?" Kim asks.

"Yeah, I'm living there," Kevin says. "Temporarily. It's near the studio."

"Oh, is your project set up at Warners?"

"Right," Kevin says. Whatever the fuck. He's sort of aware that Warner Bros. studio is down the street because he's seen the water tower with the logo. All he can think of when he sees that is Bugs Bunny. Those were good cartoons, Bugs and Porky and Yosemite Sam, and it always cracked Kevin up when Elmer Fudd would look at the audience and say, "Be quiet, be *vewy, vewy* quiet." It's what Kevin whispered to Sean the night they took out Dominic Vera as he was parked up by the reservoir looking to do the job on *them*. It had broken the tension, and him and Sean were literally giggling as they opened up on Dom.

Be *vewy, vewy* quiet.

"Well, maybe I'll see you around," Kim says. Then she puts it right out there, laughing like it's a joke, "And hey, if you have a part for a cute twelve-year-old . . ."

"I know where to find you," Kevin says.

"Yeah, you do," she says, letting him know with a frank look that she'd give it up for him, no problem, for a crack in the Hollywood door. "Well, good luck with the project."

Kevin watches as she walks out of the restaurant, checks out her hips and the backs of her legs. They're tight, muscled. Mommy Kim keeps herself in shape, a little MILFier than he'd thought checking her out from the balcony.

"Can you get his number?" Kevin says.

"Whose?"

"'Whose'?" Kevin repeats. "Bobby Bangs's."

"Yeah, I guess."

"Get it."

We should pay Bobby a little visit.

Maybe he'd, what do you call it, take a lunch.

DANNY AND SHARON go out to dinner and then to her apartment downtown. It's a nice place because she has an executive position with one of the big casinos. She hands Danny a brandy and says, "Your mother says you haven't had sex in years."

"She told you that?" Danny's horrified.

"Like you said, a sledgehammer," Sharon says. "Don't worry."

"Is it like riding a bike?"

"Did you just compare me to a bicycle?" she asks. "If that's the case, you'd better know I'm a ten-speed."

Yeah, at least.

Danny hasn't been with a lot of women. A couple of girls before Terri, and then he was a completely faithful husband. So he's nervous at first, but then biology takes over and it's pretty great.

"I needed that," Sharon says.

"*You* needed that."

She laughs. "You sleepy?"

"No."

She turns on the TV. Clicks around through a number of shows and then settles on some kind of *Entertainment Tonight* show about some actress.

A chirpy female narrator is describing Diane Carson's "release from rehab" under a still photo of a smiling Diane edging her way through a crowd of photographers. The next image shows her getting into the back of a limousine.

"Keep clicking," Danny says.

"No, I *love* her." Sharon turns up the volume.

". . . *the latest chapter in the saga of America's favorite sex symbol*," the narrator, now on camera, is saying. "*Her dramatic, almost larger-than-life story began in a small town in Kansas.*"

Still photos of Carson as a little girl, blowing out candles on a cake, then in a cowgirl outfit. Grainy video footage of her singing in an elementary school play, then twirling a baton. More stills of her as a teenager—in a local beauty pageant, at what looks to be a county fair, then what has to be her high school graduation picture.

"*As anyone who hasn't been on Mars the past ten years knows, the young Diane Groskopf married her high school sweetheart, Scott Haroldson, the son of a prominent, well-to-do doctor, perhaps as a way to escape the desperate rural poverty that she'd been raised in.*"

More still photos of a ramshackle, rural slat-board house that could have been taken straight from *The Grapes of Wrath*. Followed by a shot of a modern suburban bungalow behind a neatly cropped front lawn.

"*The couple was happy for the first two years . . .*"

The voice drops an octave in an effort at seriousness.

". . . *then tragedy struck.*"

The narration goes silent. Still photo of a young man, another graduation picture, then a shot of the same boy, obviously another graduation picture. Then a photo of the outside of a small-town courthouse, followed by video of the young man, now clad in an orange jumpsuit, handcuffed and shackled, being led out to a waiting van.

The narration picks up. *"Diane's older brother, Jarrod, attacked Scott in a drug-induced rage, slashing and stabbing him more than one hundred times. A horrified Diane came home to see this and called 911, but her husband bled to death before the ambulance could arrive. Jarrod pleaded guilty and was sentenced to life without possibility of parole."*

File footage of the outside of a prison.

Jesus, Danny thinks, no wonder the actress drinks and takes pills. Her brother slaughtered her husband in front of her.

"A heartbroken, shattered Diane moved to Los Angeles to fulfill her life-long dream of becoming an actress."

Diane's centerfold photo, with her nude body blurred out. Her face is clear, though, and she smiles at the camera with the classic girl-next-door look, a potent blend of innocence and sexuality.

"But Hollywood didn't like the name Diane Haroldson, so she changed it to . . ."

Dramatic, the-rest-is-history pause.

"Diane Carson."

"So what is it you love about her?" Danny asks.

"Are you kidding?" Sharon asks. "Look at her. Don't lie—you'd do her. Hell, *I'd* do her."

She goes on to list a bunch of movies that Diane Carson's been in, none of which Danny has seen because he hasn't been to the movies in years, either. Then, noticing his eyes glaze over, she says, "Don't worry, Danny, you don't have to spend the night. To be honest, I prefer sleeping alone."

"I'll call you tomorrow."

"Really?" she asks. "Because I thought we didn't want a relationship."

"We don't, but—"

"You feel obligated," Sharon says. "Listen, Danny, it was great, and if you want to go for another bike ride in a week or two, give me call, but otherwise . . ."

When he's dressed and about to leave, Sharon says, "Madeleine really loves you, you know."

"Is that right?"

"Come on, she thinks the world of you," Sharon says. "She says you can be anything. She says you could build an empire if you wanted to."

DANNY GOES INTO Ian's bedroom.

The boy is sound asleep.

When Danny first got to Madeleine's house, Ian was afraid of him. Or angry at him, or both, because he treated him like a stranger. Danny couldn't blame the boy; so he was patient, gentle, didn't try to push it, and pretty soon Ian started looking at him again, then sitting on his lap, then letting Danny read him a story—but not the bedtime story, he still only lets Madeleine do that.

But gradually, over weeks, Ian has warmed up to Danny, started to call him Daddy, asks him to play, wants to show him his toys.

Danny feels forgiven.

He's determined to break the Ryan dysfunctional parent cycle here, so Ian will have a real father, even if he doesn't have a mother.

He kisses Ian on the cheek and pulls the sheet up onto his neck.

BOBBY SETS UP the lunch at the Beverly Hilton.

One, if you're going to meet Kevin Coombs and Sean South, it's always a good idea to do it in a public place. Two, he gets a table out by the pool, where they'll be distracted by the female flesh. Three, he's hoping that power atmosphere might intimidate them.

After all, this is his turf and these chowderheads can't possibly know the lay of the land, the way things work, and how an industry lunch plays out.

A good plan, but flawed on the conceptual level.

One, push comes to shove, the Altar Boys would whack Santa in the middle of the Macy's Thanksgiving Day Parade. Two, the only thing they care about more than pussy is money, and three, they're not intimidated by anything or anybody in this world, except maybe, *maybe* Danny Ryan.

Anyway, Bobby shows up wearing a white shirt, open at the neck, over three-hundred-dollar stone-washed jeans, loafers with no socks, and Cobian shades. Black hair gelled back, skin freshly exfoliated and moisturized.

Kevin shows up looking like shit. A dirty, wrinkled, sweat-stained denim shirt that Bobby is sure he slept in, black jeans, and work boots. Tight wraparound shades to hide bloodshot eyes. Long, dirty hair, at least three days' growth of beard. Most people at the other tables suspend their disdain, though, until they can be certain that he's not a famous actor doing the hip, dissolute thing. Sean has at least made an effort. His green-on-white striped shirt is neatly tucked into pressed khaki trousers and he has real shoes on his feet.

The poolside dining area smells like chlorine and suntan lotion. The Beverly Hilton is old Hollywood, at least twenty years out of being hip, but Bobby has no way of knowing that. What you get here are mostly former television stars whose sell-by dates are coming at them like runaway trains, old film actors hoping to get a part as the grandfather or dotty old uncle, and aging divas whose face-lift scars are fresher than their complexions.

The whole place has the feel of a faded film star. It's a Gloria Swanson of a hotel, its former beauty tired and out-of-date, in need of a major makeover that's not going to happen, and it won't ever be ready for its close-up, Mr. DeMille.

Bobby doesn't know that, though. He parades his friends in and sits down at a table under a broad green umbrella, looks around to make sure he's been seen, and orders an Arnold Palmer.

"The fuck is that?" Kevin asks. He's relatively sober, which puts him in a bad mood anyway.

"Iced tea and lemonade," Bobby says.

"I'll try one," says Sean, eager to be agreeable.

"Give me a beer," Kevin says.

"We have some really interesting microbrewery offerings," the waiter says.

"You got Sam Adams?"

"Certainly."

"Give me a Sammy," Kevin says, glaring across the table at Bobby.

The waiter comes back with the drinks and the lunch menu. Bobby orders a duck breast roll-up with hoisin sauce and jicama. Sean gets a cheeseburger. Kevin orders a New York strip steak, rare, which he figures is sort of a down payment from Bobby. Then he gets right to it. "So this 'treatment', Bobby. . ."

Beads of sweat pop on Bobby's exfoliated, moisturized forehead. He tells himself it's the sun, but he knows better. "It's mostly taken from my memories."

"Your memories," Kevin says. "Did you remember anyone we might know?"

"I was careful."

"Careful," Kevin repeats. "Do I show up in it? Sean here?"

"Yeah, but only as minor characters," Bobby says. Realizing that this might have been a tactical error, he quickly adds, "I mean, most of it covers the time before you two were major players."

Kevin stares at him.

Bobby says, "It's mostly about Pat, Liam, Danny, those guys."

"Danny?" Sean asks. "Danny's in this movie?"

"I don't have a whole lot to do with the movie," Bobby says.

"Let's cut to the chase," Kevin says. "How much you figure to make from all this, Bobby?"

"Well, I'm not at liberty to disclose—"

"Bobby, Bobby, Bobby." Kevin shakes his head. "You're the expert on the Irish mob. You, of all people, should know how it works."

"One for all, all for one," Sean says. "What was it you wrote . . ."

He'd gotten a copy of the treatment from Ana.

It made fascinating reading. He had even memorized a passage. "'We were like brothers, wolf cubs from the same litter. We laughed together, ate together, lived together, bled together and died together.' Beautiful stuff, Bobby. I choked up."

"Except," Kevin says, "you were a little short on the bleeding side, weren't you?"

"I don't remember you doing any bleeding, Bobby," Sean says.

"But it's not too late," says Kevin. He leans across the table, points his index finger at Bobby and pulls the "trigger."

The waiter arrives with the food. Bobby's hands tremble as he dips his roll-up into the hoisin sauce. The other diners stare as Kevin lifts his entire steak with the fork, puts it to his mouth, and tears off a chunk with his teeth.

Juice running out of the corners of his mouth, he smiles at Bobby and says, "Kind of wolflike, huh?"

MADELEINE IS ALREADY by the pool when Danny brings breakfast out there in the morning.

She has a wry and knowing smile on her face. "How was your date?"

"Yeah, good."

"Are you going to see her again?"

"Maybe."

"That's a no," Madeleine says. "Well, at least you got your rocks off."

"For God's sake." He gets in a couple of bites of his eggs and bacon and then says, "She relayed your message to me."

"Message?"

In this *Whatever do you mean?* tone.

"Why do you have to be like that?" Danny asks. "Why does everything have to be a manipulation? Why can't you just be yourself? If you have something you want to say to me, just say it. You don't have to send freakin' ambassadors."

She sets her glass of grapefruit juice down on the table. "All right. For one thing, this is my last apology to you. I'm sorry I abandoned you. I've done everything I can to make up for it and you can either forgive me or not but I'm done apologizing."

"That's for 'one thing.' What's the other?"

"You're lucky to be alive," she says. " You're lucky not to be behind bars for the rest of your life."

"I agree."

"Second chances are hard to come by," she says. "I don't want to see you waste yours."

"Okay."

"I can help you," she says. "I can get you started with investments, stockbroking, real estate . . . if you need money—"

"I have money," Danny says. "I've been thinking about all this. I want to do something. Something legit. I want to pass something on to Ian. I just don't know what it is yet."

"I'm pretty sure it's not sitting on my chaise all day."

"I'm pretty sure you're right," Danny says. "Look, if we're in the way here, I can—"

"No!" Madeleine says. "I love having you here, of course. You can stay as long as you want. I'd love it if you found something in Las Vegas."

"I was thinking more California."

"Well, it's a short flight."

They each look at the pool for a few seconds, then he asks, "What's this about building an empire?"

"You could," she says. "I've known less talented men than you to build empires."

"I'm a leg-breaker from Dogtown."

"You think trust fund babies build empires?" she asks. "Let me tell you, this whole town was built by guys from Dogtowns."

Danny has a feeling she's talking about herself, too. He drove past Barstow on the way here. Pictured her growing up in a trailer park there.

"I hear you," he says.

"Do you?"

"Yeah," Danny says. "And Mom? I can find my own women, okay?"

"Okay."

She gets up and leaves him by the pool.

THE ALTAR BOYS turn Bobby into a human ATM card.

You read his printout, it's a monotonous litany of *Withdrawal, Withdrawal, Withdrawal*, as Bobby tries to leverage his skin with his cash. He got a payday of $600K on the "first day of principal photography," and it's like the Altar Boys stuck a straw in it and are sucking it dry.

Bobby, my brother, I need a little rent money. Bobby, brother, I have to buy some new threads. Bobby, brother, do you know how much it costs to eat in this town? Kevin and Sean love the concept of drive-through banks, because they can just hop in Bobby's ride on the way to the studio, have him stick the plastic into the slot, hand them the cash, then drop them off at whatever restaurant, bar, or fine retail establishment they are patronizing on that given day.

That is, until they start going to the studio with him.

It's Kevin's idea.

"We're missing out," he told Sean one day during an al fresco lunch on Sunset.

"On *what*?" Sean asked. He has food, money, booze, even love—he's practically living with Ana and things are getting almost serious. So what's there to miss?

"The whole Hollywood thing," Kevin said. "Stars . . . star pussy. Bobby's hanging with Diane Carson, we don't get as much as a look, except we're in line at the supermarket, see a magazine picture?"

"When do you go to the supermarket?"

"You're missing the point."

"Which is what?" Sean asked. He's actually mellow, enjoying his lunch, enjoying his life. He even has a tan, as much as he's ever had a tan, a sort of buff sheen underneath his freckles. "You think you're going to bang Diane Carson?"

"I don't think I'm going to bang Diane Carson," Kevin said. His plate of pasta amatriciana arrived and he watched the waiter grind fresh Parmesan cheese on it, and then said, "But I do think I can get some satellite gash."

"I can't wait to hear this."

"Satellite gash?"

"That would be what I can't wait to hear, yes."

"Babes like Carson," Kevin explained, "are like the sun. They have other almost-but-not-quite-as-hot women that orbit around them, like satellites."

"You mean planets," Sean said. "The sun has planets that orbit around it. We're on one of them, Kevin."

"You're a real pain in the ass today," Kevin said. "The point is, you maybe can't reach the sun, but you can definitely lay your hands on one of the satellites. It's a target-rich environment is all I'm saying."

Sean took a bite of his chili-encrusted sea bass and said, "My girlfriend is one of those satellites."

"Proves my point," Kevin said. "Besides, there's more money to be made here."

Yeah, money. The truth is that they have to bust Bobby out slowly. Make him fork over cash a little bit at a time, then get him to run his credit cards to the max on crap they can sell later. Bobby's made some nice bread, but he's nothing compared to the studio, and Kevin read in *Variety* that the budget on *Providence* is on the high side of $30 million.

There had to be a way to tap into that.

The Altar Boys have some money now, but more money is always better, and it's money that Danny doesn't have his hands around.

"Consultants," Kevin informs Bobby that night as he takes them to dinner.

"What?"

"We want to be consultants—"

"Technical consultants," Sean says. "We think we have a lot to offer creatively."

"I don't know, guys," Bobby says.

"What don't you know, Bobby?" Kevin asks.

"I don't know."

"That's right," Kevin says. "You don't know what you don't know, and one of the things you don't know is you don't know shit about what really went on back during the wars."

"What he said," Sean agrees.

Kevin takes a second to peruse the dessert menu. "They don't have fucking crème brûlée here? I was all geared for crème brûlée."

"Maybe they're out of brûlée," Sean says.

Kevin passes on the other offerings and orders a double espresso and a shot of bourbon. Then he says, "Talk to the director, Bobby."

Bobby talks to the director.

Mitchell Apsberger is one of the reality-freak directors. Everything has to be fucking real, based in reality, down to every last detail. So when

Bobby reluctantly approaches him with the word that two of the real Providence mobsters want to be consultants, he creams his distressed jeans.

"You know Kevin Coombs and Sean South," he says to Bobby.

"Well, sure," says Bobby, whose most profound wish at that moment is that he didn't know Kevin Coombs and Sean South.

"And they're here."

They're here, all right, Bobby thinks. God damn it.

"And they want to work on the film," Mitch says.

"They need money," Bobby says. And it would be nice, in fact, if they needed somebody's money other than his.

"Let's do lunch," Mitch says.

That's it. Mitch Apsberger, two-time Oscar winner, red-carpet regular, pop-cultural icon and a very bright man, invites the wolves into his own tent.

Lunch goes great. Kevin and Sean regale Mitch with stories that fall short of confessions but easily make it to the level of lurid violence porn. Mitch is titillated. Not an uncommon phenomenon, directors and actors vicariously getting off on the exploits of real-life gangsters. Hard to tell, sometimes, who's a groupie for whom, whether the gangsters are hanging on the Hollywood coattails or vice versa, but suffice to say that after an hour of stories and whispered confidences, if Sean and Kevin had asked Mitch to go into the men's room and suck their cocks, it's an even bet that Mitch, famed for the sexual swath he cuts through the screen actress ranks, would scuff his knees on the tiles.

"You guys actually said that?" Mitch asks at one point. "'Be *vewy, vewy* quiet?' You did Elmer Fudd on a *hit*?"

Kevin nods modestly.

"We have to get that in," Mitch says to Bobby.

"I'll make a note," Bobby says.

"So you knew Pat Murphy," Mitch says to them.

"Pallbearers," Sean says.

Which isn't true, but should be, Kevin thinks, so what's the difference?

"How about Danny Ryan?"

"Oh, yeah," Kevin says. "We know Danny."

It's a touchy subject, as a matter of fact. After all, crowbarring their way into a major Hollywood film about themselves isn't exactly being inconspicuous.

Mitch signs them as consultants on the spot. Gets on the cell, phones the studio and demands fifty grand for each of them, papers to be ready by end of business day, don't even think about arguing.

Done.

Bobby sits there figuring the over/under on how many days it will be before Kevin and Sean demand their own trailer.

(Three, as it turns out.)

You can't invite wolves to dinner and not expect them to eat.

Mitch walks them straight from lunch right over to Sound Stage 41 and onto the set. He introduces them around like an early Christian might have done with a couple of actual, original apostles, like Peter and Paul had shown up at Bible study. Gets them high canvas-backed chairs next to his and headsets so they can listen to the next take.

"Any input you have," he says, "don't be shy."

Yeah. Maybe the first time the word "shy" has been used within a ten-foot radius of Kevin Coombs. He's not shy. Not shy about offering his assistance to the actors on perfecting the difficult and unique Rhode Island accent, or about grazing the craft-services table like a one-man plague of locusts; especially not about hitting on actresses, makeup technicians, hairdressers, or production assistants.

Or extras.

"They're called 'atmosphere personnel' now," Sean advises him when Kevin tells him about the seemingly inexhaustible number of women eager to get next to anyone who's a little closer to the director's chair. "They're kind of sensitive about it."

Speaking of sensitive, Sean has a pretty delicate conversation with Ana about him showing up on the set. She was in the hair trailer when gossip came rolling through that two of the real Dogtown gangsters were on the soundstage, and when she came out to take a peek, it turned out that one of them was her boyfriend. She had wondered what Sean did for a living—all apparent evidence pointing to "nothing"—but she hadn't suspected this.

That night, back at her place, she accuses him of using her.

Sean denies it, of course, but he does point out that it's a two-way street, that the film people are using *him*, so turnabout is fair play. What can she say? She's taking home a paycheck funded in part by Sean's past, so she can hardly hold it against him. Besides, he was a perfect gentleman on the set—quiet, kind, helpful, discreet.

Kevin, on the other hand . . .

HOW LONG CAN you stare at a swimming pool before it starts staring back?

What Danny asks himself as he sits dangling his feet in the water. Ian sits beside him, copying him.

Yeah, is this what you want to teach your son? he asks himself.

To do nothing?

Be one of the idle rich?

The boy is already getting spoiled. He has the pool, the hot tub, the kid has a freakin' *pony*, for Chrissakes. Next thing he'll want a car, something with fine German engineering. It's okay for now, but if this keeps up he won't stand a chance to be anything but a useless little shit.

Like his old man? Danny wonders.

He's taking stock.

You have a high school education, he tells himself. You've been a fisherman, a longshoreman, a leg-breaker, a hijacker, a racketeer. A killer. Now you're a multimillionaire, and the reality is that you can let your money work for you.

And do what, though? Watch it?

Boring as freakin' shit, and you're not that guy.

Not that guy to get up in the morning, check your investments and go golfing with doctors and lawyers and stockbrokers. The only thing that could improve golf is snipers. Then those guys wouldn't wear those stupid clothes, and it would sure as shit speed up the game.

So you're not going to do that, Danny thinks, what are you going to do?

Move back to California, for one thing.

Be near the ocean.

And do what? What are you qualified to do?

Be a younger version of Pasco? Go fishing, play bocce ball, bridge, tell stories about the good old days.

The good old days sucked.

"You want to get in?" he asks Ian.

"Yes."

Danny hops into the pool, and gently pulls Ian around the water on his back. Every few seconds he lets go so the boy can learn to float without freaking out, then grabs him again before he sinks.

Danny knows guys from back in the day.

Guys who had made money, plenty to live on straight and just couldn't do it. They got too bored. They missed the action, the adrenaline, so they got back in. He knows guys who got back in just because they missed the other guys. Missed the hanging out, the jokes, the ball-busting, the laughs.

A few of them are spending the rest of their lives in the joint.

That ain't him.

He doesn't miss it.

At all.

He likes being with his kid.

Even likes being around his mother.

"What do you want for lunch?" he asks, although he knows the answer.

"Peanut butter and jelly."

There's the answer.

To *that* question, anyway.

IT'S THE QUILTS that keep Chris Palumbo in bed.

And, really, in Nebraska.

They're so warm, so heavy. He wants to get up and out, but he's entangled, embraced; he usually sinks back to sleep or just lies there luxuriating until the smell of coffee and bacon lures him out from under the covers and down the stairs into the kitchen, where Laura stands cooking.

She has music playing on the stereo—Bonnie Raitt, Linda Ronstadt or Emmylou Harris, shit that Chris used to hate but now has started to like. It's Bonnie this particular morning—Laura warbles along with "I Can't Make You Love Me." She fancies herself a singer, performs at open mic nights at the bar in town, is ever only one shot away from jumping into karaoke. And she's not bad, Chris thinks. She's no Emmylou, but she's not bad.

Laura usually gets up early.

First she meditates, then she feeds her chickens, then does some weird Wiccan shit, then works at her loom until she seduces Chris downstairs with coffeepot and frying pan.

Not that Laura is a great cook; she's not. She makes all this goofy vegetarian food with "legumes" and squash and beans and tons of brown rice. When she makes pasta, she makes it with some organic wheat crap, so Chris has largely taken over the kitchen duties for dinners, which he enjoys.

He can make a good marinara sauce without offending her dietary sensibilities, does some nice eggplant dishes that she enjoys, and Chris can whip up a risotto of true beauty.

No, life is good on Laura's farm. Chris had thought he'd get bored, but he really hasn't. He finds the quiet routine pleasant. After breakfast, they usually go for a walk along the fields or down the dirt road, or Laura might go to town to teach a yoga class while Chris goes to the diner and has coffee and a chat about the weather with the locals.

Afternoons feature a nap (again, the quilts), often sexual, then maybe another walk, then Chris will get dinner ready.

Nights it's television, or a trip to the bar, or a drive into Lincoln to hear some blues at the Zoo Bar or maybe hit a movie.

Then to bed.

And more sex.

"In terms of sex drive," Laura has told him, "I have a V8 engine."

It's okay with Chris.

Cathy was always great in bed, but Laura is of a different order altogether. While his wife was all flat, sharp angles and bones, Laura is lush, big breasts, big ass, and a bit of a stomach, with no inhibitions whatsoever about her body or what she can do with it.

Or what she wants him to do with it.

She's not at all shy about saying *do this to me, do that to me, right there, just like that, don't stop,* or about asking *do you like it when I do that, when I do this, oh you like that, don't you, I can tell.*

Chris knows he should leave.

Knows that he should throw off the quilt, drive down to New Mexico and pay Neto the money he owes him. Furthermore, he knows he should then go back to Rhode Island. Christ, he thinks, you have a wife and kids there, and Cathy was always a good wife, always good to you, put up with all your bullshit.

She doesn't deserve this.

And no excuses now that Peter is in the dirt.

Well, *some* excuses. Vinnie won't want him back and the other guys are probably unhappy with him over the heroin fiasco.

Part of Chris wants to go back and boot Vinnie Calfo off the throne, but a bigger part of him thinks that it's just too much work. And for what? To manage a bunch of dumb goombahs in Providence? Fill his face with stuffies down the shore? Fall asleep on the sofa after the Sunday pasta and gravy? What can he get being boss there that he doesn't have being just Chris here?

He seems to be enough for Laura; she adores him as he is and tells him so. Doesn't ask any questions, either, about who he really is or how he got there. She's just happy he's there and doesn't want him to leave.

Every time he makes noises about how he should be going, she adds a new twist—literally, often orally—to her sexual repertoire that dazzles him into stupefaction and makes him stay.

But mostly it's the quilts.

IT STARTS WITH Kim Canigliaro.

Kevin comes back to the Oakwood from the set and Kim is just getting out of her car in the parking lot. She looks tired, a little discouraged, but she looks good, too, Kevin thinks, in tight black jeans snug against her crotch like the palm of a hand and a black silk blouse that caresses her tight rack.

She sees him and waves.

He walks over to the car. "How's it going?"

"You know," she says. "It's going. How's *your* project?"

"Yeah, good," Kevin says. "Really good. You know, a lot of meetings with Mitch, that sort of thing."

"No, I wouldn't know," she says. But she doesn't sound bitter; she's just acknowledging that he's on a whole different level than her.

It kind of turns him on, and he asks, "Where's Ashley?"

"Amber?"

"Amber."

"She's with a little friend she met in her audition class," Kim says. She looks him in the eyes and adds, "She's having a sleepover."

"That's nice for her."

"It's nice for me, too," she says, in a tone that indicates it could also be nice for him. "So what are you doing now?"

Kevin shrugs. "I was gonna go up to the apartment, have a drink."

"That's what I'm going to do."

"Yeah," Kevin says. "So, you want to do it together?"

They go to his apartment. The place is a freaking mess. Empty pizza boxes and buckets of takeout chicken, dishes in the sink, an impressive collection of empty booze bottles and beer cans. Kim's not going to say anything, but wants to tell him that the complex offers maid service, which he could easily afford if he's doing a feature.

He apologizes for not having any wine, just beer and scotch. She tells him it's okay, she'd love a couple of fingers of scotch, straight up, so they sit—him in the easy chair, her on the sofa—and drink the whiskey.

"God damn that feels good," she says after she takes the first sip. "I don't like to drink around Amber."

"You're a good mother."

"I'm a shit mother," Kim says. She digs a pack of cigarettes out of her purse. "You mind if I smoke?"

"Go for it."

"You want one?"

"You know what? Yeah."

She lights his cigarette, then hers, and says, "I am. I'm a bad mother. Letting her go through all this. *Making* her go through all this. I ask myself, is it her dream or mine, you know?"

He shrugs.

She takes a drag of the cigarette and another hit of the scotch, and then looks at him for a long moment and laughs.

"What?" Kevin asks, starting to get pissed.

"I haven't gotten laid in almost a year," she says.

"That's a long time."

"Tell me about it," she says. She looks at him almost shyly, something in her he hasn't seen, and then she asks, "So . . . are you the guy?"

KIM STAYS THE night.

She sets the clock-radio alarm for nine because she has to pick up Amber at ten and take her to an open audition call at Disney. Kevin lies there and watches her put on her panties and bra and likes the way her breasts look as she fixes them in the cups. She goes into the bathroom and comes out with makeup on and then goes into the living room to put on the rest of her clothes. Kevin gets up, goes into the kitchen with her and pops open a breakfast beer.

"You're hard-core," she says.

Kevin shrugs. "You mind?"

"Hey," she says, "whatever gets you through the day, right?"

Kevin likes her. Likes the East Coast edge and what she does in bed. His dick's a little sore and his balls ache as he thinks of how she slammed up and ground against him when she came the last time, and how she stayed in there and made little circles with her hips until he finished. The woman knows what she wants and gets it, but she's fair about it, understands it's a two-way street. Not a woman who's going to step out of the batter's box. "I can make you some coffee, you want."

She shakes her head. "I need to get to my place and change. Amber's getting to the age she'd notice I was wearing the same clothes."

"And you don't want her knowing Mommy fucks," Kevin says, regretting it the second it comes out of his mouth.

"Something like that," she says. "And don't be an asshole."

"Sorry," he says, meaning it.

She walks over and kisses him on the forehead. "It's all right. You fuck *good*. See you later?"

Said lightly, laden with weight. They both know what she's asking—was this a one-night stand, which would be okay, or is something more possible? No one's thinking love here, or anything like it, but maybe they can kill a little of the loneliness together. Kevin thinks of that Tom Petty song. "*You don't have to live like a refugee.*"

"That'd be good," he says. "I'll call you?"

"How about I call you?"

Because she doesn't want Amber answering the phone, there's a strange guy on the line asking for Mom. He gets that. It's cool, it makes him respect her. Got to be weird, having a kid—everything you do, you have to think about the kid first. "Yeah, good."

He gets up and writes his number on a pizza delivery receipt, hands it to her.

"I'll call," she says.

"Good."

On the way out the door, she tosses, "Hey, if there's a part in your movie for Amber . . ."

THREE DAYS LATER, Kevin approaches Mitch about it.

The director is a little preoccupied. He's behind on his shooting schedule, the studio accountants are hovering like bottle flies on roadkill, and the actor playing Sal Antonucci wants a close-up on a simple reaction shot, so Mitch has to waste a half hour lighting a setup he knows he's never going to use.

Plus, his female lead, Diane Carson, is in her second stint at some Malibu rehab spa—the first one didn't take—and is hopefully on schedule to "graduate" in time to make her first shot but who knows? Beautiful woman, Mitch thinks, maybe the most beautiful woman he's ever seen; she has fame, fortune, and she's just as much a fucked-up ball of insecurities as every other actress he's ever worked with.

He's just hoping she can make it through the shoot before her next breakdown. So when Kevin appears over his shoulder muttering something about wanting to find a role for some twelve-year-old girl, it doesn't really register.

Kevin brings it up again at lunch the next day. He finds Mitch at his table in the commissary. Mitch and his AD, Dennis, have their heads together trying to figure out how to crunch a couple of setups together to make the afternoon's shots when Kevin sits down and says, "Mitch, about Amber."

"Amber?"

"The girl I was telling you about," Kevin says. "She's wicked cute. I brought some head shots."

He hands Mitch a manila envelope with the photos.

Mitch and Dennis exchange a quick *like we really need this right now* look, but Mitch politely opens the envelope and takes a few seconds to look at the very average shot of a very average little girl, then says, "I don't know, Dennis, do we have any parts for a twelve-year-old girl?"

Dennis shakes his head. "I don't think so."

"Could you check?" Kevin asks. Guy had a pretty quick fucking answer.

"I know the script pretty well," Dennis says. "I'm pretty sure about this."

"Sorry, Kevin," Mitch says. He goes back to looking at the shot sheet, and Kevin's left sitting there feeling like an asshole. What, these guys think there were no twelve-year-old girls in Providence? How hard would it be to stick her in one of the scenes, at the drugstore or the rink or something?

He brings this up to Mitch the next morning. Waylays the man as he's walking into the soundstage and says, "Mitch, I'd consider it a personal favor if you could find a spot for Amber in the movie. Just a line or two."

Now Mitch realizes this isn't going to go away. And he's been schooled enough in Rhode Island jargon by Kevin and Sean to understand that "personal favor" really means "obligation," that in Kevin's mind if Mitch doesn't grant the personal favor, the relationship is damaged beyond redemption. And the fact is that Coombs and South have been pretty useful, giving him all kinds of tips on how guys dressed, what they drove, how they talked. More importantly, how they didn't. All details that Bobby Bangs had been disappointingly short on. So Mitch doesn't want to offend Kevin.

Still, it's a problem on a set that doesn't need any more of them.

"It's complicated," Mitch says. "You know, you just don't throw in a line for no reason. And I'd have to get the screenwriters to do it, and then get it into the shooting schedule . . . Plus, I have a casting director whose job it is to do this kind of thing, and if I step on her toes . . ."

But he sees that Kevin is having none of this. Just hitting him with a steady gaze, as if uttering the magic phrase "personal favor" trumps all these considerations. Which, Mitch has to admit, it sort of does.

"I don't want to make you jump through a lot of hoops," Kevin says, "but it would mean a lot to me."

"You're banging the mom."

Kevin smiles and shrugs. "Yeah."

"Does the kid have her SAG card?" Mitch asks, giving up. What the hell? He's had actors' girlfriends, sisters, and mothers in movies, not to mention the porn star mistress of his last producer, who took up half a day trying to get through her one line.

"I think so," Kevin says. He seems to remember Kim telling him something about something like that.

Mitch summons his assistant and tells her to get hold of the writers and see if they'll add a line for a twelve-year-old white female.

"You got it," Mitch says. "No big deal."

Yeah, but it is. It's a huge mistake, because now Kevin gets the idea that he has influence, that he can make things happen.

So the Altar Boys have their hands on the steering wheel of a hundred-million-dollar movie and are racing it toward the abyss.

No skid marks.

IT STARTS WITH Amber getting her line and Kevin getting the idea that he has some weight on the set. He goes back to the Oakwood that night to tell Kim and the kid the good news, and Amber is so excited she goes running around the complex squealing, "I'm going to be in a movie!," provoking disingenuous congratulations and heartfelt envy from the other kids and their mothers. Kim pawns Amber off on one of the other families, then takes Kevin to her place and gives him a blow job *speciale* with all the trimmings.

Life is very good.

Until Kevin comes back from the set one night, Kim is unavailable, and he decides to take a southbound migration with a bottle of Grey Goose. Comes onto the set the next morning hungover and nasty. The caterer asks him what he wants for breakfast, even though it's already ten o'clock and he's setting up for lunch.

"What can I have?" Kevin asks.

"Anything you want."

A Hollywood mantra. Words to live by. Why everybody gets into the movies, to hear the words "anything you want."

What Kevin really wants is a black coffee, some aspirin, and maybe a vitamin B12 shot. Doesn't really know that if he asked for that, he'd get it, so he settles for the coffee and a Swiss cheese omelet that he takes a few bites of. But he's getting the idea that life can be very, very good for him on a movie set, so when Mitch arrives for first shot, Kevin feels this sense of gratitude, and with the gratitude comes loyalty. Which is good, which is fine, until later that morning when Vince D'Alessandro, the actor playing Sal Antonucci, gets into Mitch's face.

Vince is the latest Hollywood bad boy, more famous for nightclub brawls, paparazzi punch-outs, and high-priced call girls than for anything he's done on the screen. Nevertheless, he fancies himself a serious actor, the spiritual heir to Brando and De Niro, and he takes his craft seriously. So when Mitch suggests that he do something in a take that goes against his artistic vision, Vince objects to it as "commercial bullshit."

Mitch fires back that someone has to pay for Vince's inflated "quote," and that means putting asses in the seats and not just on the screen.

"Who you calling an ass?" Vince shoots back.

"Just do the shot," Mitch answers. Last thing he wants is a tabloid-tempting confrontation with one of his stars on the set.

He starts to walk away.

"Don't turn your back on me, Mitch," Vince says. "You got something to say, be man enough to say it to my fucking face."

He makes the mistake of following Mitch.

Kevin steps in his path. "What, are you a tough guy?"

"This doesn't concern you."

But apparently it does. It concerns Kevin a lot. In his head, Mitch is the guy who has given him the key to the first-class lounge, and Kevin isn't going to let anyone mess with his benefactor, especially not some punk actor who thinks he's a badass because some writer gave him some badass words to say.

He points this out to Vince. "You may *think* you're a tough guy because you're *playing* at being a tough guy, but that doesn't *make* you a tough guy. So if I were you, I'd shut my mouth and do what the man asks you to do."

Vince is scared but he can't back down here—not in front of the other actors and the whole crew. So he stands his ground, but his voice is a little weak as he says, "But you're *not* me."

"And you're not *me*, asshole," Kevin says. "And, trust me, you're not Sal Antonucci, either."

If you were, Kevin thinks, there'd be blood on the floor already.

This cuts Vince to the quick. He *is* Sal Antonucci, he's fucking *channeling* Sal Antonucci. He's done tons of research watched *Goodfellas* at least a dozen times. He even went back and screened *Mean Streets*, so this was in-depth research. He's so into Sal, Sal is so into him, that he answers, in his best East Coast Italian accent, "The fuck you know about Sal Antonucci?"

"He killed several of my friends," Kevin says.

Vince is improvising a scene now. Forgets he's not in some West Hollywood acting class and says, "So maybe you're not such a tough guy."

When Vince comes to, his jaw hurts like crazy, he's nauseated, Mitch has locked everyone inside the soundstage, and a whole crowd of people, including studio security, stand between him and this Kevin Coombs character.

One of them is Sean South, which is a good thing, because he's the one person there who actually could intervene without getting killed. He grabs Kevin by the front of the shirt and pushes him away. "Jesus, Kev."

"He asked for it."

Then Hollywood gets even more wonderful for Kevin Coombs. He's expecting the cops to arrive, assault charges, a stretch in jail for assault, but none of that happens. Vince's manager is Johnny-on-the-spot, and he makes sure none of that happens. Vince's bad boy reputation is based on him being the beater, not the beatee, and the whole studio PR machinery goes into overdrive to make sure that word of his one-punch knockdown doesn't get out.

No cops, no lawyers, no media.

No consequences.

Except for Mitch, who loses a day's scheduled shooting because his star is in his trailer with an ice pack on his swollen jaw, which proves, thank God, not to be broken. There is a certain satisfaction in seeing D'Alessandro get smacked, no question, but Mitch has a movie to make. Mitch is no pussy—he confronts Kevin about it, but he does it carefully.

"That wasn't cool," Mitch says.

"He disrespected you," says Kevin.

"Artistic disagreements happen on a set all the time," Mitch says. "You can't let them get to you. Certainly not to the point of getting physical."

Which proves that Mitch still doesn't comprehend what he has a hold of here. Vince had basically said that if Kevin had been truly tough his friends would still be alive, and that called for a physical response. And here Mitch is about two steps removed from admonishing Kevin Coombs to "use your words."

"I'm sorry," Kevin says. He's not—he's just afraid of getting booted out of a world where they throw free money, free food, and free pussy at you. If they threw free booze, Kevin would never leave. (In fact, they do, Kevin just hasn't figured out how to work that angle yet.)

"It can't happen again," Mitch says.

He walks back to the director's table, where Larry Field, the executive producer, summoned from a power breakfast, has already arrived in response to the 911 call. "What the hell, Mitch?"

This film is Larry's shot at the serious big time. At thirty-three years of age, he's done four indie films, the third of which made a small splash on the festival circuit, but the fourth of which was a surprise bust-out hit that he brought in for a slick ten million. He used that bump to get the studio to acquire *Providence* for him, pestered Susan Holdt until the deal was done, then had personally delivered the book to Mitchell Apsberger and called the man twice a week until he read it and agreed to direct if he liked the screen adaptation.

Larry then went to the writing team of Kelmer and Hoyle, fresh off an Oscar nomination for *Yellow Dawn*, got them to take a lunch, and peppered them with his boundless enthusiasm until they phoned Sue Holdt, told her they were at Osso with "the relentless Larry Field" and said they wanted *Providence* to be their next project.

The deal was made that afternoon.

Three months later Larry had an approved script that he took to Mitch. Mitch asked for a few changes, then Larry messengered the script over to Diane Carson's manager. He liked it, thought Diane should do it, but the actress was in rehab and not reading scripts at the moment. Larry, script in hand, was literally waiting outside the gates of the Malibu facility—along with a score of paparazzi—when Diane came out, shoved his way through, then helped Diane's security ease her through the crowd and got in her car with her.

"Do I know you?" she asked.

"I'm the guy who has your Oscar," Larry said, laying the script in her lap.

Two days later her manager called and they got the deal done. With Diane attached to play Pam, Larry got Sam Wakefield in a male lead role, Pat, with Vince D'Alessandro in a featured role to play Sal, and even talked Dan Corchoran—Oscar for Best Supporting two years ago—to take a small but tasty role as Danny.

It was a dream package with Apsberger directing those stars, and the studio fast-tracked it. Now, with Diane back in rehab and two thugs throwing their weight around on the set, it's threatening to go off the rails.

"I want these guys off the set," Mitch says.

Larry says, "We just paid them a hundred grand to be *on* the set."

"Then give them another hundred to get them *off*."

Yeah, that's not going to happen.

That might work with a businessman, who would look at an offer like that and figure he's scored two hundred grand for doing nothing and step away from the table.

But that's not the way a criminal thinks.

A criminal thinks that if you offer him $200K for doing nothing, you must have a lot more money to spend, so he should stick around and tap into the main source. The criminal gets almost insulted that you're offering him chump change for doing nothing. He truly feels that he deserves a lot more for doing nothing.

This is where the film industry and the criminal class intersect.

A serene choir in a pitch-perfect harmony of indolence and greed.

Larry knocks on the door of Kevin and Sean's trailer and hears a sullen "Come in."

Kevin sits on an upholstered bench, a cold beer in one hand and a shot of Walker Black in the other. When he's popping the scotch, he holds the beer against his punching hand, which is raw and slightly swollen. The producer makes the pitch: *We've decided to go in a slightly different direction, but we want to make sure you're fairly compensated for your work to this point.*

Sean and Kevin want to make sure they're fairly compensated, too. Actually, they want to make sure they're *unfairly* compensated, so they decide that they want to go in a slightly different direction.

"We want a producer credit," Sean says.

"A producer credit," Larry repeats, genuinely dumbfounded. He doesn't even know how these guys know an industry phrase like "producer credit." In any case, it's out of the question. It's not just a matter of having their names scroll on the screen—they would have to be paid a healthy producer fee. They might even be asking for—is it possible?—a piece of the movie. These two employees want to be your partners?

Yup.

Welcome to organized crime.

You want reality? It doesn't get any more real than this.

But Larry doesn't understand that yet. He looks at these two guys like they're crazy. Granted, he may not know their world, but they sure as hell don't know his. They don't know that you don't just come on a major feature film as consultants and then become producers. And they expect this for doing what? Beating up one of the stars?

Apparently yes, because Sean continues, "We think it's fair. See, Bobby wrote about it, but we lived it. You're making money off our lives, and we think we should be compensated for that."

"Also," Kevin adds, "with us as producers, feeling a sense of owner-ship, you wouldn't have to worry about the sort of security problem you had this morning."

"What?"

"If I hadn't been there," Kevin says, "that actor, that Vince, would have had a clear shot at your director. I don't know where your security was, but it wasn't where it should have been. With us fully on board, you have no worries."

So now the mobster is taking credit for punching out the star, like it's a *good* thing.

"On the other hand," Sean says, "without us . . . ?"

He frowns and shrugs, as if he's trying to indicate that that would be a very risky proposition.

Which is exactly what he is trying to indicate. Call it extortion, pro-tection, whatever you want, the inference is clear: Cut us in on the action, via a producer credit—or bad things are going to happen.

Larry's been around just long enough to remember the last time the mob tried to work its way into the film industry, back in the early sev-enties, via the stagehands' union, and they had modest success until the Organized Crime Control Commission shut them down. But these two punks? Are they freelancing it or do they represent somebody bigger?

This is the same question the studio head asks when Larry tells her the problem. He'd stalled for time, told South and Coombs that it was complicated, that he'd have to talk with the studio execs, then fetched Mitch off the set and went into the president's office.

Susan Holdt is already sick of this damn movie. Sure, it's supposed to be Mitch's long-overdue Oscar, and a box office boon, but so far it's been nothing but headaches—Vince D'Alessandro's endless adolescence, Diane's relapse, and now a couple of punks that Mitch hired as consultants are trying to shake more money out of a project that's already overburdened with participation deals.

Susan knows about participation deals. She cut more than a few of them herself as an independent producer, and then as an exec as she made hit after hit that finally propelled her into the big chair at the ailing studio. As a woman in the top spot of an industry that, despite its liberal, politically correct affect, is notoriously sexist, she's been called all the names that get hung on successful women—"bitch" and "ball-buster" being the mildest among them. At forty-three, she's inured to it. She worked her ass off to make it to this place. Now rich, attractive, and powerful, she has life by the throat and she's not going to let go. A huge house in the Hills, a respectable writer husband who knows where his bread is buttered and therefore tolerates the string of young lovers she meets at the Beverly Hills Hotel, regular appointments at José Eber, and, most of all, a job that, while it's high-stress, is at least never boring.

Now she asks, "Are these guys mobbed up?"

Mitch shrugs. "They used to be."

"Which is not the question I asked, Mitch," Susan says. "I want a water. Does anyone else want a water?"

Mitch shakes his head. He doesn't want a water—he wants a double martini and a week at his house in Maui.

"I'd like a water," Larry says.

Susan buzzes her assistant and asks for two waters. She's trying to drink eight bottles of the shit every day, which her trainer assures her will drop those last stubborn five pounds. Donnie comes to her house at 5:30 A.M. every MWF to torture her into shape.

The assistant comes in with two bottles of designer water.

"I need to know," Susan says, "whether these guys are connected and could possibly cause us union problems, in which case we take them seriously; or whether they're just two punk freeloaders, in which case we throw them off the lot and call the cops."

"I don't want to wake up with a horse head in my bed," Larry says.

"More like Mr. Potato Head," Mitch says.

"What?"

"Bad Irish joke," Mitch says.

"In any case," Susan says, "there's no way we give them producer credit. This project is already top-heavy. Just Diane's piece . . ."

"Have you heard from her?" Mitch asks.

"She's allowed phone calls now," Susan says. "She sounded good. Upbeat. She invited me to her graduation ceremony."

"You going?"

"Sure." She and Diane Carson had their first mutual hit together. In a sense, they owe each other their careers, and they're still close friends. It was Susan who persuaded Diane to go back into rehab this last time.

Larry says, "Hello? Our little gangster problem?"

Susan smiles. "Did one of them really punch out Vince?"

"Yup," Mitch says.

"I should send the guy a muffin basket," Susan says. "Have the lawyers start negotiations with these guys."

Larry says, "You're not really going to—"

"Of course not," Sue says. "But it will buy me a little time to figure out how to really deal with them."

Mitch gets up off the couch. He's done three films with Susan and knows from her tone when a meeting's over. Besides, he's already two hours behind, with no chance of making his day, and he has to sit down with the AD to reconfigure the shooting schedule.

"Thanks, Susan."

"You're welcome," Susan says. "Next time, Mitch? Maybe a historical drama about dead people?"

"You got it."

Susan polishes off her water and wonders how she can get rid of these clowns.

THE CLOWNS AREN'T going anywhere.

The clowns in question, aka the Altar Boys, are shocked and delighted how easy it was to shake down the movie people.

"One punch," Kevin says.

"Amazing," Sean agrees.

So it's good being Sean South and Kevin Coombs.

Sean takes his producer role fairly seriously. He shows up on the lot in time for first shot every morning, puts in a full day of offering his advice and experience to make sure the film is true to life, then goes home with Ana for a quiet dinner, a little wine, and some sex before they turn in early to do it all again the next day.

Kevin works it a little differently. He gets to the set in time for lunch, watches a take or two, then goes to his trailer and makes cell phone calls to Larry Field or the studio legal department to find out how the negotiations are coming.

It doesn't take him long to figure out that the studio is stringing them along.

"What do you want to do?" Sean asks him when Kevin gives him the bad news.

Kevin knows exactly what to do. He goes to the shop steward of the stagehands' union on the set, shows him his ILA card and drops a few names. Maybe he also drops a couple of grand with hints at more where that came from, brother, once his deal goes through.

Next day the shop steward finds two health-and-safety violations on the set; the day after that, two more. And work starts to slow down, the gaffers take their time getting from setup to setup, and it gets worse as the shoot goes on location, subbing downtown L.A. for certain Providence scenes. The trucks are slow getting there, the drivers' breaks have to happen on the dot, the offloads are slow and require every piece of safety equipment. A heater in a truck isn't working properly, so the truck doesn't roll and a new one has to be found. Actors are kept waiting in trailers while the drivers of the shuttle vans take their breaks. Trucks get lost or stuck in traffic.

The production starts to suffocate.

With the Altar Boys' hands around its neck.

"Things are really bogging down," Larry says to Kevin one day, trying to bring the subject up as subtly as he can. They're standing in an alley outside the Biltmore Hotel in downtown L.A., pretending it's an alley in Dogtown. The art designer has sprinkled it with specific Providence trash—Del's cups, White Castle wrappers, crushed cans of 'Gansett, even a Providence Reds hockey program smeared with fake mud. If it weren't seventy and sunny instead of thirty and gray, Kevin would swear he *was* in Providence.

"Must be something in the air," he says. "My negotiations are taking forever, too."

Like, Connect the dots, dumbass. Slick Hollywood gyppo, think you can bone the ignorant chowderheads who don't know how things work and that are going to run off the road at the learning curve. Well, let me teach *you* how things *really* operate, in the real freaking world, you water-sipping, salad-crunching, meeting-taking motherfuckers.

Mitch is pulling his distinguished gray hair out. He might as well wipe his ass with the shooting schedule, the budget's inflating like third-world currency, Vince D'Alessandro is afraid to come out of his trailer (God only knows what stupid shit he's dreaming up in there to try to make his dick grow back), Diane Carson is going to emerge from rehab onto a set that isn't ready for her, and the last thing you want to hand to Diane is leisure time.

He puts in a 911 to Susan Holdt.

She's too smart to come down to the set and give Kevin and Sean the (correct) idea that they're pushing buttons.

The studio is owned by a multinational conglomerate that sends a retired FBI agent named Bill Callahan, their head of security.

They meet downtown at the Los Angeles Athletic Club, of which she's a member. He would have come to her in Burbank, except she doesn't want gossip columnists stumbling on their lunch, and none of them cover the old-fashioned, nothing-close-to-trendy LAAC. Nevertheless, he arranges for a private room.

Callahan is impressed with Sue Holdt. She projects power and confidence and she orders a martini and a rare steak instead of the frou-frou shit he'd expected.

"They make a good martini," Holdt says, "but I have a private stock of single-malt scotch here."

"You're on," Callahan says.

She doesn't waste time with small talk. "I need your help with my Coombs and South problem," she says.

"You don't have a Coombs and South problem," Callahan tells her. "You have a Danny Ryan problem. Pardon my language, but Coombs and South wouldn't take a piss without Ryan giving the nod."

"So what are you going to do about my Danny Ryan problem?" Holdt asks.

Callahan says, "In your interest, in the studio's, in the parent company's . . . hell, Susan, in *my* interest . . . I have to tell you that you need to be a little patient about this situation."

"Patient?" Holdt says. "Bill, I have a movie hemorrhaging money here. Time is not my friend."

"I understand."

"Apparently you don't, because—"

"I'll take care of your problem, I promise. But I need a little time to work it out."

"Work *what* out?"

"A sit-down between you and Ryan," Callahan says. "Will you take it?"

Turns out she will.

Callahan puts in a call to Madeleine McKay.

FOURTEEN

I F DANNY FEELS OUT OF place in Las Vegas, Bill Callahan looks like an alien who's crashed his spacecraft.

Danny watches him get out of the car in his brown suit, white shirt too tight around his neck and tie that literally cinches the deal. The man is already sweating, his face red, even though Danny can hear the air-conditioning blasting as he opens the door. Callahan's a Boston guy transplanted to L.A., Danny knows, so Vegas must be another planet.

Danny knows the feeling.

What he doesn't know is what a former high-ranking FBI executive wants with him, or why he asked Madeleine to arrange the sit-down. She shares information and influence with any number of politicians, law-enforcement figures, and business moguls, so he's not surprised she knows Callahan.

She walks out and greets the agent in the driveway and escorts him in.

"Danny Ryan," Madeleine says, "Bill Callahan."

They sit down in the living room. Callahan accepts the offer of a cold beer, then Madeleine says, "I'll let you talk," and leaves.

Callahan kicks it off. "First of all, I'm not interested in anything that went down in Providence or anything that may or may not have happened regarding Domingo Abbarca."

Jesus, Danny thinks, he knows about the deal with Harris. "Okay. But why are you here?"

"Two of your old crew—Coombs and South—have gone off the radar, am I right?"

Danny nods.

"Well, they showed up."

Callahan lays out what the Altar Boys have been up to in Hollywood, about Sue Holdt reaching out to him for help, hence his reaching out to Madeleine to arrange this conversation.

"You want me to rein them in," Danny says.

"It's in everyone's best interest."

It is, Danny thinks. South and Coombs going cowboy could raise a lot of dust from the past that's best left settled.

"Do you still exercise influence with them?" Callahan asks.

"I think they'd listen to me."

"So you'll do this?"

"I'd want to talk to Sue Holdt first," Danny says.

"She sent me."

"If she wants me to talk to my people," Danny says, "she can talk to me. Otherwise . . . I mean, I'm not the one coming with the ask, am I?"

They both get the power dynamic—Holdt needs Ryan, Ryan doesn't need Holdt.

"I'll talk with her," Callahan says.

MADELEINE WAITS FOR Callahan to leave before she comes back into the living room.

When she sits down Danny tells her about the conversation with the FBI agent and asks, "What do you think?"

"All things being equal," she says, "I think you should do it."

"Why?"

"Because influence is power," Madeleine says. "There are worse things than a major studio chief owing you a favor."

"What can she do for me?"

"You never know."

Danny thinks for a moment and then says, "I hate to leave Ian again."

"Take him with you."

"A three-year-old in Hollywood?"

They're *all* three-year-olds in Hollywood, Madeleine thinks. She says, "They have babysitters in Los Angeles. Nannies. I'll arrange it. It will be a bonding experience for you."

She hates the idea of Ian leaving, even for a short time, but she has another agenda—Ian getting a new mommy. Danny, a rich widower with a cute child? Catnip for young eligible women.

Irresistible.

THREE NIGHTS LATER. Danny Ryan sits in the passenger seat as Callahan negotiates the narrow, curvy road into the Hollywood Hills.

At Sue Holdt's recommendation, Danny is staying at the Peninsula in Beverly Hills.

He was already checked in when he and Ian arrived at the front desk, and the concierge took them up to a suite, which had two large bedrooms, a sitting room, and a private deck that looked out over Los Angeles.

The nanny arrived shortly after, a competent and professional young lady named Holly.

Madeleine was right about the bonding—without her there as a buffer,

Ian engaged with his father through the exciting and scary new experience of the airport and the flight and delighted in naming for Danny everything he saw.

Ian was also delighted—the childhood-education types would call it "overstimulated"—by the hotel suite, and he and Danny went up to the rooftop pool and got in the water together, Danny pulling the boy around on his back, teaching him how to float, Ian even taking a few tentative dog paddles into Danny's arms. Then they sat by the pool eating hot dogs and chips, and when Danny left that evening for the meeting, Ian cried a little but soon settled happily into one of the games that Holly had thought to bring.

Now Callahan stops at a polished wooden gate. He opens the window and talks into a speaker. A moment later, there's an electric buzz, the solid gate slides open, and Callahan pulls into the driveway.

Holdt's house sits on the right, downhill side of the driveway. It's a one-story modern with huge picture windows, a wraparound deck, and a sprawling lawn below. Danny gets out of the car and follows Callahan on the flagstone walkway that edges the softly lit swimming pool.

Callahan rings the doorbell and a few seconds later Holdt appears at the door, holding a huge old greyhound by the collar. The dog's head comes up to Danny's chest and it nuzzles its nose into his stomach.

"He's friendly," Holdt says. "Just exuberant. Come on, Midnight."

She pulls the dog aside as she extends her other hand to Danny. "I'm Sue Holdt."

"Danny Ryan. It's nice to meet you, Ms. Holdt."

"Susan," she says. "Nice to meet you, too. Please, come in."

She points toward a sunken living room. "Would anyone like coffee or tea or anything?"

"No, thank you," Danny says.

Callahan waves his hand no.

He and Danny sit down on a large sofa facing a picture window that provides a startling view of the city. The lights of Los Angeles sparkle below, as if you're sitting above the sky and looking down.

Holdt is dressed deliberately casual in a faded black blouse and old jeans. She sits in a large, overstuffed chair, pulls her bare feet underneath her and sips from a mug of green tea. A hardcover book is splayed open on the side table beside her.

He's not what she expected. She thought she'd be seeing a slightly older version of Kevin and Sean, or a classic wiseguy. But Ryan is understated—a soft-spoken man in a quiet gray business suit, with a white shirt open at the neck, but no chains. His shoes are dull black oxfords—shined but not shiny. His brown hair is short, clean, recently cut.

"Danny," she says. "Bill says you might be able to help me with a problem I'm having."

"First of all," Danny says, "if Coombs and South have caused you any trouble, I apologize. I haven't been in contact with them for a while. But I'm here now. Your problems with them will end tomorrow."

"In exchange for . . ."

"Kevin and Sean do have a point," Danny says. "In a sense, you've taken our lives and you intend—or hope, anyway—to profit from them."

Right, Holdt thinks. My problems with Coombs and South end to-morrow because my problems with you start tonight. You're simply going to take over their extortion effort and make it more efficient.

"We legitimately bought the rights to a film treatment," Holdt says. "As such, we have every right to profit from that acquisition. I would suggest that your problem isn't with us, it's with Bobby Bangs."

"I'll handle any problem I might have with Bobby myself," Danny says. "You bought the rights to his work. That doesn't give you the rights to my life."

"Any character in our film is strictly fictional."

"We both know that's not true."

"You can pursue that through litigation," Holdt says. "What you can't do is shake down my production."

Danny likes her. There's no bullshit and she doesn't back down. He says, "I'm not a litigious person and I'm not interested in a shakedown, I'm interested in a partnership."

Sue laughs. "You want me to give you a piece of the film. It amounts to the same thing."

"I don't want you to give me anything," Danny says. "I want to buy it."

Danny's pleased that she looks surprised. He continues, "You're behind schedule and over budget. You have one star in rehab and another who should be going in. Your board of directors is breathing down your neck because you've bet the studio on this film. Not to mention your career."

He's done his homework—asked his mother to have her people do research, and then he studied it.

Hard.

Holdt doesn't know where he's getting his information, but it's accurate. Just this morning she floated her need for more money to the corporate guys and it was a lead balloon. She doesn't have the funds to finish the film and then promote it in any meaningful way, and she's about to launch into the pirate-infested waters of private financiers. If *Providence* goes down, the studio goes down with it, and she'll be in professional limbo for at least five years before the stink of failure fades.

"I'm listening," she says.

"I have available money," Danny says. "More than enough to make up your deficit. I'll invest it in your movie, a straight-up percent of the budget for a straight-up percent of the gross, first-dollar profits."

"Is this an offer I can't refuse?" she asks. "What if I say no?"

"You won't, because you're too smart," Danny says. "But if you do, I'll still call Kevin and Sean off and you'll never hear from them or me again. You also won't be able to finish your film, but that's your business."

"These monies," she says. "They're . . ."

"Clean."

Callahan says, "Mr. Ryan is not the subject of any prosecution nor a person of interest in any investigation whatsoever."

Sue turns back to Danny. "You must have other conditions."

"I do," Danny says. "My accountant moves into your finance office with access to all the books, and he monitors every penny that goes out and comes in."

"I can live with that," she says. "What else?"

Because there has to be something—a girlfriend who he wants in the film, an actress he wants to date, a consulting fee, tickets to *The Tonight Show* . . .

"I want to come on the set," Danny says, "to see what I'm buying into. If it's a complete mess, the deal is off."

"You mean if Diane Carson is a complete mess," Sue says.

"That's what I mean, yes," Danny says. "I've known junkies all my life, Sue. I'm not betting a fortune on one of them."

"Diane's not a 'junkie.'"

"Good," Danny says. "I hope that's what I think after I've seen her."

They have a brief stare-down, then Sue says, "You're certainly welcome on the set. Any time."

"Then we have a deal?"

Sue nods.

They have a deal.

DANNY COMES ON the lot.

Personally escorted through the security gate by Holdt, he also has Jimmy Mac and Ned Egan flanking him. Good to have a little backup if Kevin and Sean decide they want to get stroppy.

Ned's in L.A. anyway, and even though Jimmy's in the process of moving his family to San Diego, he's always going to be there for Danny.

It's bizarre, Danny thinks, walking down the "street" that's been replicated to look like Dogtown. Like someone took your life, your memories, and built them in a life-size toy set. There's the front of the old drugstore, McKenzies Cigars, Wong's Chinese chop suey joint. There's Pat Murphy's house, and then, shit, there's *his*.

Danny stops and stares. He can almost see his old man sitting out there, smoking a Camel and sipping on a pint. Can also see himself there, as a kid, reading comics with Jimmy and Pat, talking shit, plotting how to get fifty cents to buy that special *Superman* anniversary issue.

"Did we get it right?" Holdt asks.

"Yeah," Danny says. "Yeah, you did."

They walk down toward the soundstage. What impresses Danny is the sheer *business*. Workers everywhere, moving urgently, trying to keep their schedule. Rolling around equipment that Danny doesn't recognize— lighting rigs, reflector screens, cameras, mic booms. Wires and cables spread all over the place. Everywhere people moving, moving, moving.

Hustling.

Throbbing with energy.

"You guys work hard," he says.

"We do," Holdt says. She talks him through a little bit of what he's seeing, but Danny's only half hearing her. He's lost in the pure strangeness of it all, seeing his own life replicated, but more so. Everything's a little prettier, a little shabbier, a little more colorful . . . just a little more than real life.

Or my memories of it, anyway, Danny thinks. Which brings up a question—is the Hollywood version brighter, or are my memories muted?

"This is freakin' amazing," he says to Jimmy Mac.

"Yeah, it is."

"Can't escape the old days," Danny says. "No matter where we go."

Jimmy looks awed, his neck craning around to take it all in. Ned's head is on a swivel, too, but for a different reason—crowds of people and lots of activity make him nervous. He doesn't like it.

"Would you like to meet yourself?" Holdt asks Danny.

"All my life," he says.

"Come on."

Danny follows her to the periphery of a set that is—

Shit, Danny thinks. It's the Glocca Morra.

Half of it, anyway. To his right is another set that's the opposite half. It is so fucking weird, standing at the edge, looking through the small crowd of technicians and another knot of people clustered around a large camera on a wheeled dolly, all intently watching the action on the set.

Four actors sit at the booth in the back.

That old wooden booth, Danny thinks, where Old Man Murphy would hold court like an ancient Celtic king. And indeed, the old Harp is sitting there, his glass of whiskey on the table in front of him, a cigarette glowing in a chipped ashtray.

The detail, Danny thinks. Somebody did their research.

The old man is talking to—

Fuck, that's *me*, Danny thinks. He looks at the actor, dressed the way he would have been, his hair long and unkempt, his body wrapped in the old navy peacoat even though he's inside. And the guy sitting next to him—that's Pat. That has to be Pat—handsome, charismatic, earnest. Danny vaguely recognizes the actor playing Pat, has maybe seen him in a movie or two. The actor playing *him* he doesn't recognize at all. Figures, he thinks, chuckling to himself. I wasn't a star in Dogtown. I'm not a star now.

The fourth actor in the scene has to be Liam Murphy. A pretty boy with the lady-killer smile. Has to be Liam. Fucking Liam, who started it all. Fucking, fucking Liam Murphy.

Danny looks back at "himself." Holdt sees him staring at the actor, smiles and points a finger at Danny's chest. Mouths, *That's you.*

Danny nods, then shakes his head, like *This is so weird.*

Holdt takes a headset off the camera rack, puts it on Danny's head and now he can hear what the actors are saying—

You care more about this piece of gash than you do about your family.

Don't call her that.

Liam, it's true. If you could keep your snake in the cage—

I love her.

"Love." The fuck . . .

"I" don't say anything, Danny thinks. Typical—the good soldier. He looks over at Jimmy, who looks back at him, smiles and mouths, *Pisser.*

We gotta hit back.

They can put so many more guys on the street.

I'm not giving her up, Dad.

Danny remembers the conversation. It actually went something like that, except it was in the Murphys' backyard, not the Gloc, and Old Man Murphy didn't slap Liam. But I guess this way is more dramatic, Danny thinks.

Cut!

A sharp buzz comes through the headset and brings Danny back into the present. The set is moving again, technicians changing lights, cables, and camera lenses as the guy who seems to be in charge says, "Let's grab the close-up."

"What do you think?" Holdt asks him.

"Amazing."

"Let's introduce you to you."

She walks him to the side of the set where the actor playing him stands, sipping from a plastic bottle of water.

"Dan Corchoran," Holdt says with a glint of mischievous pleasure in her eye, "meet Danny Ryan."

Corchoran looks gobsmacked. "Really?"

Danny puts out his hand. "Nice to meet you."

"Nice to meet you," Corchoran says. "I mean . . . Jesus . . . how weird is *this*?"

"Weird enough," Danny says.

"Listen," Corchoran says, "I'd love to have a chance to sit down and talk with you. Pick your brain. Uhhh, do you have lunch plans?"

"He does," Holdt says. "Another time?"

"Sure."

"Danny," she says, "would that work for you?"

"Sure."

"Cool," Corchoran says. "Well . . ."

"Yeah," Danny says.

"I want you to meet Mitch," Holdt says.

"Who's Mitch?"

"The director," Holdt says. "He works for you."

They go meet Mitch. It's clear to Danny that the man's been briefed, that he knows Danny is taking care of their Kevin and Sean problem, that he's putting a cash transfusion into their hemorrhaging budget. So Mitch stops everything to have a polite conversation with him. "Are we getting it right?"

"Too right," Danny says. "Tell you the truth, it's a little painful."

"Good."

"Don't let me get in the way," Danny says. "I know you're on a tight clock."

"Spoken like a producer," Mitch says. "I appreciate it." He shakes Danny's hand again and goes back to work. Same scene, except this time the camera is pushed in on Old Man Murphy.

"Watch the monitor," Holdt tells him.

Danny does. He looks at the little television screen beside the camera and watches the actor say, *You care more about this piece of gash than you do about your family.* Watches his reaction as Liam says, *Don't call her that* and Pat says, *Liam, it's true. If you could keep your snake in the cage—*

I love her.

The actor's face twists into a disgusted, bitterly amused sneer. He sucks on his cigarette, carefully sets it back in the ashtray and snarls, *"Love." The fuck . . .*

They got Old Man Murphy just right, Danny thinks. He loved money, and power, and his boys, and that was it and that was all.

Cut!

"Are you offended," Holdt asks, "that you don't have many lines?"

"No," Danny says. "I was pretty much quiet."

"Taking it all in."

It's a challenge as much as an observation. He doesn't rise to it. "No, I just didn't have a lot to say in those days."

The Murphys did most of the talking, Danny remembers. Liam especially. Liam liked the sound of his own voice; what he didn't like was the sight of his own blood. For all the good that did him. No, Liam was the talker, Pat was the doer. Pat was the Murphy brother who took it all on his shoulders. Paid for Liam's sins.

"Where did you just go?" Holdt asks.

"Back there," Danny says.

A red light goes on and the set becomes quiet.

The camera is focused on the actor playing Liam, and Danny watches as he says, *I love her.*

I remember, Danny thinks.

I'm not giving her up, Dad.

But I wish to hell you had.

Then a shaft of light hits him, and Danny is, literally, starstruck.

DIANE CARSON COMES on the set like a queen.

The soundstage door opens and she walks through, backlit by the sunshine. Her court—an entourage of hairdressers, makeup artists, a dialogue coach, an assistant, a security guard, two agents, and a lawyer—buzzes around her.

She's beautiful.

No, Danny thinks, she's more than beautiful—suddenly he understands the appellation "star," because she shines in a way that average people don't. The golden halo of hair, the high and chiseled cheekbones, full lips, and cornflower-blue eyes that, well, shine. And her body is so sexual, even clad in a plain dark gray wool sweater and old jeans.

He walks right up to her.

Puts out his hand and says, "Ms. Carson, I'm Danny Ryan. It's a pleasure to meet you."

"*The* Danny Ryan?" she asks.

Her hand is warm and strong in his and she doesn't let it go.

And her voice—deep, throaty, intelligent. A challenge and a welcome at the same time. A voice for the living room and the bedroom, a voice you want to hear in the morning.

"Sue has told me so much about you," she continues.

"Good things, I hope."

He looks her straight in the eyes and she likes that. She likes him, right away. He's soft-spoken and strong. Gentle, but there's a danger not so far from the surface, and he knows who he is. Most others she meets are trying so hard to play larger versions of themselves, but he's not playing anything.

He just is.

And he's handsome. Chestnut hair and deep brown eyes with a trace of sadness in them. The broken nose that disturbs what would be an almost feminine symmetry. Ruddy Irish cheeks. Strong chest, strong arms, a strong hand that holds hers almost protectively.

She says, "Mostly good. Enough bad to be intriguing."

"I'm embarrassed to say I've never seen any of your movies," Danny says.

"See, we already have something in common," Diane says. "Neither have I."

"You're making fun of me."

"No," Diane says. "Seriously, I can't stand to see myself on-screen. I look fat, I look old, I can't act to save my life . . ."

"Two Oscar nominations."

"Oh, you've done your homework."

"I always do my homework, Ms. Carson."

"Diane."

"Danny."

The diminutive nickname has to go, she thinks. He's not "Danny"—he's "Dan," maybe even "Daniel." She resolves to work on it, and then she asks, "This is last-minute, I know . . . pretty rude . . . but do you have plans for Saturday afternoon? I'm having a little get-together at my place. Just a few friends, and I was wondering if maybe . . ."

"I'd like to," Danny says, "but my kid's with me . . ."

"Bring him," Diane says. "It's going to be a very PG party. I'm just out of, you know . . ."

"I heard."

"Yeah. I'll see you there, then." She lets go of his hand with a little squeeze and walks into the "Glocca Morra."

And Danny has this feeling that his life just changed.

He watches Mitch talk her through the scene, then she slides into a booth next to "Liam."

Lucky Liam, Danny thinks, then he turns around and sees Kevin and Sean, who are standing there looking sheepish and guilty.

"Kevin," Danny says. "Sean."

The Altar Boys nod.

"We should have a conversation," Danny says.

"We can go to my trailer," Kevin says.

Your *trailer*, Danny thinks.

Okay, what the hell.

When in Hollywood . . .

KEVIN OFFERS DANNY a drink.

Danny turns it down, suggests Kevin should, too.

"You look a little shaky, Kev," Danny says. "You been hitting it hard?"

"No, I'm just surprised you're here," Kevin says.

"I'll bet you are," Danny says. "Sit down, Kev, take a load off."

Kevin sits down on a padded bench, Sean beside him. Two schoolboys waiting in the principal's office. Ned Egan doesn't sit at all. He just stands there and gives Kevin the hard look. Jimmy leans against the trailer door, guarding them from intrusion.

"So you're okay," Danny says.

"Yeah, we're good."

Danny reaches into his jacket. Kevin flinches, but Danny pulls out a copy of *Entertainment Weekly*, opened to a certain page, tosses it onto the table and points. "You both look pretty good in that picture."

Kevin looks at it. It's an article about Diane Carson coming back from the drying-out tank, and in the background on the set it's him and Sean, pigging out at the craft services table. Sean has a bagel in his mouth.

"A guy's gotta eat," Kevin says.

Ned takes a step toward him, but Danny holds a hand up to stop him. He leans across the table. "That's a low profile? A picture in a magazine?!"

"I was gonna tell you, Danny."

"Really?" Danny asks. "When?"

"I couldn't find you," Kevin says. "I didn't know where you were, how to get hold of you."

Lying sack of shit, Danny thinks. You went on a binge, and when you woke up, this movie thing dropped into your lap and you knew I wouldn't approve. So you just kept on the down-low, hoping I wouldn't find you.

He gives Kevin a long, hard look, letting him know how bullshit he is.

"We were afraid maybe you were—" Sean stops suddenly. It sounds undiplomatic.

"Dead?" Danny asks. "You were afraid, or you were *hoping*, Sean?"

"*Afraid*, Danny. Jesus."

"Because it looks to me," Danny says, "like the two of you have your own sweet little operation going here."

The truth is you couldn't expect them to resist the temptation of this weird movie thing. On the other hand, he can't let them go cowboy like this, not without consequences. Once you loosen the grip, you never get it back.

"I have your kick-up, Danny," Kevin says. "I've been saving it for you."

"Don't insult me, Kevin. Any more than you already have." Danny lets the silence sit for a minute to let the anxiety rise. Then he says, "I'm not interested in what happened, I'm only interested in what happens from this point on. One, the shakedown stops. Yesterday. I love you both like brothers, but I swear on my father's immortal soul that I will walk you out of here and put you in the dirt."

He makes a point of looking them each in the eyes to reinforce his sincerity, then he goes on. "Two—you can go off on your own, take your shares of the Mexican payday and do your own thing. But you do it without me—without my knowledge, approval, guidance or protection. You're on your own. We say goodbye today—no hard feelings, but if we ever bump into each other on the sidewalk, you cross the street. We don't know each other."

He pauses for a second to let it sink in, then he says, "Or, you come back into the fold, you invest *half* your shares of the Mexican money into this film. We become legitimate partners, *earning* our own way. We'll take that profit and reinvest it in other legitimate businesses. Our mob days are over."

He looks at them for a second, then repeats, "*Over.*"

Danny opens up the little refrigerator, takes his time looking through it, then grabs a plastic bottle of water, the kind the movie people seem addicted to. He twists the top off, tosses it in a trash can, takes a sip, and then says, "If you do stay in, you stay in under my guidance, protection, and *authority*. I'll expect your loyalty and obedience."

Danny steps right in front of them and looks down.

"If this is it, then this is it," he says. "You have my gratitude for everything that you've done. If you decide the other way, I look forward to working with you again."

He walks out.

Past the drugstore, McKenzies Cigars, Wong's Chinese chop suey joint, and his old house.

Out the gate and into the real world of Hollywood.

FIFTEEN

YOU EVER TOLD ME BACK in Dogtown, Danny thinks, I'd buy a shirt that cost eighty bucks . . . hell, you told me there *was* a shirt that cost eighty bucks . . . I'd have laughed in your face.

Nevertheless, he puts on the designer shirt he bought at the hotel gift shop. It's black and looks good over the jeans and loafers.

Getting Ian dressed is another question; trying to get a squirming, giggling kid into a shirt, pants, and shoes is like wrestling Jell-O, but he finally gets it done, calls the parking valet to bring up the rented Mustang and heads out to Diane Carson's party.

There's a security gate with a guard at the bottom of Diane's driveway. He politely asks for Danny's name and when he hears it, waves him right in. When they get up to the house another parking valet takes the car.

The front door is open and they walk right in, greeted by a waiter with a tray of hors d'oeuvres. Another waiter comes up with a tray of drinks.

Danny asks, "Are these—"

"Soft," the waiter says. "They all are. This is a sober party."

Danny takes a Coke.

Diane sees them from across the room, makes a point of breaking off the conversation she's having and walks over. She looks radiant in a white summer dress, her hair down over a turquoise necklace.

She gives Danny a hug and a peck on the cheek, then extends her hand to Ian and says, "Hi. I'm Diane."

Danny says, "Can you say hello, Ian?"

"Hello."

"Ian," Diane says, "I have a puppy. Would you like to see him?"

Ian nods.

She walks them outside to a piece of lawn where a golden retriever puppy is happily chewing on a toy. "This is Pre, Ian."

Ian giggles as the puppy licks his face.

"Pre?" Danny asks.

"I named him for Steve Prefontaine, the runner," Diane says. "I was into running for a while."

"Got it."

"I think he really likes you, Ian," Diane says.

"I like him."

"Would you like to help me feed him?"

"Yes."

"Let's go get his food, then." Diane takes Ian's hand, and to Danny's surprise, the boy walks away with her without even looking back at him. She glances over her shoulder at Danny.

He mouths, *Thank you.* She shakes her head and then blows him a kiss.

Danny wanders around the "small" party. There are probably fifty or sixty people there, all casually but expensively dressed, a few he vaguely recognizes from movies or television. The conversation, unlubricated by alcohol, is quiet and a little subdued, but people seem to be having a good time.

So this is Hollywood when it wants to be laid-back, Danny thinks. Hardly the cocaine-snorting orgy that the stereotype would have you believe. Maybe everyone's on their very best behavior, with Diane just out of rehab. Or perhaps the no-booze thing is enough of a novelty to keep them interested for a while.

But it's nice, Danny thinks. The atmosphere is nice, Diane's friends supportive and happy that she's back and in good shape. And though it's quiet, the laughter is real, and the conversations seem animated, even if no one is going out of their way to engage him. He doesn't mind—it's all right to be a ghost at the party, the unobserved observer.

A number of people stand around the pool. A few others are swimming or knocking a volleyball around. A cook tends to some chicken breasts and salmon fillets on an open grill.

Danny takes a glass of some kind of fruit-juice mix from a waiter and sits down on a lawn chair. He leans back, lets the sun hit his face and enjoys the warmth. Tired suddenly, he feels as if he could just go to sleep.

Maybe I'm not tired, he thinks. Maybe I'm just actually relaxed.

Can let down a little.

It feels good.

He closes his eyes, just for a second.

When he wakes up, he looks through his sunglasses and sees Ian and Diane sitting at the far end of the pool in animated conversation. Ian is actually talking—a mile a minute, judging by his lips—and Diane dangles one foot in the water and listens to him intently, giving him all her attention, nodding and smiling, now and again reaching out and touching the top of his hand.

Suddenly Danny is ravenous, grateful that the chicken and salmon are being served, along with piles of fresh vegetables, salads, cold new pota-toes and corn bread. He gets a plate and joins the line.

"Are you having a good time?" Holdt asks him, appearing behind his shoulder.

"I am."

"Is that your boy over there with Diane?" she asks.

Danny spears a piece of salmon, then a chicken breast, and puts them on his plate. "That's Ian. I think he's smitten."

"So is she," Holdt says. "You be careful, Danny Ryan. You be careful with my friend."

Whatever that's supposed to mean, Danny thinks as Holdt walks away. He takes salad and some potatoes and walks over to rescue Diane from Ian.

"I don't have to tell you that you have a wonderful son," she says. "He's so sweet, and funny. You must be very proud."

"I am," Danny says. "Thank you for being so nice to him."

"It's easy."

"You have a beautiful place," Danny says.

"I think I'm going to sell it," she says. "It's too big for me and I'm trying to simplify my life. I have a little house on the beach. That should be enough for anybody, right?"

"It would be enough for me."

"I'm sort of trying to reinvent myself," Diane says.

"Is that hard in Hollywood?"

"Hollywood's all about reinventing yourself," Diane says. "It's the American dream, isn't it? You can come out here and become anything you want to be. Then, when you don't like it anymore, you change yourself again. It's expected out here, accepted."

"Are we talking about you or me?"

"Both of us, I guess."

She takes his arm and makes a point of introducing him around. *This is Danny Ryan, an investor in my current project. Hey, guys, meet Danny, he's helping with* Providence. She steers the conversation away from his background, his connection to the old days in Dogtown, but Danny sees behind the polite smiles that they know. The gossip has reached them about Bobby Bangs and the Altar Boys' attempt at extortion, that he'd been called in to put a stop to it—and had. They treat him with a kind of deferential curiosity—they're pleasant and polite, but they want to keep a little distance from the danger.

Danny doesn't mind. He knows it's going to take some time to "re-invent" himself.

Even in this land of metamorphoses.

Later, when the sun is just slipping down over the hills, a guy who's apparently a big recording star pulls out his acoustic guitar and starts to play, and people sit around just like they did back in the seventies, all *mellow*, *grooving* on the sound.

The guitar player is a neo-hippie, singing songs about nature—the ocean pounding out rhythms, rivers running through redwood forests, lovers walking on rocky beaches, romance disappearing into the fog and reemerging with the morning sun. He sings about surfers, hitchhiking bards, midnight meals in all-night diners, early-morning cigarettes in lonely motel rooms.

But it's nice, it's pretty, and Danny enjoys sitting on the grass next to Diane. The gentle light, her scent—he doesn't know if it's her perfume or just her—the feel of her close, warm and real, it's all working on him.

Danny likes it here.

EASY, GIRL, DIANE thinks.

It's too soon, way too soon, and what did they tell you in rehab and at the meetings? Don't get into a relationship for two years? Not two *weeks*, dummy, two *years*.

Two years without love, without sex? she'd asked.

Your vibrator won't get you drunk, her sponsor, Patty, told her. Actually gave her one. *It will always get you off and it doesn't want breakfast, just batteries.* More wisdom from Patty. Yeah, Patty, but it won't hold you, kiss your neck, bring you coffee in the morning. It won't give you kids. *Another good thing about it*, Patty said.

But I want children, I want a family, she thinks as she washes her face.

The man is a father, she thinks as she gets into bed. You invite him to a Hollywood party and he asks if he can bring his kid. And not divorced, a widower. Something so compelling—admit it, sexy—about those sad brown eyes. No Peter Pan syndrome, commitment phobia with this guy.

Easy, easy. Slow. Patty's right, they're all right, it's always been sex that has gotten you into trouble. It's always been that way, ever since . . .

Diane pushes that memory out of her mind. Suffice to say that sex and love have always led to problems. You're your own country-western song.

So take it slow.

She pulls the sheet up under her chin.

Her rise to stardom was neither quick nor steady.

Diane was quickly cast upon her arrival in Hollywood and did three low-budget sexploitation films in rapid succession. The camera loved her. Dressed, nude, or somewhere in between, when Diane was on the screen she was all you saw, and the films broke out at the box office.

Two more bad films followed, then her all-too-predictable protest to the media that she wanted to be considered a serious actress. A howler, it drew the usual jokes and derision from late-night talk show hosts, but then

Diane did a gutsy thing—she appeared on one of her tormentors' shows dressed provocatively in a skintight, low-cut dress, and she *killed*.

She made fun of herself and him, teased him, made him blush and stutter; her segment ended with thunderous applause from the studio audience and raves from the radio shows the following morning. Hollywood columnists made references to Marilyn Monroe.

Overnight, women *got* her, liked her, rooted for her.

A famed, "serious" director called her later in the week and offered her a role in his next film. It was a small part, but featured—the sadly funny whore with a heart of gold that the writer hero visited as much for conversation as for sex, although she had a love scene of subtle yet powerful sexuality that became watercooler talk across America, and not just among men.

The role won her a Golden Globe and an Academy Award nomination for Best Supporting Actress. She didn't win the Oscar, but she did win the red carpet and the press conferences, and the Diane Carson jokes were history, especially after the famed director asked the media, "Do you know how smart you have to be to play stupid?"

Now the media compared her to Marilyn Monroe *and* Judy Holliday. She sifted through the scores of scripts that she was offered, looking for that next, critical role that would define the future of her career. It had to be perfect—a female lead, sexy but not exploitative; serious but with a sense of humor; above all, intelligent. Something that would let her show her range. She turned down dumb blonde after dumb blonde. Turned down hooker roles, mistress roles, passed on so many parts her agent at CAA warned her that she needed to get on the screen again before the public forgot who she was.

The media took care of that problem, linking her romantically with every up-and-coming actor in the business, star quarterbacks, and rock singers. She played that part—hit the clubs, the parties, the red-carpet premieres that kept her in the public eye.

Then *the part* came to her.

Sue Holdt brought it. Fresh off three successive hits, Sue was the hot young producer—smart, ambitious, unyielding. She literally brought the script to Diane's house on Doheny, just south of Sunset. The two women sat out on Diane's little lawn and Sue read her the script out loud.

It was the opposite of glamorous—a period piece set in the Depression. Diane was to play Jan Hayes, a young wife on a struggling farm. Two little kids. Her husband was killed on page fifteen when his tractor flipped over and trapped him beneath. Jan was left to try to hold on to the land. Couldn't make it on what the farm produced, so she went to work in the local meatpacking plant—minimum wage, unsafe working conditions. Reluctantly, Jan started to organize her fellow workers. She was fired, she sued, she eventually won.

There was no love interest, no romantic possibility other than a friendship with a lesbian coworker that went, however, no further than an ambiguous conversation over a coffee break. The costuming was deliberately shabby and unattractive—denim shirts and jeans in the early scenes, white overalls smeared with blood later, wardrobe by Kmart for the courtroom sequences.

But it was Jan's story—a single-lead script.

Diane's film to carry.

Her agent *begged* her not to do it. Literally, down on his knees in his office, pleading with her that *Jan Hayes* would ruin her career.

She took the role.

It damn near killed her. Sue insisted that they shoot on location in South Dakota. The weather was brutal, the shooting schedule on a single-lead film even more so. Diane was on the set twelve, fourteen hours a day, six days a week. On the seventh day she rested, yeah, but she was so geared up from the previous six that it was hard to come down and sleep. She started taking pills to put her out, then more to get her up.

She and Sue went to New York for the premiere. You know how a movie is going to do in the first three hours—from six to nine on the first Friday night in Manhattan. The women waited together in the lobby of Cinema 1 on Third Avenue, across from Bloomingdale's, their mutual futures at stake.

The lines started to form at five o'clock. By five thirty, they stretched around the block. By six, people were buying for the ten o'clock screening. Diane and Sue stood in the back of the theater. The film ended to thunderous applause from the audience. It came in second for the weekend, a surprise hit just behind a huge action film with two male stars.

It won the next weekend.

Another Golden Globe, another Oscar nom, this time for Best Actress. *Jan Hayes* won Best Picture, Best Director. The media chirp was that Diane was robbed, that the statue went to an older actress as a makeup for not winning earlier.

It didn't matter—the film was a critical and commercial smash.

Diane Carson was a serious actress.

A major star.

Men loved her for her looks and sexuality, women for her intelligence and beauty.

But Diane's personal life was a train wreck. She wed the director of *Jan Hayes*—the marriage lasted seven months. Next, she got involved with a country-western star who drank and cheated on her. Diane finally broke it off when he knocked up a twenty-year-old centerfold. She did a rebound wedding in Vegas with an actor—it was true love this time, the real thing—two weeks later they had it annulled.

"We were drunk," the actor smirked to the cameras.

She was tabloid fodder, a paparazzi wet dream. Diane couldn't go anywhere without a flock of them descending on her like starving crows and, increasingly, she hid in the Malibu beach house that *Jan Hayes* paid for.

Al Jolson built the home, Roy Orbison lived there, later, Bobby Vinton. Diane stayed in her house, looked out at the ocean and wondered why nobody loved her with the intensity with which she loved them.

The run-of-the-mill rumors, none of them true, started to circulate: She'd earned her first film roles on her knees, giving blow jobs to every B-movie producer in town; she made porno films that were circulated at private parties. Diane ignored them. She understood that being a movie star was to be simultaneously vestal virgin and sacred temple whore in the American secular religion.

Her response was to work, following *Jan* with a romantic comedy in which she shined, then a dark, sexy suspense film in which she did another torrid nude scene.

"I didn't want people to forget I have nice boobs," she said on the same late-night talk show. It was funny, the audience laughed, it made the watercooler symposiums the next morning, but so did speculations that she was drunk or high when she said it.

Possible, very possible, because Diane was hitting the trifecta of sleeping pills, speed, and vodka. She started presenting a challenge to the makeup people—her face puffy in the early morning, lines left from sleeping so hard and long without moving. Vodka put on weight, which the camera picked up, so she started adding diet pills into the mix, stopped eating, started purging.

More gossip followed—anorexia, bulimia, alcoholism, drug addiction. The comparisons to Marilyn took on a different slant. *When will we find Diane Carson dead in her house at the beach?* They didn't, but they did find her sprawled in her trailer when she didn't show up for a shot. An ambulance rushed her to the E-room, arriving just before the paparazzi. She stayed for two days, then went to a rehab just up from her house in Malibu.

When she got out two months later, Larry Field met her with the script for *Providence.*

Both Diane and Sue think it's her Oscar.

Sleeping without the pills and alcohol is hard and Diane lies awake for a long time.

Part of it is thinking about Danny Ryan.

Easy, girl, she tells herself.

Slow.

DANNY LEARNS THAT a film set is one of the most boring places on earth.

Most of the time is spent setting up lighting, so there isn't a lot to look at. Unless you're actively engaged in making the movie, there's nothing to do and Danny quickly tires of feeling useless.

Sometimes he goes over to the accounting office to check in on Bernie, who is ensconced deciphering the seemingly impenetrable intricacies of Hollywood accounting, which he has described as "a wonderment."

But Bernie's technique is pure persistence, the dogged drip-drip-drip of the Chinese water torture, and he simply wears the studio people down to a genuine accounting of real numbers.

Danny doesn't understand half of what Bernie tells him, so he feels pretty useless there as well. And keeping the Altar Boys in their traces is simply a matter of putting in an appearance, so there's little to keep Danny occupied at the studio.

He moves out of the Peninsula (Bernie won't justify the expense and Danny feels out of place there anyway) into an apartment complex in Burbank. It's good to have the larger space for Ian and a kitchen, too, so that a peanut-butter-and-jelly sandwich doesn't have to come up from room service. The complex has a pool and play court, which keep the boy happy and engaged, and the ever-efficient Holly comes over a few hours a day to give Danny a break and Ian a change of faces.

Yeah, but a break to do what?

Wander over to the set and stand around like a jerk-off? Go bother Bernie? Drive around L.A. just to . . . drive around L.A.?

He's restless and he knows the reason.

Diane Carson.

Danny doesn't want to be that guy, the pathetic schmo who thinks he has a chance with a movie star. Or the *I put millions into your movie so you have to date me* guy.

But he can't get her out of his head.

He thinks about calling her, asking her out, thinks better of it, thinks about it again, drives around L.A. some more.

Then Diane calls him.

"You knew Pam Murphy personally, didn't you?" she asks.

"Sure."

"I wonder if you could give me some insight into her," Diane says. "What she was really like, what drove her. Kevin has told me a few things, but, you know . . ."

"I do know," Danny says. "Should I come by the set?"

"Actually," she says, "I'm not shooting on Saturday. I thought maybe we could go for a drive, you could tell me about Pam, I could show you around L.A., two-birds-with-one-stone sort of thing."

"Sounds good."

"Pick me up, I don't know, around noon sometime?" she asks. "We'll grab lunch?"

"I'll be there."

SHE LOOKS STUNNING in her simplicity.

A faded purple denim shirt, white jeans, her blond hair tied up in a ponytail under a blue L.A. Dodgers cap.

Subtle makeup, if any at all.

He opens the car door for her.

"Oh, my," she says. "L.A. guys don't do that."

"Rhode Island guys do," Danny says. "Am I being sexist?"

"No, I like it."

He follows her instructions to drive down to the Pacific Coast Highway and then north toward Malibu.

"The Dodgers, huh?" he asks.

"I suppose you're a Red Sox fan."

"It's a sad fate," Danny says, "but it's mine."

Sad fate, right, Danny thinks. I'm driving a Mustang convertible up the coast with the ocean on my left and a beautiful woman on my right.

California.

Diane asks him about Pam Murphy.

It seems like a different life; it *was* a different life, he reminds himself. But he tells her about his memories of Pam, how he first saw her come out of the water at the beach, how beautiful she was, how surprised he was when she turned out to be Paulie Moretti's girlfriend.

"Why was that?" Diane asks. "Why do you think this Connecticut, aristocratic, trust fund baby dated a mafioso?"

"Rebellion?" Danny shrugs. He goes on to tell her about that night, when a drunk Liam Murphy felt Pam up, and how the Moretti brothers and a couple of their thugs beat Liam half to death.

"And then Pam showed up at the hospital," Diane says.

"I was there," Danny says. "I about swallowed my tongue when I saw her."

He tells her how Pam left with Liam when he was discharged, how she moved in with him, married him on a quick trip to Vegas.

"And that started the war," Diane says.

"It was the excuse, anyway," Danny says. "The Morettis always wanted what the Irish had—the docks, the unions. Pam just provided a convenient pretext."

"Why Liam?"

"Liam was charming," Danny says. "Handsome, funny. He was a piece of shit, but women seemed to love him. I think Pam did, to a point. Until she flipped on him."

"What?"

"Bobby didn't put that in his book?" Danny says. "I guess he didn't know. Yeah, Pam called the feds on Liam. That's how they got him."

"I thought he killed himself," Pam says.

"That's one theory."

"What's the other?"

"That it was an 'other-assisted suicide,'" Danny says. "Anyway, you know that Pam went back to Paulie."

"What I don't know is why."

Danny says, "I'm not a shrink, but I know Pam always felt guilty about all the killings that happened. She blamed herself. I think going back to Paulie was sort of . . . penance."

"Self-punishment," Diane says. "I know a little something about that."

She gives him directions to her beach house in the Malibu Colony. "I thought we'd have lunch there, if that's okay. I had my assistant leave some groceries."

It can be a hassle, she explains, eating out in a restaurant.

The house, like most of them in the Colony, is long and narrow, closely packed amid its neighbors, but fronts onto the beach with a large balcony. Diane gets right to work in the kitchen and makes them a salad and turkey sandwiches. She has a bottled iced tea but offers him a beer.

"I'll have tea," Danny says. "Should you really have beer around the house?"

"Probably not," she says. "But I was never a beer drinker."

They take the food outside.

The ocean is beautiful on a classic sunny California day.

"I think I could live here," Diane says.

Danny laughs. "A lot of people would give their right arms to live here. It's everyone's dream, right?"

"Is it yours?"

"Yeah," Danny says. "Kind of it always has been. I love the ocean."

After lunch, they go for a walk on the beach.

"I brought you a present," Danny says.

"You didn't have to do that."

"I wanted to, but . . ."

"What?" she asks.

"It's maybe a little too personal."

"Oh, then I really want it," Diane says.

He digs into his pocket and puts a little metal disk in her hand.

"A ninety-day medal," she says. "How did you know?"

Danny says, "I figured I was close, anyway."

"You're dead on," she says. "Ninety days today. But how do you know about this? Are you a friend of Bill's?"

She hopes he isn't. Two alcoholics in a relationship—not good, not good. Not at this phase, anyway.

"No, I'm Irish," he says.

Diane laughs. "Right. Gotcha."

"I hope this wasn't . . . presumptuous."

"No," she says. "It's perfect. Thank you."

She leans over and kisses him on the cheek.

THE SQUALL COMES up quickly.

A sudden blackening of the sky and then a deluge.

Danny and Diane are soaked within seconds.

Laughing, they hold hands and run up the beach and under her deck. Their sodden clothes cling to their skin.

As sudden as the storm, as inevitable, Danny kisses her, she kisses him back. He unbuttons her blouse, feels underneath, then unsnaps her jeans and pushes them down. He lifts her, moves her against a pylon as she unzips his jeans, and then he's inside her.

Rain hammers the deck, drowning out their sounds.

And that's it, they're in love.

SIXTEEN

THEY'RE DISCREET AT FIRST.

Danny and Diane keep a cordial distance when he comes on the set, which is less and less. They meet only at her beach house, after shooting hours or on her days off.

At first, that's the fun, the clichéd cheap thrill of sneaking around.

Danny hadn't been a perfect husband, but he'd been a perfectly faithful one. There'd been Terri and only Terri. He'd been that young married guy in a small city where everyone knew each other, wed each other, socialized with each other, went to church, weddings, christenings, and funerals with each other. He lived in a closed circle, sexually and socially, and if he was being honest with himself, a restlessness had set in the moment he saw Pam step out of the ocean.

Now he's in L.A., in Hollywood no less, dating a movie star (the irony that she's portraying Pam isn't lost on him), the sex is incredible, the intimacy intense, the secrecy a frisson.

They decide to keep their romance on the down-low because they don't want the interference, the advice, the knowing smiles, the smirks.

Diane especially doesn't want the tabloid stories and the paparazzi; for his part, Danny is so used to living off the radar that secrecy comes as a natural instinct.

But it gets old in a hurry.

They're in love, they want more. They want to go to restaurants and movies, to clubs, to parties.

They're like kids, they want to shout it to the world.

They don't have to.

The world finds out on its own.

A look exchanged on the set gets noticed. Speculation becomes rumor, rumor becomes fact. A production assistant calls a tabloid, which dispatches photographers to stake out Diane's houses. One gets lucky at the beach place, nails a shot of Danny going in.

The photograph appears in the paper that week with the cut-line DIANE'S MYSTERY MAN.

They know his name, but the Mystery Man angle is too good to give up and they stay with it as they publish a grainy photo of Danny driving through the studio gate under the line WHO IS DIANE'S GENTLEMAN CALLER?

"You're my 'gentleman caller,'" Diane says to Danny one night in bed. "I kind of like that."

Diane might; Sue Holdt's not so sure.

She comes to have lunch one day in Diane's trailer and says, "You and Danny Ryan?"

"What about it?"

"So it's true?"

"The *National Enquirer* printed it," Diane says, "so it must be."

"Is this a set romance," Sue asks, "or is it serious?"

Diane says, "I don't know yet. I can tell you that it *feels* serious."

"Be careful, huh?" Sue says. "I don't want to see you get hurt."

The tabloids already dine out on Diane's past, Sue thinks. Add Ryan's past to that, it's a virtual smorgasbord.

It takes no time at all, because film sets are leakier than old wooden boats. The tabloids get the word that a minor character in *Providence* is actually based on Danny Ryan.

DIANE CARSON—REAL-LIFE GANG MOLL

IN "PROVIDENCE," DIANE CARSON PLAYS THE GIRLFRIEND OF A MOBSTER, BUT NOW SHE SEEMS TO BE TAKING METHOD ACTING TO A WHOLE NEW LEVEL, DATING A REAL GANGSTER RIGHT FROM THE SCRIPT. IS IT RESEARCH OR ROMANCE?

Sue finishes reading out loud and then tosses the paper on her desk.

Mitch Apsberger sits on a sofa in her office. So does the head of publicity and the studio's in-house legal counsel.

The lawyer kicks in first. "The studio has no standing to sue. That would have to come from Diane or Ryan himself. The depiction of him as a 'mobster' and 'gangster' is legally dubious, as he's never been charged, much less convicted, of any crime. At the same time, he's been portrayed in Bangs's book as such, and there is a character in the film based on him. But I would strongly recommend against litigation, as the discovery process might bring out damaging information and/or expose Ryan to the jeopardy of perjury."

"Diane suing would only shine a brighter light on this," Sue says. "Ben?"

The head of publicity says, "Can I be honest here? I love this. I mean, you can't buy this kind of media. Any more of this, we'll have to add six hundred screens."

"If Ryan is some sort of Damon Runyon, *Guys and Dolls* lovable gangster," Sue says, "it works in our favor. But if darker things come out it could turn in a heartbeat."

"If it's *Godfather*, it's one thing," Mitch says, "if it's *Goodfellas*, it's another."

"Danny Ryan isn't Al," Ben says, "but he's not Ray, either. And he's certainly not Bobby."

"We're not casting Ryan," Sue says.

"We sort of are," Ben says. "I mean, Diane has cast him for us."

"The movie's not even in the can yet," Mitch says. "It won't be out for another six months. By that time, everyone will have forgotten about Danny and Diane."

"Unless they're still together," Sue says.

"Even if they are," Mitch says.

Sue isn't so sure. And she's not just worried about revelations regarding Danny Ryan and Diane Carson. What, she thinks, will happen if it's discovered that Ryan has money in the film?

Corporate will go bleeding-from-the-nose crazy. It's the kind of thing that gets studio heads fired.

"Use some of our tame reporters," she tells Ben. "Get some different stories out. 'Danny Ryan was a minor player who had to flee the mob. He's a widower with a small child.' That sort of thing. And Mitch, see if you can't clamp down on your set. Stop the chins wagging."

The lawyer and the publicity guy leave.

"I'll talk to Diane, ask her to cool it," Sue says. "Can you talk to Ryan?"

Mitch says that he'll try.

DANNY'S A DECENT guy.

The last thing he wants to do is hurt Diane, damage her career. Walking on the beach with her and Ian after his conversation with Mitch, he says, "Look, if this is a problem for you, I understand. I'll go away."

"No," Diane says. "I don't want you to. I want to be with you."

Neither of them has dropped the L-word yet, but it's in the air between them like a moist heavy sky waiting to rain.

"I spent most of my life doing what other people wanted me to do," he tells Diane. "No more. That's over."

So they don't cool it.

Danny being Danny and Diane being Diane, they go the other way with it.

All out.

Full tilt.

They go out to lunch at Chateau Marmont, dinner at Musso and Frank, shopping on Rodeo Drive. They don't even try to duck the paparazzi, they just let them snap away.

It's a new world for Danny.

He's spent his whole life staying in the shadows. Now he's out there, in the L.A. sunshine, in the spotlight, not hiding a damn thing.

It's strange at first, weird, off-putting.

He doesn't like it.

Danny feels the temptation to push the photographers out of his way, shove those cameras back into their faces; he feels especially protective of Diane. But she just laughs and tells him to let it go.

"Ignore them," she says. "It's what I do."

Harder to ignore when they photograph Ian, who's with Danny and Diane more and more. The photographers scare the little boy, and one afternoon Danny finds himself walking up to them and saying in a calm and reasonable tone, "Hey, guys, Diane and I are fair game, but you have to give my kid a break, okay?"

He's surprised when they do back off and shoot with longer lenses when Ian's there.

And Danny's smart enough to realize that the media can be allies as well as enemies, that a little cooperation gets him better coverage, that he sees "mobster" and "gangster" less and "survivor" and "widower" more.

One columnist writes, *Who among us doesn't have a past? Danny Ryan certainly does, but he's put it behind him.*

If it's a war, it looks like Danny and Diane are winning.

They're everywhere—with Ian at Santa Monica Pier and Disneyland, behind home plate at a Dodgers game (Danny conspicuous in his Red Sox cap), laughing together at the Comedy Store, dancing at Café Largo.

It's Danny unleashed.

For so many years the good soldier, the loyal husband, the dutiful son, the responsible father, for the first time in his life he's doing exactly what he wants to do.

Even Danny will admit he goes a little crazy.

But being a little crazy feels good.

Being out there feels good.

Loving Diane feels good.

IT DOES TO her, too, and she tells Sue this during their conversation at Sue's house.

"I've been with so many jerks," Diane says. "I've been with too many L.A. boys. Danny is a man."

"With a past," Sue says.

"I'm the last person who should judge anyone about their past."

Sue tries a different tack. "Diane, if this film tanks, both our careers could go down with it."

"So that's what this is all about."

"I'm just being realistic," Sue says. "I'm not saying don't be with him, I'm just asking you to keep it on the down-low for a while."

Too late for that.

It's out there.

They're out there, and they're not going back into some dark cave.

They're too happy in the sunlight.

•   •   •

BUT NOTHING IS more persistent, more patient, than the past.

After all, the past has nothing but time.

CHRIS PALUMBO STANDS in line at the little grocery store in town.

He likes doing the shopping. Who knew? Likes planning the meals, strolling up and down the aisles, shooting the shit with the clerks. And he likes doing it by himself, so he can take his time and so Laura doesn't bust balls about his Jimmy Deans.

So now he waits with his red plastic basket—it has his Jimmies, a bunch of veggies for her, a couple of boxes of penne pasta he talked the owner into stocking (before Chris, the locals thought all pasta was spaghetti), a dozen eggs, brown rice—and looks at the rack of magazines and newspapers.

Then he sees it.

Danny Ryan's smiling mug.

Chris grabs the tabloid.

And son of a bitch, there's Ryan with his arm around some gorgeous blond chick. DASHING DANNY, the headline screams and DARLING DIANE, and as Chris reads he learns that Danny Ryan is dating a movie star.

Fucking Danny, Chris thinks, shaking his head. That Irish donkey hump could fall face-first into a pile of shit and come up with a diamond in his mouth. Chris doesn't know what kind of angel Danny has sitting on his shoulder, but it has to be one with some heavy swag.

"Joe?"

"Huh?"

"*Joe*. You want that paper?" Helen asks. Her gray hair, which looks a little blue, is tightly permed.

"Uh, yeah."

He starts laying his stuff on the counter.

"Danny and Diane," Helen says as she rings him up. "Quite the couple. I guess he was some kind of a gangster. What a world, huh?"

"It's the one we got," Chris says.

He likes Helen. He likes just about everybody in town, and they like him back. They make fun of his accent, that he doesn't pronounce his *r*'s, asking him if he's *pahked his cah*, and Chris always answers, *Yeah, outside the bah*, and they all laugh, even though it's about the seven-thousandth time they've done it.

Chris takes the groceries to the car and sits and reads the article.

Christ, they're making a fucking *movie* about the war?! And Danny's involved with it? The fuck is that dumb bastard thinking?

Then he wonders, Am I in the movie?

If I am, who's playing me?

Better be some good-looking son of a bitch.

REGGIE MONETA READS the stack of tabloids on her desk.

And laughs.

Danny Ryan, the man no one could find, then the man no one *wanted* to find, surfaces as a media star.

They say there are no second acts in American life, but Ryan is having a beaut. Dating a movie star, living it up all around L.A., a tabloid darling, he's freaking Joe DiMaggio now.

Good, she thinks.

Let him have his fun.

Every second act, Reggie knows, is followed by a third.

She picks up the phone.

IN WASHINGTON. BRENT Harris and Evan Penner go for another walk, this one in Rock Creek Park.

"What does your boy Ryan think he's doing?" Penner asks.

Harris doesn't like the depiction of Ryan as his boy. For a couple of reasons—first, Ryan isn't anyone's boy; second, he doesn't want Ryan's actions tied to him. "Living his life, I suppose."

"In the public eye?" Penner asks. "Don't you think that's a problem?"

Of course I think it's a problem, Harris thinks. The tabloid media are one thing, but if the serious press gets into it, they're going to dig deeper than the obvious superficial titillation of the gangster-and-the-movie-star story. If the *Times* or the *Post* gets hold of Ryan's investment in the film, they're going to want to know where that money came from. So yes, it's a problem.

As usual, Penner is ahead of him. "My sources tell me that Ryan put considerable monies into this film project. That makes the corporate types very nervous."

"Maybe they should have thought of that before they took the money," Harris says.

"Sadly," Penner says, "few shiny baubles are as irresistible as ready cash. The reality remains, however, that we cannot afford to have Danny Ryan linked to us."

"I understand."

"Do you?" Penner asks. "I wonder."

Harris wonders, too.

BERNIE SHOWS DANNY the billings. "They're robbing you."

The old accountant lays it out. The catering company that provides meals for the production when it's out shooting on the street is billing for meals it doesn't deliver.

"How do you know?" Danny asks.

"I went to the set, I checked," Bernie says, as if it's obvious. "Look, see here? 'Seven dozen chicken breasts'? No, five. Tenderloin, crab legs, the same. They're even shorting you on macaroni and cheese. Now look at this . . ."

Bernie shows him bills from UR Peein'.

"The hell is that?"

"Porta-potties," Bernie says. "They bill you for five, they deliver three."

"Why haven't the studio accountants picked this up?"

"They don't leave the studio," Bernie says. "I tracked down both companies, both are owned by the same person, Ronald Faella."

The next morning, 5:00 A.M. sharp, Danny's waiting on the location set when the catering van pulls up. Danny walks up to the lead guy. "You're fired."

"What?"

"What about 'fired' don't you understand?" Danny asks. "You've been ripping us off. I have another company coming in."

"I gotta call my boss."

"Call whoever you want," Danny said. "But get your trucks off my set."

Forty-five minutes later, a very annoyed Ronald Faella pulls up and seeks out Danny. He looks like someone woke him up, his hair is disheveled and he hasn't shaved. "You Ryan?"

"Yup."

"So what's the problem, chief?"

"The problem is you're a crook."

"Whoa."

"I look like a horse to you?" Danny asks.

"Obviously there's been some sort of misunderstanding here," Faella says.

"No misunderstanding," Danny says. "I pay for seven, I get seven. I pay for three, I get three."

"You better talk to someone at the studio," Faella says.

"Who?" Danny asks. "Who should I talk to? Give me a name."

Faella stares at him but doesn't say anything.

"What I thought," Danny says. "Anyway, I just fired you."

"We have a contract, my friend."

"Call your lawyer," Danny says. "I'll call ours. I'm sure everyone will have a good time going over your books."

"Do you know who I am?" Faella asks.

"Don't *you* know who you are?" Danny asks. "We have an amnesia problem here?"

"Do you know who I'm *with*?"

Shit, Danny thinks. It's always the same old, same old. "I don't care who you are, I don't care who you're with. The party's over, the grab bag is closed. I don't care who else you rip off, it's just not going to be me."

Faella's not ready to give it up. "Twenty minutes after I leave, the union steward is going to find safety violations."

"No, he's not," Danny says.

I already explained it to him.

"DANNY *WHO*?" ANGELO Petrelli asks.

"Ryan."

"Doesn't ring a bell."

Angelo and Ronnie Faella are sitting at the nineteenth hole of the Westlake Village golf course sipping Long Island iced teas and eating club sandwiches.

The West Coast mob is not the East Coast mob.

"You remember a couple of years ago," Faella says, "the Providence people had a problem with some Irish crew? Ryan was one of them."

"That was Peter Moretti?"

"Yeah."

"He's dead, right?"

"I guess," Faella says. "I think there's still a brother. Seriously, haven't you read about this guy? It's all over the papers. He's banging Diane Carson."

"*A salut.*" Angelo lifts his glass. "Other than the fact that it's him instead of me, why do I care?"

He's sleepy. The combination of sun, exercise, food, and booze makes him want to take a siesta.

Faella tells him about what happened on the set.

Now Angelo cares. Ronnie Faella kicks up to him, so now this Ryan guy is lightening his pockets. "We got a union guy there, don't we?"

"Dave Keeley," Faella says. "I went to talk to him, two of Ryan's guys were there."

"What did they say?"

"Nothing, they just looked at me," Faella says.

"They *looked* at you?"

"You know what I mean," Faella says. "Keeley basically told me there was nothing he could do."

Angelo doesn't like it all. Some guy comes out of the East Coast—Providence, no less—and sets up camp in L.A.?

No.

"YOU ARE RECEIVING a telephone call from an inmate at El Dorado Correctional Facility. Do you accept the charges?"

"Yes," Diane says.

It's been a long time.

Then she hears, "Hello, sweetheart."

DANNY WATCHES THE sunset from Diane's deck.

On the beach below, Ian is running around in circles with Holly, and Danny thinks he'll go down there in a minute to join them.

But it's been a day, and it makes him sad and tired.

I came out here to get away from all this wiseguy bullshit, he thinks, and here it is waiting for me. I came here to be a different person, and here I am right back in the middle of it.

He only hopes now that this Ron Faella will give it up and just go away. Nevertheless, he had the Altar Boys go check him out, see how much of a threat he really is, who he's *with*, if he's with anyone. Maybe he's just another big-mouth wannabe like Danny used to run into in Rhode Island all the time, the type who's always bragging about knowing a guy.

Diane comes through the slider and sits down beside him.

They have a quick kiss, a peck, and she asks, "So how was your day?"

"Yeah, fine. Yours?"

"Good."

They're lying to each other.

That's how it starts.

KEVIN COOMBS IS not impressed with Ronnie Faella and Angelo Petrelli. It took him two days, but he tracked them down to a bakery in Westlake Village where they usually meet for a late breakfast.

"Guess what they were eating," he says to Sean.

"Do I have to?"

"Croissants," Kevin says with disgust. "The fuck kind of mob guys eat croissants?"

"What do you want them to eat?"

"Bacon and eggs," Kevin says. "Mob guys eat bacon and eggs, okay, maybe sausage, the Italians. But *croissants*? Sean, come on. And you know what they were wearing? Pastel polo shirts."

"So what?"

Kevin shakes his head. "Mob guys wear black. Captains and above, black suits. Below, black leather jackets."

"It's ninety degrees out."

"Doesn't matter," Kevin says. "There are standards. And the next morning, my hand to freakin' God, one gets *oatmeal*, with *berries*, the other? *Yogurt*. A so-called boss. Yogurt. How are we supposed to take these guys seriously?"

"Danny takes them seriously," Sean says.

"All we got to do is run Ned in front of them," Kevin says, "they'll piss themselves."

"Yogurt *is* good for the urinary tract," Sean says.

The next morning, Kevin sits in a car in the parking lot of the strip mall where the bakery is located and watches Faella and Petrelli munch on *muffins*. He's disgusted and not happy anyway at this time of the morning because he's wicked hungover.

Then Faella gets up and starts walking toward him.

Kevin lays his hand on his gun.

Faella gestures for him to roll down the window. When Kevin does, he asks, "You South or Coombs?"

So they've done some homework, Kevin thinks. Good for them.

"Coombs."

"My boss would like to talk with your boss," Faella says. "A friendly sit-down. You think we can work that out?"

"I can ask."

"You do that," Faella says. "You ask."

He goes back to his freakin' muffin.

Kevin sets down his gun.

DIANE FLINCHES.

"Cut!" Mitch yells.

They're shooting the first love scene between Pam and Liam today—in fact, probably for the next three days. Mitch has waited until relatively late to schedule this scene because it's difficult and delicate and he wanted to give Diane time to get comfortable with Brady Fellowes, the actor playing

Liam. And she has been, their previous scenes have shown great rapport and sexual chemistry, but now, as Brady touches her shoulder, easing her blouse off, she's flinched for the third take in a row.

"I'm sorry," Diane says.

"No problem," Mitch says. "Let's take a five."

The set is almost empty, Mitch having closed it—essential personnel only—for the sex scene.

Diane sits down in the chair to have her makeup and hair refreshed.

"You okay?" Ana asks.

"Yeah."

But she's not. Diane feels terrible. She knows she's letting everyone down, costing the production money, getting Mitch behind on a shooting schedule that's already behind. And she knows how quickly the rumors can start, the questions. Is Diane high again? Is she back on drugs? On alcohol?

She isn't, but it's the first time in a while that she's felt the urge.

Mitch comes over.

Ana doesn't need to be told to walk away.

"How are you?" Mitch asks.

"There's an old joke," Diane says. "On their wedding night, the groom asks the bride if it's her first time. And she says, 'Why does everyone keep asking me that'?"

"Funny," Mitch says. "But you seem, I don't know, jumpy. Is it Brady? Do you have a problem with him?"

"No. Brady's great."

Mitch lets the question hang.

Diane says, "I don't know, Mitch. I don't . . . I'm just jumpy."

"Yeah, look," he says, "maybe we bring in the body double for the close-ups. And you know, for the rest of it, I'm framing up from the shoulders."

"Thank you."

But, Diane thinks, the passion has to be there. Without the sexual attraction, the compulsion, the Pam-Liam story makes no sense. Without that, the whole film doesn't work.

And I have to deliver that.

The body double can't.

It's on me.

She tries to focus, tries to get into Pam, leave herself behind. But the voice on the phone keeps coming into her head.

Hello, sweetheart.

DANNY GOES TO Petrelli's breakfast place.

He doesn't mind, he's not into playing the status game and settling on a neutral location. And there's no risk to coming here—nothing is going to happen in Westlake Village at ten thirty on a Thursday morning.

Westlake Village doesn't even feel like Los Angeles, it feels more like an upscale suburb.

Danny's done his research.

Angelo Petrelli is the boss of the L.A. mob, which isn't saying a lot in itself. Back in the day, the day being from the twenties through the fifties, the L.A. family was something, with powerful guys like Jack Dragna, Mickey Cohen, Benny Siegal, and Johnny Roselli.

Then in the seventies and eighties, guys started flipping on each other, a lot went to prison, sending the L.A. family into a tailspin from which it's never recovered. Now some of those people are out, including Petrelli, and the family is trying to make a comeback, mostly by reinfiltrating the studios and moving to take a piece of Las Vegas.

But what L.A. really is, Danny learned, is a semiofficial colony of the Chicago Outfit, and that's a problem.

Danny doesn't want a problem with Chicago.

No one does.

So Danny goes to the meeting.

He goes alone. His crew was against it, but Danny thought he'd actually look stronger if he was confident enough to show up by himself.

Petrelli's already outside, sitting at a table with Faella. He stands up and greets Danny warmly. "Danny, thanks for coming."

Because Angelo's done his homework, too. He knows that Danny Ryan is a serious person, that he boosted forty kilos of heroin from Peter Moretti, that he took at least two guys, maybe more, off the count, and, most of all, he's an old friend and protégé of Pasco Ferri. The former New England boss is in retirement in Florida, but he stays in touch with all the major families, including Chicago.

So Angelo shows Danny Ryan some respect.

"You want anything, Danny?" he asks. "A coffee? A pastry? Ronnie, get Danny here a coffee. Sit down, Danny."

Danny sits down.

Faella goes into the bakery.

"Danny," Angelo says, "if you had a problem, I wish you'd come to me first."

"I didn't know," Danny says.

"But see, that's the problem," Angelo says, "with just showing up in a place. You don't know what you don't know."

"You make a point."

Angelo smiles. "So look, forget about it. You let Ronnie back in, life goes on, everything is forgotten."

"No."

The smile disappears. "No what?"

"No, I'm not letting Ronnie back in," Danny says. "Would you let a thief back in your house?"

Danny lays it out—phony food costs, overcharging on equipment that wasn't there, charging for employees who never showed up. It amounted to tens of thousands of dollars.

"What do you care?" Angelo asks. "It's not your money. But look, if this is about you wanting to dip your beak, okay, we can talk about that. You want to skim off the skim, I can talk Ronnie into that, maybe you call Pasco and tell him that we treated you right out here."

"You're not talking to Pasco," Danny says, "you're talking to me."

Faella comes back with a coffee and a Danish that he sets in front of Danny. Then he sits down.

Angelo says, "Danny and I were just working things out."

"The movies are a big table," Faella says. "We can all eat. As long as you don't get greedy, Danny."

Danny removes the plastic lid from the coffee cup, takes a sip, and puts the lid back on. "This movie is my table. I didn't invite you."

"We were there before you were," Faella says.

"And now you're not," Danny says.

"Are we really going to argue over some mac and cheese?" Angelo asks, starting to get angry. "This catering stuff, no offense, Ronnie, it's small potatoes. But this is my turf. You want to earn on my turf, you kick up to me."

"I'm not moving onto your turf," Danny says. "I don't want a piece of your gambling, dope, women, the unions, loan sharking, nothing."

"What *do* you want?"

"Only my movie business," Danny says. "This film or any film I decide to make."

"We have interests in the film unions," Angelo says.

"Go with God," Danny says. "Just not on my sets."

"You want protection," Faella says, "you pay for protection."

"Except I don't and I won't," Danny says. He gets up. "Thanks for your time. Thanks for the coffee."

He walks back to his car.

Gets on the phone to Jimmy. "I want someone on the set at all times. Tell everyone to keep their heads on a swivel."

"You want someone with you?"

"No, I'm good."

I'm not, though, Danny thinks.

I'm shitty.

This is the last thing I wanted.

When he pulls into his apartment complex, a car is waiting for him.

TWENTY-THREE TAKES.

And it's still not good, Diane thinks as she leaves the soundstage. Twenty-three takes and I sucked in every one of them. Mitch tries to disguise his unhappiness, but he's even a shittier actor than I am. The whispers have started, the phone will be ringing in Sue's office.

Diane's exhausted.

All she wants to do is go home and sleep.

HARRIS SITS IN Danny's car.

"When an extremely low profile is called for," he says, "you have adopted an extremely high profile."

"Whatever that means."

"It means dating a movie star and going out in public," Harris says. "I don't get it. You're not a stupid person. You could have taken that money and lived a happy, quiet life."

"That's what I want."

"Despite all evidence to the contrary?" Harris asks. "Have you told her anything? Anything she shouldn't know? Pillow talk?"

"For Chrissakes—"

"She's unstable," Harris says. "She has a history of drugs and alcohol, depression, mental illness in the family. Her brother—"

"I know about that," Danny says. "No, I haven't told her anything."

They sit silently for a few seconds and then Harris says, "Some people in Washington are very concerned."

"What people?"

"Come on, Danny."

"I don't work for you," Danny says. "I don't work for 'some people in Washington.' We had a deal. I lived up to my part."

Harris says, "You need to stay out of the media. You need to drop this relationship, or—"

"You threatening me now?" Danny asks.

"I'm trying to help you."

"Don't."

Harris opens the door. "You need to break it off with her, Danny. You need to break it off now."

He gets out.

DANNY THE DOPE DEALER?

Danny's stomach flips as he sees the headline. Then he reads:

CHARMING DANNY RYAN MIGHT NOT BE SO MUCH SKY MASTERSON AS HE IS SCARFACE. RELIABLE LAW ENFORCEMENT SOURCES TELL US THAT WHEN DANNY IS SQUIRING OUR SWEET DIANE AROUND TOWN, HE MIGHT BE DOING IT WITH MONEY FROM A GIGANTIC HEROIN DEAL.

The story goes on to talk about the bust of the Glocca Morra, the twelve keys of heroin and John Murphy's arrest.

OUR SOURCES TELL US THAT DANNY IS JOHN MURPHY'S SON-IN-LAW, AND WAS A FOOT SOLDIER IN THE IRISH GANG THAT FOUGHT A LONG WAR AGAINST THE MAFIA IN RHODE ISLAND. DANNY WAS A

"PERSON OF INTEREST" IN SEVERAL MURDERS, ALTHOUGH PROSECU-
TORS HAVE NEVER BEEN ABLE TO PIN THEM ON HIM.

NOW HE MIGHT BE A DOPE DEALER, TOO.

DOES OUR DARLING DIANE KNOW ABOUT HER BOYFRIEND'S PAST?

Danny wants to throw up.

SUE HOLDT FEELS sick, too.

It's a disaster.

The PR guys don't think it's such a good thing anymore, and the lawyer tells her that they still have no legal standing to get involved, that it's
between Ryan and these newspapers. And even if Ryan decides to sue, it's
a two-edged sword, because it would keep the story going.

And what if it's true?

She looks across the office at Mitch. "I saw the recent dailies. Diane
is a mess."

"I don't know what's going on with her," Mitch says. "It's not drugs or
alcohol. She's clean. But her head . . ."

"Can she finish the film?" Sue asks. "How many more days of shooting do you have with her?"

"Nine or ten if her head's on straight," Mitch says. "If it isn't, who
knows?"

"This isn't going to help," Sue says.

"No, it's not."

"IS IT TRUE?" Diane asks.

She came to his apartment straight from another shit day on the set.

"Parts of it are true," Danny says.

He's glad Ian's in bed.

"I read about the heroin in Bobby's book," Diane says. "It's in the script. What I didn't know was that you were involved."

"There are things about my life," Danny says, "I want to keep away from you."

"Why?"

"Because if I show you those parts of me," Danny says, "you'll leave me."

"Danny," she says, "if you *don't* show me those parts of you, I'll leave you."

Danny tells her the whole story. How he let Liam talk him into hijacking the Moretti heroin shipment. Forty kilos. How it was a trap, a setup. How he was in the hospital with his wife when the Glocca Morra bust happened.

Then he tells her the rest, how he went down and picked up his share of the heroin.

"So it is true," she says.

"I threw it away," he says. "I dumped it in the ocean."

"You expect me to believe that?"

"I don't know what I expect you to believe," Danny says. "I can only tell you the truth."

In the book, in the movie, it all ends with Liam's suicide.

After Pam leaves him.

"That's not what really happened," Danny says. "Pam flipped on him, turned him in to a fed named Jardine. Jardine murdered him to get to the heroin."

"How do you know this?"

"Jardine told me."

"He was murdered."

"He was killed," Danny says.

"Did you do it?"

"Diane, don't ask me questions you don't want to know the answer to," Danny says.

"So that's a yes."

Do you tell her? Danny asks himself. That you gave Jardine a chance to walk away, that he decided to shoot you, that it went your way instead?

No, you don't.

You don't make her a witness.

"There's a lot you don't understand," he says.

"Make me understand."

He shakes his head.

She says, "So now you shut me out?"

Danny knows it's a mistake when he opens his mouth and says, "You knew I wasn't a Boy Scout when you got involved with me."

"Got it."

She turns and walks out the door.

IT GETS WORSE the next day.

DID DANNY RYAN KILL A COP?

The story goes into the murder of Phil Jardine. It doesn't directly implicate Danny, but it implies that he could have been there on the beach that morning, that maybe he was an informant of Jardine's, that maybe he had flipped on his friends and then the relationship went south.

Or, that maybe Jardine had found him with the heroin and Danny killed him.

It doesn't come out and say it, it just asks the questions.

Then it turns on Diane. Recounts her history with drugs and alcohol, and then—

So, is Diane Carson, whose own brother murdered her husband, now dating a cop killer?

Phones start ringing like alarm bells.

• • •

MADELEINE WAITS FOR Evan Penner to get on the phone.

She doesn't have to wait long and she gets right to it. "Who is doing this to my son and why?"

"What do you mean?"

"Someone is planting false stories about Danny and I want it stopped," Madeleine says.

"We're trying to find the leak."

"Nonsense," she says. "You know who the source is—this Moneta person."

"I have to say, Madeleine, that Danny hasn't helped by putting himself in the spotlight. He's made himself a target."

"Shut this down," Madeleine says. "Ms. Moneta isn't the only one who has stories to tell."

The threat is very real, Penner knows.

Madeleine McKay could tell a lot of stories. The sexual peccadilloes of public figures being perhaps the least of them. She could also talk about under-the-counter political contributions and insider trading.

She could destroy careers, even put people behind bars.

"We will shut her down," Penner says. "But Madeleine, I don't know how we get this toothpaste back in the tube."

Madeleine doesn't, either.

She hangs up knowing that it's out there, that Danny is exposed and vulnerable.

And Evan is right, the first step is to get him out of the spotlight.

Get him out of Hollywood.

Away from Diane Carson.

PASCO FERRI GETS phone calls, too.

All about Danny Ryan.

Just two days ago, some L.A. mook named Angelo Petrelli got on the

phone and whined about Danny moving in on his territory and then re-
fusing to show respect.

Pasco was annoyed because: one, he was trying to enjoy his retirement; two, he didn't even know this Petrelli guy, and the Los Angeles
family barely qualifies as a family, more like the West Coast wing of Chicago; and three, Danny Ryan was supposed to be getting out of this thing.

He only took the call because of Chicago, and Petrelli was all over
him, wanting him to use his influence to make Danny either pay up or
ship out. Pasco said that he knew Ryan a little back in the day, didn't even
have his phone number, but he promised to look into it and do what he
could.

Pasco intended to do absolutely nothing.

To hell with this *paisan*, he thought. If he has a problem with Ryan,
it's his problem, not mine. Let him handle his own business.

Except this morning he gets calls from bosses in Chicago, New York,
Detroit, and Kansas City all asking him what the fuck is up with this Ryan
guy and why are they reading about him in the newspapers.

Because nobody needs this shit.

All the families are getting pounded by RICO, guys are flipping like
pancakes, freaking bosses are going to jail, and the last thing anyone needs
is headlines about dope and murder.

Pasco knows only too well that bodies in New England are best left
buried, and now because Danny is dipping his dick into some Hollywood
gash, people are out there with shovels digging up the past.

He remembers back in the sixties, was it, when Momo Giancana was
banging one of the McGuire sisters and getting in the papers and the
Chicago Outfit didn't like it and threw him out of the corner office.

Then Momo got mixed up with the Kennedys, the CIA, the Cubans,
God only knows what. There's some people who even say that he was involved in the JFK assassination.

He was in the spotlight.

Eventually, the Outfit had to put a bullet in his head.

The poor son of a bitch was frying up some *sausiche* or something when they did him.

And now Danny.

Hell, wiseguys have been fucking actresses since before there were even movies—it's expected—but you keep it under wraps.

This thing, you can have a damn fine life if you're smart.

Danny's being stupid.

And most of the calls about him are pretty much the same thing—they want Danny clipped. They don't say it—nobody's saying anything over the phone these days—but that's what they want.

But it isn't, Pasco thinks.

If they thought it through, they'd realize that the last thing in the world they want is headlines about Danny Ryan's body being found face-down in the Los Angeles River.

The papers would love that.

No, what they want—what everyone wants—is for Danny to knock this shit off, go away and let this thing die down.

Danny will listen to sense.

And if he doesn't . . .

REGGIE MONETA DOESN'T even bother to plead innocent.

Nor does she yield to the not-so-subtle pressure that Evan Penner puts on her during a tête-à-tête lunch in Georgetown, alluding to her future in the Bureau or in the private sector.

"If you want to open up cans of worms," she tells Penner, "we'll open all of them. We'll open Central American cans, we'll open Operation Aetna cans, we'll even open Domingo Abbarca cans. So if you want all those worms squirming around Washington, Mr. Penner, issue me more veiled threats."

"These leaks need to stop," Penner says.

"They have," Moneta says.

She's satisfied. There's nothing left to tell. The wine has been poured and they can't get it back in the bottle.

"As far as I'm concerned," Moneta says, "Danny Ryan is a drug trafficker and a murderer and not enough bad things can happen to him. And, by the way, you can tell that to his mother. Yes, we know all about Madeleine McKay, and there are certain investigations on which we can bring her in as a witness, if you'd like us to do that."

Speaking of veiled threats.

Or unveiled ones.

She knows that what she's saying isn't going to get Danny Ryan indicted.

It's going to get him killed.

ANGELO PETRELLI WASN'T happy with his phone call to Pasco Ferri.

He knows when he's being blown off, and that old wop breezed him like foam off a beer.

Angelo thinks about taking this up with Chicago, except he knows it's not a good look. They already think he's weak, and if he has to go to them with every little thing, it will only make him look weaker.

Besides, he thinks, this Ryan cocksucker is in a jam now, what with his face all over the papers and being linked to a cop killing. He's become a problem, and the bosses of the big families might be kindly disposed if I handle a problem for them.

Make it go away.

What Angelo really wants is a piece of the move back into Vegas, which Chicago is spearheading. Impressing them by handling this Ryan business might be his invite to the party.

"Give it to someone," he tells Faella.

"Who?"

Angelo glares at him over his smoothie. "Do I want to know?"

Somebody good.

EVEN DANNY'S OWN crew isn't happy with him.

Kevin Coombs is pissed first because it's Danny boffing Carson instead of him, and then he's even more pissed when Kim, now that he got Amber a part in the movie, dumps him.

"It's nothing personal," she tells Kevin after what turns out to be a farewell fuck. "We're moving to New York."

"New York?"

"Amber's been offered a repeating role in a television series," Kim says. "It shoots there. We feel it's a good move for her. She wants to be a real actress, not just this superficial L.A. stuff. The shooting schedule will allow her to do Off Broadway."

The main thing is that Kevin's bored.

Sure, the money from the drug heist is good, life around the set has been sweet, but Kevin wants to get active again, he wants to do work, and Danny isn't allowing any of that because he wants them off the radar.

So it really fries Kevin's balls that Danny has become a huge blip on everyone's screen while he's telling his people to lie low.

"It's . . . what's the word?" he asks Sean.

"Hypocrisy," Sean says. "Hypocritical."

Sean, he's not happy with Danny for pretty much the same reasons, but his major concern is maybe getting indicted for stuff he did back in Rhode Island, and also that Ana is all over his ass about Danny not treating Diane right.

"He's going to wreck her career," Ana said the other night.

He's going to wreck everyone's career, Sean thinks now, sitting at Burger King with Kevin. He's going to get us all freakin' whacked if the big families decide to shut his shit down.

Bernie Hughes is just worried.

That's what Bernie does, he worries, but this time he really has something to worry about. Danny's gone off the deep end and he could take them all down with him. But mostly he's worried for Danny, because Danny is Marty's son.

It's Jimmy Mac who confronts Danny. He's bringing Angie and the kids out here. He found a nice house in suburban San Diego, in a good school district with nice parks.

Now he's not so sure.

"Me and the guys have been talking," he says one day at a fish-and-chips place Danny found in Burbank that's passable.

"You and the guys?" Danny asks. "What about?"

"You know."

"Yeah, I think I do," Danny says. "But why don't you spell it out for me."

"Okay," Jimmy says, "we think maybe it's time to move on."

"From . . ."

"All this," Jimmy says. "This Hollywood stuff."

"Hey, you want to go, go."

"You have to go, too," Jimmy says. He pours more vinegar on his fries and contemplates them.

"Why is that?"

Jimmy's had it. "Because you're the problem, Danny. This thing with Diane, you have us all over the papers, even TV. It has to stop. You're going to get us all killed. You're supposed to be the boss of this family, and you're letting us down."

Fuck you, Danny thinks. I put the money in your pockets, the food in your mouths. I'm the boss here, not you, not "the guys." I say when and where we go, what we do. You don't like it, there's no lock on the door.

Then he thinks better of it.

Jimmy's your oldest friend, he's always had your back.

You owe him. Honesty, anyway.

So he says, "I love her."

"You know the last guy I heard say that?"

Yeah, Danny thinks.

Liam.

Fucking Liam.

I'm him now.

"Ask me anything," Danny says. "Ask me for money, ask me to do a job, but don't ask me that."

"What did you tell Liam," Jimmy says, "about Pam?"

"I told him to leave her."

Jimmy shrugs.

There you go.

DANNY'S PHONE RINGS. "Yeah."

"Danny Ryan," the guy says, "you don't know me, but our mutual friend in Pompano Beach asked me to come talk with you."

Pasco, Danny thinks. "Okay."

"Is there a time and place we could meet?" the guy asks.

"Do you know L.A.?"

"I know the airport," he says. "I just got in."

"Santa Monica Pier," Danny says. "Two o'clock. How will I know you?"

"I'll know you."

HE DOES.

Danny has just stepped onto the pier when a short, slim guy, maybe in his early fifties, in a trim charcoal-gray linen suit walks right up to him. "Thank you for coming, Danny. I'm Johnny Marks."

They walk past the big Ferris wheel out onto the pier.

"What's this about?" Danny asks.

"Our friend wants you to know he thinks you're doing the wrong thing here," Marks says. "He thinks it's time for you to move on."

"I don't."

"Let me put it another way," Marks says. "You know speed limit signs?"

"Yeah." What the hell, Danny thinks.

"We think of them more as suggestions, don't we," Mark says. "This isn't a speed limit sign, this is a stop sign. And at a stop sign, you stop."

"Please tell Pasco, with all love and respect," Danny says, "that I appreciate his concern, but this is none of his business."

"It is, though," Marks says. "He went to bat with the big families for you. Don't put him in a difficult spot."

"I have business here."

"The film business," Marks says. "It's not for you. Look, you know Pasco, he wouldn't reach out with empty hands. Friends of ours are moving back into Vegas. I know you have strong connections there. Pasco's offering you a piece of that."

"I don't want it."

"You have a son," Marks says. "You need to think about Ian, his future. This Vegas thing, you're talking generational wealth."

"I'm going legit."

"Hollywood?" Marks asks. "Please. You think wiseguys are crooks? When we skim, we have limits—these movie *ladri* eat with both hands. You want to be with strangers instead of people who love you?"

Yeah, Danny thinks, the Italians love me.

"This was a friendly conversation," Marks says. "If you see me again, it won't be a conversation. And if you see me again, you *won't* see me. Don't take too long on this. Have a good day."

Danny watches him walk down the pier.

Sean will pick him up there, follow him to wherever he's going.

So, Danny thinks, I'm in a freakin' jam.

Three people have threatened to kill me—Petrelli, Harris, and now Marks, in that order of danger.

Petrelli will be your basic mob hit, he'll farm it out to an underling, probably Faella, who'll go out and get another wiseguy to do it.

Standard stuff.

Harris is a different thing. Government, CIA shit. They have their own killers, military types, but they're not above working with OC.

Then there's Marks, who speaks for Pasco, who speaks for the big bosses. If they want me dead, I'm dead. Even if I take out Marks, they'll send someone else, then someone else, and it won't ever stop.

But you can stop it, he thinks as he walks to his car.

You can stop it today.

Leave Diane.

Leave L.A.

Which is what you should do. Save yourself, save your guys, because even if you tell Jimmy Mac and Ned and the rest to walk away, they won't do it. They'll go down with you because they're New England guys and that's what they do.

So you'll get them killed, too.

Just like Liam got guys killed over a woman.

And you hated him for it.

So end this now.

Then he thinks, No, fuck that.

I love her.

We belong together.

• • •

DANNY MAKES THE car following him before they hit the PCH. Doesn't care, they know where he lives anyway, and besides, Jimmy Mac is just a few cars behind the guy, with Kevin riding shotgun.

These guys, Danny thinks. Do they think they're playing with children? Did they think I was going to show up without cover?

He decides to take the guy for a drive, all the way through Malibu Canyon, then back on the 101 to the Oakwood.

The guy drives past him, like he's looking for a place to park.

Danny goes straight to the pool, where he knows he'll find Ian with Holly. He pays her, then plays with Ian in the pool for an hour or so.

Pulling Ian across the water, Danny looks across to a man-made berm with a fence and a bunch of trees and sees a guy trimming bushes. A white guy, which would be the first guy he's seen in California doing yard work who wasn't Mexican.

He isn't trimming bushes, Danny thinks.

He's lining up his shot, doing his research.

They go upstairs and Danny makes fish sticks and instant mashed potatoes, which Ian loves, the little mick.

He gets a call from Sean. "Marks left you and went and met someone else. You wanna guess who?"

"Why don't you just tell me, Sean?"

"Harris."

Danny takes that in.

It makes sense that Pasco and Harris would find each other, work together on this, he thinks. They have a common interest—me. And if Harris is going to have me whacked, he has to make it look like he wasn't involved or he has to deal with Madeleine. If it's a mob hit, he doesn't.

And Pasco, he works with the government, he gets protection on it. And for God knows what else.

It's good news and bad news. Bad because they're a powerful combination with limitless resources, good because it reduces the threats he has to deal with from three down to two.

"Okay," Danny says. "Where did he go?"

"The Biltmore," Sean says. "Downtown."

"Stay on him."

"You got it."

Danny calls Jimmy.

"The guy who was tailing you checked into a Best Western on Santa Monica," Jimmy says. "Kevin has eyes on it. The car's a rental."

"So he flew in."

"My guess."

"You think he's with Petrelli or this guy Marks I met with?" Danny asks.

"Hard to say. We got photos, though."

"Run them through Bernie," Danny says. "See if any of our connections can ID him."

"He's already on it."

If Danny has to bet—and he does—he goes with Petrelli. Marks wouldn't have had the conversation and then instantly put a tail on him.

Jimmy says, "If you want, me and Kevin can just go take care of it."

"No," Danny says. "I want you to come over here, pick Ian up, drive him to Madeleine's."

He knows that Pasco's people wouldn't hurt Ian, and he doubts that Petrelli's would, either. The Italians aren't Domingo Abbarca, they don't hurt families. But you never know—a missed shot, a ricochet.

Danny's not taking the chance.

He hangs up and says, "Ian, how would you like to go see Grandma?"

Ian's face lights up. "Gramma!"

"Uncle Jimmy's going to drive you," Danny says. He sees the boy frown, tears well up. "Don't worry, I'll be there in a couple of days."

"Two sleeps?"

"Two sleeps," Danny says.

He packs a few of Ian's clothes and some toys and then reads him a story until Jimmy gets there.

A few minutes later, Bernie calls. "Your man's name is Ken Clark, out of Phoenix. He has connections to the L.A. family, but all the major players use him. Army sniper, Vietnam; he's good, Danny."

"Okay, thanks."

HALF AN HOUR later, Danny sits with Harris in the agent's car in the Oakwood parking lot.

"What's so urgent, Danny?" Harris asks.

"Why don't *you* tell *me*?"

"What do you mean?"

"You have something you want to tell me?" Danny asks.

"These latest stories," Harris says, "linking you to Jardine. They're bad, Danny, what do you want me to tell you?"

How about the truth? Danny thinks. How about that you and the big families are in bed together and the pillow talk is about taking me out? How about that? But he doesn't tell Harris what he knows. Let him think I'm living in blissful ignorance.

"You ever see *On the Waterfront*?" Harris asks.

"I dunno. Maybe. Why?"

"There's this famous scene," Harris says. "Brando and Rod Steiger are in a car, and Steiger says to Brando, 'Take the money, kid, before we get to . . .' And Brando asks, 'Before we get to where? Before we get to where?' Because he knows that when they get there, Steiger, his own brother, is going to have him killed."

"So?"

"So take the money, kid, before we get there."

Danny gets out of the car.

KEN CLARK GOES out to get some chicken.

Popeyes.

Extra spicy.

Which is a mistake, because when he gets back to his room, Kevin Coombs hits him on the back of the head with a sap, and when Clark wakes up on the floor, Danny Ryan is sitting in a chair looking down at him.

Danny asks, "Who hired you, Ken?"

"They'd kill me."

"Least of your worries right now," Kevin says.

Then Danny gives him a *shut up* look and Kevin shuts up and goes back to eating Clark's chicken. Ned Egan doesn't say anything, but he rarely does. He just holds his .38 on Clark's head.

"It's simple," Danny says. "Tell us who hired you or we'll kill you."

"You'll kill me anyway."

"No," Danny says.

"How do I know?"

"You don't," Danny says. "But if you tell us, you have a chance of living. If you don't, you don't. Do the math."

"Ronnie Faella."

"Okay," Danny says. "Get up. Go in the bathroom."

"No, you said—"

"Do what I say."

Kevin lifts Clark off the floor and half drags him to the bathroom. The guy still doesn't have his legs under him.

Danny turns the volume on the television up and then rummages through Clark's suitcase. "Hey, Ken, you have any clean socks? Never mind, here we go."

Clark has a pair of white gym socks, neatly rolled together. Danny walks into the bathroom. "Open your mouth."

"Come on, please. I told you what—"

Danny jams the socks into Clark's mouth.

"You want me to do him?" Kevin asks.

"Ken, here's the thing," Danny says. "If I let you live, you might come after me again."

Clark shakes his head, tries to say, "No."

"I can't take that chance," Danny says. "Stick your hand in the door."

Clark shakes his head again.

"It's either that or a bullet in the head," Danny says.

Clark lays his hand against the doorjamb.

Danny kicks the door shut.

Clark screams under the socks. His fingers are shattered. Two of the bones poke through the skin. He drops to his knees, holds his wrist and whimpers.

"The other one," Danny says.

Kevin grabs Clark's other wrist and holds his hand against the doorjamb. Danny kicks it again. It'll be a long time before Clark aims a gun.

Danny waits until the screams stop and then takes the socks out of Clark's mouth. "These guys will drop you off in front of the E-room. Tell Faella and Petrelli that if I didn't want peace, you'd be dead and so would they."

He takes Clark's car keys and looks inside, opens the trunk.

No rifle.

So one down.

Still one to go.

•　　•　　•

DANNY GOES TO the beach house. Diane walks into his arms. "I'm sorry."

"Me too."

"The whole world wants us to split up," she said.

"Fuck the world," he said. "I'm more thinking about going the other way with it."

"What other way?"

"After you finish the movie," he said, "we go to Vegas, one of those wedding chapels . . ."

"Is that a proposal?"

"I don't have a ring on me," Danny said. "But I'll get one. Do this right."

LATER. LYING IN bed, facing each other side by side, holding each other tight, her face in his chest, he feels every inch of her skin against him.

Then she goes tight.

Stiff.

Says softly, "You know my brother, Jarrod, killed my first husband."

"I know."

"Do you know why?"

"Your brother was on drugs or something," Danny said.

"No," she says, "that wasn't why."

For the next half hour, Danny listens to her tell him, her voice like a slow-running stream, soft but steady, flowing.

He hears her say that they were always close, Diane and Jarrod, always a team, a unit allied against the fighting and yelling that went on downstairs, their detached father, hypercritical mother. They used to lie in bed at night and tell each other stories, make each other laugh, but it started when she was about twelve, her brother sixteen, and as sort of a joke, her and Jarrod practicing kissing, getting ready for the boyfriends and girlfriends they were going to have, and it was funny and they giggled but it felt good to her and that's what you have to know, Danny, I have to have you know that I was never raped, that would be the easy lie, it felt good, it always did even when I knew it was wrong and he knew it was wrong and the first time he touched my breast it was thrilling, I was thrilled I was wet and when he touched me down there for the first time I came for the first time and I loved it and I loved him and the first time he went into me it was from behind so I could pretend it was someone else and he called me "sweetheart" but I didn't pretend, I knew who it was I knew it was him and I whispered his name and it went on for years, it went on for years not all the time not every night and sometimes we would stop, for months sometimes but never longer than that because we loved each other and even if we had other people sometimes we loved each other and always came back to our bed and if you don't want to touch me anymore, Danny, I understand if you don't want me anymore I understand I do it's disgusting it's horrible it's sick what we did but I don't want to lie because I've stopped lying to myself I lied myself into booze and pills I liked it I let it happen because I liked it and I loved him.

Danny lies perfectly still, afraid that if he moves she'll fall apart, and he listens as she tells him that she left home, she left home and got married and when she got married she told Jarrod it had to stop and he said of course it did, of course, but he was angry he was hurt she never realized never knew how sick he was and when the family got together he would laugh and make ugly jokes and when he got her alone he'd tell her that he missed her that he missed it that Scott never had to know nobody ever had to know but she said that she wouldn't, she couldn't anymore and he got angrier and angrier and one night she came home and Scott was lying on the floor dead there was blood everywhere and Jarrod was sitting in the easy chair with the knife in his hand and he looked up at her and said, *This is your fault, sweetheart.*

At the sentencing hearing Jarrod made up a story that he asked Scott for a loan and he wouldn't lend him the money and he lost his temper and just went berserk but from the stand he would look at Diane as if they had a funny secret and Danny, I understand if you don't want me anymore I understand.

Her tears are wet against his skin, her body stiff and tight, and as they lie there pressed together they each understand that they are two damaged people who found each other.

"It's all going to come out now," she says.

"What do you mean?"

"He phoned the other day."

Hello, sweetheart. I've been reading about you. You're having a pretty great life, aren't you? You found another guy. While I'm here in this hole. In this hell. Well, it's going to stop, sweetheart. I'm going to tell the world about us. I'm going to tell them how you fucked me, year after year. Your own brother. Then we'll see what kind of life you have. Bye, sweetheart.

Danny holds her tighter.

SEVENTEEN

DANNY GETS UP EARLY. WITH the sunrise just a promise.

Goes and sits out on the deck.

Couldn't sleep because he doesn't know how to help her.

Danny doesn't know anyone in El Dorado.

If Jarrod were in the Rhode Island ACI, any joint in New England—even a federal lockup somewhere, it would be one phone call, maybe two, and the problem would be solved.

But El Dorado is in Kansas, a state facility, and Danny doesn't know anyone there.

Diane comes out and says, "You're still here. I thought you'd run away during the night."

"I'm not going anywhere," he says. "I mean, I am, I need to get back to Ian, but on the larger scale of things . . . We all have pasts, Di, we've all done things we're not proud of."

"Danny, when this comes out," she says, "when Jarrod—"

"We'll jump off that bridge when we get to it," he says. "It hasn't happened yet. He might have just been jerking your chain."

Danny says this but doesn't believe it. If her brother just wanted to torture her, he'd have done it already, he'd have kept doing it over the years.

I have to figure out how to get to him, Danny thinks.

Diane goes in to get dressed. A car will come and take her to the studio. They kiss goodbye, and Danny goes for a walk on the beach.

He doesn't know what to do.

The people who I could ordinarily reach out to, he thinks, aren't in the mood to do me any favors and I have no leverage, nothing to trade.

Yes you do, he thinks.

You have everything to trade.

CHRIS THINKS PSYCHICS are bullshit.

But he doesn't want to piss Laura off, so he plays along when she brings over one of her friends from the coven for a "reading."

"Gwendolyn is *won*derful," Laura said. "She predicted that I'd meet you."

Yeah, Chris thought, she probably said that you'd meet a man, which, given your sexual history, was a high-probability bet. Chris would take that number and give points.

Anyway, now he sits across the kitchen table from Gwendolyn, who has wilder hair than Laura and is dressed like a drag queen who hit a San Francisco Goodwill store around 1969.

"You're an exile," she says. "A refugee."

Yeah, Chris thinks, my car has Arizona plates and I'm living in a one-horse town in Nebraska, so I'm not impressed.

"I keep seeing the letter *P*," Gwendolyn says. "Does that mean anything to you?"

"Pneumonia?" Chris says. "Psychology?"

But Laura shoots him a look, so he knocks it off.

"Yeah, maybe," Chris says.

"Can you see into his future?" Laura asks.

Gwendolyn goes into what Chris guesses is meant to be a trance, and then says, "I can tell you that you will be going home. I'm seeing some kind of a throne there . . . maybe an office . . ."

Now maybe Laura doesn't think Gwendolyn is so wonderful. "When? When will he be going home?"

"I can't tell," Gwendolyn says. Then she remembers which side her bread is buttered on and adds, "Not soon."

But now Chris thinks maybe this psychic stuff isn't such bullshit after all. The *P* could be for Providence. And him taking a throne? An office? Yeah, not while Vinnie Calfo is alive and out of the joint, but who knows what happens?

"There are people from the other side who want to contact you," Laura says.

"The other side?" Chris asks.

"The deceased," Laura whispers.

Great, Chris thinks. There's more than a few dead people who, if they can talk, he hopes they lie.

"Your mother wants you to know that she's well," Gwendolyn says. "But missing you killed her."

Of course the old bag would want to stick the knife in and twist it, Chris thinks. Even from the damn grave . . .

"I'm seeing another *P*," Gwendolyn says. "Maybe Paul? Or Peter?"

"Probably Peter," Chris says, all in now.

"He wants to tell you that his wife . . . Oh, this is horrible."

"What?" Chris asks.

"Well, that his wife had him murdered," Gwendolyn says. "Does that make any sense to you?"

It does if you know Celia, Chris thinks. But how does this babe know?

"No."

"I'm seeing a Sally," Gwendolyn says. "But it's a man."

"Sal," Chris says.

Sal Antonucci. A Moretti family captain and a good friend. Fucking Liam Murphy shot him when he was coming out of some fag's apartment.

Who knew Sal was a pipe fitter?

"He says to thank you for taking care of things."

Chris and Frankie had stuffed the fag into a car trunk and dumped it in a pond. "Tell him he's welcome."

"He's worried about his children," Gwendolyn says.

"Tell him they're fine," Chris says.

He has no idea how the kids are, but if Sal doesn't know, either, what's the harm in making him feel good?

After Gwendolyn leaves, Laura is *pissed*.

"You're going to leave me," she says.

"I'm not."

"Gwendolyn said—"

"What does the *chiacchierona* know?"

But over and over and over again: *You're going to leave me, You're going to leave me, You're going to leave me*, with the tears and the sniffling. And over and over and over again, Chris says, *I'm not gonna leave, I'm not gonna leave, I'm not gonna leave*, even though now he's kind of thinking about it, what with what Gwen said about the throne and that.

In bed, Chris reaches out for Laura, but she moves away. He goes to touch her breast, she rolls over; goes to touch her hand, she moves it; tries to kiss her, she turns her head away.

The first time since he got here that she doesn't want to fuck like a mink.

Psychics are bullshit, Chris thinks.

Or maybe not.

•   •   •

DANNY LEAVES HIS car with the valet at the Biltmore Hotel on Fifth and Grand.

The Biltmore is old Los Angeles, Raymond Chandler Los Angeles. Movie stars used to dance in the ballroom, they used to hold the Oscars there; Elizabeth Short, aka "the Black Dahlia," was last seen in its lobby.

It's just the kind of place an old-school guy like Johnny Marks would stay.

Danny walks through the lobby to the bank of elevators and rides to the eighth floor. Knocks on the door of room 808.

He knows that Marks is looking at him through the peephole.

The door opens the width of the chain lock.

"I just want to talk," Danny says.

Marks lets him in. He sits down in the desk chair and gestures Danny toward the sofa.

"I'll stand," Danny says. "I won't be long."

"Suit yourself." Marks raises an eyebrow, asking *What do you want to say?*

"I'll leave L.A.," Danny says. "I won't pursue the movie business."

"What about the woman?"

"I'm leaving her, too."

"These are good decisions," Marks says.

People are going to be happy. Relieved.

"I WANT ONE thing in return," Danny says. "It's nonnegotiable."

JARROD GROSKOPF GOES out to the basketball court where he usually shoots around with guys from the Aryan Brotherhood.

They're out there, six of them, playing a pickup game.

Jarrod strips off his sweatshirt to join in, nods a hello, holds his hands up for the ball.

Then he notices something odd.

The guards leave.

The two of them just turn their backs and walk away.

Jarrod drops the ball. Starts to run, but it's too late.

The boys mob him, surround him, stab with shanks fashioned from razor blades, metal from the tool shop, melted-down toothbrush handles sharpened to hard points.

By the time the guards start to run back, yelling into their radios, Jarrod has already bled out.

"DID YOU DO this?" Diane asks.

"No," Danny says.

They're standing on the deck of her beach house.

She's crying.

"Just tell me the truth," Diane says. "Please, Danny. Did you have anything to do with my brother's murder?"

Danny looks her straight in the eye. "No."

"So it was just a coincidence."

"I guess so."

She turns away from him. "I don't know what to think anymore. I don't know what to think about you anymore."

"You don't have to think anything," Danny says.

She turns back to him. "What do you mean?"

Then she takes a long look at him and says, "You're leaving me, aren't you? I can see it on your face. I've seen that face before."

"We're done," Danny says.

The look of hurt in her eyes is brutal.

But there can't be anything between us now, Danny thinks. She knows I had someone slaughtered for her. There's blood in our bed. And they're all right—I'm wrecking her career. There's no point in saving her from her brother if I destroy her myself.

Be honest, he tells himself. This love of ours is destroying you, too. They'll kill you, they'll kill your crew, and you owe your guys more than that. And you owe your son more than leaving him without a father.

Her face twists in pain. "It's because of what I told you, isn't it? About my brother and me."

It isn't, Danny thinks.

It isn't that at all.

You could tell her, tell her you made a deal to save her, but that would kill her, too. She'd still love you, but she'd die inside.

Better that she hate you.

So he says nothing.

Diane goes into a rage. "So, go! Get out! Get out of here! I loved you, you son of a fucking bitch! I loved you!"

Danny doesn't say anything.

She screams, "Get out! Go! I never want to see you again. I hope you die! Do you hear me?! I hope you *die*!"

She walks back into the house.

The slider shudders as it slams shut.

DANNY GIVES THE orders.

We're pulling out of L.A.

"Thank freakin' God," Kevin says.

He's had it with Hollywood. The guys are all half fags and the women watch themselves fuck to see how they look.

He's ready for something new.

"Where are we going?" he asks when Jimmy gives him the word.

Jimmy says, "Danny wants to go to Marty's grave down in San Diego and give him a proper send-off."

Kevin approves. "The boss is getting back to himself. The pussy poison must be seeping out."

"Don't let him hear you say that," Jimmy says. "Don't let him even hear you think it, son."

Sean, he's ready to go, too. Now that Danny's done with her boss, Ana's done with Sean; she can't see how they can stay together. It's all right with Sean; it was good, but it was getting old and he's looking for something new.

A blowout in Dago sounds good.

Bernie's happy, looking forward to getting back to nice, quiet Rancho Bernardo, with its clean chain restaurants and sidewalks.

Jimmy's freakin' ecstatic.

The family's going to fly out to San Diego and then stay. He'll find a nice place in the suburbs.

Thank God that Danny has come to his senses.

EIGHTEEN

SOMEONE, PROBABLY IT WAS PAULIE, once said that Frank Vecchio wasn't the sharpest spoon in the drawer.

Any fucking idiot (well, apparently not *any* fucking idiot) who had been through what Frankie had been through would put as many miles between himself and the Abbarca organization as possible. He'd get out of San Diego—Popeye's backyard—as soon as he had bus fare. He'd go to Seattle, Duluth, Ulan Bator, anywhere where he'd be less likely to be found.

Especially when he has to know that Abbarca's people in the greater San Diego–Tijuana metropolitan area have to be looking for the one outsider they know was at the stash house before the *tombe*, and who wasn't there after.

The only thing that Frankie has going for him, through no virtue of his own, is that Neto Valdez isn't going to make him a high-profile target because it was Neto who was responsible for Frankie's presence at the stash house in the first place, and he doesn't particularly want that known.

So Neto is keeping his search for Frankie personal and quiet.

But he's looking for him.

He didn't expect him to be so close.

Frankie was adrift in California with no money and no way of making any. Not any real money, anyway. Sure, he picked up some chump change getting a few odd jobs here and there. The problem is that chump change made him feel like a chump.

That's the thing about jobs—they're work.

And wiseguys don't become wiseguys to work.

That is not their way of being in the world.

Frankie tried, he did.

He got a J-O-B at the Golden Arches and a room at the Golden Lion, an SRO in downtown San Diego, and his gratitude at just being alive lasted for more than a month. His streak of luck continued when the day manager of the hotel had a stroke, thereby creating a job vacancy that Frankie was happy to fill. He was even happier to learn that he could actually sell some of the residents their mail, especially the ones who didn't speak such good English.

But all good things come to an end, and Frankie's state of grace faded as the boredom ensued and the unreasonable expectation that he put in regular, scheduled hours behind the desk became onerous.

Back in Providence, Frankie had shown up when he wanted to show up. And what he mostly did was hang around the vending machine office shooting the shit with Peter and Paulie and otherwise sticking his beak into everyone's business. He had his card games, his loan-sharking, his protection racket. He had his *gumars* and the occasional stripper blow job that was comped.

He was happy.

Now he spends his days putting up with winos, psychos, immigrants, and other undesirables; there aren't enough antibiotics in the world to let him fuck any of the crack whores he charges a commission to use the vacant rooms; and he doesn't have the escarole to take a classy woman out on a classy date, even if he could meet a classy woman in this shit dump, which he can't. He's reduced to bringing a roll of quarters into one of the porn shops in the Gaslamp and feeding them into a slot with one hand while jerking off with the other in a booth watching some grainy video.

Talk about feeling like a chump.

Frankie's whole world smells like vomit, piss, come, and Lysol.

And even if he had the scratch to get a ticket back to Rhode Island, he can't go because the word is that he's gone into the Witness Protection Program, which doesn't actually function very well in Providence—which has more of a Protect Yourself against a Witness Program—and anyway, his fed protector got himself croaked.

Fucking Danny Ryan ruined everything.

And then Chris, that two-faced motherfucking cocksucker, left him high and dry with the Mexicans. Went away and never came back, and Frankie hopes the redheaded piece of shit is dead and in a ditch somewhere with crows pecking at his liver for what he did.

There is no fucking friendship in this world, no loyalty.

So he does something desperate.

Desperate and dumb.

He goes looking for Neto.

This is how Frankie thinks, this is how his wiseguy mind works—he figures he has something that Neto wants, something of value that Neto is willing to pay real money for.

Frankie has information, and this has always been his real bread and butter.

But any fucking idiot (well, apparently not *any* fucking idiot) knows that when a miracle comes from nowhere and pulls you out of a bad situation, you stay out. When people who should by all rights have killed you let you live, you thank God and leave those people alone.

Yeah, not Frankie.

Chalk it up to desperation.

Or to being fucking stupid.

What Frankie does is he walks over to East Village to a corner where they're clearly slinging H and asks the Mexican kid on the corner if he knows Neto Valdez.

The kid is too smart to answer that.

"Whatever," Frankie says. "Tell him that Frankie V wants to talk to him."

And then Frankie actually says that he's living at the Golden Lion Hotel.

Spoon. Drawer.

TWO NIGHTS LATER. Frankie is hanging from a meat hook in a warehouse in Chula Vista.

"Who was it?" Neto asks him. "Who robbed the stash house? Was it Chris?"

Frankie has balls, you have to give him that.

More balls than brains.

He says, "A hundred grand and I'll tell you."

"Frankie, you're going to die," Neto says. "But you have a choice. You can die slowly and in great pain, or you can die quickly. Up to you, I don't care. But you are going to tell me who robbed the safe house and you are going to tell me the truth, because I'll know. Now, what's it going to be?"

It's going to be Danny Ryan.

"Who?" Neto asks.

Neto doesn't read the tabloids or watch a lot of television.

But within days the word is out among the whole drug world.

BOLO for Danny Ryan.

DIANE BUILDS A fire on the beach.

Ana helps her gather some wood and they construct a little pyre. Then Diane soaks it with starter fluid, tosses a match, and it goes up in satisfying flames.

The fire crackles.

Ashes spiral up into the night sky.

Then Ana helps her gather the few things that Danny left behind—a toothbrush, a couple of shirts, a pair of swim trunks—and they feed them to the fire. The last items to go are photos of her and Danny, and Diane watches her own image twist, blacken, and then melt in the fire.

"Good," Diane says. "He's gone, we're gone."

"Are you okay?" Ana asks.

"I'm good," Diane says. "In fact, I'm great."

So Ana leaves.

Diane stands by the fire until it's out, then goes back into the house.

She thought she was good, she thought she was great, but then the emptiness hits her, this gaping hole in her heart, and the profound loneliness settles on her like the fog at night, heavy and chill, and she goes into the bedroom, digs around in the back of her closet until she finds the bottle of Smirnoff hidden there and before she can stop, before she can become fearful, she opens it, tilts it to her lips and drinks.

And knows it's not going to be enough, it's not enough, never enough, and as she drinks she rummages through clothes, through jackets, sweaters, jeans, until she finds the bottle of Valium tucked away and she puts one on her tongue and then washes it back with vodka and after that she loses track of how many she takes or how much she drinks but the cold fog dissipates, the harsh solitude softens, she lies down on the bed wanting only to sleep, to sleep and forget that she's alone, she's alone she will always be alone because she is a broken thing, a doll ravaged beyond repair and her hands get numb and her lips fuzzy and she does fall asleep and that's how Ana finds her the next morning, splayed out on her bed, still and lifeless.

PART THREE

What the Dead Souls Want

San Diego
April 1991

. . . what does it mean, this thronging toward the river?

What do the dead souls want?

Virgil
The Aeneid
Book VI

NINETEEN

I wish I was in Carrickfergus,
Only for nights in Ballygrant . . .

STANDING AT THE GRAVE SITE, Danny thinks about one of Marty's favorite old songs, one that he must have heard a thousand times over the years.

Rosecrans Cemetery is beautiful, set on a long ridge overlooking the Pacific, as if so many of the bodies buried there can look across the ocean and see where they died.

Harris fulfilled this promise, Danny thinks. He took care of my father's burial.

But the sea is wide,
And I can't swim over,
And neither have I the wings to fly . . .

Well, you always said you loved San Diego, Danny thinks, probably because you got drunk here on your way to and from the war. You always said you liked the sunshine. So here you are now, I hope you enjoy it.

> *I've spent my days in ceaseless roving,*
> *Soft is the grass and my bed is free,*
> *Oh, but to be back now in Carrickfergus,*
> *On that long winding road down to the sea . . .*

Danny knows his feelings are complicated, conflicted. For most of his growing up his dad was a neglectful, abusive drunk. When Danny grew up, Marty was just a bitter old man. It was only since Ian was born that Marty started to show a little heart, and he was more of a father in the last year or so of his life than in all the years before.

Still, it's those last months that Danny thinks of now.

He isn't going to cry for Marty; hell, Marty would just laugh at him for it, call him a pussy.

But he wants to cry.

Now he pours Bushmills on his father's grave.

Not the whole bottle, most of that he saves for himself. He's never been a heavy drinker, the Irish disease seems not to have been passed down from Marty, but now Danny goes at it hard.

Has been for two days, since he heard about Diane's death.

Wonders about his role in it. Classic Danny Ryan, he thinks, you tried to save her and ended up killing her.

The newspapers were careful to write that it was an overdose, not suicide, the tabloids that so recently crucified her discreetly removed the nails in their prose and printed elegies, the studio knows that the finished film it has in the can is worth vastly more than it was yesterday, and the public feels the sorrow and satisfaction of knowing that a woman who found love has been punished for it.

Now in Kilkenny it is reported
On marble stone there as black as ink
With gold and silver I would support her
But I'll sing no more now till I get a drink . . .

Danny takes another swig and then pours some more on the grave. "*Sláinte.*"

He hands Ned the bottle and Ned takes a swallow, then passes it along to Jimmy Mac, who in turn passes it on to Bernie.

Then Sean, then Kevin.

They all stand respectfully silent as Danny says his goodbyes. The bottle comes back to him and he takes another long drink.

Hears his father's voice—

Because I'm drunk today and I'm seldom sober,
A handsome rover from town to town,
Ah but I'm sick now, my days are numbered,
Come on, you young men, and lay me down.

Danny pours the rest of the bottle on the grave.

"Rest in peace, old man."

SUNLIGHT COMES THROUGH the window like an assault.

Hits Danny's eyes and he knows it must be afternoon for the sun to be striking a west-facing window of a hotel room on the beach. Danny clenches his eyes shut and then gives up and slides out of bed. The hangover picks up where the sun left off, stabbing him in the side of the head. He shuffles into the bathroom and splashes cold water on his face.

Marty's wake had gone on in the hotel suite.

Danny remembers few details of the night. There'd been an impromptu moonlight swim in the ocean, a footrace down the beach, at some point Sean and Kevin got into a fistfight that they wouldn't break up until Danny threatened to take on the winner.

Embarrassed, he recalls that there would have been a marksmanship contest with bottles set up on the balcony railing, but a relatively sober Bernie had put a stop to it before they started shooting.

Jesus, Danny, he thinks.

Get your shit together.

Guilty questions are a constant theme with small variations—

Why are you alive and she isn't? Why are you alive and she's dead?

Danny doesn't have any answers.

He's shaving when Angie MacNeese calls asking if she can come over for a talk.

They sit out on the deck.

"Jimmy would be wicked pissed if he knew I came to talk to you," Angie says.

"What's up, Angie?" They've known each other since high school.

"Jimmy doesn't want to go to Las Vegas," Angie says. "He wants to stay here."

"Why hasn't he told me that?" Danny asks.

"You know Jimmy," she says. "He's too loyal. He's a follower. First it was Pat, now it's you. But, Danny, he's been banging around for years now, pillar to post. It hasn't been good for us, for our family. We're tired of moving, we just want to settle down."

"You can't settle down in Vegas?" Danny asks. "One more move, Angie. We settle there, and we'll be totally legit."

"You were going to be legit here," she says. "How did that work out?"

She makes a point, Danny thinks.

"Jimmy wants to take his money," Angie says, "open a nice little business, live his life and raise his family."

"It's not like he's in the Mafia," Danny says, "not like we pricked his finger and he took an oath. He can leave when he wants."

"But he needs your blessing, Danny," Angie says. "He needs to hear you say it's all right, otherwise it won't be."

She's right again, Danny thinks.

But life without Jimmy?

They've been together since kindergarten.

"I'll talk to him," Danny says.

TURNS OUT BERNIE, he doesn't want to go, either.

"I like it here," Bernie says. "It has a Mediterranean climate. In the desert, if you want to walk, it has to be very early in the morning. No offense, Danny, but I'm an old man. I don't want to work anymore."

Danny doesn't take offense, but it's ironic. He made so many decisions based on protecting his crew and now it's falling apart on its own. He'll miss Bernie, his wizardry with numbers, his common sense, but the man has earned the right to dictate the terms of his retirement.

Ned's coming, of course. He's spent most of his life protecting Marty Ryan; he'll spend what's left of it protecting Marty Ryan's son.

It don't matter where.

The Altar Boys are in, too. Are you kidding? Vegas? Booze, gambling, hookers—it's a trifecta, an unholy trinity.

Danny warns them, though. They have to play it straight. He's going into legitimate business and he'll find roles for them, but the Altar Boys have to keep their noses clean.

Before he leaves, Danny goes to talk with Jimmy. They meet outside a doughnut shop in a little strip mall in the San Diego suburbs.

"What I wouldn't give for a Dunkin's," Jimmy says.

"You're a California guy now," Danny says. "Starbucks, In-N-Out Burger, you'll be eating sushi next time I see you."

"What do you mean, 'next time'?" Jimmy asks. His eyes narrow with suspicion, the freckles crinkle on his cheeks.

"You don't want to come to Vegas," Danny says. "You'd freakin' hate it there. Everything's phony, and you're the realest person I know."

"You don't want me with you?" He looks hurt.

"Of course I do," Danny says. In fact, he thinks, I don't know what I'm going to do without you. "But probably better we split up for a while. Safer. You do your thing here, let everything cool down."

Jimmy knows what Danny's really doing. They both do. He says, "You know if you ever need me—"

"I know that."

"—it's a forty-five-minute flight."

They leave it at that.

No goodbyes, no hugs.

Just "Take care of yourself, huh, Danny?"

"You too, Jimmy."

Then Danny gets in the car and drives.

TWENTY

PETER MORETTI JR. COMES HOME from the war. And now he's home in Providence. On leave, his deployment finished, but with two years left on his stint in the Corps.

A decorated marine.

He was there on the front line the night the Iraqi armor rolled into Kuwait. At first he was scared shitless when the tanks came at them, he wanted to piss himself, but he held his position and fired back.

He did his duty, did his job.

Semper Fi.

And now he's home in Providence.

First time he's been back since his father's funeral. It's been a tough time for Peter Jr.; he's buried his sister and his father and fought a war.

A Marine buddy, discharged a few months ago, picks him up at the airport. Tim Shea was right beside him when the Iraqis attacked, was still right beside him when they ran back.

Peter Jr.'s not ready to see his family yet. What's left of it, anyway. He knows he should go straight home to his mother, that's what he should do, but for some reason he doesn't want to. Maybe it's he doesn't want to see her with her new husband, Vinnie.

My stepfather, he thinks.

Jesus.

Tim gets it. His own stepdad was one of the reasons he went into the corps, he was so sick of the asshole's endless bullshit. "Where to, then? You want to get a drink, hit a strip club? Remind yourself what American pussy looks like?"

"I'd like to go to my dad's grave," Peter Jr. says. "Is that weird?"

"Not weird at all," Tim says.

They drive out toward the Gate of Heaven Cemetery over in East Providence.

"So what you been doing since you got out?" Peter Jr. asks.

"Little of this, little of that," Tim says. "Mostly that. Drinkin' and jerkin' off. If you think you're going to get a hero's welcome, don't hold your breath. Nobody gives a fuck."

"We didn't do it for that, though, did we?"

"So what did we do it for?"

"Freedom," Peter Jr. says.

"Okay." Tim laughs.

"What?"

"You're fuckin' funny, Pete," Tim says. "You never change."

They get to the cemetery.

"I'll wait in the car," Tim says.

Peter can see the headstone, more of a monument, from the parking lot. It's big, with angels and cherubs and shit carved into it, and the Virgin Mary engraved looking down at his dad.

Then Peter spots a woman laying flowers on the grave.

"Heather?" Peter asks.

She turns around. "Baby brother. When did you get home?"

"An hour ago."

"Look at you," Heather says. "I hardly recognized you. All grown up, a marine."

It's true. He's the epitome of the lean, clean-cut marine. Short-haired, shaved, hardened. A young man, not a teenager anymore.

They hug.

"Have you been home yet?" Heather asks.

"No," Peter Jr. says. "How is it?"

"It's weird," Heather says. "With Vinnie there. Playing the man of the house. I don't go around much."

"They *are* married, Heather."

"Too quick, if you ask me," she says.

"You want Mom to be lonely?" He doesn't know why he feels a need to defend her.

Heather snorts. "I wouldn't worry about Celia being lonely."

"What's *that* mean?" And when did she start referring to Mom as "Celia"?

"I don't want to fight with you, baby brother," she says. "How'd you get here?"

"A friend brought me," Peter Jr. says. "He picked me up at the airport."

"Why didn't you call me?" Heather asks. "I'm hurt."

"It's just strange, you know?" Peter Jr. says. "Being back here."

"Fuck this place," Heather says. "It's creepy and sad. Let's go get some drinks."

Peter Jr. and Tim meet her at the Eddy back downtown and start doing shots.

"Does Celia know you're home?" Heather asks.

"I told her I was coming," Peter Jr. says. "I didn't tell her exactly when."

"She's going to be wicked pissed when she finds out you didn't go straight there," Heather says.

"I'm not sure she cares that much," Peter Jr. says. "You know how many times she wrote me when I was overseas?"

He holds up one finger.

"Don't take it personally," Heather says. "She's half in the bag most of the time."

They order another round.

Somewhere around the fourth shot Tim says, "I'm going to leave the brother and sister to get reacquainted. You'll see this dumb jarhead gets home all right, Heather?"

The brother and sister talk about their memories of their dad, their grief, their sorrow, about Vinnie taking his place, both in his house and in the business. Peter notices that Heather seems more angry than sad, and she's holding it back. "What?"

"Nothing."

"What?"

She hesitates, thinking about whether she really wants to say this, and then leans across the table so her face is just inches from his. "They killed him, you know."

"I know someone did."

"No," Heather says. "Vinnie and our cunt of a mother. *They* killed him."

"Heather, Jesus." He can't fucking believe she said that.

"It's true," Heather says. "You don't believe me, ask your godfather."

"Uncle Pasco knows about this?"

"What *doesn't* Pasco know about it?" Heather says. "Listen, I don't know if Mom actually killed him. But she practically pushed Vinnie through the door. She even almost admitted it to me one night, when she was drunk."

Peter Jr.'s head is spinning, not just from the shots. "Jesus fuckin' Christ, Heather."

"Forget it," she says. "Forget I said anything."

"How can I forget it?!"

"Look, what are we going to do about it, anyway?" Heather asks. "Go home, baby brother, let her make a fuss over you, throw a party . . . I'm sure Vinnie will find you something, if that's what you want."

Peter doesn't go home. Instead, he calls Tim and asks for a ride to the shore.

To Pasco's house.

Pasco is surprised to see him but lets him right in. Sits him down at the kitchen counter and offers him a sambuca. "We're all proud of you, Peter Jr., what you did over there."

"Thank you."

"You looking to get set up now?" Pasco says. "I'm sure if you talk to Vinnie—"

"Did he kill my dad?"

"Peter—"

"You're my godfather," Peter Jr. says. "You have to tell me the truth."

"The truth," Pasco says, "is that I don't know. I've heard that, yes. But I can't prove it."

Peter Jr. takes that in. "I heard my mother was in on it."

Pasco sighs. "Your parents had a troubled marriage, you know that. It was complicated."

Which is Pasco saying it's true.

Peter Jr. shakes his head, holds back tears. "What would you do, Uncle Pasco? If you was me?"

Pasco gives him the simplest answer. "You're your father's son."

Peter Jr. is ripped in half. Whatever I do, I'm fucked, he thinks. If I kill Vinnie, I'm a murderer. If I don't, I'm a punk. *You're your father's son* —that was Pasco telling me to do it, giving me the green light. If I don't do it, I'm a piece of shit.

He says his goodbyes and goes out to the car, where Tim is waiting. "Where to now, boss?"

"My house," Peter Jr. says. Then he asks, "Are you heavy?"

"I got some hardware in the trunk," Tim says. "A twelve-gauge and a Glock nine. Why, you gonna knock over a liquor store or something?"

"No," Peter said. "You ever hear anything about my dad's murder?"

"It's Rhode Island," Tim says.

Meaning everyone hears everything.

"I have to take care of that," Peter Jr. says.

"You gotta do what you gotta do."

It's a short drive, maybe ten minutes to the mansion in Narragansett. Doesn't give Peter much time to think, it's like the car keeps driving in that direction, taking him with it.

"Just drop me off," Peter Jr. says when they get near the house.

"No," Tim says. "Go one, go all. Semper Fi. If he has guys there, I got your back."

"You sure?"

"Not my first rodeo, cowboy," Tim says. "You remember?"

Peter Jr. remembers. Lying in the dark, muzzles flashing red, Tim laughing like a bastard.

They've killed at night before.

There's a kiosk at a stone gate now.

Since when, Peter wonders, did my mother get a freakin' gate? And a guard? The guard steps out and stops the car. Peter remembers him as one of his father's minor soldiers. The guard recognizes Peter Jr., too, in the passenger seat. "Peter Jr.! Welcome back! Does your mother know you're here?"

"I want to surprise her," Peter Jr. says.

The guard hits a button and the gate swings open. They park right up by the front door.

Tim opens the trunk and Peter Jr. takes the shotgun, steps up to the door and rings the bell. It takes a couple of minutes—the happy couple, the king and queen, are upstairs in bed.

Peter Jr. holds the gun behind his back.

The view slot slides open.

Then the door.

Vinnie is in a robe with nothing underneath, and Peter Jr. has a fleeting, obscene thought that the guy's been fucking his mother.

"Peter Jr.," Vinnie says, "we didn't know you were here. When—"

Peter Jr. swings the gun out.

Vinnie turns and tries to slam the door.

Peter Jr. fires.

The blast hits Vinnie in the back of the neck, almost severing his head.

Peter Jr. steps into the house, looks up and sees his mother standing on the staircase. She holds a blue silk robe around her, the belt hanging loose. Her hair is disheveled.

Tim walks in and kicks the door shut behind him.

Celia runs back up the stairs.

Peter Jr. chases her, finds her in her bedroom, fumbling in the dresser drawer. He pulls her away from the dresser and turns her around. She backs into the dresser, not noticing or maybe caring that her robe falls open.

The room smells of her perfume.

It's nauseating and he thinks he might throw up. There are butterflies on her robe, butterflies and flowers, and he sees the triangle of hair between her legs.

"What are you doing?" she asks, crying. "Peter Jr., what are you doing? Oh my God . . ."

"He killed my father. Your husband."

"No."

"Don't lie." He pumps a round into the chamber.

"I'm your mother," she says. "I gave birth to you."

"You killed my father!" Peter Jr. yells. "I'm fucked up! I'm so fucked up!"

"My baby. My baby boy."

She opens her arms to him, beckoning him in.

He freezes.

She steps toward him.

He pulls the trigger.

The blast slams her against the dresser. She slides down, smearing blood, sits with a thud, looks at her intestines spilling into her fingers, then looks up at him.

He pumps in another round and blows her head off.

Then he runs down the stairs.

"We gotta get outta here," Tim says.

They get in the car and race past the guard, who's running in.

Peter Jr. freaks out. "What did I do? *What did I do?!*"

Now he throws up. Pukes again and again.

PASCO ANSWERS THE frantic knocking.

He already knows who it's going to be, he got the phone calls—someone murdered Celia and Vinnie Calfo.

And he knows who did it.

Now Peter Jr. stands in his doorway, crying, his shirt spattered with blood and God knows what else. "You have to help me, you have to help me."

Pasco doesn't let him in. "*Help* you?!"

"You told me," Peter Jr. says. "You told me to do it."

"Did I tell you to kill your mother?" Pasco asks. "What kind of animal does that?"

"I don't know what to do," Peter Jr. sobs. "I don't know what to do. Please . . ."

"Turn yourself in," Pasco says. "Or run. Or blow your own brains out. But don't come here anymore."

"Uncle Pasco . . . Godfather . . ."

"You're not my godson," Pasco says. "I'm ashamed of you. You're an *animale. Bruto.* A sick animal."

He shuts the door.

Peter Jr. staggers away from the house.

There's no car in the driveway. Tim has taken off.

Peter Jr. runs.

TWENTY-ONE

DANNY DRIVES THROUGH THE DESERT.

On a back route to Las Vegas, away from the freeway, a two-lane blacktop through the Anza-Borrego Desert.

He drove out of San Diego into the backcountry, through the little mountain town of Julian and then down fifteen miles of sharp switchbacks down onto the desert floor.

Maybe not the smartest route, he thinks, just thirty or forty miles north of where I did the Abbarca *tombe*, but Popeye is dead and gone, no one knows I'm out here, and I need some space to clear my head.

He wants to be alone, and the desert is empty and beautiful.

His thoughts aren't.

The ifs torture him. In the vast emptiness, they have space to run riot. *If I had been there . . . if I hadn't left her . . . if I hadn't abandoned her . . .*

She'd be alive.

The guilt racks him.

He imagines the what-if scenarios, sees himself going back to the house, finding her unconscious, dialing 911, giving her CPR, feeling her heart beat again, seeing her breathe.

Or he gets there sooner, *before* she picks up the bottle, the pills.

Or, he thinks, you never left her at all.

He has images of the flip side, other things he didn't see but now imagines: Diane reaching for the pills, opening the bottle, lying dead on the bed.

Danny has killed five people in his life.

But now he makes it six.

He doesn't feel guilty about the others, they were self-defense.

So was this, Danny tells himself.

Right, you killed her to save yourself.

A few miles out of the town of Borrego Springs, he sees a young woman on the side of the road.

She wears a peasant blouse, faded jeans, and sandals. Long blond hair flows straight down under a leather shepherd's hat. A backpack sits at her feet. Heat waves shimmer around her ankles.

Her thumb is out.

Danny pulls over.

She hefts the bag, trots to the car, opens the door and gets in. "Thank you!"

"It's dangerous out here," Danny says. "You could die."

"I'm used to it," she says. "Where are you headed?"

"Vegas," Danny says. "You?"

"East a few miles," she says. "Where I live. I guess you could call it a commune."

"I didn't know those still existed."

"This one does," she says. "I'm Cybil."

"Danny." They shake hands.

She bends down and pulls a joint out of her backpack. "You wanna get high?"

At first, Danny thinks no, but then he thinks, why not? It's been years, since before Ian was born, since he's smoked grass, or weed, or whatever they call it now. "Okay."

"Cool." She lights up, takes a hit, and hands it to him. "Hit it easy, it's strong."

Yeah, it is. Just a few seconds after Danny takes a toke (do they still call it a toke?) he feels it. He hands the joint back and Cybil takes another hit. Back and forth three times until Danny is *high.*

Cybil plays with the radio dial. "I'm kind of a Deadhead. I follow them around when they tour."

"Who?"

"The Grateful Dead," she says, laughing.

"I'm pretty much a Springsteen guy," Danny says.

"Blue collar, working class, East Coast . . ."

"There you go."

Twenty minutes later they come to a dirt road that leads off to the right.

"This is my turnoff," Cybil says.

"I'll take you there."

"You sure?" she asks. "It's about five minutes."

"It's all good."

The commune is on an abandoned mining site. Small, ramshackle buildings of adobe and timber with tin roofs, an old tower and two big wooden water tanks. Several mine shafts, framed with wood, are dug into a hill behind.

Two tepees stand out in front, next to the inevitable VW van parked under a ramada made of poles and branches. A second ramada shelters a decrepit picnic table at which a young woman sits weaving a bracelet.

Two people come out of a tepee. One is a white guy who looks to be in his midthirties, his brown beard long, his hair braided into locs. The other is a young Asian woman with long straight black hair hanging to her waist.

They look wary until they see Cybil open the car door.

"It was nice meeting you," Danny says.

"Don't you want to hang out a little?" Cybil asks.

Danny hesitates.

Cybil laughs. "Don't worry, we're not the Manson family. You must be hungry, right?"

"A little."

A little? Danny thinks. I have the munchies so bad I could chew on the car seat.

"So stay and have some food." She hugs the man and woman. Then she says, "Danny, this is Harley and Mayling. Guys, this is Danny. He gave me a ride."

"Welcome, man," Harley says as Danny gets out of the car. Then he looks to Cybil. "Did you get the . . ."

She nods and taps her backpack. "Is there any food? We're starving."

Danny follows her to the ramada where the picnic table sits and sees an oil drum cut in half with a grill on it. A big pot sits over wood embers and Cybil ladles out two bowls. "Vegetarian chili."

Maybe, Danny thinks, but it tastes like dirt. He wolfs it down anyway.

Harley sits down next to him. "Danny, what's your story?"

"I'm not a cop, if that's what you're wondering," Danny says.

"So what are you?"

"A businessman."

"A businessman just driving through the desert," Harley says. "Interesting."

"Taking the back road to Las Vegas," Danny says. "I get tired of the Fifteen."

"It's pretty ugly," Harley says. He looks Danny over hard. "See, I could swear I know you from somewhere. Have we met before?"

"Not that I remember," Danny says, thinking the guy might have seen his picture on a tabloid at the grocery store or something.

"Must have been another life," Harley says.

"That must be it," Danny says. He wants to change the subject. "So what do you guys do out here?"

"'Do'?" Mayling says. "We *live*."

Two more people wander over, Hannah and Brad, the woman Danny saw weaving and another young guy who looks like he just got up and is getting used to the sunshine. Collectively, the group tells Danny how they "live"—they do crafts, they do arts, they do music. Once a week or so they go into Borrego Springs and buy supplies, but mostly they dumpster-dive.

"The restaurants waste so much food," Cybil says.

Danny thinks he might puke up the vegetarian chili, but the grass helps him keep it down. "What do you do for money?"

"We don't have a lot of use for it. Mostly we barter," Harley says. He has jagged teeth and his smile is almost lupine. "Sometimes maybe we deal a little weed."

He juts his chin south toward the border.

Danny tries to figure out the deal here, two guys and three women living together.

Cybil sees it and laughs. "We're poly."

"I have no idea what that is," Danny says. He knows, like, Pollyanna, Polly wants a cracker . . .

"Poly*amorous*," Cybil says.

"Monogamy is ownership," Mayling says. "Exclusivity excludes."

Okay, Danny thinks. He wonders what Terri would have said about exclusivity excluding, like, *That's the idea, dummy.*

"Well, thanks for lunch," Danny says. "It's been nice meeting you."

"Hang out for a while," Cybil says.

"I should be going."

"Las Vegas will be there," Cybil says. "Slow down, sleep off the grass. That's what I'm going to do."

I *am* tired, Danny thinks.

Tired, stoned, the alcohol still toxic in his system. The urge to lie down, to sleep, is powerful. There's something else; this idea about just living, setting down his responsibilities and just living for a little while.

He follows Cybil through the camp. Two outhouses remain from the mining days; a Lister bag hangs from a wooden tripod to serve as a shower. Danny notices Christmas lights strung around, and then sees a propane-powered generator.

"We turn it on some nights when we want electricity," Cybil says.

She stops in front of a mine shaft dug into the ridge. A palo verde branch, spray-painted gold, serves as a door.

"A personal touch," Cybil says as she pushes it aside.

She stoops to go in.

Danny has to get on all fours to follow her inside.

It's pitch-black.

"Wait here," she says.

Danny hears her moving around and then candlelight appears and he sees her living quarters. A sleeping bag, a pillow, a dozen candles, a crate that serves as a bookshelf with a few paperbacks and some old hardcovers. A stack of tape cassettes and a Walkman.

A mandolin.

Cybil peels her clothes off, then lies down and pats the sleeping bag, inviting him.

He lies down beside her.

"I'm way too wasted to want to fuck, though," Cybil says.

"That's okay."

He's asleep within seconds.

HARLEY TAKES A long draw from the pipe and then hands it to Kenny. "I know I know that guy. From someplace."

Brad says, "I know who he is."

"You do?"

Harley waits for Brad to elaborate, but Brad just sucks on the pipe and stares off into space.

"Who is he?" Harley asks.

"I saw it in a newspaper last time we went to town," Brad says. "He's like some mob guy dating this actress. They're doing a movie together or something."

"You have a name?"

"Gimme a second." Brad goes into deep concentration. Then he says, "Danny Ryan."

The name strikes a chord. "You sure?"

"Yeah, why?"

Harley has heard the name. Not from some fucked-up Hollywood fantasy, but from his drug connections.

"I'm taking the van, going into town," Harley says.

"Okay."

Harley has to make a phone call.

CYBIL KNEELS ON the sleeping bag and reaches under the pillow. "Danny, do you want to get *really* high?"

She pulls out a handful of small, light-brown mushroom caps. "Magic mushrooms. Hallucinogenic. Sort of like acid, but natural. We're all going to do it tonight."

"No, I don't think so."

"Come on," she says. "Loosen up. It'll get you into your head."

"I wouldn't go into my head," Danny says, "without a flashlight and a gun."

"You'll have me," Cybil says. "I'll be your guide."

She holds her hand out, a cap pinched between her fingers, like a priest offering the host at communion.

Introibo ad altare Dei.

Danny takes the mushroom. "What do I do with it?"

"Chew it," she says. "Then swallow."

He does. It's bitter and his face twists. Cybil chuckles and takes one herself. Then she hands him a second one.

"Yeah?" Danny asks.

"Oh yeah."

Danny takes the next cap, chews and swallows.

This is my body.

PETER JR. WRAPS his arms around his chest and rocks. Sitting against a tree off the side of Route 1, he doesn't know what to do now.

Can't believe what he *has* done.

"What did you *do*, what did you *do*?" he asks himself as he rocks back and forth.

You killed your own mother, he thinks.

He thought that Pasco would come to his aid, that his godfather would have used his power to hide him, help him get away until things blew over. That Pasco would have been proud of him for killing Vinnie, and would have smoothed things out.

But he called me an animal, a monster.

Maybe I am.

It's cold out and he shivers. He sees a car coming down the road, gets up and sticks out his thumb.

The car pulls over.

Peter Jr. jogs to it.

The passenger window rolls down. The guy asks, "Where are you headed?"

"Wherever you're headed," Peter Jr. says.

"I'm going as far as Westerly."

He unlocks the door and Peter Jr. gets in. Westerly is on the Connecticut border, he thinks, so at least I can get out of state.

"Pretty late at night to be out here hitchhiking," the guy says. Older
guy, maybe a fisherman.

"A buddy ditched me."

"Not much of a buddy."

"No," Peter Jr. says.

Semper Fi.

The guy drops him off downtown and Peter Jr. finds a phone booth
and calls Heather.

"The police were here," Heather says. "God, Peter, you shot Mom?"

It's "Mom" again now, Peter thinks. "I don't know what happened.
She came at me. I don't know what to do, Heather."

"I don't know, either."

"Can you come get me?" Peter asks. "Take me somewhere?"

"The police were *just here.*"

"But they're gone now," Peter Jr. says. "So you can come, right?"

Silence.

"Heather, *please.*"

More silence.

Then a dial tone.

That's it, Peter Jr. thinks.

I'm on my own.

A hunted animal alone in the night.

TWENTY-TWO

DARKNESS.

No, not darkness.

Blackness.

So black you can't see out, you can only see in. Inside my head, Danny thinks, inside the fucked-up head of Danny Ryan, a flashlight and a gun, a flashlight and a gun won't we have fun a flashlight and a gun. Oh Danny Boy the pipes are calling . . . the summer's gone and all the roses falling, all the roses fallen around my feet, petals crushed underfoot, smell of dead blossoms rotting without sun, sweet sickly stench of death never leaves the nose, the memory you dug Pat days dead from his shallow grave from the dirt from the earth fallen flower all the roses dying if I am dead as well as I well may be ye'll come and find the place I'm lying and kneel and say an Ave there for me we didn't kneel we didn't sing Jimmy and I dug you up and wrapped you in a blanket and threw you in the back of the car oh Pat oh Pat oh Pat the pipes are calling maudlin Irish bullshit nostalgia never saw the ould sod myself what's it to me Oh Danny Boy O'Crocodile tears oh give me a freakin' break get drunk on St. Paddy's Day St. Paddy's is for

amateurs the pros get drunk every day every night my drunk of a father
drunken old man bitter chowderhead the real Rhode Island stuff with
clear broth not with that baby-puke cream or heaven forfend tomato sauce
which is an abomination unto the Lord, Christ I'm fucked up, fucked
up, fucked up *introibo ad altare Dei* come to the altar of God fucked up
like this do you remember when Pat was in his want-to-be-a-priest phase
would put a screen door up in the closet and take confessions but you had
to make up sins not real ones because that would be a mortal sin so you'd
say stupid shit like you assassinated Lincoln or killed Superman or stole
the Hope Diamond and Pat would give you penance three Our Fathers
five Hail Marys a sincere act of contrition his I-want-to-be-a-priest phase
ended when he saw Sheila's tits under a tight white blouse and then he
was in I-want-to-get-my-hand-under-that-blouse phase, same phase you
went through with his sister Terri although for God's sake you'd never say
it would get punched in the nose remember one time Pat asked are you
fucking my sister you said not exactly he said what the hell does that mean
you said it means not exactly just third base. Terri good Catholic girl good
daughter not going to give it up the nuns said to put a phone book on a
boy's lap if you had to sit on it in a car so you didn't feel his thing and the
Italian guys would say for the Irish you'd only need a newspaper and not
the Sunday one either.

Terri poor Terri another fallen flower diagnosis that filthy word that
evil word what kind of God punishes the good with the bad Terri never
did anything he remembers her face when they got the word the diagnosis
the tests that always came back bad couldn't catch a break not one the
chemo the drip drip drip the shit into her arm her veins her blood left her
there dying Danny on the lam Danny on the run Danny abandons his
wife to the diagnosis winter when they buried her in cold hard ground
probably used a blow torch to thaw enough to dig God couldn't let her die
in soft warm summer it is so dark so black.

Danny crawls on his belly, reaching forward as if he can pull himself into a light that doesn't exist.

Death.

He feels it all around him, in him. Death, disease, the cancer that killed his wife, the rot that ate away at his father, he feels it on his skin, in his bones, in*side* his bones, deadly marrow, rot in the being, rot in the bone, born to sin, to corruption.

Monsters now, the devils and demons of his childhood the nuns told him about Satan's minions poking prodding pitchforks into his skin as it burns, burns without cease forever and ever amen he sees their hideous faces now grinning at him their fangs sharp and bloody he hears them hissing he says *Oh my God I am heartily sorry for having offended Thee and I do detest all my sins* and hears *Too late, dumb fuck* he pulls the gun from his belt shoots red muzzle flashes stab the dark make it bloody he'll kill them all but Cybil says They're only in your head so he stops shooting now he hears water rushing, crashing waves on a shore but no it's not the ocean it's a whirlpool, spinning swirling mud and filth the detritus of his life his sins he sees Jardine dirty cop filthy his beard grown in death, his fingernails long his clothes tattered now hanging off him he stands on a boat to cross the channel Danny recognizes it now it's the old channel, the passage between Goshen and Gilead and he knows he has to cross it but then from behind him come the dead rushing toward the channel running over him trampling him they're most of them there the dead from the long war running toward the ferryman, the boatman but Danny remembers no ferry on the old channel they used to just jump in and swim across letting the current take them to the rocks on the other side and he asks Cybil What are they doing? Where are they going? she says They want to cross but they can't because they aren't at peace and now Danny's at the channel's edge Jardine says You can't cross, motherfucker, you're not dead Cybil says You have to pay him, How much? Danny asks You owe me millions Jardine says You took my money you took my life and Cybil says You know the golden branches in front of my place I'll give them to you take him over Danny gets in the boat beside Jardine but now it's not Jardine it's Liam fucking Liam Liam who started all this and Liam gaping hole in his head looks at Danny says You fucked my wife Danny says I didn't I never did Liam says In the movies I mean you fucked her in the movies which is bigger better that should have been me I'm movie star handsome everyone said so not you you mutt and then Danny hears dogs howling it makes no sense dogs down here but they're not dogs they're coyotes and he follows their howling.

Out of the mine shaft into the open air a party in progress people dancing under the moonlight *spirits in the night spirits in the night, stand right up now* Danny off all fours onto his feet like a person a human being not an animal crawling in the dark stands up and sees bodies lit red by a bonfire twisting to music weird music flutes and guitars maybe Grateful Dead maybe grateful not to be dead he sees Cybil in front of him beckoning beckoning him out onto the desert floor the dance floor he follows her out away from the fire out into the raw night and then

Danny sees Peter Moretti black hair wet and dripping I heard you were dead Danny says They shot me in the bathtub can you believe that Peter asks Guy can't even take a bath anymore Cassie's lying there in the tub her hair splayed like seaweed floating on the tide two neat holes in her forehead she sees Danny she says I tried to warn you he says I'm sorry, I'm so sorry I didn't listen she says Did you hear the one about it started raining soup and the Irish ran outside with forks, good one, huh?

Pat walks up Are you trying to fuck my sister Not this one Danny says the other one Pat says Both my sisters are dead Pat his best friend more than a brother-in-law more than a brother Pat dragged behind a car pieces of him scraped onto the street pieces of Pat pieces of Pat now he says Jesus Danny you screwed the pooch shit the bed I left you in charge what did you let happen? Danny says I'm sorry Pat I did my best it wasn't good enough I'm not you I never was I never will be You have to be Pat says Why? Because there's no one else.

Just Danny Ryan Danny Ryan Danny Ryan the pipes the pipes, Pat says You know the difference between you and me, Danny? You'll see the sun come up again, and then he's gone.

Danny walks farther away from the camp out into the desert alone away from Cybil away from his guide he sees Terri.

Not tied to tubes the fluids draining out the morphine seeping into her blood but she's lying on the sand the way she used to lie on the beach on her elbow her hand propping up her head she says You left me he says You told me to you told me to take our son and go and she says Sure maybe the only time you ever did what I said and she laughs and says I told you you wanted to fuck her he asks Who she says The woman coming out of the water, Pam, that day all this started I saw you checking her out looking at her tits and I knew you wanted to do her and you finally did and he says he's sorry Terri says No, good on you, Danny, if I could fuck Robert Redford I would but I can't because I'm dead here but good on you honest to God I didn't think you had it in you it makes me kinda hot come on down here and do me he says Let's go back to the cottage she says No right here on the beach but when he goes to lie down with her to feel the soft hair on her arms smell the sweet vanilla scent behind her ears there's only sand and he gets up again and goes looking for her in the stars look so close here like you could reach up and grab one so close in this soft desert night he walks farther out farther away and then there's

Diane walking, drifting on the sand in the muted moonlight, dim, misty, her eyes fixed on the ground Danny follows her walks after her calls out to her but she won't stop walking, walking away from him not seeing him or pretending not to see him Danny says Was it my fault? I'm sorry, I never meant to hurt you like that, I didn't want to go, to leave you, I had to, to save us both but I never thought you'd do . . . what you did I never dreamed that don't walk away from me Diane please talk to me tell me you forgive me tell me you hate me say something to me talk to me please Diane but she keeps walking, she won't look at him, she walks away. He's loved two women in his life two women gone now gone gone rose petals off the stem floating floating away away.

Danny stands and cries face in hands tears running through fingers hunched over he sobs can't stop can't stop grief pouring out of him like a wave rushing in breaking into white water rushing past his ears salt water in his nose his mouth the pain in his chest heavy heavy pulling him down the wave pressing pushing him down weighing him his tears flow away with the other water hot tears in cold ocean salt to salt.

The wave rushes onto the beach washes him up washes him on the sand Cybil is beside him they can still hear music mandolins guitars drums cymbals flutes she moves with the music she is harder than he thought hard edges bones, hard muscles on her belly but so soft inside so soft and moist sticky soft warm his dick swells swells she says It's okay I want you to he does he dies in her.

More howling, human now, whoops hollers song and music and then Cybil beckons him to come to the party celebrate the moon and stars, the pussy, the cock, the shit, the piss the dirt the sand the life of it but he doesn't want to be with people I want to see my father he says My father, I want to find my father Cybil says You can see whatever you can imagine your head will take you where it wants to go he gets up and staggers along a path, a ravine up into the hill behind the camp into there it is an oasis green grass and even a few trees he climbs to the top of the hill.

A fire now, back from the camp, tall flames rise in front of the towers, embers swirling into the night sky angels returning to heaven cleansed by fire from this earthly hell.

I'm not an ember, Danny thinks, I'll never rise like that none of us will none of us the thieves, the hustlers, the dealers, the racketeers, the killers. The forgiven fly, the unforgiven are earthbound, chained to the ground by our sins those heavy chains we groan here we die here.

Still high though, still so high, Danny tries to fight his way out of it, struggle from this cocoon but he's trapped and he hears himself say The sun is coming up now rose red and Marty is there, sitting facing east, says The fuck are you doing with some hippie broad, dipshit, you some kind of crunchy granola tree hugger now? Danny goes to put his arms around him but Marty leans away I wish I was in Carrickfergus Danny says I only want a hug. You a fag now, too? Jesus. They sit silently, look out across the desert, empty, quiet until Marty says The fuck you doing, mushrooms. You have a kid. Why are you sitting here, dumb fuck? You have a kid a family to take care of Danny says You never took care of yours never took care of me Marty says I'm taking care of you now, you wanna be like me you want to live with those regrets those sorrows those pains only for nights in Ballygrant. Get the fuck up, fuckup.

Get up, Danny thinks. Get up get up get up Marty that shitty father is right you have a son you have to get back you have to be his father don't do to him what your old man did to you it has to end somewhere sometime it has to end now you have to end it there is no one else.

Danny stands up.

Walks off the ridge down the ravine the sun just coming up now he turns his back to it walks back toward the camp coming down he thinks he's coming down off the high too but then he sees the worst hallucination, the worst images, the worst monsters the bodies naked tied to the poles arms stretched out above them, wrists tied ankles bound to the posts Brad, Hannah, Mayling. Harley, naked, his dick obscene his face twisted in rage and terror. Cybil, her long lean body hard edges taut to the breaking point tears streaking the dust on her face her shoulders heave as she sobs and Danny knows he isn't back from the land of the dead yet because in front of him he sees a huge one-eyed man a cyclops.

Popeye.

Danny walks up to him, asks, "Are you dead?"

"I look dead?"

"I don't know."

But he's not dead, he's alive and real.

Danny sees other men, standing around with guns. A semicircle of SUVs, in an arc, like wagons in the old western movies. He recognizes the man standing beside Popeye, remembers him from the *tombe*, the man zip-tied on the floor.

Neto Valdez looks back at Danny and says, "I told you. You and your whole family. *Muerte*. And not fast, either."

Harley screams, "Not me! I'm the one who called you!"

He twists and squirms.

Arms grab Danny, kick him to his knees, zip-tie his hands behind his back.

Popeye talks to him. "This is your family? Your little hippie family?"

Danny should have killed them all.

He knows that now.

But that ain't Danny Ryan.

It's always been his problem—he still believes in God. Heaven and hell and all that happy crap.

He's on his knees with a gun to his head. The others are tied, bound wrists and ankles, stretched on poles, looking down at him with pleading, terrified eyes.

The desert air is cold at dawn and Danny shivers as he kneels in the sand with the sun coming up and the moon a fading memory. A dream. Maybe that's all life is, Danny thinks, a dream.

Or a nightmare.

Because even in dreams, Danny thinks, you pay for your sins.

An acrid smell pierces the crisp, fresh air.

Gasoline.

Then Danny hears, "You watch while we burn them alive. Then you."

So this is how I die, he thinks.

Popeye nods to Neto.

Neto picks up a big can of gasoline.

Cybil screams and begs *Please please please nooooo!*

"Her first," Popeye says.

Someone grabs Danny's chin from behind and wrenches his face up, forcing him to look.

He sees Cybil's eyes, wide in terror.

Neto hefts the gas can.

"*Pleeeeaase!*" Cybil bellows. "*Noooooooo . . .*"

Neto pours the gas over Popeye's head.

Then he flicks a match onto him.

DANNY SEES POPEYE twirl, a whirling torch.

The men laugh.

"Sick of his shit." Neto spits on the sand. "Good riddance."

He looks down at Danny. "Don't worry, *pendejo*, I'll make it quick for all of you."

He pulls a pistol.

"Leave them be," Danny says. "They had nothing to do with it."

"Even the one who dimed you?" Neto asked. "You don't want revenge?"

Danny shakes his head.

"You could have killed me, you didn't," Neto says. "Let's call it even."

He holsters the gun, snaps orders in Spanish.

Hands untie Danny.

He falls on his face.

Hears footsteps, car doors, engines.

When he looks up again, they're gone.

The dream fades.

The long night is over.

The day is breaking.

ACKNOWLEDGMENTS

NO ONE WRITES A BOOK alone.

That's an illusion.

When I come downstairs in the morning, flip on the lights, make that first essential pot of coffee and then fire up the computer, I am already beholden to the skills and labor of thousands of people whom I don't even know.

I do, however, know a great number of people without whom my work would not only be impossible, but would also lack both quality and joy.

To my friend and agent, Shane Salerno, I can't adequately express my appreciation, so a simple "thank you" will have to suffice. We've put together quite a run, brother.

To Deb Randall and Ryan Coleman and the whole crew at The Story Factory, please know that I appreciate you.

To Liate Stehlik at William Morrow, your trust and confidence in me means more than you can imagine. You have given a somewhat itinerant author a home.

To my editor, Jennifer Brehl—without you this is not a novel, merely a manuscript, and this book owes much to your taste, discernment, enthusiasm and support. I can't thank you enough.

To my copyeditor, Laura Cherkas, please accept my contrition for all my sins and my gratitude for your redemption thereof. You have saved my from many blush-worthy embarrassments.

To Brian Murray, Andy LeCount, Julianna Wojcik, Kaitlin Harri, Danielle Bartlett, Jennifer Hart, Christine Edwards, Andrew DiCecco, Andrea Molitor, Ben Steinberg, Chantal Restivo-Alessi, Frank Albanese, Nate Lanman and Juliette Shapland, please accept my thanks for all your hard and great work on my behalf.

To all the marketing and publicity staff at HarperCollins/William Morrow, I know that I don't have my job unless you do yours, and you do it so well and so tirelessly.

To my lawyer, Richard Heller, my great appreciation.

To my followers on social media, @donwinslow on Twitter, the #DonWinslowBookClub, and the troops of the #WinslowDigitalArmy, my sincere thanks for walking beside me on this road. Forward.

To all the booksellers—I don't know where I'd be without you, but it wouldn't be where I am. Thank you for all the years of support, hospitality and friendship.

To my readers, my humble gratitude for the inspiration, support and warmth that you have shown me throughout my career. You have made it possible for me to do what I love for a living, and at the end of the day, you are what this is all about.

To the many people and places that have given me so much friendship, fun, food and much more: David Nedwidek and Katy Allen, Pete and Linda Maslowski, Jim Basker and Angela Vallot, Teressa Palozzi, Drew Goodwin, Tony and Kathy Sousa, John and Theresa Culver, Scott and Jan Svoboda, Jim and Melinda Fuller, Ted Tarbet, Thom Walla, Mark Clodfelter, Roger Barbee, Donna Sutton, Virginia and Bob Hilton, Bill and Ruth MacEneaney, Andrew Walsh, Jeff and Rita Parker, Bruce Riordan,

Jeff Weber, Don Young, Mark Rubinsky, Cameron Pierce Hughes, Rob Jones, David and Tammy Tanner, Ty and Dani Jones, Deron and Becky Bisset, "Cousin" Pam Matteson, David Schniepp, Drift Surf, Quecho, Java Madness, Jim's Dock, Cap'n Jack's, The Coast Guard House, Las Olas, Peaches, The Seaview Market and Right Click—thank you all.

And, course, to my son, Thomas, and wife, Jean, without whom . . . well, you know. You are more than I ever dreamed of.

No one writes a book alone.

READ ON FOR AN EXCERPT FROM

CITY IN RUINS,

THE NEXT AND FINAL VOLUME
IN DON WINSLOW'S
BESTSELLING TRILOGY

PROLOGUE

DANNY RYAN WATCHES THE BUILDING come down.

It seems to shiver like a shot animal, then is perfectly still for just an instant, as if it can't bring itself to acknowledge its death, and then falls down on itself. All that's left of where the old casino once stood is a tower of dust rising into the air, like a cheesy trick from some lounge act magician writ large.

"Implosion," they call it, Danny thinks.

Collapse from the inside.

Aren't they all, Danny thinks.

Most of them, anyway.

The cancer that killed his wife, the depression that destroyed his love, the moral rot that took his soul.

All implosion, all from the inside.

He leans on the cane because his leg is still weak, still stiff, still throbs as a reminder of . . .

Collapse.

He watches the dust rise, a mushroom cloud, a dirty gray brown against the clear blue desert sky.

Slowly it fades and the disappears.

Nothing now.

How I fought, he thinks, what I gave for this . . .

Nothing.

This dust.

He turns away and limps through his city.

His city in ruins.

PART ONE

Ian's Birthday Party

But devout Aeneas now—the last rites performed and the grave-mound piled high . . . sets sail on his journey . . .

Virgil, *The Aeneid*

ONE

Las Vegas, Nevada
June 1997

DANNY'S DISCONTENT.

Looking down at the Las Vegas Strip from his office window, he wonders why.

Less than ten years ago, he thinks, he was fleeing Rhode Island in an old car with an infant son, a senile father, and everything he owned jammed in the back. Now he's a partner in two hotels on the Strip, lives in a freakin' mansion, owns a cabin up in Utah and drives a new car every year that the company pays for.

Danny Ryan is a multi-millionaire, which he finds as amusing as it is surreal. He never dreamed—hell, nobody who knew him back in the day ever dreamed—that he'd ever have a net worth beyond his next paycheck, much less be considered a "mogul," a major power player in the major power game that is Las Vegas.

Whoever doesn't believe that life is funny, Danny thinks, doesn't get the joke.

He can easily remember when he had twenty bucks in his jeans pocket and he thought he was rich. Now the clip he keeps in one of his tailor-made suits usually has a thousand or more in it as walking-around money. Danny can recall when it was a big deal when he and Terri could afford to go out for Chinese on a Friday night. Now he "dines" at Michelin-starred restaurants more than he wants to, which partially accounts for the shelf developing at his waistline.

When asked if he's watching his weight, he usually answers that yes, he's watching it slide over his belt, the bonus ten pounds he's gained from living a mostly sedentary life at a desk.

His mother has tried to get him into tennis, but he feels stupid chasing a ball around just to whack it and have it come right back at him, and he doesn't play golf because for one thing it's as boring as shit and for another, he associates the game with doctors, lawyers and stockbrokers, and he's not any of those.

The old Danny used to sneer at those types, looked down at those effete businessmen from beneath. He'd jam his toque down over his shaggy hair, climb into his old peacoat, grab his brown bag lunch with pride and a chip on his shoulder, and go to work on the Providence docks, a Spring-steen kind of guy. Now he listens to *Darkness* on a Pioneer stereo system that ran him a bill and a half.

But he still prefers a cheeseburger to Kobe beef, good fish-and-chips (impossible to get in Vegas at any price) to Chilean sea bass. And on the rare occasion when he has to fly anywhere, he goes commercial instead of taking the corporate jet.

(He does, however, fly first class.)

His reluctance to use the company's Lear pisses his son off no end. Danny gets it—what ten-year-old doesn't want to fly on a private jet?

Danny has promised Ian that the next vacation they go on of any distance, they'll do it. But he'll feel guilty about it.

"Dan is a chowder-head," his partner Dom Rinaldi said one time, meaning that he's an old New England, practical . . . well, *cheap*, guy . . . for whom any kind of physical indulgence is deeply suspect.

Danny deflected the issue. "Try getting a decent bowl of chowder here. Not that milky baby puke they serve, but *real* chowder in the clear broth."

"You employ five executive chefs," Dom said. "They'll make you chowder from the foreskins of virgin Peruvian frogs if you tell them to."

Sure, but Danny won't do that. He wants his chefs spending their time making the guests anything *they* want.

That's where the money comes from.

He gets up, stands by the window—tinted to combat the relentless Las Vegas sun—and looks down at the Lavinia Hotel

The old Lavinia, Danny thinks, the last of the hotels from the '50s building boom—a relic, a remnant, barely hanging on. Its long-gone heyday was the era of the Rat Pack, wiseguys and showgirls, counting room skim and dirty money.

If those walls could talk, Danny thinks, they'd take the Fifth.

Now it's on the market.

Danny's company, Tara, already owns the two adjacent properties to the south, including the one he's standing in. A rival group, Winegard, has the casinos to the north. Whoever ends up with the Lavinia will control the most prestigious location left on the Strip, and Las Vegas is a prestige kind of town.

Vern Winegard has the purchase all but sewed-up, Danny knows. Probably for the best, probably not wise for Tara to expand too quickly. Still, it *is* the only space left on the Strip, and . . .

He buzzes Gloria in the outer office. "I'm going to the gym."

"Do you need directions?"

"Funny."

"Do you remember that you have a lunch with Mr. Winegard and Mr. Levine?"

"I do now," Danny says, although he wishes he didn't. "What time?"

"Twelve-thirty," Gloria says. *"At the Club."*

Even though Danny doesn't play golf or tennis, he's a member of the Las Vegas Country Club and Estates, because, as his mother instructed him, it's pretty much mandatory for doing business.

"You have to be seen there," Madeleine said.

"Why?"

"Because it's old Las Vegas."

"I'm *not* old Las Vegas," Danny said. He's been here for just six years and is still considered "the new kid in town."

"But I am," she said, "And, like it or not, to do business in this town, you have to do it with old Las Vegas."

Danny joined the club.

"And the bouncy castle will be delivered by three," Gloria says.

"The bouncy castle."

"For Ian's birthday party?" Gloria says. *"You do remember that Ian's party is this evening."*

"I remember," Danny says. "I just didn't know about a bouncy castle."

"I ordered it," Gloria says. *"You can't have a kid's birthday party without a bouncy castle."*

"You can't?"

"It's expected."

Well, then, Danny thinks, if it's expected . . . A horrifying thought hits him. "Do I have to assemble it?"

"The guys will inflate it."

"What guys?"

"The bouncy castle guys," Gloria says, getting impatient. *"Really, Dan, all you have to do is show up and be nice to the other parents."*

Danny's sure this is true. The ruthlessly efficient Gloria has teamed up with his equally methodical mother to plan this party, and the two of them together are a terrifying combination. If Gloria and Madeleine ran the world—as they think they should—there would be full employment, no wars, famine pestilence or plague, and everyone would always be on time.

As for being nice to the guests, Danny's always nice, affable, even charming. But he does have a justified reputation for sneaking off at parties, even his own. All of a sudden someone notices his absence, and he's found in a back room by himself, or wandering around outside, and on more than one occasion, when a party has gone late into the night, he has simply gone to bed.

Danny hates parties. Hates schmoozing, small talk, finger-food, standing around and all that shit. It's tough, because socializing is a big part of his job. He pulls it off, he's good at it, but it's his least favorite thing.

When The Shores opened, just two years ago after three years in construction, the company threw an opening night extravaganza, but no one can remember seeing Danny there.

He didn't give one of the several speeches, he didn't appear in any of the photographs, and the legend started that Danny Ryan didn't even attend the opening of his own hotel.

He did, he just stayed in the background.

"Ian's going to be nine," he says now. "Isn't that too old for a bouncy castle?"

"You're never too old," Gloria says, *"for a bouncy castle."*

Danny clicks off and stares out the window again.

You've changed, he thinks.

It's not just the excess pounds, the slicked-back Pat O'Reilly haircut, the suits from Brioni instead of Sears, cufflinks instead of buttons. Before Las Vegas, you only wore suits at weddings and funerals. (Given the hard facts about New England in those days, there were more of the latter than the former.) It's not just that you have folding money in your pocket, that you can pay for a meal without worrying about the tab, or that a tailor will come to your office with a tape measure and "swatches."

It's the fact that you like it.

But there's this sense of . . .

Discontent.

Why? he wonders. You have more money than you can spend. Is it just greed? What was it the guy in that dumb movie—his name was like some lizard or something—said, "Greed is good"?

Fuck that.

Danny knows himself. With all his faults, his sins—and they are legion—greed isn't one of them. He used to joke with Terri that he could live in his car and she'd retort, "Have a good time."

So what is it? What do you want?

Permanence? Stability?

Things you've never had.

But you have them now.

He thinks of the beautiful hotel he built, The Shores.

Maybe it's the beauty you want. Some beauty in this life. Because you've sure as hell had the ugly.

A wife dead from cancer, a child left without a mother.

Friends killed.

And the people *you* killed.

But you did it. You built something beautiful.

So it's more than that, Danny thinks.

Be honest with yourself—you want more money because money is power and power is safety. And you can never be safe enough.

Not in this world.

DANNY HAS LUNCH once a month with his two biggest competitors.

Vern Winegard and Barry Levine.

It was Barry's idea and it's a good one. He owns three mega-hotels on the east side of the Strip across from the Tara properties. There are other casino owners, of course, but these three form the nexus of power in Las Vegas. As such, they have shared interests and common problems.

The biggest one now is a looming Federal investigation.

Congress just passed a bill to create the Gambling Impact Study Commission to investigate the effects on the gaming industry on Americans.

Danny knows the numbers.

Gaming is a trillion-dollar business, grossing over six times the amount of money than all other forms of entertainment combined. Last year, players lost over $16 billion, seven billion right here in Las Vegas.

The idea is gaining steam that gambling isn't just a habit, or even a vice, but an illness, an addiction.

When gambling was illegal, it was organized crime's breadbasket, by far its biggest profit center after Prohibition and bootlegging ended. Whether it was the "numbers" racket hawked on every street corner, or the race wire, the sports books, or backroom poker, blackjack and roulette games, the mob raked in vast amounts of money.

The politicians saw that and of course wanted their taste. So what once was a private vice became a civic virtue as state and local governments muscled in on the numbers with their own lotteries. Still, Nevada was about the only place that a gambler could legally play table games or bet sports book, so Las Vegas, Reno and Tahoe pretty much had a monopoly.

Then the Native American reservations figured they had a loophole and started opening their casinos. States, particularly New Jersey with Atlantic City, started doing the same thing and gambling proliferated.

Now anyone could just get in a car to go lose the rent or mortgage money. Some social reformers are likening gambling to crack cocaine. So now there's going to be a Congressional investigation.

Danny's cynical about the motives, suspicious that it's just them trying to stick their noses into the trough. President Clinton has already floated the idea of a 4% federal tax on gambling profits.

For Danny, the tax isn't the worst of it.

As it stands, the bill will give the Commission full subpoena power to hold hearings, call witnesses under the penalty of perjury, demand records and tax returns, look into shadow corporations and silent partners.

Like me, Danny thinks.

The investigation could blow the Tara Group to bits.

Force me out of the business.

Maybe even put me in jail.

I'd lose everything.

This subpoena threat isn't just an annoyance or another problem—it's a survival issue.

"A 'disease'?" Vern asks. "*Cancer* is a disease. *Polio* is a disease."

Polio? Danny thinks. Who the hell remembers polio? But he says, "We can't be seen to be fighting this. It's a bad look."

"Danny's right," Barry says. "We have to do what the alcohol industry has done, big tobacco—"

Vern won't let it go. "You show me the craps table that's given anyone cancer."

"We put out some PSAs about gambling responsibly," Barry says. "We stick brochures for Gamblers Anonymous in the rooms, we fund some studies on 'gambling addiction.'"

Danny says, "We can issue our *mea culpa*s, throw some money along the lines that Barry suggested, fine. But we can't let this commission go on a fishing expedition into our businesses. But we have to shut down the subpoena power. That's the line in the sand, as it were."

No one disagrees. Danny knows that neither of them wanted their financial laundry aired in public. Those sheets wouldn't be squeaky clean.

"Here's the problem," Danny says. "We've only been donating money to the GOP—"

"They're on our side," Vern says.

"Right," Danny says. "So the Democrats see us as the enemy. If they're on this committee they'll come after us with a vengeance."

"If Dole wins, we can forget about this Commission shit," Vern says. "It goes away."

"You read the polls?" Danny asks. "Hell, do you read our own odds-makers? Clinton will get re-elected, and he's one vindictive SOB. He'll let that committee jam scopes up our asses. You want to testify, Vern? You want to be a daytime tv star?"

"So you want to give money to our enemies," Vern says.

"I want to hedge our bets," Danny says. "Keep giving to the GOP, but get some quiet money to the Dems, too."

"Bribes," Vern says.

"Never entered my mind," Danny says. "I'm talking about campaign contributions."

"You think we can persuade the Dems to accept money from us?" Vern asks.

"You think you can persuade a dog to accept a bone?" Barry asks. "It's an election year, they're walking around with their hands out. The president's coming here soon for some kind of meeting. I can organize a lunch. But he'll want a guarantee of a contribution before he agrees to attend."

Danny hesitates, then says. "I invited his guy to the party tonight."

Dave Neal, a major player in the Democratic Party who holds no official position and is therefore free to maneuver. The word is if you want to get to the President, you could go through Neal.

"You think you might have talked to us about that first?" Vern asks.

No, Danny thinks, because you would have objected. It was one of those permission-forgiveness things. "I'm talking to you now. If you don't think I should make an approach, I won't. He comes to the party, he eats and drinks, he goes back to the hotel—"

"At this level," says Barry, "a comped suite and a blow job aren't going to do it. These guys are going to expect some real money."

"We'll ante up," Danny says. "Cost of doing business."

There's no disagreement—the other two men agree that they'll come up with money.

Then Vern asks. "Dan, are wives invited to this thing tonight?"

"Of course."

"No, I didn't know," Vern says. "You don't have to worry about that, you lucky prick."

Danny notices Barry wince.

It was an insensitive remark, everyone knows that Danny is a widower. But Danny doesn't think that Vern meant any harm or offense—it was just Vern being Vern.

Danny doesn't dislike Vern Winegard, although he knows a lot of people who did. The man has the social graces of a rock. He's abrasive, generally disagreeable and arrogant. Still, there's something to like about him. Danny isn't sure exactly what, some vulnerability under all that posturing. And although Winegard is a sharp businessman, Danny has never heard of him cheating anyone.

But he feels this little stab in his chest. Once again, Terri won't be there to see her son's birthday.

But the meeting went well, Danny thinks. I got what I wanted, what I needed.

If money will kill this subpoena thing, great.

If not, I'll have to find something else.

He glances at his watch.

He just has time to make his next appointment.

• • •

DANNY WAKES TO tendrils of sable hair on a slender neck, musky perfume, beads of sweat on bare shoulders even in the chilled air of the air-conditioned bedroom.

"Did you sleep?" Eden asks.

"I dozed off," Danny says. "Dozed" bullshit, he thinks, starting to come to. You dropped off like you were dead, a short but deep post-coital sleep. "What time is it?"

Eden lifts her wrist and looks at her watch. It's funny, it's the one thing she never takes off. "Four-fifteen."

"Shit."

"What?"

"Ian's party."

"I thought it wasn't until six-thirty," she says.

"It isn't," Danny says. "But, you know, things to do."

She rolls over to face him. "You're allowed pleasure, Dan. Even sleep."

Yeah, Danny has heard this before, from other people. It's easy to say, it's even rational, but it doesn't acknowledge the reality of his life. He's responsible for two hotels, hundreds of millions of dollars, thousands of employees, tens of thousands of guests. And the business isn't exactly nine-to-five—there are famously no clocks in casinos and the problems are twenty-four-seven.

"You of all people know I take time for pleasure," he says.

True, she thinks.

Mondays, Wednesdays and Fridays, two o'clock sharp.

Actually, it works for her. Fits perfectly into her schedule, because she's on a Tuesday-Thursday teaching schedule with one night class on Wednesdays. Psych 101—General Psychology, Psych 416—Cognitive Psych and Psych 441—Abnormal Psych.

She sees clients late afternoons or evenings, and sometimes wonders what they'd think if they knew that she just got out bed from one of these matinees. The thought makes her chuckle.

"What?" Danny asks.

"Nothing."

"You laugh at nothing a lot?" Danny asks. "Maybe you should see a shrink."

"I do," she says. "Professional requirement. And 'shrink' is derogatory. Try 'therapist.'"

"You sure you don't want to come to the party?" he asks.

"I have clients tonight. And besides . . ."

She lets it trail. They both know the deal. It's Eden who wants to keep their relationship a secret.

"Why?" Danny asked once.

"I just don't want all that."

"All what?"

"All that comes with being Dan Ryan's girlfriend," Eden said. "The spotlight, the media . . . First of all, the notoriety would hurt my work. My students wouldn't take me as seriously and neither would my clients. Second, I'm an introvert. If you think you hate parties, Dan, I *hate* parties. The faculty do's that I have to go to, I arrive late and leave early. Third, and no offense, casinos depress the hell out of me. The sense of desperation is soul-killing. I don't think I've even been on the Strip in two years."

Truth be told, it's one of the things that attracts him about her, that she's the exact opposite of most of the women who set their cap at him. Eden doesn't want the glitz, the gourmet dinners, the parties, the shows, the presents, the glamor, the fame.

None of it.

She put it succinctly. "What I want is to be treated nicely. Some good sex, some good conversation, I'm good."

Dan checks those boxes. He's considerate, sensitive, with an old-school sense of chivalry that just borders on paternalistic sexism but doesn't cross the line. He's good in bed and he's postcoitally articulate, even though he's clueless about books.

Eden reads a lot. George Eliot, the Brontës, Mary Shelly. Lately she's been on a Jane Austen kick, in fact, for her next vacation she already booked one of those tours of Austen country, and will go blissfully alone.

She's tried to get Dan interested in literature outside of business books.

"You should read Gatsby," she said one time.

"Why is that?"

Because it's you, she thought, but said. "I just think you'd like it."

Eden knows a little about his past. Anyone who ever waited at a super-market checkout counter did—his affair with movie star Diane Carson was tabloid fodder. And when Diane Carson committed suicide after he left her, the media went nuts for a while.

They called Dan a gangster, a mobster, there were allegations that he'd been a drug trafficker and a murderer.

None of that squares with the man she knows.

The Dan Ryan she knows is kind, gentle and caring.

But she's sufficiently self-aware, and trained, to know that she enjoys the frisson of danger, of disrespectability that comes with his reputation, whether true or not. She was raised in an utterly respectable, normal back-ground, so of course she'd find the difference attractive.

Eden feels a little guilty about it, knows she's flirting with immorality. What if the stories about Dan are true? What if even some of them have a basis in reality? Is it still right for her to be literally in bed with him?

An open question that she's unwilling at this point to resolve.

Dan's affair with Diane Carson was six years ago, but Eden thinks that he really loved that woman. Even now, there's an air of sadness to him. She knows he's a widower too, so maybe that's it.

They met on a fund-raising walk for breast cancer, each of them en-gaging to walk twenty miles a day for three days. Dan got his rich friends and colleagues to sponsor him for bucks up and God knows how much money he raised.

But he walked, she thought, when he could just have easily written a check.

She said so to him. "You're committed."

"I am," he said. "My wife. My . . . *late* wife."

Which made her feel like shit.

"And you?" he asked.

"My mother."

"I'm sorry."

He asked her about herself.

"I'm a walking stereotype," Eden said. "A Jewish girl from the Upper West Side who went to Barnard and became a psychotherapist."

"What's a New York psychiatrist—"

"Psychologist—"

"*Psychologist*—doing in Las Vegas?"

"The university offered me a tenure track position," she said. "When my New York friends ask me the same question, I tell them that I hate snow. And you? What's your story?"

"I'm in the gaming industry."

"In Las Vegas? You're kidding!"

He held his hand up. "The truth. By the way, I'm Dan—"

"I was joking with you," she said. "Everyone knows who Dan Ryan is. Even I do, and I don't even gamble."

That was on the first day's walk. It took him until day three, after a good ten miles, to ask her out.

What surprised her was that he was so bad at it.

A man who'd had an affair with a movie star, one of the most beautiful women in the world, a billionaire casino owner who had access to all kinds of gorgeous women, he was incredibly awkward.

"I was wondering if . . . I mean, if you don't want to, I get it . . . no hard feelings . . . but I thought . . . you know . . . maybe I could take you to dinner or something sometime."

"No."

"Right. Got it. No problem. Sorry to—"

"Don't be sorry," she said. "I just don't want to go *out* with you. If you'd like to come over and bring dinner . . ."

"I can have one of my chefs—"

"Takeout," she said. "Boston Market. I love their meatloaf."

"Boston Market," he said. "Meatloaf."

"I have next Thursday night free. Do you?"

"I'll make it free."

"And Dan," she said. "This is just between us, okay?"

"You're ashamed of me already?"

"I just don't want my name in the gossip columns."

Eden stuck to that. The occasional dinner, fine, the three-times-a-week matinees, fine. Beyond that, no. She wants a quiet life. She wants Danny on the down-low.

"So I'm basically a booty-call," Danny said one afternoon.

She laughed at him. "You're not allowed to be the woman in this relationship. Let me ask you, is the sex good?"

"Great."

"Is the companionship good?"

"Again, great."

"Then why do you want to mess it up?"

"You never think about marriage?"

"I had a marriage," she said. "I didn't like it."

Frank was a good guy. Faithful, nice, but so needy. And the neediness made him controlling. He resented the evenings she spent with patients, the alone time she wanted with her books. He wanted her to go out to too many dinners with his law firm partners, tables at which she had nothing to say and less to hear.

The offer from Las Vegas came at the right time.

A clean break, a reason to leave both Frank and New York. She knew he was probably relieved, although he would never say so. But she wasn't the wife he needed.

To her immense surprise, Eden likes Las Vegas. She had thought it would be her rebound location, a pit-stop to heal from her failed five-year marriage before moving on to a place with more culture.

But she's found that she likes the sun and the heat, likes to lie out by the pool at her condo complex and read. Likes the ease of living there as opposed to the endless competition that is New York—the fights for space, for cabs, a seat on the subway, a cup of coffee, everything.

She drives to her office on campus and has a designated parking spot. Same with the covered parking structure at the medical building where she sees her clients. Same with the condo.

It's easy.

So is grocery shopping, always a hassle in New York, especially in the snow and sleet. Ditto going to the pharmacy, the dry cleaners, all the mundane errands that took up so much time in New York.

Which lets her focus on the important things.

Her students, her patients.

Eden cares about her students—she wants them to learn, to succeed. She cares about her patients—she wants them to get well, be happy. She wants to bring all her intelligence, education and skills to bear to achieve these things, and the ease of living her allows her the energy to do that.

Students are pretty much the same, so are the patients. The neuroses, the insecurities, the traumas, the same steady drumbeat (heartbeat?) of human pain. There are a few local Las Vegas twists—the gambling addicts, the high-end call girl—but those are about the only infusions of the casino world in Eden's life.

Well, except for Dan.

Her New York friends ask her, "What about the museums? What about the theater?"

She tells them that they have museums and theater in Las Vegas, and let's be honest, the struggles of working and living in New York left them little time to go exhibits and plays anyway.

Aren't you lonely? they'd ask.

Well, not anymore, she thinks.

The arrangement (can you call it a relationship? she asks herself. I suppose so) is perfect. They give each other affection, sex, companionship, laughs. But now he wants me to come to his son's birthday party? Where all of power Las Vegas will be present? Talk about jumping into the deep end . . . But, knowing Dan, he probably doesn't really want me to come, he just doesn't want to hurt my feelings by not inviting me.

"Dan," she says, "I don't feel like you're hiding me. I want to be hidden."

"Got it."

"Does that hurt your feelings?"

"No."

Danny has loved two women in his life, and they both died young.

His wife, Terri—Ian's mother—the breast cancer had been unforgiving, unrelenting, capricious and cruel.

Danny left her comatose and dying in the hospital.

Never had a chance to say goodbye.

The second woman was Diane.

In an earlier era Diane Carson would have been called a "goddess of the golden screen" or something like that. In her own time she was a movie star, the stereotypical sex symbol that everyone loved but who could never love herself.

Danny loved her.

It was his one blazing affair as they trotted out their love for the world to see, a feast for the tabloids, the clicking of camera shutters the leitmotif of their life together.

It was too much.

Their different worlds pulled them apart, *ripped* them apart. Her fame couldn't tolerate his secrets, his secrets couldn't abide her fame. But in the end, it was a secret of hers, a deeply held shame, that destroyed them.

Danny left, thinking he had saved her by going.

She overdosed, the tragic Hollywood ending.

So the last thing that Danny wants now is love.

But he's always been a one-woman man, he doesn't have the desire or the time to "chase tail," even of the professional sort, and he needs a routine.

So the afternoons with Eden work.

Eden is great.

Drop-dead gorgeous—lush black hair, full lips, dazzling eyes, a figure out of an old *noir* movie. She's funny, full of wit and charm, and in bed, well . . . One time, shortly after they first went to bed, she offered him *"la spécialité de la maison"* and it was certainly special.

Now Danny hops out the bed and gets into the shower. He's in there for maybe a minute, then comes out and gets dressed.

Typical Dan, Eden thinks.

Always efficient, no wasted time.

"You're sure about the party?" he asks.

"I am."

"There'll be a taco bar."

"Tempting."

"And a bouncy castle."

"A combination with immense potential," she says. "But . . ."

"I'll lay off," Danny says. "Monday?"

"But of course."

He kisses her and leaves.

MORE FROM DON WINSLOW

THE FORCE

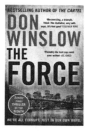

"*The Force* is mesmerizing, a triumph.
Think *The Godfather*, only with cops.
It's that good." —Stephen King

Based on years of research inside the NYPD, this is the great cop novel of our time and a book only Don Winslow could write: a haunting and heartbreaking story of greed and violence, inequality and race, crime and injustice, retribution and redemption that reveals the seemingly insurmountable tensions between the police and the diverse citizens they serve.

THE BORDER

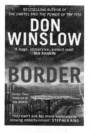

"One of the best thriller writers
on the planet." —*Esquire*

The explosive, highly anticipated conclusion to the epic Cartel trilogy, *The Border* is a shattering tale of vengeance, violence, corruption, and justice. This last novel in Don Winslow's magnificent, award-winning, internationally bestselling trilogy is packed with unforgettable, drawn-from-the-headlines scenes. Shocking in its brutality, raw in its humanity, *The Border* is an unflinching portrait of modern America, a story of—and for—our time.

BROKEN

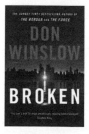

"A master of thrills shows his range, and his bite. . . .
[Winslow is] a writer from whom others can learn
the ropes." —Janet Maslin, *New York Times*

In six intense short novels connected by the themes of crime, corruption, vengeance, justice, loss, betrayal, guilt and redemption, *Broken* is #1 international bestseller Don Winslow at his pulse-pounding best. In *Broken*, he creates a world of high-level thieves and low-life crooks, obsessed cops, private detectives, dope dealers, bounty hunters and fugitives, the lost souls driving without headlights through the dark night on the American criminal highway.